MW00596642

The QUEEN'S LIES

ALSO BY OLIVER CLEMENTS

The Eyes of the Queen

The Queen's Men

All the Queen's Spies

The QUEEN'S LIES

An Agents of the Crown Novel

OLIVER CLEMENTS

LEOPOLDO & CO

ATRIA

NEW YORK LONDON TORONTO SYDNEY NEW DELHI

An Imprint of Simon & Schuster, LLC
1230 Avenue of the Americas
New York, NY 10020

This book is a work of fiction. Any references to historical events, real people, or real places are used fictitiously. Other names, characters, places, and events are products of the author's imagination, and any resemblance to actual events or places or persons, living or dead, is entirely coincidental.

First Leopoldo & Co/Atria Books hardcover edition August 2024

LEOPOLDO & CO/ATRIA BOOKS and colophon
are trademarks of Simon & Schuster, LLC

Simon & Schuster: Celebrating 100 Years of Publishing in 2024

Interior design by Kyoko Watanabe

Manufactured in the United States of America

1 3 5 7 9 10 8 6 4 2

Library of Congress Cataloging-in-Publication Data has been applied for.

ISBN 978-1-9821-9748-3
ISBN 978-1-9821-9749-0 (ebook)

To the incredible architect Leopoldo Francisco Goût Ortíz de Montellano, my father, who is now at work in the grand blueprint dance of the universe.

Who always said, "*Big ideas can only manifest under tall ceilings . . .*"

PROLOGUE

Fotheringhay, Northamptonshire, February 8, 1587

John Dee thanks God for the thick mist that rises from the frigid water this morning, for though he has poled a punt before—once, many years ago, when he was a child—the lives of others did not then depend on his skills as they do now. He lifts the pole and feels the freezing runoff drench his arms, then lets the pole slide smoothly through his palms, soft and steady, as if it were made of glass, until its end kisses the river's muddy bed, and he pushes, and on they go, eastward through the deserted fenland toward the sea.

He prays for a soft, slow English dawn; for that ridiculous little dog that stands on the prow as if he is somehow the captain of the ship not to yap; and for the woman who lies slumped in a royal blue traveling cloak, out of sight in the well of the boat, to wake from her drug-addled dreams with a smile, and that she, too, will remember her last words before she passed out:

"In my end is my beginning."

⌖

PART | ONE

Eighteen months earlier

CHAPTER ONE

Aboard HMS Resolute, *somewhere in the English Channel, September 1585*

It is a late summer's day, with a stiff wind from the southwest blowing across a fast-running sea the color of split flint, and under a full press of spanking new canvas, Her Majesty's Ship *Resolute* tacks hard to cut behind the French privateer *Neaera*. Doctor John Dee stands balanced on the rear deck, smothered in an oiled-cloth cloak, and he grins at Sir Francis Walsingham, who is just then vomiting vivid green bile onto the toes of his boots. A few paces away the shipmaster stands, teeth clenched, grappling with the wheel, and beyond him, braced easy against the gunwale, stands John Hawkins, Her Majesty's Treasurer of the Navy, who considers Walsingham with disgust.

Meanwhile, on the deck below, *Resolute*'s gun crew is gathered about the ship's single armament—a particularly large culverin of unusual design—watching suspiciously as John Dee's laboratory assistant, Roger Cooke, loads it with the first of his newly invented missile canisters. When it is done—from the rear of the cannon, rather than down the length of its muzzle; and with what looks like a brass tube rather than the usual ball and black powder—they run the cannon out over the starboard gunwale and then every man aboard steps back to leave the deck clear for Cooke to stand alone with hammer and pin.

From the rear deck Dee gives him an encouraging sign.

You'll be fine, he mouths.

Cooke scowls at him, but they've made the cannon much stronger since those first tests back in June, in Thomas Digges's garden in Mortlake, haven't they? And they've lengthened the thread on the breech block, too, so really, it should be fine.

Now all eyes turn to the *Neaera*, two hundred paces off the port bow, every scrap of sail up, running fast for the safety of Honfleur, but the *Resolute* is closing thrillingly fast.

"Wait for it!" the bearded gun master advises Cooke from behind his water barrel. "Wait for it! On the upward roll! Fire as you bear!"

But Cooke doesn't need to hear this, for these new missiles are of his own design, and he knows that when the pin hits the canister's tail, the powder within explodes instantly, and the missile in the canister's nose is forced at an impossible speed along the cannon's barrel, in which Dee has had machined grooves to set the missile spinning, so that when it emerges from the muzzle it cuts through the air like a screw rather than a nail. If it then hits its target, a second chemical reaction will occur, similar to the first, and the actual missile itself will fragment and tear itself—and everything within a ten-foot circle—to shreds.

So goes the theory, in any event.

They've tested the cannon on dry land, of course, at home in Thomas Digges's garden in Mortlake—shooting across the river with admittedly mixed but not absolutely disastrous results—but this is the first time they have hoisted her aboard a ship and taken her beyond prying eyes out to sea, where famously anything can happen. Dee has spent six months cajoling John Hawkins, the Treasurer of Her Majesty's Navy, to attend this trial with a view of impressing him into ordering more of the cannons—ten? twenty?—so as to equip each of the navy's newly designed race-built galleys with at least one. The English navy could not only blast the Spanish galleons out of the water, but also provide him with a fortune enough to last him the rest of his life.

Again, so goes the theory.

Until half an hour ago they'd been towing an old pinnace, which they intended to set free and use as a target, but then the lookout saw a ship he recognized as the *Neaera*, which had recently attacked Lyme Regis and had been harassing English shipping hereabouts, so, despite only having this one untried cannon aboard, Hawkins ordered the shipmaster to abandon the pinnace and set off after the privateer, and now here they are, closing on the sleek stern of what is to all intents and purposes a powerful French warship on which its name is picked out in red letters.

"She'll maybe have four guns on each side," the master warns, "and a couple out back, so keep your heads down."

Just then a puff of gray smoke appears above that sleek stern and a moment later something dark skips across and dips into the heaving waves ahead.

"Falconet," the master announces. "Small caliber."

"Harmless," John Hawkins confirms. "Unless it hits you."

Well, quite, Dee thinks.

Roger Cooke is crouched below the gunwale, peering along the length of the cannon, hammer and pin at the ready. He has to make this shot count. If only because the canisters are so dauntingly expensive—especially for a natural philosopher of uncertain means, recently returned from Bohemia to find his house ransacked and his possessions carried off by creditors—that they only have two. If Cooke misses, it will destroy any credit Dee has left with Hawkins and Her Majesty's navy. And now, since they've picked a fight with the *Neaera*, the stakes are suddenly higher still.

The *Resolute* is now within a bowshot of the *Neaera*'s stern. It will be a difficult shot in a rising sea, and Dee can only pray as he watches Cooke, who is waiting . . . and waiting . . . before *whack!* Cooke hammers the pin into the cannon just as the *Resolute* rises from a deep gulley between two rolling waves and instantly there is a deafening retort. The cannon leaps back in a billowing froth of gray cloud, and a stout spike of thick brown smoke erupts from the ship's side to leap across the span of sea toward the *Neaera*.

Roger Cooke is thrown back and lies stunned on the deck for a moment, so he is the only man unable to watch the missile's trail of smoke as it rises and shoots straight over the privateer's stern castle through the mess of her unbroken spars to vanish somewhere beyond.

The groan from Dee outdoes all others.

The master swears lustily and grapples with the wheel, turning the *Resolute* hard to port, away from the privateer's portside battery, but there's another puff of smoke in the privateer's stern and a moment later a crash and a cry of pain from above. A sailor tumbles from the ratlines to bounce on the deck mere feet from Roger Cooke.

Hawkins ignores him.

"About we go, Master English," he instructs, "and spill the wind, if you will?"

Walsingham looks ever more sickly.

"Can we not just leave her be and find that pinnace again?" he begs.

"No one ever died of being seasick, Sir Francis," John Hawkins barks.

"The thought of dying is the only thing keeping me alive," Walsingham tells him, retching again. Up in the rigging the other sailors are at work letting out some sails, furling others, and the *Resolute* slows to a dawdle, and the *Neaera* once more pulls ahead, but then on another command from the boson those sails that were let out are hauled back in, and those that were furled are unfurled, and so the *Resolute* once more takes wing after the privateer, steering a course back across her stern to the windward side. The master laughs, delighted at the speed and agility of this new ship.

"We'll get her this time, Roger," Dee shouts to encourage his laboratory assistant, who has loaded a new canister and is busy straightening the silver pin.

"Hit the pin harder/softer/sooner/later/on the down-roll/on the up-roll," and so on comes all sorts of advice from men behind cover, and Roger Cooke crouches once more to sight the cannon as the *Resolute* gains on the privateer, and just before they are broadside to broadside, and just as the *Resolute* is coming down from the crest of a swell, he hammers the pin.

This time he gets it right.

The cannon leaps, and the smoke billows, and once more Cooke is thrown back, but the trajectory of the missile streak is fast and flat, and it strikes the privateer's rudder just above the waterline with a flash of dirty orange flame. When the smoke of that explosion clears, a great bite is taken from the privateer's stern. Her name and steering are gone, but there then follows a second explosion, even louder than the first, and then even a third within the ship, deep and rumbling, and the *Neaera* seems to almost swell, to expand beyond its space, and then it flies apart in a thousand individual pieces: masts and spars and planks and God knows what else are flung flaming from the center of the blast, hard and fast across the sea, and then the wave of the blast reaches the *Resolute*, removing Hawkins's hat, dishing the sails, setting the ship's bell ringing.

For a long moment every man is silent, staring agape at where the *Neaera* used to be until Hawkins speaks.

"Fuck me!"

CHAPTER TWO

Pelican Inn, Portsmouth, same night

It is not until that evening, after they have made landfall in Portsmouth, with the *Resolute* safely tied up and Dee's new cannon safely wrapped in back in the cart, that Sir Francis Walsingham is able to sit up and think straight. It is just the three of them—him, Dee, and Hawkins—in a private room over roast rabbit and ale that tastes of autumn hedgerows.

Hawkins's smile remains fixed in place as if by pegs, and his dark, deep-set eyes are fixed on Dee with an unsettling kind of intensity that Dee—still pale with shock—is doing his best to ignore. Hawkins is a small, hard knot of something malignant, Walsingham thinks, warped like bog oak, and he rubs his hands and speculates with glee on how many Spanish galleons such a cannon will send to the bottom of the sea, each with its complement of soldiers and sailors.

"Hundreds," Hawkins hisses through his bad sailor's teeth. "Thousands!"

Hawkins hates the Spanish with a fever that has raged since

he sailed to the Indies nearly twenty years previously, where the Spanish broke a truce and near destroyed his little fleet at San Juan de Ulúa. After a four-month voyage he arrived back to England with a scant fifteen men left alive, each burning with an unquenchable enmity for Spain. Walsingham is no lover of Papists himself, but Hawkins's lust for Spanish blood is unquenchable.

"It is only a shame none of the privateer's crew lived to tell the tale," Walsingham suggests.

"Why?" Hawkins spits.

He had actually laughed when the *Resolute* beat back into the wind through the spread wreckage of the *Neaera* to see there were no survivors, nor anything worth salvaging save scorched timbers and fire-blackened stores bobbing in the water among a great quantity of corpses.

"Well, we might have picked one or two up," Walsingham supposes. "Put them in a pinnace and pointed them at Honfleur to spread news of our cannon."

"Why do you want news of it spread?" Hawkins asks. "Let the Spanish bastards discover it for themselves when it's too late! When they are roasting or drowning off Selsey Bill!"

Walsingham remembers this tension when Her Majesty forced Dee to reinvent Greek fire: Do we let them know we've got it, so they do not invade? Or do we surprise them with it, and utterly destroy them? Walsingham never made up his mind, but he distinctly recalls Dee being on the side of the former.

"How many such cannons can you make us, Doctor?" Hawkins asks.

Walsingham knows Dee's finances are a wreck as usual, but he has at least learned to suck his teeth like any good horse trader.

"That depends," he says, "on how many you'd need, and when you'd need them by?"

"You'll find me a plain-speaking man," Hawkins tells him. "I want fifty, by this time next year."

Dee hides a splutter of surprise in a cough. This is obviously many more than Dee had anticipated. He takes a drink to give himself some time and then hits on his answer: "My ironmaster tells me there is an iron rule of forging, which is that you can only have two of the following qualities: quick, good, cheap. You seem to have chosen the first two, so it follows that the cannons will not be cheap."

Walsingham might laugh, for before his very eyes, Dee is transmuted into a wheeler-dealer! But Hawkins has saved an enormous amount of money in his painful and radical reorganization of Her Majesty's navy precisely against this sort of opportunity, and he knows a bargain when he sees one.

"I will pay fifty pounds for each cannon."

Dee is almost too stunned to smile.

"And a pound for each canister," Hawkins goes on. "Of which I would require ten per cannon, minimum."

"That is three thousand pounds!" Walsingham calculates. A vast sum. Enough to buy one of Hawkins's new fighting ships! Surely he is not going to give that to Dee? There is no telling what the man will do with it. Hawkins seems to know what he is thinking, and before Walsingham can say anything, Hawkins grips his wrist with a hand like a manacle and pins it to the table.

"I want those cannons, Walsingham," he barks. "I want them. With enough of them in my ships, we can blast the Spanish out of the water! So now is no time for any knavish penny-pinching!"

Even Walsingham is helpless under Hawkins's ferocious glare and can only shrug his agreement. Hawkins relinquishes his arm and turns on Dee.

"Docter Dee," he says, his face still wrought as a pickled walnut in the low light of the candle, "I believe we have a deal."

He thrusts his hand out to be shaken. Dee rises to his feet, takes it, and winces as his fingers are crushed.

"I will need an advance," he manages to squeak.

Hawkins glares at him with what might be disgust, or it might be admiration, and he seems to squeeze even harder on the scholar's fingers.

"I'll have a thousand silver crowns delivered here first thing tomorrow," he says, and then he moves closer, so that his face is an inch from Dee's and Dee cannot escape his breath. "And I will expect the cannons to be delivered here, as agreed, on the day agreed, when I will pay the balance."

Dee can only nod.

"And if you fail me," he goes on, "then on that day, I will reach up your fundament, Doctor Dee, and I will pull out your liver. Do you understand me?"

It seems Dee does, and he manages a weak nod. His hand is released.

"Good man."

A thump on the shoulder, and then Hawkins turns back to Walsingham.

"Master Secretary," he snaps in farewell. He bangs on his hat, gathers up his cloak, and is gone, stamping off into the unlit recesses of the inn. A door slams. The candle flickers. There follows a long moment of silence, Dee standing thunderstruck, holding his aching hand, his face a reflection of his conflicting thoughts: an advance! But also: his liver.

"He doesn't mean that literally, does he?" Dee wonders.

"Oh yes," Walsingham murmurs. "Very much so. It's how he gets things done."

CHAPTER THREE

Dungeons of the Chateau de Joinville,
seat of the de Guise family, same day, September 1585

Of course she is naked—it is the very first thing you'd do to anyone, man, woman, or child who comes in here—and she's spread facedown on the tenter frame, her wrists and ankles tied to each corner, and even in the umber light of the dungeon's brazier and torches, the Duc de Guise cannot help but be struck by the absolute beauty of her form, of her skin, of her whole being. Everything is perfect; she is perfect.

Which is a shame.

"Do you know," he begins, taking a stool by her head so that she can hear him properly above her stifled sobs and the woof of the smith's bellows, "that when I had no more than twelve winters to my name, I watched my father's surgeon cauterize the wound in his back where he was hit by the ball from a Lutheran's pistol? His surgeon—Monsieur Paré was his name—used a silver rod taken fresh from the very heart of a brazier and he plunged it into the hole in my father's back—just here, can you feel?—where you cannot scratch either by going up over your shoulder, or around under your arm?"

He places a gloved finger where he means, and the woman's skin seems to crawl from his touch.

"And despite all the brandy he'd drunk," he goes on, "and despite the leather strop he clenched between his teeth, I remember to this day how my father screamed when that tip went into his flesh. I remember how he screamed and screamed and how he did not stop screaming until the moment he died, four days later, and never once, not for a single moment, did he let up."

Beneath him the woman twists, and writhes, and is racked by more of her own desperate sobs.

"Sometimes," he tells her, "I believe I can still hear those screams, just as I can smell his burning flesh."

He always makes a point of explaining this to the people he intends to burn. It's not to excuse himself, or to make them understand that he has suffered and so is damaged in some way, nor, really, is it to warn them of their agonies to come, though that would be a nice thought. No. It is to alert them to the fact that they can expect no mercy from a man who saw his father—the man he loved above all others—reduced to a screaming wreck, shitting himself and begging to be allowed to die.

He doubts such a thing can ever be topped for horror.

And so what he wants them to know is that although what is going to happen to them will come to define their life, for him it will mean nothing, and their cries, however ghastly they are, will land with him no more than would the disputatious chat of sparrows.

"I'm sorry," the woman now breaks her incoherent sniveling. "I'm sorry!"

De Guise sighs.

"You are only sorry you are here, Mademoiselle de Fleurier, rather than for defying my wishes."

"I'm sorry," she sobs again.

He lets out a gusty, exasperated sigh and looks up at the others who are gathered in the small low-ceilinged dungeon: two nervous men and a less-nervous woman.

"You"—he nods to one of the men, the tallest, whose head nearly scrapes the dungeon's ceiling—"Master van der Boxe."

The man swallows hard and glances at the other two as if for help that does not come, and he steps forward, filled with fatal hesitancy.

"Go on, then," de Guise orders. "Take one."

And he nods toward the brazier, five paces away, from which bristle three little-finger-thick, wooden-handled pokers. The tall man approaches the brazier and slowly reaches out a hand toward one of the pokers. He is looking sick as he slowly pulls it out. The color along its length changes from black toward the handle through ruby to cherry red and then to searing white at its tip. He stares at it for a long moment, and then across at the woman in the tenter frame. And then back at it. And then across at the woman. He takes a small step toward her. He holds the glowing poker up before him, takes another step, and moves the poker toward her naked back. There is a long moment when the struggle within looks as if it might go either way, but then there is a hardening of the shoulders, of the spine, and the man closes his eyes and shakes his head minutely. He'll not do it.

"Get out!" de Guise bellows.

The man tosses aside the poker, letting it clatter into the drain that's set in the stone flags in case of runoff, where it hisses disappointment, and he turns and hurries into the darkness at the end of the dungeon.

"You," de Guise says, addressing the other man.

The other man actually pulls at his collar. Above his beard his face is mottled, as if he might be sick at any moment. He does not even reach for the poker but shakes his head and steps back into the shadows after that first man, leaving only the woman.

"Mademoiselle Báthory," de Guise says.

Mademoiselle Báthory stares back at him, long and level, her hard face very sharp. Her expression is unreadable, but her actions are plain and swift: after hardly a moment she strides forward, withdraws a poker from the brazier with a short yank, and she steps over to the woman in the frame. She holds the poker out before her, over that stripped naked back, and she looks de Guise in the eye, a special kind of challenge, and then she places the poker's searing point firmly in the spot where Kitty de Fleurier will never be able to scratch.

The hiss of flesh is drowned out by the unearthly howl as Kitty de Fleurier writhes in her bonds and Mademoiselle Báthory presses the poker down harder as if to still her, and through the whorls of human smoke, Mademoiselle Báthory's gaze never leaves his, and his never leaves hers.

Whenever he has done this sort of thing in the past—be it to man, woman, or child—afterward he has been like a satyr, consumed by an almost inexhaustible need to rut, to penetrate, and with an erection that remains ramrod for hours. In the past he has exhausted his wife as well as three, four, five women in quick succession, going at each like a possessed bull, the one after the other, until they scream, or faint, or beg for mercy. He shows them none. No tenderness. No care. No discretion. Today is no different, save today this woman is his equal in every manner of depravity, matching him in every desperate carnal endeavor until two hours later they both collapse exhausted on the Turkey rug of de Guise's private salon, each battered and bruised, pinched, bitten and reamed, their bodies glazed with every kind of bodily excretion.

He had known Mademoiselle Báthory would be the one to pass this test. She'd been the only one of the three who had shown any remorse—in the form of a burning thirst for revenge—after they were foiled in the scheme to lure the emperor into joining an invasion of heretic England. He would have those other two failures meet their ends in agony, he thought, but for Mademoiselle Báthory, he has more interesting plans.

CHAPTER FOUR

Her Majesty's Privy Chamber, Richmond Palace, England, same day, September 1585

It is another perfect late summer's early evening, and the light falling through the glazed west windows has a golden quality that sets Her Majesty's hair aflame and brings to mind past glories. She stands, alone for once, with the looking glass her father gave her so many years ago and she studies what she sees therein, turning the glass this way and that, convinced there must be some new thing in her face—some unnoticed crack perhaps—that has been taken by certain gentlemen at court as a sign of her weakness,; as a sign that they might ignore her wishes, as a sign they might defy her will.

How else to explain it?

A subtle cough from behind a curtain.

She turns.

"Come."

"Master Beale is here, Your Majesty," Mistress Parry announces.

Queen Elizabeth says nothing for a long moment, still turning the glass, still looking at her reflection.

"I think more ceruse," she says. "Here. Here. And here."

"Very well, Your Majesty," Mistress Parry says. "I will send for your ladies."

And she steps back through the curtain, leaving the Queen to continue studying her reflection as the golden light through the western window slowly fades.

Late evening now, and cool enough for a fire, and Her Majesty has decided on magenta silk, with long loops of pearls, and those extra layers of ceruse give her face a bone white, otherworldly mask of command. When at last she enters the room, the halberdiers bang the butts of their weapons on the floorboards, and Master Robert Beale stiffens and bows his head while she takes her place on her throne.

"Master Beale," she says.

"Your Majesty," he replies.

He has aged well, Master Beale. Gray temples now, but he has kept himself fit and healthy, has largely abjured the pleasures of the table and shows no sign of smallpox. He pays for a good tailor, too, who has the sense to keep things simple. He has a reputation for being a sentimental, enthusiastic lover of beautiful women, including, she knows, Dorothy Perrot, while the woman's husband enjoys his spell in the Tower.

She asks him first if there is any word from Antwerp.

"None since its fall, Your Majesty."

His eyes are averted and she supposes he must be one of those who blame her for not sending a proper army to the Netherlands to support the city's Dutch defenders against the Spanish, or for offering only token support, and even that too late to prevent the Duke of Parma from taking it after an extremely costly—in blood and gold—yearlong siege. She knows they blame her hesitancy on her womanhood; and that they say if England had a king, then he would have sent an army five, ten, fifteen years ago, and a proper one at that—not just a token force of five thousand foot and a thousand horses—and under a proper general, not the Earl of Leicester, who cannot be trusted to do what is right, and when oh when will she ever learn to do what they say?

"And will you volunteer to go to the Netherlands with my lord of Leicester?" she wonders.

He thinks not, he tells her: he is too old for campaigning.

"I am happy to hear it," she says.

And he looks up at her quizzically, and it seems he cannot help himself starting when he sees her, and she is convinced it is because she is, if nothing else, very striking this evening. She sees him fumbling for the right words to use to ask why she might be so happy to hear he is not going to Holland with Leicester.

"For we need you here in England with us," she forestalls. "Which is why we have summoned you to us this evening,"

Ahh.

"If there is any particular service I may perform, Your Majesty, then Your Majesty surely knows she need only say the word, for I am hers to command."

True, she thinks.

"Master Beale," she starts, "did you by any chance let Sir Francis know you were called to attend upon us here this evening?"

"Not as yet, Your Majesty," he tells her. "He is gone to Portsmouth, on some errand to do with John Hawkins and Doctor Dee, and of course your pursuivant was very specific that I should tell no one. He stood over me until I was ready to attend."

She nods. *Good*, she thinks, *good*.

"And how is our master secretary?" she begins and notes Beale's instant wary stillness as he fumbles for an answer.

"He is tired, I should say, Your Majesty. And suffers with his kidney stones but there is no one as loyal to your person, nor as selfless and as tireless on your behalf, as Sir Francis."

"That is a very honorable answer, Master Beale," she tells him, "and I commend you for it."

Though she does not think it entirely true, for she is becoming ever more certain that Sir Francis is not laboring tirelessly on her behalf, as he should be, but is actually working against her expressed interests and has resumed his efforts to entrap Mary of Scotland in some treachery. This has ever been Walsingham's aim: to bring Queen Mary to trial, to find her guilty, and to have her executed, not, as he claims, in defense of England, but in reality to show the world that she—a queen!—is subject to the laws of the land. And if they might judge and condemn Mary of Scotland, then what is to stop them judging and condemning *any* monarch? Even Elizabeth of England?

This is the unspoken battle in which she and her personal private secretary are engaged, and despite the fact that she needs him now more than ever as a bulwark against her many foreign enemies, it is a battle that she intends to win.

Which is why she has summoned Master Beale.

"We worry that Sir Francis is overworking himself," she starts, knowing that she sounds like a draper's wife gossiping after Mass on a Sunday. "And we are particularly worried that he overtires himself especially in regard to the affairs of Queen Mary, our cousin of Scotland."

At which Beale exhibits the particular stillness of a man trying to divine what is really being said by someone who is saying something else.

"Despite our entreaties," she continues, "that she be left in peace to enjoy—whatever it is she is supposed to enjoy."

"But Your Majesty," Beale starts, "the Scottish queen is the pintle about which every plot to usurp you from your throne has ever hinged. All these assassins who come from France or our homegrown variety, they do so only to put her in your place. James Hamilton; Francis Throckmorton; the Guild of the Black Madonna; John Somerville; William Parry: they all acted with the specific intent of putting Mary of Scotland on your throne. It would be a dereliction of duty were Sir Francis not to keep her under constant surveillance."

The Queen has heard all this before.

"Surveillance is one thing," she counters, "but we are concerned that he overreaches himself in an effort to force our hand when he full well knows our thoughts on this matter, which we have time and oft clearly expressed, which is that she is not to be schemed against."

"I am certain Sir Francis is cognizant of those wishes, Your Majesty."

"Ahh, yes. Cognizant, certainly, but obedient?"

"I am certain he is," Beale says.

"Are you? How certain are you, Master Beale, if you do not mind our pressing?"

"As certain as I can be, Your Majesty."

"Good," she says. "Good. Then you will not mind our asking you to act as our man in this matter?"

Beale's eyebrows rise in alarm.

"To act as your man, Your Majesty?"

"In this matter."

Beale's mouth opens and closes as he casts around for somewhere to look, somewhere to rest his eyes.

"I am not sure I understand, Your Majesty?"

As usual, when it comes down to it, it is much easier than she thought it would be. "We cannot afford to lose Sir Francis's services," she spells out. "But nor can we have him defying our wishes, especially in this matter, so we are asking you, for the sake not only of your country and your queen, but also for the friendship you bear for Sir Francis, that you ensure—by whichever methods you deem most appropriate—that he makes no progress in any scheme that threatens the life of our cousin of Scotland."

Beale swallows.

"You wish me to work against Sir Francis?"

"Not against him. We wish you to channel his dwindling energies away from Queen Mary into more profitable areas. You can be Queen Mary's champion. We know you have been to see her in Tutbury or wherever, and you may do so again, quite properly. You might advise her in caution, for example, should you divine that she flies too close to the sun."

"And should Sir Francis learn that I am thwarting his strategies, then—"

"What strategies, Master Beale? You say yourself: there are no strategies. He has none, in this regard."

Beale stands openmouthed for a moment, but if he is gathering himself to resist or even defy her wishes, she has the very thing to put an end to that.

"And how fares our dear Dorothy?" she asks before he can speak. "Or Lady Perrot now, as we shall have to learn to call her, although Dorothy Devereux did have a real ring about it, didn't it? So dashing."

Beale still stands openmouthed.

"You have been spending some time with her, we understand?" she continues. "Consoling her while her husband is given the run of our amenities?"

She means Sir Thomas Perrot, of course: Devereux's husband, who is as famous for his temper as he is for his skill at arms, and who has been under lock and key at Her Majesty's pleasure these last few years for impetuously marrying his beloved Dorothy without seeking Her Majesty's say-so, which was unwise, perhaps, but not as unwise as Beale jumping into bed with this same Dorothy while Perrot's back was turned.

"Will you pass on our greetings?" the Queen continues. "And do tell her that we are considering whether to pardon Sir Thomas his crime and let him work his way back into polite society?"

Beale closes his mouth with a clack.

She dismisses him with an airy wave.

"Will you send in Mistress Parry on your way out, Master Beale?"

CHAPTER FIVE

The Pelican, Portsmouth, dawn,
next morning, September 1585

Dee had hoped to dream of all the money that would soon be coming his way from the navy's treasury, and of all the things he intends to do with it, but instead he dreams of John Hawkins pulling his liver out of his backside. He wakes an hour or so before dawn, filled with fearful apprehension, and he must force himself to think of returning to Mortlake to tell Frommond that all their worries are over. He also forces himself to imagine telling Thomas Digges that his name will resonate through history as the man—one of them, anyway—who saved Protestant England from the Inquisition. Then he tries to picture himself striding through Somerset, being guided to the whereabouts of the wondrous treasures of King Arthur with the help of the new and—supposedly—wonderfully sensitive divining orb that he can now afford from the dealers off Cheapside.

When he falls asleep again this time, he actually does dream of money, of actual silver crowns: a great pile of them, toppling on him, pressing him flat, as if he were being done to death in the old

French way of *peine forte et dure*, and he wakes with a shout to find a cat is sitting upon his chest.

"You all right, Doctor?"

It is Roger Cooke, lying on the other side of the fire's embers, gray-faced in the dawn.

"Yes, thank you, Roger, I was just dreaming about—"

Before he can say another word there is a thunderous pounding on the back door of the inn.

"Jesu!" Dee exclaims, used to such things at home, of course, where bailiffs hammer on his gate most mornings, but that they should follow him to Portsmouth? Cooke is relieved not to have to hear any more of Dee's dream, and he gets warily to his feet. He, too, has seen all this a thousand times before.

"Shall I tell them you are not at home?" he asks.

"Tell them I am at home," Dee whispers.

The innkeeper comes shuffling and opens the door before they can stop him, and there in the cool gray light stands not just any old bailiff, but John Hawkins, Her Majesty's Treasurer of the Navy, all in black; no collar or hat even, but sworded and seabooted and carrying a black hardwood staff with a pommel of the size and shape you'd choose to dent a man's temple.

"Where's Dee?" he snarls, though he means nothing by it, for that is just his manner.

"God give you good morrow, Master Hawkins."

Four men stand behind him in the yard: one is a whey-faced clerk of sorts; two are defined by their arquebuses and swords, and the last by his sword and the tether of a sorry-looking donkey that is overloaded with heavy saddlebags.

"A thousand pounds in silver crowns," Hawkins tells him. "You'll sign for it."

Jesu! Dee's gaze locks on the donkey's bulging saddlebags. No wonder the poor thing looks so sad. A thousand pounds!

With that they might buy, say, a castle!

The clerk comes forward with a tightly rolled sheaf.

"Shall we go in?" Dee wonders, indicating the hall of the inn where there might be tabletops for ink flasks and celebratory mugs of warm spiced wine, but Hawkins is having none of it. The clerk passes Dee a document, shows him where to sign, then turns and offers his back so that Dee might use it as a desk. Evidently this is normal. Dee takes the proffered stub of feather and signs and cannot resist adding his monad.

"The fuck is that?" Hawkins demands.

Dee begins to explain, but Hawkins cuts him off.

"Remember, Dee: those cannons, delivered here by Michaelmas next, or you'll answer to me for them."

Dee can only nod, for he doubts not that Hawkins will do as he says. Then the donkey is led forward and the swordsman hands over the tether.

"What?" Cooke calls from the door. "That's it? A thousand pounds and no guards nor nothing?"

"You've got the donkey, haven't you?" Hawkins barks. "What more do you need?"

"A dozen horsemen armed to the teeth'd help."

Hawkins doesn't trouble to answer. The clerk has rolled the document into his bag, and the delivery party turn and trail Hawkins stamping his way back toward the docks whence he came. The problem of getting the money and the cannon safely back to Mortlake is evidently not theirs.

"Where's Walsingham?" Cooke asks Dee.

"Called away in the night," the innkeeper answers for him. "Ridden for the Northern Parts, he said."

Leaving Dee to pay their bill, of course.

He and Cooke look at each other, then up at the sky. It's early yet, but they have a three-day journey ahead, over the downs and across Surrey, with a thousand pounds in silver and a heavy cannon.

"We'd best get going then," Dee supposes.

⌖

The Portsmouth road cuts straight up the bluffs of the South Downs, and Nurdle—Thomas Digges's brewer's horse they'd borrowed to bring the cannon down from London—has no great interest in hauling the cart with the heavy gun barrel in its bed and half the silver back up the steep and dusty track to the top, but after three grueling hours and many carrots, they crest the hill, and before them lies the great forested swath of Surrey.

"Always said we should've come by sea," Cooke reminds Dee, wiping the sweat from his eyes.

Dee is beginning to think he is right.

"But imagine if we were overtaken by pirates? Or the Spanish, God forbid? Then they'd have our cannon and then—well. Let's not even think about that."

"We could have tossed it overboard before they'd taken us?"

"Then we'd never be able to find it again," Dee says, "and copy it fifty times, and then just think what Hawkins would do to us."

"To you."

They walk on under the sweltering late summer sun. The road is fairly busy, with all sorts of merchants and their loads coming up and down from London. Most are accompanied by one or two guards, if not more, but are moving too swiftly for Nurdle and the donkey, not to say Dee and Cooke, and those who do stop to offer help are those they trust the least.

"It is just some old turnips we are taking to market," Dee tells any who ask, indicating the canvas-shrouded cannon. "Should we be robbed, they'd be doing us a favor!"

Cooke tells him they do not look like turnip traders.

"We do not look as if we are the richest men in Christendom, either."

"Even so. You'd be better off going full Doctor Dee. You know: companion of witches and conjurer up of hellhounds, that sort of thing. Scare them off."

"That won't work in Surrey," Dee tells him. "They like all that sort of thing."

Cooke still thinks they should have hired a couple of guards in Portsmouth.

"Good luck finding an honest man in Portsmouth," Dee tells him. "They'd have tipped off every highwayman from here to Westminster, and we'd soon find ourselves rolled in a ditch with our throats split from ear to ear."

On either side are deep woods and tangled underbrush, and as the day wears on there are long stretches of the road where they are all alone save for birdsong. These are perfect haunts for the robbers who are known to infest these parts, and so they are relieved to reach the little village of Liss where there is an inn with what Cooke claims is his name all over it.

"Your name is the White Hart?"

Cooke laughs: it is the end of a long day, with ale in prospect.

That night Dee takes his turn to sleep in the stables with Nurdle and the donkey—and the cannon and the money—and in the night there are stealthy, probing footsteps in the yard, but a word from Dee and they scurry away leaving him to his thoughts, which turn to the cannon, naturally enough, and what happened to the *Neaera*, the French privateer for whose crew he ought to feel no sympathy, and that night the shades of the dead seem to crawl onto dry land and present themselves to him, one by one, showing him their awful wounds, and he can say nothing more than *je m'excuse, je m'excuse.*

⌖

"You see?" he tells Cooke when morning comes and the cannon and silver are still there. "Safe as houses. One more night and we'll be home and dry."

Cooke perhaps took too much ale the night before and finds today hard going, which is why, as they trudge through the heathland and up the hill from which a great scoop seems to have been taken, he listens less attentively to Dee's account of the myths and legends that surround what is known locally as the Devil's Punchbowl, and why he does not hear the horse's hooves until they are almost upon them.

"Heavy load you have there," the rider observes as poor Nurdle wheezes in his straps.

He keeps to their left—always a bad sign—and despite the warmth of the day he wears a capacious soldier's cloak, the mossy cloth of which is whorled about with sea salt stains, and a tall felt cap studded with tarnished silver buttons. On his saddle bow, artfully exposed as a warning, two pistols—what look like wheel locks—hang ready in leather loops.

"Turnips," Cooke mutters, climbing up into the cart.

"Heaviest turnips I ever saw," the man says.

"Yes," Dee agrees cheerfully. "Perhaps we should give poor old Nurdle a rest, eh, Roger?"

He pats Nurdle's nose and gives him a carrot as if he has not a care in the world.

"Aye," Cooke agrees, and then he adds without too much thought, "Our friends will be along by and by."

Dee knows they are in trouble when the man makes a show of shading his eyes and peering back down the length of the forested, deserted road.

"By and by?" he asks, almost jocular. "If your friends travel more slowly than yourselves, then their turnips must indeed be weighty."

He's a big man, about forty perhaps, with a big dark-bristled chin and a hooked nose, and he looks like he has knocked about a good deal. Dee supposes he must have a sword on the hip he cannot see, and he wishes he had one himself, though what good would that do against a couple of wheel locks?

"Told you," Cooke mutters. He means hiring guards. Too late for that now.

"Sir Francis Walsingham has promised to catch us up before we reach Guildford," Dee announces.

The man grins.

"The devil, you say! Then I'd best be about my business."

The first pistol is unsheathed and pointed unwaveringly at Dee.

"Ah," Dee says.

"Yes," the man says, "so let's have a look at these magical turnips then, shall we?"

The sun is in Cooke's eyes while he squints at the man. His face is very red and sweaty and he is hungover and truculent and he has no time for an idiot in a silver-buttoned hat, pistol or no pistol.

"Fuck off," he says.

The horseman flushes and looks—can it be?—stung by Cooke's words, and he turns the pistol on him.

"Brave talk," the horseman says, "for a fat man."

Cooke's face seems to gather weight. Dee distracts the horseman by pulling back the sailcloth with a flurry, and the movement startles the man's horse, which stamps and snorts, and tosses its head, and the horseman's pistol wavers as he fights to control his mount.

That's when Cooke lunges.

But he is, as the horseman has said, a fat man, and slower than once he was. As Cooke comes at him, the wheel whirs and the powder flares and the pistol leaps in the horseman's hand with a flash of flame and a dull retort. The bullet catches Cooke. It checks him, and he lurches sideways from the cart to hit the road under the horse's flailing hooves.

"No!" Dee cries, and he throws himself between Cooke and the horse, making himself loom as large as he may—the companion of witches; the conjurer of hellhounds—and the horse's hooves are inches from his unprotected face. To stop himself falling backward the rider discards the pistol into the dirt and clings to reins and Dee advances, shouting nonsense, hoping to scare the horse enough to throw the rider.

But the rider regains his saddle, brings the horse under control, and wheels it around. He draws that other pistol and pulls the trigger. The wheel whirs again and just as the powder catches with a boom, Dee throws himself back. The ball clips his hat off but misses his head, and the horseman slips that pistol back in its loop and pulls back his cloak to draw the sword at his hip. Dee scrambles to his feet and starts to back away as the horseman heels his horse forward. Dee runs from him, staggering past Nurdle's nose, and the horseman follows. He hauls himself along the other side of the cart, around behind the donkey, who is tethered to the rear of the cart's rear, carrying just half the silver crowns.

"Kick him!" Dee implores the donkey.

When he comes back onto the road, he sees Cooke lying facedown in a spreading pool of dark blood. He forgets the horseman and his sword, and he drops to kneel by his old friend.

"Oh Jesu, Roger!"

The horse surges past, and instinct makes Dee duck just as the sword tip would have cleaved his skull. He rolls Cooke onto his back. The bullet has entered his chest and there is blood everywhere: all over his clothes, spilling from his mouth. Dee suppresses a sob and presses his fist into the hole in Cooke's doublet. Blood welters from Cooke's mouth. He grips Dee's arms.

"Don't let him've killed me!" he splutters.

But it is too late for that.

"I'm so sorry, Roger," Dee tells him. "I'm so sorry."

The horseman has come back around the back of the cart and dismounted.

Dee only glances up at him, over his shoulder. The horseman comes to stand behind Dee and he lays the blade against Dee's cheek. Dee ignores the man. He holds Roger Cooke through his last spasms, careless of the blade; careless of the blood that splatters his cloak; careless of everything except keeping hold of his old friend while he dies, never looking away, until Roger's shudders cease, and the life goes out of him. Only then do Dee's tears splash, mingling with the blood, and only then does he look up to find the horseman, the donkey, and the rest of the silver crowns in the cart, all gone.

In his haste, though, the horseman has forgotten the dropped pistol. It lies scratched, and even still smoking, on the ground where it fell. Dee kicks it away as if it were a serpent, as if it were its fault that Roger is dead, not the man who pulled its trigger. In the distance is the dot of the horseman leading off the donkey, both staggering under the weight of the silver. Otherwise the road is deserted, and he can hear the plaintiff cries of buzzards, circling high above, and there is a sudden thin wind to stir the heather by the roadside.

Oh Jesu.

What does he do? Abandon the cannon and the body of his old friend and set off after the murderer though he still has no sword, nor balls for the pistol and is on foot?

He looks down again at Roger Cooke, peaceful now, though his beard is full of blood, and he bends and slips his arms around him and tries to lift him. It is impossible. He stands for a moment, studying the problem. In the end there is only one way: Dee hauls Roger out onto the road and lays him flat, with one knee cocked. Then he stands at his feet, takes a few steps back, and comes at him quickly, dropping down, grabbing the cocked leg and rolling over Cooke's body, squeezing the last of the blood from him, and hauling the leg with him as he twists over, so that he now lies prone on the ground, with Roger sprawled on his back. Then he gradually straightens up, and lifts Roger, and then kneels, and then stands, and he staggers with his friend to tip him onto the back of the cart, to lay him down next to the cannon, with his legs hanging off the end, then Dee climbs up and hauls him up into the cart so that he appears comfortable, and then he covers everything with the sailcloth.

When that is done, he drops to the ground.

"Well, Nurdle," Dee addresses the horse, "it is just you and me now."

He takes the horse's lead and is about to set off when he stops and collects the pistol.

Just as he thought: on its handle is scored a cross, and the words *Deus Vult*.

God wills it.

CHAPTER SIX

Mortlake, same day, late September 1585

It is already the golden hour when the light is low and the cows are being brought back along the lane when Jane Frommond—Mistress Dee—offers to help Sarah, her maid and cook, by taking Arthur down to the vegetable garden to see if there is anything worth picking to reinforce tonight's pottage. Sarah thinks that will be nice, and so Frommond walks down through the garden holding her son's hand, relishing the late-summer sun, past the tree where his various rabbits lie buried, and down toward the orchard, where the vegetable plot is fenced off behind hazel panels.

There are a few things worth collecting, she thinks, but Arthur is never very interested in this sort of thing, and quickly leaves her to it, and she picks away alone while he wanders down through the apple and pear trees to the river's edge.

A moment later she hears him calling, and she looks up to see him pointing upriver.

"A barge," he says.

"Whose is it?" she asks, for he is good at identifying them now.

"It's the Queen!" he squeals. "The Queen!"

Frommond smiles. It is not unheard of, of course, for Her Majesty to move between her various palaces along the river, but still she brushes the earth from her hands and her skirts and steps over the hurdles to come to stand with Arthur to watch the Queen of England being rowed by. But then from across the dipping water comes a low call, and the early evening sunlight catching on the painted oarsmen's flashing blades shows them dragging in the water to slow the barge, and then the men begin to backrow, and the barge—long and black, with red and gold painted details and a glazed cabin at the stern—drifts on the river's current.

"She's coming here!" Arthur squeals.

And sure enough, with some skillful helming, the barge comes to a graceful halt against Dee's water steps. A man in blue with red piping leaps out. He quickly ties the barge off with a red-dyed rope.

"Are you expecting anyone?" Frommond asks her son.

Arthur ignores her joke.

A gangplank is sent out, and four Yeomen of the Queen's Guard stamp ashore with halberds lowered and at the ready in case of—what? They are in an orchard in Mortlake. The worst that could happen to anyone is to be hit by a windfall. Still, they are quite a sight as they fan out and secure a cordon around the steps, and Frommond would admit that her heart is racing when the familiar person of the Queen emerges from the cabin, diminutive next to her Yeomen, and is helped up onto the gangplank by some courtier or other. Her Majesty is dressed in vermilion today, with a dark cloak and hood that she has raised as if she wishes to pass unnoticed, and there is, in fact, Frommond thinks, something altogether surreptitious about her movements, too, and she cannot help wonder at what is afoot.

It can only be to see John, she supposes, as she effects a deep curtsy in the grass.

"Your Majesty," she says.

Out of the corner of her eye she sees Arthur execute a very fair bow before coming to stand behind her skirts. Meanwhile the Queen descends the steps and smiles—her teeth yellow against the blanched white of her face—for even before Frommond saved her life under London Bridge, she was fond of her lady-in-waiting and was both happy and sad when Jane Frommond left court for the marriage bed of Doctor Dee.

"Mistress Dee," she says, "we miss you every day at court."

Frommond laughs.

"I'm sure that is not true, Your Majesty, but I thank you for saying it, for I confess I do oftentimes think of our past times together with great pleasure."

This is also a lie, and they both know it, but it is what the Queen expects to hear so she doesn't listen, and Frommond watches her gaze dance over every detail of what she sees, and it is possible to read a flicker of envy in her expression, for the freedom and ease of Jane Frommond's life is a far cry from the Queen's own, but also a certain amount of contempt, for it is not much, is it, when all's said and done? A scrubby garden, and an orchard of ten or so apple trees.

"But I am sad to have to say that my husband is not here to welcome you, Your Majesty, for I know how honored he would have been to have received you."

It is as tactful a way to explain that the Queen's visit is wasted, but Her Majesty now surprises her again.

"But it is not John we've come to see," she says.

"Oh, then?"

"It is you, Mistress Dee. We have a particular favor to ask of you."

"Anything, Your Majesty," she says, though her mind spins: Why has the Queen come to her in this curious manner? Why has she not just summoned her to Whitehall, say, or merely sent word of her request? What manner of favor is this going to be? She will not be going to Prague again, that is certain.

"Walk with us," the Queen says. "Show us the highlights of your estate."

Frommond laughs.

"This is the highlight," she says, turning and placing a hand on Arthur's head. The Queen is not good with children and almost freezes in horror, and Frommond recalls too late that it is almost treason to present anyone to the Queen unless she has specifically asked for it.

"Run back to Sarah," she must tell Arthur, who is relieved to be released, if he is honest, for he was only ever interested in the barge and the Yeomen's halberds. When he is gone, the Queen summons Frommond to her side and becomes confidential as they step out along a rough path between the trees.

"We find ourselves in need of your services, Mistress Dee," the Queen tells her. "As a favor not just to us, but to our royal cousin, Queen Mary of Scotland."

Frommond frowns to hear the name, and the thought that Her Majesty might wish to do Mary any favors.

"Your Majesty need only say the word," Frommond says, just as she must, and just as the Queen expects.

"We understand from Sir Amyas Paulet—who is our cousin's keeper in the north—that our cousin has turned in on herself," the Queen begins, "and is in poor spirit."

As would you be, Frommond thinks, *if you'd spent the last eighteen years locked up, rarely if ever being allowed to take exercise or air, with no purpose in life save to pass the hours until . . .*

"So as a gift to her, from us," the Queen goes on, "or a favor, rather, we would like to send her something to divert her inward thoughts and cheer her through the coming winter."

Dear God, yes; winters in the Northern Parts are famously grim.

"That is very thoughtful of you, Your Majesty. I am sure Queen Mary will be most touched and grateful."

When Her Majesty nods, there is a little symphony of clicks and tinkles from her jewelry.

"And so naturally," she goes on, "we thought of you."

"Of—me?" Frommond asks, alarmed.

"Yes. We thought you might join her household, for but a few short months, to cheer and energize our cousin."

It is not a question or a request: it is an order.

Frommond is too stunned to speak for several moments, but then gathers her thoughts.

"I have nothing to wear" is her first.

"We have brought all that you will need."

"Nor have I any maid," she says, thinking of Sarah, who is altogether too natural a spirit for any sort of polite society. "Or none that would do."

"Ah!" The Queen almost laughs. "We have already found the perfect maid: Mistress Pargeter. I am sure she will provide great comfort and consolation, for not being a run-of-the-mill maid."

The Queen sounds pleased with herself for this piece of farsightedness, but Frommond is breathless with panic. She concentrates on placing one foot in front of the other. She does not want to go back to court ever again; not any court, but most especially not one of an exiled queen in captivity, with duties to cheer her during the coldest months, and in the Northern Parts. Her life, for better or worse, is in Mortlake, with John Dee, who for all his chaotic financial affairs, is her beloved husband, and her son, Arthur. The thought of sitting all day suffering endless complex formal dinners followed by nothing save embroidery until supper makes her want to throw herself in the river.

Nevertheless, she cannot now say no.

"So we will send you Mistress Pargeter," the Queen continues, "who will bring all that you need, and money besides. Our cousin is in Tutbury, in Staffordshire, and so I will also lend you a carriage and escort so that you may arrive in proper state. I believe our cousin of Scotland places great emphasis on such things."

Frommond feels as if she is being softly robbed.

"And when would Your Majesty wish me to go?"

"This next week."

Frommond nearly emits a squeal.

"My husband—"

"Will understand."

And now it is as if she is swallowing feathers.

"So . . . I . . . well . . . ," she begins, and the Queen turns on her, and her hooded eyes are adamantine, and Frommond remembers how vengeful she can be when crossed or checked, and so she must yield, though, Jesu, she still has many a question to ask.

"Of course, Your Majesty," she says with a bow. "It is my pleasure to serve."

And so that is that: she is to pass the winter among strangers, in a strange place far from home, and with a maid not of the usual sort, whom she has never met.

CHAPTER SEVEN

Tutbury Castle, Staffordshire, same day, September 1585

A crow caws on her windowsill, dragging her down from a diaphanous dream in which she was back by that house above the loch: the gray stone farmhouse under its thatch of heather by which she'd hesitated all those years ago, struck by its modest perfection, and the way the air smelled of pine trees and peat smoke, where the linen on a line billowed in the warm summer breeze, and she had thought: *Yes, this would do me*. But she could not linger, for her men were crowding behind her, drums and fifes and twenty or thirty war banners, and so on they'd gone, ten thousand or more of them, marching across the moor toward their fate, but she'd looked back at that house in the bracken until it was out of sight.

And now she is awake, and still here, still under heavy, damp blankets—still enclosed within the dark damask hangings of her unhappy bed—and when she tries to move her swollen legs, she is further reminded of just who she is and where she is by the pain that racks almost every part of her body. She lies still for a long moment, only breathing, letting her tears dry, and then she extends a hand to where lies under her pillow a slim fold of gold in which is kept a miniature portrait not only of her younger self, but also of a young man with fair skin and coppery hair, beautifully dressed, staring impassively at the viewer as if daring her to make of him what she will.

She studies this second face for a long moment, and then is about to press it to her lips by habit when she hesitates and allows the tears to flow once more as she thinks of him, her son, James, whom Mary has not seen since he was a babe in arms. He is eighteen now—a man—and until very recently she was certain he would send for her and lead her back to Edinburgh, where he and she—she and he—would reign together with all due dignity and honor, until the time came that she would ride south, to take the throne of England by right of being Queen Elizabeth's only natural heir.

But this is not to happen. Recently she has learned that her son has—or, rather, her son's advisers have—made a treaty with the English behind her back, and in return for a measly pension, her son has entered Scotland into a "League of Amity" with England that pits the two countries against the Catholic powers of Christendom, the very powers who would seek to have her released and to have England restored to the one true faith. His advisers have painted her as a die-hard Catholic, and therefore unsuitable to take the throne of England, whereas James was brought up a Protestant, and so it is he who should be considered the next in line to the English throne. He has in effect trampled over her every right and ensured her continued captivity, against all honor and civility, so that he can take the English throne after Elizabeth when by rights it should first go to her, to Mary.

So she will no longer be kissing his portrait.

When she first heard of her son's—his advisers'—betrayal, her heart broke, and for a month or two she was left speechless, powerless, unable to move, eat, or drink without aid. It was only thanks to her household—and in particular Master Nau, who assured her that James would soon see the error of his ways, eject his advisers from Holyrood, and summon her to his side—that she is alive, and indeed even managing to entertain slender hopes that she will hear from the boy someday soon.

Until then, though, she must ring a little silver bell to summon her women of the privy chambers to help her start her day, and when she has done so her maid of honor, prim and bitter Mary Kennedy, who brings her Cache-Cache, Queen Mary's lapdog, a delicate streak of pure white curled fur, with a bright pink tongue and dark eyes that seem to look into her soul and read everything beautiful within, and who is no larger than a cat.

Kennedy also brings in the smell of the middens that are overflowing in the castle bailey, an ever-present feature of this disgusting place.

"But it's Thursday, Your Majesty," Kennedy says with a quick smile, and Queen Mary, too, manages one in return, for today is indeed Thursday, the day around which her whole week has come to turn, the day during which the messenger arrives from London. She relies for her sanity on the company of her maids, of course, and particularly upon Mary Kennedy, but her life's chief delight now is this correspondence which comes through the offices of the new French ambassador in London, Guillaume de l'Aubépine, Baron de Châteauneuf, in whose diplomatic bag are brought letters from such well-willers across Christendom: Bishop Beaton, her ambassador in Paris; Thomas Morgan, her business agent, also in Paris, who manages the various disbursements from the money she still receives as dowager queen of France; her cousin, Henri, Duc de Guise, whose polite, formally framed missives promise nothing, but leave her without doubt that he strives behind the scenes for the restoration of her fortunes.

And, of course, Mary still clings to the hope that she will hear once more from her son in Edinburgh.

An hour later she has said her prayers, broken her fast, and is dressed in ruby red silks, with her wig curled to her satisfaction. There is nothing immediate for her to do save to hobble on aching legs from her privy apartment, across the Turkey carpets on the floor of the Presence Chamber, to find her throne upon its dais, and there await under her cloth of state for the packet of letters to be delivered.

It has not always been like this: she was once used to more freedom under her old keepers, but this new man, Sir Amyas Paulet, is a fierce, unbending puritan who would pride himself—were pride not a sin—on his pitilessness.

"Enough to make a milksop of Calvin," Mary Kennedy says of him.

Paulet breaks open every letter Queen Mary sends or receives, she is certain of it, and his men go through everything she is sent from Paris, unpicking the seams of her dresses and cutting holes in the heels of her shoes to see there is nothing hidden within; he makes her cooks and her laundresses strip down to their shifts whenever they enter or leave the castle in case they are smuggling in letters, and he conducts searches of all her rooms at various times of the day. Worst and most offensive of all is that whenever he enters the Presence Chamber—with hardly a by-your-leave—he tears down her cloth of state that hangs over her throne, each time telling her there is but one queen in England.

The morning passes slowly, as do all her mornings, and Mary entertains herself with the thought that one day all this will be over, and that when her son is restored to his senses, he will send for her, and she will travel north in a new-spring caroche, and she will dispense alms to the needy as she enters her own dear country and word will be spread that the queen is returned from the south, ready to rule once more, and all will be well.

She will enter Edinburgh and the crowds will come out for her, just as they used to, and she will scatter coins, and pieces of cloth, and hanks of wool, and the poor and the needy will bless her, and then she will ride on up to Stirling, with her son by her side perhaps, but there the dream ends, or becomes watered down, for despite all that she has said and done as to the plan of Association—by which she and he agree to rule the country together—she cannot really picture it, or not in her mind's eye. Where will he sit in relation to her, and she to him? And it is always then that she remembers that little farmhouse above the loch, with the heather-thatched roof, and the laundry billowing in the sweet-scented air.

There is a movement at her window. The messenger perhaps. But it is only the brewer, bringing his cartload of barrels from Burton.

Mary calms herself and plays with dear little Cache-Cache's ears, and she soothes herself by watching her secretaries, Masters Nau and Curle, playing a desultory game of billiards, and also her various ladies at work embroidering the panels for her new cloth of state, which she has designed herself, for this year she decided to change her motto; gone is the old one—"One Like the Lioness"—and in its place her mother's, "In My End Is My Beginning."

She is adopting her symbol, too, that of the phoenix.

Time inches by, and still the messenger does not come, and then it is dinner—for which Mary chooses capon for the first course and kid lamb for the second, with white and then red wine—and it is not until she is in her postprandial slump that a susurrus passes through her chambers that the messenger has finally come.

Her secretaries ready themselves to hand over the packet of letters she has had them write to France and to Scotland and to take those that have come, knowing that both those coming and those going will have either been read through already or are about to be read through by Sir Amyas's cypher clerks, who occupy the west wing of the castle.

Ordinarily the handover is done in the castle bailey, but today Sir Amyas comes himself, stamping into her Presence Chamber, with her entire senior household gathered there in witness. He's a foursquare little fellow, like a frog, she thinks, but carved from granite. He stops before her, ignoring her cloth of state for once, for there is obviously some news that he feels he must deliver in person, and her heart races in the hope that it is something from her son to summon her home, or from Queen Elizabeth perhaps, to say that she is to be released and allowed back to Scotland, or to France, but then she sees Paulet carries but one very small piece of paper and on his face is an expression she has never seen before, and she thinks: *Dear God, can it be that he is actually sorry for me?*

He jerks his head in an impression of a bow.

"Sir Amyas," she says, "God give you good morrow."

"Ma'am," he says, very seriously. "I have been sent word from London, from the office of Her Majesty's principal private secretary."

Walsingham, that devil!

"Sir Francis bids me inform you that in the light of the recent attempt on the life of Her Majesty Elizabeth by Grace of God Queen of England, you are henceforth no longer to be permitted to send or receive any correspondence of any nature with any person, and that from henceforth the services of the diplomatic pouch of the Baron de Châteauneuf are to be denied to you."

There follows a thick, incredulous silence, then a scrape of a chair as Monsieur Nau, her first secretary, sits as if filleted. Cache-Cache starts yapping, but no one rushes to quiet him. Sir Amyas stands as everyone in the room stares at him, all save he enraged and inflamed at this latest injustice.

"You cannot do that," Monsieur Nau finally speaks up. "You cannot cut Her Majesty off like that."

"This will be her death!" Mary Kennedy squeals before clamping both hands over her mouth.

"Why do you not just put Her Majesty in an oubliette and have done with it?" someone else calls out.

Sir Amyas nods very slightly.

"I am merely Her Majesty's messenger," he says. "But I acknowledge this is a great hardship, and as God above is my witness, I wish it were otherwise. However, it is as it is. God give you good day, Lady."

And with that he turns and stalks back out of the Presence Chamber, his back turned on the queen of Scotland. Mary feels the floor pitch, and the sky darken. The ceiling presses down on her. Cache-Cache keeps yapping until someone at last hushes it. Then there is total silence. All eyes are on her. She can feel the tears gathering.

"Get out," she says quietly, but loudly enough for Mary Kennedy to hear. "Get out, all of you, please. Leave me. Leave me be."

Mary Kennedy shoos the others from the room but then returns, creeping to Mary's side, and even her footsteps sound concerned across the spread threshes.

"So," Mary says. "I am to be let die, am I? Is that it?"

Mary Kennedy cannot deny it.

"It is beyond cruelty, Your Majesty."

"They have taken everything," Queen Mary manages to say between sobs. "Everything, everything I have. Taken from me. I cannot live like this anymore. It is the end. I can feel it, Mary, I can feel it. His fingers around my throat. I cannot breathe."

And with that she breaks down into hysterical sobs. Mary Kennedy knows she means Walsingham's fingers, and she steps up onto the dais and, unseen by any other member of Queen Mary's household, takes the woman in her arms and rocks her gently to and fro, to and fro as the light and life fade from the room.

⌖

CHAPTER EIGHT

Dee's house, Mortlake, west of London,
that evening, September 1585

It is nearly curfew by the time John Dee leads Nurdle and the brewer's cart back up the lane toward his house in Mortlake, trying to come up with something better to tell Frommond than the base truth: that not only has he lost a fortune in silver crowns, but Roger Cooke is dead.

That is when he hears the low growl by his shin: a dog on a leash held by a man he has not seen for a few years.

"Why, Bob!" he croaks.

A bailiff.

"It's Bill, actually, Doctor. We always was easy to mix up, weren't we? But sad to say Bob passed out of this world two years ago this last Saint Dunstan's."

Dee is sorry to hear it.

"But I am bringing his boy up in the trade, though," Bill goes on. "Young Bob, come and meet Doctor Dee, one of our regulars."

An oddly stout boy of about twelve steps out of the gathering shadows. He has the face of someone who enjoys pulling wings off flies, and his hand, when he has wiped it on his breeches and taken Dee's proffered palm, is chillingly moist.

"And a new dog, too, I see?"

Which has attached itself to the hem of Dee's cloak, trying to pull it from his shoulders, and growling throatily.

"Clever of you to notice, Doctor. This one shows great promise, don't he? Can always spot what's worth a bob or two and what ain't."

He means Dee's cloak, which he borrowed from Thomas Digges, and which Bill now steps surprisingly nimbly around behind Dee to unhook.

"For old time's sake?" Dee hopes.

"'Fraid not, Doctor. We've come about the small matter of twelve pounds, eight shillings, and sixpence outstanding since Lady Day in favor of James Duckett, bookseller, of Paternoster Row."

What was that for? Ah. Yes. *La Cosmographie Universelle*, André Thevet's book of all things from animals to trumpets to goldmining. Interesting, but surely, he paid for it? It strikes him that if he had not lost all the silver he might now dip a hand into one of the pouches and come up with coin enough to astonish even the hardest-hearted bailiff, but, of course, he cannot.

"Well, come in," he tells Bill. He can imagine Frommond's face when she sees whom he has brought with him, and it almost comes as a relief when Bill places his hand on the wagon and suggests that it and its contents will do for now.

"We don't want to go upsetting Mistress Dee," he says. "Do we?"

Dee is grateful for the consideration these sorts of men usually show Frommond. It is as if they understand the problems of having taken such a man as himself to husband.

"But you don't even know what's in it," Dee says, nodding at the cart. "It could be turnips."

"Anything heavy enough to make a horse sweat like this 'un will do us," Bill says, and he pulls back the sailcloth only to step away, startled.

"Well, stone the crows, Doctor, if that is not poor old Master Cooke."

He takes his hat off and instead of crossing himself, he runs a hand across the bristles of his mostly bald head. Dee notices a hole in the sole of Cooke's boot through which one might put a finger. He tells Bill what happened.

"Pity," Bill says, "and a shame you didn't let us know you was transporting such large amounts of money across the country, Doctor. We could have helped with the security and the like but as it is, we'd not be wanting to take the body with us at this point in time."

Dee understands that means they wish to take the cart, and the cannon.

"What do you suggest I do with Roger?"

"Bury him?"

"Well, of course. Jesu."

In the end they take everything else.

"Even the cannon?"

"Is that what it is?"

And they give him a prewritten receipt "for items to the value of twelve pounds eight shillings and sixpence" that neither Bill nor Young Bob can read.

"But the horse and cart are worth almost that much alone."

"Not nearly, sad to say, Doctor."

"Well, the cannon definitely is."

"But it's too heavy to take off the cart, isn't it? Just us three? No, no. Doctor. We'll keep her safe and sound, until you come along to the yard and pick her up when you've raised the ticket."

And they help Dee sling poor Roger Cooke over Dee's shoulder, hanging with his hands down by Dee's heels, and they loop poor old Roger's bag around Dee's neck, and with a cheerful but solemn wave, they leave him standing outside his own gate, a week after he set off with such high hopes, with nothing to show for his endeavors save a huge debt, and his friend's dead body.

When she greets him in the hall, Frommond claps her hands to her mouth and can hardly speak for sorrow.

"Poor old Roger," she says when they have him maneuvered into the house and laid him out on the Turkey carpet before the fire in Dee's library.

"Who did it?" she asks.

Dee shows her the pistol.

"A Catholic?"

"With salt stains on his coat."

"So just come from France, then. English?"

"Definitely."

She blows out air and straightens Roger's coat for him. His face is mottled the color of cheap tallow and his cheeks are sunken.

"Have you told Walsingham?" she asks.

"He is gone up to north."

"Then Burghley? He will have to know."

"Tomorrow," Dee promises. "First thing. I just need— It has been a long journey."

And he leaves Cooke lying there and hurries down to the laboratory Cooke used while he was working on the canister missiles. There is no sign of a single written note, and nothing to say what went into them, or how they were constructed at all.

Can it be that Cooke has taken their secret to the grave?

CHAPTER NINE

Dunkirk, Flanders, last week in September 1585

Mademoiselle Báthory has never seen the sea before, and when she does, after five long days in the saddle from Joinville, she is left entirely unmoved. It is an obstacle to be overcome, that is all, and crossing it will either be easy, or not; will either kill her, or not; and all she need do is find the boat master to take her across it to England. The air stinks of sea coal and fish guts.

She swings her leg off the horse and drops stiffly to the ground outside an inn overlooking the harbor.

"You there!" she calls to a boy.

"M'sieur?"

"Master Duroc?"

The boy hesitates and glances at her again, either because her voice is not deep enough to be a man's, or because he knows of Master Duroc's reputation.

"Tell him Monsieur Báthory is here," she commands, tossing the boy a coin, and she wheels her horse around and leads it through the inn's gate to find the ostler. When that is settled, she takes a table in a corner and she sits with her back to the wall and her eyes on both entrances. She places her rapier on the bench next to her, but she cannot keep her hands off its hilt. She has enjoyed passing as a man these last few days, especially carrying the sword, though her face is very dry from the walnut juice she's rubbed onto her skin to darken her chin and cheeks.

Duroc comes before she has ordered another cup of wine.

He describes the problem of the wind.

She tells him she does not care, that he must get her to England before Saint Michael's or she'll find someone else who can.

"And I will send word to the duke," she says, meaning de Guise. "To tell him that you have let him down and are no longer to be trusted."

The boat master contemplates what that might entail, and he supposes they might try.

"Dawn, tomorrow."

She takes a private room and sleeps with the rapier unsheathed next to her and her stiletto under her pillow, and the other blade hidden in her sleeve as usual. She wakes to find her right hand on the sword hilt, her left on the dagger, and is pleased with her instincts.

Outside it is a flat gray morning, with scarcely any wind, and the canvas of Duroc's two sails hangs as damp rags in a hawthorn tree. He and his boy—the same from yesterday—use long oars to inch the unnamed craft out of the harbor and into the scrambled swell of the Narrow Sea where Báthory finds she must fight nausea.

"How long will we be?" she asks.

The boy has been told not to look at her, and to keep his mouth shut, but it does not stop him rolling his eyes at the stupidity of her question. The boat master raises a hand as if to backhand him.

"He means nothing by it, Monsieur. He's just a boy."

She says nothing because it does not matter what they think or say.

By about midmorning, when they can row no more and are still scarcely two bowshots from the harbor, the sun breaks through the cloud and the sails flutter in the faintest of breezes. The boat master is quick to abandon his oar and adjust the canvas sheets above her head, and under her feet she feels the boat quicken. It even leaves a faint trail in the sea to mark its progress. The boat master smiles hopefully, hand on a tiller, and by way of apology the boy passes Báthory some ale in a stinking costrel. The rest of the morning wears by; the clouds slide back over again, though still the wind picks up further, cupping the sail, and the water becomes ever more choppy, slapping at the boat's gunwales. Rain sets in, cold and hard, but sometime later the boat master points ahead: a dim and dirty line in the distance.

"England," he says, under low cloud, shrouded in mist, but he knows the coast; knows where his passenger wants to be put ashore, and they make good progress through rough water until they reach the harbor under a low cliff on which sits an ugly church. Dusk is rising now, and the rest of the fishing fleet is coming in, five or six boats under full sail pursued by a hundred gulls apiece.

"Let them get ahead," Báthory tells the boat master.

"The English keep watch on the cliffs," he tells her. "They'll still know you are come."

She doesn't care who sees her come.

"Drop me there," she says, pointing to a stretch of the quay that is sheltered from view of the village and the other boats by a tall hut from which hang fishing nets. As they come in, and the boy is taking down the foresail, she moves quickly behind, so the boat master cannot see her, and she stabs the boy hard in the back. She can feel the dagger slip between two ribs and she knows she has struck the boy's heart by the quantity of blood that follows when she twists the blade and then pulls it from him. He tumbles into the boat as if filleted and she thinks it a shame he did not suffer longer.

"Emile?"

The boat master supposes he's tripped, caught his foot in a rope, but then the sail collapses in salt-stiff folds and he sees the blood and the blade in her hand, and he swears and reaches for some kind of ax that is kept on hand, maybe for just this purpose. Mademoiselle Báthory cannot fight. She can only kill. But the boat master is no longer as young as he was, and he has lost his sense of where the boat is in relation to the jetty, and when the bow thumps into its timbers, he is pitched forward, and must scrabble to keep his footing. The ax comes down on the thwart with a clack as he stretches to save himself, and that is when Mademoiselle Báthory strikes with that infinitely fine blade, a quick dart into his back, aiming to the left of his spine, low down, aiming to kill him, but only slowly. He seethes with the pain of it, ax tossed aside, hands clamped to his back and his belly, his teeth clenched as he flails in the boat like a landed fish. She dips the blade very quickly in the sea and then wipes it on his breeches before sliding it back into its scabbard.

She takes from her saddlebag the long cloak that covers her from chin to shin, and then she is quickly out and along the jetty, never once glancing back at the boat master, who is still reeling. She slips quickly between the stone cottages and an inn above the low door of which swings a wicker basket, into a noisome little alley, and is swiftly into her kirtle and her hood, and though she will need a maid to properly tighten her points and pin her waistcoat, they will do for now. She modifies the cloak so she is back to being a woman again, albeit a drab one, and with a sword hidden in her skirts.

Báthory enters the inn, as if ducking out of the rain, in through the heavy door and into the gloomy hall where smoke from the central hearth hangs heavy, and the one or two men not stupefied by exhaustion or drink look up from their cards to study her, but she hunches herself so that what they see is a bearded crone. She knows it is unconventional for a woman to travel with no maid, but she is here to meet a man whom she has been told will provide all.

And there he is. John Ballard.

Moss-green coat, silver buttons on the hat that sits on his table. He is big, she thinks, and striking, with a dark beard and a fleshy nose. She had been told he is a priest, now very active in the cause of placing the Scottish queen on the English throne, and of returning England to the Catholic fold, but the way he looks at her, she knows that if he is a priest, he is not the sort that keeps his vows. On the table before him are two tankards of battered pewter. She joins him on the bench, and they sit shoulder to shoulder as if they are married five years, and she is just back from the privy. After a long moment, such desultory chatter as there was in the hall of the inn resumes. It is just three or four men too old to be out in the boats, anyway, sitting around a candle and a single jug of ale, and the innkeeper and his wife.

"Any problems?" Ballard asks, just as if indeed they have known each other their whole lives.

"No."

"Nor me," Ballard tells her though she did not ask. "Just the opposite in fact."

He gives the saddlebag under his table a gentle kick. It gives a distinctively heavy clink. She notices gold brocade on the faces of his doublet, the new silver buttons in his hat.

"What have you said?"

"They know me as Captain Fortescue, and I have told them you've been ill. In the room above the stables. It has outside steps. I told the servant to tell the wife. You know."

He nods at the innkeeper's wife, who is staring.

"You've told them I am your wife?"

He pulls a face to suggest "not quite."

"Your whore?"

"Somewhere in between," he corrects, and he takes a deep draft of his ale. Báthory considers this: that these men and that woman think she might be this man's lover. She'd rather die, she thinks.

"Can I ask what brings you to England?" he asks, putting down his mug and turning to her as if making polite conversation.

"I need to find a Jew wizard," she tells him.

Ballard scratches his cheek. He smiles uncertainly, glancing around to see if she is overheard. She's not, though the men at the other table have noticed her subtle transformation into a youthful beauty, albeit with mottled cheeks.

"A Jew wizard?" Ballard wonders.

"A Jew wizard from a place called Mortlake."

"You don't mean Doctor Dee? The alchemist?"

"You know him?"

Ballard knows of him.

"Do you, though?" he asks, and he is perhaps about to go on to tell her who Dee really is, but she doesn't want to hear it. She knows enough about the man who snatched Kitty de Fleurier from her in Prague, undoing many months of careful work that were about to yield up a great triumph.

"What for?" Ballard wonders.

"He owes me something," she says, "and he owes the Duc de Guise something."

She does not tell him that Dee owes them his life, and that she will take it, but not before she has killed every member of his family, and disgraced him, and his name, and all memory of him.

"Don't just kill him," de Guise had said. "Don't just kill them;

I want you to plow salt into his fields. I want to see him ruined; I want everything about him ruined, even his name, so that if anyone ever remembers who he is in the centuries to come, they will laugh, and think him a pitiful fool; a credulous deluded idiot; a raving lunatic."

"The searchers will have seen the boat," Ballard tells her. "They'll soon come calling."

She nods and takes a drink and nearly spits it out. English ale, thick and sweet and nutritious but, by Jesu, disgusting.

A moment later and there is a crash against the door. The innkeeper slaps a rag over his shoulder and marches over to find out what is going on. As he touches the handle, the door swings open, and a man staggers in. It is the French sea captain, Duroc. He would fall into the innkeeper's arms, save the innkeeper steps back and lets him fall hard, facedown on the rushes. A dog starts barking. The Frenchman's breeches are sodden with blood and they all see the ragged hole punched through the cloth on his back.

"Is he dead?" the innkeeper's wife asks.

Báthory slips her cloak off her shoulders and is on her feet and coming around the table.

"No, he's not dead," she says.

Now she wants to be noticed.

"Pass me that," she tells the innkeeper, gesturing at his bar cloth. "Quick!"

He flips the rag off his shoulder and passes it to her. She balls it and presses it onto the wound, but with her thumb pressed deeper into the wound. The Frenchman gasps, flapping like a river-banked salmon, and his blood flows quick and hot.

The innkeeper bends to look in his face.

"Who's done this to you?" he shouts as if the man were deaf. "Who's done it?"

Báthory knows this is the risky part.

"*Un homme*," the Frenchman manages. "*Un gentilhomme qui—qui n'était pas un homme. Un lache.*"

"A man who is no gentleman? A coward?" Mademoiselle Báthory translates. "A coward for stabbing you in the back?"

Duroc tries to correct her.

"*Une française*," he manages, before she stabs her thumb into the hole again. A Frenchwoman. He writhes and shrieks with the pain. He is trying to indicate, to move his arm, perhaps to point at her, but her boot is in the way. She covers it with her skirt so that none see the salt stains.

"What?" the innkeeper says, bending his ear to the whimpering Frenchman's mouth. "What? Francis? His name's Francis?"

Another piteous wail from the Frenchman cuts off any answer and Mademoiselle Báthory feels the life go out of the man under her thumb, a collapse of will that signifies the transition from man to meat. The innkeeper stands abruptly and shakes his head.

"He's dead," he says, and he nearly crosses himself in the old-fashioned way.

"Raise the hue and cry!" his wife shouts.

And so the men stumble to their feet and follow the innkeeper uncertainly out through the door. One man draws his knife. Another lantern is lit. There may be a coward out there, but they aren't desperate to face him.

"You did your best, Mistress," the innkeeper's wife calls over. "More'n anyone else would do for a stranger. Especially a Frenchy."

Where they think she comes from, with her harsh accent, she can only guess.

"My wife is very brave," Ballard announces, and on surprisingly light feet he has come to stand by her side and places a heavy hand on her shoulder, which she cannot stop herself shrugging off. She lets out a sob and stares at her bloody hands.

"Who was he?" she wails for show.

The innkeeper's wife doesn't know, of course.

A moment later and there are shouts from through the open door.

"There's another one!" someone calls through. "Another one in the boat out here. Dead an' all, too!"

The innkeeper's wife bustles through the door after the rest of them and now the inn is deserted, all save Mademoiselle Báthory, Ballard, and a dog sniffing at the Frenchman's blood. Báthory bends and offers her hands to the dog. It licks her fingers very thoroughly, and when they are clean she wipes them on the hem of the dead man's shirt.

"You are playing with fire, Mademoiselle," Ballard mutters.

"They will only remember me as your whore, trying to save this fool's life," she tells him, standing up. "They'll have forgotten when I came in."

She kicks the dead man's body. How did he know she was a woman? Française? Spying on her when she told him she was taking a shit from the back of the boat, that is how. She is glad he is dead, and now his boy too.

When the men return to their ale they have found no sign of the murderer.

"They must've killed each other," she suggests.

"Typical Frenchies," Ballard adds. "Stabbing each other in the back!"

"Let's keep it to ourselves," one suggests. "We keep the boat, sell it, split the price between us."

"The fuckin' searcher'll have seen it come in, won't he? Like as not he'll be on his way right now."

At this she nudges Ballard. He finishes his ale in a gulp and she watches as he approaches the bar where the innkeeper is about to tap another barrel. He invites him into a huddle and they confer among themselves. While Ballard explains something in hushed and secretive tones, she sees the innkeeper glance over at her and back to Ballard, and a repellent smirk crosses his face as his suspicions about her virtue are confirmed, and she sees a coin exchange hands, and then another, and then Ballard comes back to her while the innkeeper tucks the money away with a salacious leer.

The rest of the men in the inn have gone silent and watch as Ballard gathers his hat and gloves, and the hand of the woman whom they have now understood is not his wife.

"Where are you two goin'?" one of them asks. "There's been a murder."

The innkeeper steps in.

"Hush now, Matthew," he says. "This poor gent and his good lady wife aren't caught up in this. They aren't from round here, so can't serve on any jury, and you know they was in here buying you ale when the dead Frenchy come in, wasn't they?"

At which point another coin appears in Ballard's fingers.

"And for your understanding, gents, I shall buy you each another jug from that new barrel there."

As a further coin changes hands, there is grumbling pleasure at this prospect.

"After all," Ballard continues with a wink, "a lady's reputation depends upon it."

At which they all turn to Mademoiselle Báthory, and she manages a very pretty blush, and a cheer breaks out as Ballard—whom they seem to know as Captain Fortescue—gathers up another man's beautiful wife and bundles her from the inn.

Later, when she is up in the saddle of the horse Ballard has brought for her, Báthory notes he has a pistol in the bow of his saddle, and there is a loop for another, but she has no time to think about that, for as they are making their way up through the little gap in the cliffs, beyond the church, they see a party of horsemen come riding, and they turn off the path, behind two hovels, and must duck low while the horsemen clatter past down into the village.

"Searchers," Ballard confirms.

They resume their journey, trotting now, and after a long while, as if he has been thinking about it, Ballard asks her why she could not have come ashore at Selsey, say, just as he had, or any one of the other countless deserted beaches on England's southern shore?

"Why did you need to kill two men? Why take such a risk?"

"I did not want to wet my feet," she tells him. "And it will give them something to think about."

She doesn't tell him how she enjoyed it, the pleasure she took in risking everything, the way it excited her and how it made her blood glow.

CHAPTER TEN

Robert Beale's house, Barnes, last week in September 1585

Thomas Phelippes is Sir Francis Walsingham's decipherer in chief, ordinarily to be found at his desk smoking a foul-smelling pipe of tobacco while grinding his way through pile after pile of encrypted intercepts, but today he is winning a noisy game of bowls with another of Walsingham's men, Arthur Gregory, out on Robert Beale's lawn.

"Five: two to me," he says, sweeping the balls to one end with his foot.

Beale sticks his head out of his window.

"Have you two really nothing better to do?" he asks.

"Not since the master secretary stopped the packets for Tutbury," Gregory tells him. He means the letters that used to come for Mary Stuart from Paris that it was his job to open so that Phelippes could go through each one for hidden messages and invisible writing and so on, and then his job to seal up again, so it looked like no one had.

"I'll be out of practice soon," he goes on. "Unless you've got something good for me?"

Beale hasn't, but that doesn't mean there isn't much else to do, for sitting on his desk this morning are two reports. One, concerning Doctor Dee and the murder of his laboratory assistant, is accompanied by a wheel lock pistol carved with a cross and the words *Deus Vult*, which even Beale can decrypt as being Latin for "God wills it."

Christ, Beale had thought when he read the report, *another blood-crazed assassin on the prowl about the southern counties.*

But at least they have his pistol.

Then he'd read on.

At least they have *a* pistol.

The murderer still has the other.

Beale had set the report down and then he had set about writing eleven identical messages in very curt terms to the various men Walsingham employed to monitor those who come and go along all the many roads and pathways that crisscross southern England: they are to search for a dark-complexioned man who might or might not be wearing a green coat and have silver buttons in his hat. He is to be killed or apprehended on sight, though care should be taken, for he is believed to be armed with a wheel lock pistol.

These messages he summoned a secretary to dispatch immediately.

The other report came from an espial across the water in France, at the English College in Rheims, where the treasonous Father William Allen trains Catholic malcontents to slip back into England either to sow sedition or make attempts on Her Majesty's life. The report described how the arrival at the school of a man named Gilbert Gifford has exacerbated tensions between the English and Welsh factions at the college to such an extent that insults—both penned and spoken—have graduated to physical blows.

Good, Beale had thought, for Gilbert Gifford is one of Sir Francis Walsingham's men.

Then he had sat back to steeple his fingers and think of each report through the prism of his newly imposed priorities: Did either suggest anything that might involve Sir Francis Walsingham scheming to bring Mary Queen of Scots to trial?

He could not see anything, so he had rolled each up again, and put them in his bag, along with the pistol, ready to take to Barn Elms, Walsingham's sprawling house upriver where the man himself has been on his sick bed after overexerting himself on his ride from Portsmouth to Tutbury and back to London in the span of a week.

"What's he up to—old Walsingham—do you think?" Phelippes asks when Beale emerges. "Blocking her messages? He's never going to catch her conspiring in anything that way, is he?"

Since he first heard of Walsingham's newly imposed ban on Queen Mary's correspondence Beale has wondered the same thing himself.

"Perhaps he doesn't want to catch her in anything?" Beale suggests, watching the other man send his ball toward the jack at the end of the lawn. "Perhaps he is just trying to protect her from herself?"

It is not clear if it is Gregory's delivery of his ball that inspires Phelippes's snort of derision, or the suggestion that Walsingham's motives might be anything but impure.

"He hates that woman more than he hates the pope," Phelippes reminds him, sending his ball to nestle perfectly against the jack.

Beale takes the last horse in his stables and rides the half mile to find Walsingham in his bed in Barn Elms.

"Kidney stones," Lady Ursula tells him when she sees him in the anteroom. "They always come on when he's been overdoing things."

Walsingham's wife is a handsome woman, intolerant of nonsense, but very anxious about what is next to happen in the Netherlands, where her son-in-law is almost certain to go with the Earl of Leicester. Beale has no news for her.

"Antwerp is still fallen, obviously, but there are reports of the Duke of Parma not putting its people to the sword."

Which feels hopeful.

"Perhaps Her Majesty will not send her army after all?"

"I hope not," Beale agrees. "It's the only one she's got."

And it is not much good anyway.

Lady Ursula shows him to Sir Francis's door.

"And remember: don't overtax him," she says.

Walsingham lies in his dark curtained bed looking dreadful—sallow and sweaty, with crusts around his yellow eyeballs and in obvious pain—and the room smells just as bad. He can hardly raise his eyes to greet Beale and can only whisper.

"What have you got for me?"

Beale sits by his bedside and moves the candle closer to tell him about Dr. Dee's laboratory assistant being shot dead.

"Jesu! When was this?"

"Ten days ago."

Walsingham groans and tries to raise himself onto his elbows.

"I must get up," he moans, but he cannot, and he flops back onto the pillow.

"You must rest, Sir Francis. Lady Ursula will kill me if you die."

Walsingham lets out a windy sigh and closes his eyes.

"So what happened? Why do we only learn of this now?"

Beale explains all he knows. Walsingham is furious.

"He told no one for two days! Why didn't he come to see me?"

"You were away."

Which is true, of course: Walsingham has been to Tutbury and back. Which is why he is now laid up sick.

"Did he manage to get his gun home?" Walsingham wonders.

"His gun? Other than this one, I am not sure."

Walsingham is about to explain something, but when Beale takes out the wheel lock pistol, he is distracted, and both men stare at it, fascinated, and the mood becomes very somber. To think that it was used to kill a man.

"How does it—?"

"I'm not sure," Beale answers the unfinished question. "I think you load it normally, but then you put a piece of pyrite in here, and then pull it back here, so it touches this wheel, and when you pull the trigger the wheel turns and the pyrite sparks and catches the powder. Or something."

Beale finds he cannot keep his fingers from playing with the pistol's ornate mechanism, and he points the barrel at the fire and almost says the word *bang* aloud. He has never fired one of these things, but he would like to. He remembers the almost comical pleasure Mistress Devereux took in firing that gun from the top of the tower in Orford, and in other circumstances he might laugh. Beale shows Walsingham the cross carved in the pistol's handle and the motto. Walsingham pulls a face and waves the pistol away, and Beale must return it to its bag.

"So a Catholic then?"

Beale nods.

"And Dee described him as looking more like a Spaniard than an Englishman, with silver buttons in his hat."

It is Walsingham's turn to nod.

"It certainly sounds like John Ballard," he agrees.

The man John Ballard has been on a list of "wanted men" for some time now, ever since he was seen meeting Queen Mary's agents in Paris this last month, when it was learned he was an old soldier, and therefore likely to present a more than usually active threat to Her Majesty's life and limb. He's the one they've been dreading coming to England.

"And there were salt stains on his coat, too," Beale continues, "as if he has recently been at sea."

"Which fits with him leaving Paris," Walsingham supposes, placing his fingers over his eyes. "So there's another one. Christ. And this one with a pistol."

He means another assassin on the loose.

"I've sent word this morning to our searchers along the south coast," Beale tells him. "And to all the sheriffs in Surrey and the southern counties generally. But he could be anywhere by now."

Walsingham is silent for a moment, thinking.

Then he asks if when he leaves here, Beale will go and find Dee.

"Find out if Hawkins paid him any money—well, he must have, if Dee had any to steal—and if so how much, and how much of it was stolen, but most of all will you check that he managed to get that cannon back to Mortlake?"

"Cannon?"

Only then does Walsingham give him the bare bones of the sinking of the *Neaera*, and Hawkins's reaction. Beale actually laughs, very quietly so that Lady Ursula does not hear.

"Hawkins? Hawkins gave Dee a thousand crowns?"

Walsingham cannot help but smile too.

"I know. I know. Absurd, isn't it? I'd not trust him with three. But that is my point. Dee is as reliable as—as—as my own kidneys, and if he has even the smallest amount of money in his purse he will be off after some new scheme or discovery instead of—instead of knuckling down and doing what he should be doing."

Beale has always been fascinated by Walsingham's relationship with Dee, whom he consistently vilifies, but who has saved Walsingham's reputation, skin, and country time after time.

"So just make certain he is in his workshop, will you? Tinkering away with his alchemical hammer or whatnot. Or gone to the Weald to consult his ironmaster. I don't want him getting up to anything astrological or wizardy, because Sir Christopher Hatton is still intent on having him burned to death for the amusement of the denizens of Smithfield."

Beale nods and is about to gather his papers together when Walsingham brings up the matter of Gilbert Gifford and the English College in Rheims, and both laugh at the thought of the Jesuits fistfighting among themselves.

"And so surely now is the time to move him on to Paris?"

At this, Beale stiffens. By Paris, Walsingham means into the orbit of Thomas Morgan, Queen Mary's business agent. It means putting Gifford a step closer to Queen Mary, which is the very thing Queen Elizabeth has instructed Beale to ensure does not happen.

"Surely we should leave him be, if he is doing such a good job in Rheims?" he tries. "And you know how suspicious Morgan is."

Walsingham's bruised eyes settle on Beale for a moment longer than Beale finds comfortable.

"It was your idea getting him in with Morgan in the first place, remember?"

Beale makes a show of sucking his teeth doubtfully.

"That was before Morgan was thrown in the Bastille."

As a courtesy to the English, the French have jailed Thomas Morgan for his part in a plot to kill Her Majesty that they managed to foil the year before, but Morgan has continued his work for Queen Mary, managing her money—to his own advantage, of course—from his cell, where the French ensure he has all he needs, and visitors may come and go as they please.

Walsingham is now tiring visibly.

"Well, Robert," he murmurs. "I shall leave it to you."

Beale nods, relieved.

"I will see what Gifford says," he says, though he knows he won't.

And with that Lady Ursula bustles in, and Robert Beale's audience with Her Majesty's principal private secretary is concluded.

On his way home, Beale wonders how he can stop Gilbert Gifford going to Paris and inveigling himself into Mary's household in exile. More than that, he wonders how he can do so without Sir Francis noticing that it is he—Beale—who has done so. He tries to think what advice Sir Francis would give him were he to go to Sir Francis with the problem.

Throw yourself into some other work, he'd probably say. *If you are elsewhere, then you cannot be expected to know what is happening, can you?*

When Beale gets home, Phelippes is still there, but sitting at his desk now, eyeglasses on and smoking that filthy pipe, and he is about to instruct him to send word to Gifford in the usual way, which is in alum water on the back of a letter to Her Majesty's ambassador to the court of King Charles in Paris, when he bites his tongue.

"I am going down to Surrey," he tells him instead.

"Surrey? Why?"

"To speak to the sheriffs about Ballard—if it is Ballard—myself. I'll see if Mistress Devereux will come," Beale goes on.

"Ahhh."

Now Phelippes understands.

"Good idea," he says. "See if Surrey likewise falls for her charms."

And so it is that Robert Beale also forgets for the moment Walsingham's instruction as to the activities of Doctor Dee.

CHAPTER ELEVEN

Mortlake, October 1585

Finally, Thomas Digges is home! He's out in his garden, examining what the rabbits have done to his herbs, when Dee spots him from where he has been waiting for him, perched on the roof of his house.

"Where have you been?" Dee calls down with little or no ceremony.

"Ah! John! I did not see you up there! God give you good day, sir! What news of our cannon?"

"Stay there!"

Dee hoicks himself up and balances his way to the gable end, where he takes hold of an oak branch that extends from Digges's garden, and he swings onto it, and then, branch by branch, descends to land more heavily than he used to in Digges's garden, right in his onion patch.

"Did Roger leave any notes with you?"

"Roger? No. Why?"

Dee realizes that since Digges has been away with his cousins in Northamptonshire he knows nothing of Dee's recent misadventures; knows nothing of Cooke's death, the theft of the money, the confiscation—if he can put it that way—of the cannon, as well as Nurdle and the cart. When he tells him, Digges is stunned into silence. They are now walking in the long grass down by the river at the bottom of Digges's garden. Digges's head is bowed in sorrow, but there is also anger and disappointment.

"I'm sorry, Thomas," Dee says. "I really am."

"How much do you need to get it all back?" Digges asks.

"Just fifteen pounds for the cart, Nurdle, and the cannon. I will repay you when I have—when I have recovered the money."

"And how will you do that?" Digges wonders.

Dee is not certain.

"That is not our principal problem," he says. "Our principal problem is that poor old Roger seems to have taken to his grave the secrets of the canister missiles."

"You know nothing of them?" Digges wonders.

Dee shakes his head.

"I steered him toward certain conclusions, but it was his project, and his alone. He was very proud of it and I didn't want to intrude."

"He must have left something somewhere? In one of the laboratories, surely? Or his chamber?"

"If he did, I cannot find it. Perhaps it went up with your shed?"

The two men stare at the blackened stumps of the shed that are now almost hidden in the long grass. Dee feels his shoulders slump. To go through all that again, and this time without Roger Cooke. It doesn't seem possible.

"But you should have seen it, Thomas," he reminisces aloud. "One shot in the stern of the privateer, and the whole thing went up like a bomb. It was utterly terrifying."

"He must have tweaked the recipe since we hit the dean's water steps," Digges supposes, gesturing across the river to the crater that marks where the steps used to be. "Or hit their powder store."

Dee nods and they are silent for a while, each lost in their thoughts.

"So," Digges says eventually. "Fifteen pounds, and you will return Nurdle to Master Dollington?"

"Dollington?"

"The brewer. It is his horse."

"Of course. Of course. I will do so now."

Dee has of course oftentimes in the past had cause to visit the bailiffs' "depot," as Bill calls their scruffy little yard, to collect various items that have been taken from him before they've been sold on. Books, mostly, but once an astrolabe, and on one occasion a model of the solar system made for him by Gerard Mercator. The depot is upriver, behind a boatbuilder and a tanner, between a carpenter's workshop and a cooper-cum-wheelwright. When Dee finds his way there today, under a low sun, the first thing he sees is Nurdle, her nose in a bag of oats. The second thing is the cart, empty. And the third thing is young Bob.

"Where's the cannon?" Dee asks.

"What cannon?"

"The bronze thing that was on the back of the cart."

The boy shakes his head.

"Search me," he says.

"But you can't just lose something like that. Where's Bill?"

The dog growls at him.

Bill emerges from a lean-to.

"Why, Doctor Dee!"

"Where's the cannon?"

Please don't say what cannon, Dee prays.

"What cannon?"

Ahhh, Jesu!

Bill removes his greasy russet cap and rubs his bristly scalp. He looks about the yard through small porcine eyes at the piles of this and that; the stacks of farming implements; a small tower of unlabeled barrels; three cart wheels; some stone statuary left over from the Augmentation Office, perhaps; and even some of the worthless black ore that Frobisher brought back from the New World. There is no cannon though.

"Thing is, Doctor, I didn't really expect you'd come back for it," Bill explains, one eye cocked shut against the gravity of the situation.

"So what has happened to it?"

"Sold it to a smith, didn't I?"

Dee claps his hand to his head.

"When?"

"To be honest, Doctor," Bill says, shifting from foot to foot, "I took it straight there after we collected it from outside yours that night, didn't I? No point in unloading it here, I thought, because as you said yourself it was heavy, and I know they're always after anything iron or brass or what have you, and as I say, I didn't think you'd ever raise the ticket, did I? I mean, in a way, how was I to know? I thought I was doing you a favor in fact, because they paid more than I thought it was worth, so I owe you three shillings, which if you'd care to accompany me to my office I can pay you now, and so cancel all debts to me. How does that sound?"

Dee can feel the hair standing on his head.

"If that cannon is melted into pig iron, Bill, then it'll be to Her Majesty's Treasurer of the Navy you'll have to answer, so send Young Bob to tell the smith not to touch that cannon. Tell him that it is Admiral Hawkins who wants it back, safe and sound!"

At the mention of Hawkins, Bill flinches.

"Saints!" he hisses. "You didn't tell me it belonged to Hawkins!"

"Because I'd just seen poor old Master Cooke killed, hadn't I? And I didn't think you'd have the bloody thing melted down. Who bought it?"

"Ralph Hogge," Bill admits. "From Buxted, in the Weald."

"Oh Jesu."

Hogge is one of those ironmasters who wouldn't give Dee credit when he was trying to get the cannon made in the first place. Now he will have to ride to Buxted, today, with not a moment to lose, and if Hogge has not already melted it down, then Dee will either have to buy the cannon back, or persuade him to replicate it forty-nine times, and take payment on delivery.

"Right," he says, turning to Bill. "Give me the money Hogge paid you for it, and I'll take the horse and cart as well."

Bill counts the coins back into Dee's palm, and when Dee is reunited with Nurdle, and the cart, he climbs up onto the driver's bench and flicks the reins to stir Nurdle into action.

As luck would have it, outside his own gate, he meets Thomas Digges come riding the other way. Digges greets him with less warmth than hitherto beforehand.

"No cannon, I see?"

Dee can only shake his head.

"But I have your money," he says, and he repays Digges the fifteen pounds from before. He calculates fifteen pounds will not make much of a difference to Master Hogge, and he still has the money Bill gave him. With that he will rent a horse, or something, and perhaps he will still be able to afford that divining pendulum from the dealer off Cheapside. Then, as he is telling Digges what has happened, another idea strikes him.

"Thomas," he says, "might I trespass on your already much trampled good nature and borrow your horse? It will take Nurdle a week to plod to Buxted, and—"

And when it is done, and Digges has reluctantly yielded his own horse, Sparrow, and agreed to return Nurdle to the brewer Dollington, Dee leads Sparrow into his own yard to collect things he might need for the journey and to explain his departure to his wife, Jane Dee, née Frommond, whom he oftentimes thinks of as just Frommond.

"Jane?"

He meets her in the yard where she stands with another woman, who flinches when she sees him. Dee recognizes her, though he cannot recall where from.

"Mistress Pargeter," Frommond tells him. "She is to come with me to Tutbury."

In all his mad anxieties Dee has not asked after Frommond's activities, but now he does.

"Tutbury?"

He listens in astonishment as Frommond explains, but half his mind is trying to remember how or why he knows Mistress Pargeter, who was certainly called something else when he knew her. Perhaps that is why she is evading his gaze, because he is certain she knows who he is, and how they know each other.

"And what about Arthur?"

It turns out Sarah, Frommond's maid, has taken their son to stay with Frommond's brother, Nicholas, and his cousins in Cheam.

"You were not here to be said good-bye to," she rebukes.

Dee apologizes to both women, most especially to Frommond for being so absent, but also to Mistress Pargeter, for staring.

"I am sure we have met before?" he probes.

She tells him no, she thinks not, and if he were a betting man—he sometimes is—he would put money on the fact that she was speaking with a put-on accent.

But Jesu! The cannon! It will be melted by now! He has no time for this. He tells them he will see them both shortly, perhaps, and will send word to Tutbury, before he swings himself into Sparrow's saddle and sets his heels for Kent.

CHAPTER TWELVE

Tutbury Castle, Staffordshire, October 1585

Autumn now, this far north, with an edge to the wind, and the hills more brown than green, and Sir Amyas Paulet stands in Queen Mary's preference room and says nothing, for there is nothing to say. If she were any other person in the world, he might tell her to get up; get up, go out, and get some exercise in the fresh air before it is too late. If she were a child of his, he might grip her ear and drag her to the door and push her out into it, but he cannot do that, for she is the queen of Scots, and at the Queen of England's command—and his obeisance of that command—she is not permitted to go out and must sit cooped up like this all day, with not a single thing to occupy her hands or her mind save billiards and embroidery, of which she is respectively bored and incapable, and so no wonder she is looking so wretched. Anyone would.

Her women and her secretaries glare at Sir Amyas as if it were his fault, and Master Bourgoing, her surgeon, has been to see him privately to voice his concerns, with which Sir Amyas entirely agreed: the last few weeks have been very hard on Queen Mary and, yes, she has deteriorated in body and mind far faster than might have been anticipated. He has written of course to Queen Elizabeth and explained how things stand, but has not Queen Mary agreed to do anything that Queen Elizabeth thinks best?

She has, of course.

And this is what Queen Elizabeth feels is best, and until such time, et cetera, et cetera, then there is nothing further or different that Sir Amyas can say or do. He has his instructions: Queen Mary is to stay within her chambers, for her own safety, and she is not to communicate with the outside world for everyone else's safety.

"But Her Majesty is sending a new companion for you, ma'am," he announces, aware how hollow this will sound. "The wife of a man named Doctor Dee, who is supposed to be marvelously quick and witty."

He's not sure about this, if he is honest, but there has to be a reason why another two women are coming to put further strain on the castle's already struggling sewers, and, anyway, Queen Mary barely stirs when she hears the news. She remains slumped in her chair, almost like a dolt, and there might even be a link of drool connecting her slack mouth to the fur of her tippet, which she has taken to wearing against the rising cold and the damp that has already started to seep through the castle walls. Her feet have swollen so that she can no longer wear any of the hundreds of shoes she has had sent from Paris and London, and her hands, too, lie heavy and useless in her lap where they surely used to be shapely and nimble—dainty even, for the love of God! while now each finger would feed a family of four—and despite the best efforts of Barbara Mowbray and others, the queen's face reminds Sir Amyas of nothing so much as the full moon in August, only it is a dull mat of lifeless clay in which eyes like dark berries betray nothing but anguished pain.

"She will not last another week of this," he tells his wife when they are together. His wife looks at him shrewdly. Both know not to air their speculations on Queen Elizabeth's intentions, but some words need not be spoken aloud to be understood. Sir Amyas cannot hold his wife's gaze. That it should fall to him to oversee the slow murder of a woman who was once so lively and filled with grace! It is not how he imagined passing the late years of his life, he would admit, and were it not that Her Majesty had entrusted him with this duty especially, there are times when he would rather go anywhere else—to the Netherlands with Leicester, to take his chances against the Spanish tercios—than continue here. *Oh, to be back in Jersey*, he thinks, where he was able to govern in peace, or even Paris again. Anything is preferable to Tutbury, with its whistling winds and stinking middens.

"What would you do in Queen Mary's shoes?" his wife asks.

He stops to think, to try to imagine what it might be like to have had such an extraordinary life—she can speak six languages; she wore a steel helmet and led an army in battle; she escaped from a castle on an island; she was married two or three times depending on which rite you believed in, witnessed murder, perhaps committed murder; she endured mayhem and managed to rule Scotland—notoriously impossible—and all the time while being a woman—and now here she is, a wreck, washed up like one of those seals on this beach of enforced idleness.

So what would he do?

He honestly has no idea.

"Pray," he supposes.

PART | TWO

CHAPTER THIRTEEN

The Cock and Key, Fleet Street, London,
day before All Hallows' Eve, October 1585

"This is where the Dee lives?"

It is just after noon on a gray autumn day and they are standing on Fleet Street, looking at what is obviously to Mademoiselle Báthory's eye an inn under the swinging sign of a painted chicken and a carved key as long as her leg.

"No," he admits.

"Then why are we here?"

Her patience is running out with Ballard, whom she now believes is not only a braggart and a liar, but playing the role of Captain Fortescue, a gallant old soldier with many a tall tale to tell not because it is a good cover, but solely for his own pleasure, and also hampering her mission here in England, which is a country she detests.

"We must meet some friends of mine," Ballard tells her, and he taps his nose to signal that they are not ordinary friends, but men caught up in whatever scheme he is scheming on behalf of the

Duc de Guise, from whom she has brought Ballard two or three messages that she opened on her way through France, fearing they might contain instructions that she was to be murdered. They were encrypted in a code so basic that it would fool only women, children, and rustics, and which Báthory deciphered while on horseback, though each has taken Ballard many a painful hour to go through.

"I have no time for this," she tells him.

"It will be but half an hour," he tells her. "Please. I must speak with them, on behalf of a certain gentleman known to us both."

It seems to amuse him, this nonsensical way of referring to the duke.

"And besides," he goes on, "I want to show you off."

There is nothing to show off, of course. On that first night on the road from wherever it was Mademoiselle Báthory came ashore, Ballard tried to climb into her bed, and if she bothered to look at him now she would see that there is still a scab the size of a small coin below his chin, which she knows will keep coming off against his collar every time he turns his head, each time reminding him that somewhere on her person—he still cannot decide where—she carries a very sharp knife and knows precisely how to use it.

But since she is hungry, and Ballard is her only contact in England, she cannot refuse, and he gallantly allows her to proceed into the inn before her, where she finds what she always does in the taverns they have visited since her arrival: a large smoky room filled with long tables and benches at which ugly stupid men are lined up like pigs over troughs, eating foul food and drinking filthy ale.

Just as in Kent, today all inane chatter ceases when she enters, and all eyes turn ravenously upon her, as if they have never seen a woman before. Ballard, in his role as Captain Fortescue, has in the past stepped forward to shield her, and to chide the men for their rough manners and ungentlemanly welcome, and then he has always offered them all ale, and he has winked at the innkeeper who has always so far cleared them both a place by the fire and brought them a jug of something nasty, and the choicest bits he has—sausages, usually, foul and corrupted with gristle, but sometimes just bread and stew. And then "Fortescue" has poured her some ale or wine or whatever it is and tried to feed her himself in a grotesque show of affection that makes her sick, but then within the half hour he has always been on his feet again, lying to anyone who'll listen about how he singlehandedly breached the defenses of Brielle, or how he poured boiling tar on the Spanish tercios at Alkmaar, or how he boarded a Spanish galleon alongside his Portuguese brothers in arms at the battle of Ponta Delgada.

This afternoon, though, perhaps because they are finally in London, Ballard is not playing Fortescue.

"Too many of Walsingham's watchers about," he tells her, as he steers her through the crowd, "and so as of now, I am Master Turner, a mercer, if you please, and humble as you like!"

She does not smile. To be in his company makes Báthory sick, and she must also concentrate on not stabbing the hands that stretch out to grope her as she passes on her way to a table in the corner at which sit three glum-looking men in sober cloth, narrow collars, modest hats, and polished boots, who greet this "Turner" awkwardly, as if they do not quite know how to greet a man pretending to be another man, and when they turn to her, she knows straightaway that all three are virgins.

"My friends! My friends!" "Turner" murmurs, shaking each man's hand in turn. "Well met! Well met, indeed!"

When Ballard names them, she would forget each instantly, save that she is very good at remembering names and faces. Chidiock Tichbourne (short, florid, close-set eyes and with a forked ginger beard that is so ugly she wants to tear it from his chin by its roots);

Robin Poley (a slender man/woman, as insubstantial and unreliable as morning mist); and last, Anthony Babington (the most English person she has ever met: tall, mousy, blue-eyed and flush-cheeked, whose soft hands are yet to work a day). Apart from their virginity, they seem to have little else in common, and she knows instinctively that whatever it is they are plotting, it will come to nothing.

And to be fair, they look as if they feel the same way, too, for they stare needily at Ballard, like harrier chicks opening their mouths to be fed, as if hoping he brings morsels of good news, something to give them heart and put fire in their bellies. Which is why he is here in the first place, of course, and why he is taking up her time when they should be finding Dee.

A stool is brought, and the three men budge up and she and Ballard sit, and ale comes for which Babington pays, after which, Ballard settles down, elbows on table, and when he invites their confidence, they quietly admit they are fearful of their futures.

"We are abandoned," Tichbourne whines. "On our miserable island, in our miserable state."

"No, no, no!" Ballard reassures them. "No, no, no!"

"Yes, yes, yes," Babington takes up the tune. "All these people you say care for our cause: the pope—"

"Shhhhh!"

"—the king of Spain; the Duc de Guise; they are too caught up in their own affairs to save us."

"Not a bit of it!"

"Yes they are," Tichbourne tells Ballard, slightly vexed. "We are cut off from the true religion, but not tidings! We know what is happening across the Narrow Sea. In France and in Italy."

"But I do assure you, sirs—" Ballard tries.

"And even if they were not taken up so, then—then none of them possesses an army powerful enough to take all of England by conquest."

"But with the help of all Englishmen loyal to the one true faith?"

"They will not rise against the Queen that is," Tichbourne is certain. "Not in number."

At which "Turner" beams and ushers them to bend close.

"But this is it," he whispers in their ears. "For even now there is a plan afoot to rid us of the usurping serpent."

At which Babington and Tichbourne sit back, skeptical, as if they have heard it all before; but Poley leans forward, interested, as if to hear more.

"I cannot talk further," Ballard confides, "for your own sakes, but suffice it to say that a good man with a wheel lock dag is come from France."

Mademoiselle Báthory supposes that a *dag* is another word for a pistol, which de Guise's coded letters mentioned Ballard had been sent to give to some marksman named John Savage, who is supposed to be waiting for him at a church called Saint Giles-in-the-Fields, wherever that is, from nine of the clock until ten of the clock every day this coming week. She understands that Ballard believes the importance of his errand—delivering those pistols to a man who is prepared for martyrdom in his attempt on the English Queen's life—trumps hers, though she believes he is wrong. And she knows he has lost one of the pistols.

"And there is more," Ballard goes on.

"Such as?" Poley asks.

"A certain gentleman has sent me letters," Ballard announces, tapping his new doublet in which she has seen him put the letters she brought him from de Guise. "He has asked me to assure you that everything is in place. Twenty thousand tercios wait in Antwerp where the Dutch are now well-beaten, and there is a Spanish fleet assembled in Bilbao waiting for the word to bring them over. More than that, there are men in Ireland—good men, ready and willing—waiting for the word to sail for Harlech. All they need is one spark! One spark! And they will come."

The letters from the Duc de Guise said nothing of the sort, of course, but the three men look at one another with gathering confidence, as if they are indeed nourished by Ballard's clearly untrue words, and if it were possible, Báthory's contempt for them deepens. The letters cautioned patience for now, for de Guise's scheme to get the backing of Emperor Rudolf had, of course, recently failed—thanks to Dee—and he did not want his allies in England to waste their chance "for fear of reprisals taken against our beloved cousin," by whom she believes he means Queen Mary of Scotland. When she read the letters—before resealing them—she interpreted them to mean that de Guise was not ready to come to England himself, and since she knows him to be determined to lead the army that conquers England, he does not wish for any "spark" to set in motion a process he cannot control.

So in a sense the three men were right to doubt the chance of help from abroad, though Ballard's made-up words have persuaded them otherwise.

"Yes, yes," the ginger one says, and he pounds a fist into a palm to show how inspired he's become. His cheeks are now ruddy and his eyes glassy, and she supposes him to be the sort who is disgusted by himself when he yields to his own base appetites and then writes about this in verse in the morning. She cannot even bring herself to despise him. The other one, though—Babington—leans forward and asks, as if this is the most important thing:

"And what tidings have you of *Regina Futura*?"

Ballard takes a moment to understand what he means.

"Reg—? Ah. The Queen That Will Be. Yes. Though her bonds be tight, her spirits be high! And do you know why, gentlemen? For she has received word of your endeavors on her behalf, and though she knows you do not undertake such risks as you undertake with any thought of reward come the happy morn, she wishes me to tell you that when the deed is done, and she sits where she should sit, then she will lift you up to be among the highest in the land!"

At which the three become dewy-eyed and smile shyly at one another, as if brothers in arms in some noble enterprise, while Ballard darts her a look of the sort that is both deniable, and undeniable. She cannot decide whom she hates more, him or them.

The money he has stolen is burning a hole in Ballard's purse, and so she knows it is only a matter of time before he will offer to buy them all dinner and ale, and when he does so, she places a hand on his sleeve.

"No," she says. "We must be about our business."

He opens his mouth to overrule her, but then he looks into her eyes and is cowed. He knows what she can do, with or without a knife, but it is more than that: hers is fundamentally a stronger mind with a stronger desire. He stands and bows to the three men, and they stare at him, looking something between aghast and abandoned, and he covers his surrender with a speech about the transports of desire that come with cupid's dart, and if Mademoiselle Báthory cared what any of these men did, or said, or thought, she'd probably have stabbed him, there and then, and then them. But she doesn't. Instead she turns on them and walks away without farewell, leaving Ballard to catch her up.

It is mid-to-late afternoon now, and the day is dimming, yet still they must get to Mortlake.

"The fastest way?" she asks Ballard.

"River," he says, and they walk south past a building site and soon she can smell the water, damp and cold and fetid, and it reminds her of home. When they emerge on its bank, there are the lights of one or two wherries and barges following the tide upstream, with lanterns already alight at their sterns, and a little way to their right is a set of water steps above which hangs another lamp.

Below is a wherry in which sits a short fat man wrapped in a voluminous cape.

"You'll take us to Mortlake?" Ballard asks.

The man groans.

"Not going to see Doctor Dee, are you?"

Even she must hesitate at the man's foresight.

"No," she recovers. "But do you know where he lives? I have heard much of him."

"Do I know where he lives? Bloody hell, I spend my life ferrying him to and fro. Down to Greenwich, up to Whitehall, then to Richmond and back to Mortlake. Never tipped me yet, do you know? Anyway. No. I'll not do it. Tide's against us."

"No, it isn't," Ballard says. "And I'll give you a crown."

"A crown? Fuck me, sir, in you get!"

They climb down and the man watches them settle.

"Been in a wherry before have you, Mistress?" he asks before unlooping his rope and easing his little craft out into the rising tide.

CHAPTER FOURTEEN

Mortlake, London, day before All Hallows' Eve, October 1585

It is now late evening, past curfew, with a thin sliver of moon risen in the eastern sky, when Doctor Dee finally returns home, bone-weary and empty-handed from the Weald. He would dearly love the pleasure of sitting by his own fire with a cup of something hot and strong, and listening to his wife and his son telling him what they've been up to since he set off on his entirely unsuccessful trawl through the Weald of Kent and Sussex, but he knows they are gone—Frommond to Tutbury; Arthur to Cheam—and so he will have to make do with Roger, he thinks, before he remembers Roger is dead. He then considers how long the muscle of the mind takes to adjust from habit, and he reconciles himself to the thought that at least Sarah will be there, and he envisages her having made leek soup or something, and he will sit and listen to what she has to say, and that will be quite nice enough after the—

But then he sees something is wrong: every chimney of every household in Mortlake is letting slip a winding scarf of pale wood-smoke, so why isn't his? Surely to God he paid the wood merchant?

He swings down from his saddle and hammers on the gate, and he has to stop himself calling out for Roger.

"Sarah!" he shouts. "Open up! It is me!"

There's no reply. No sound of any movement within.

Ordinarily he might suppose her out or gone to stay with her mother down the road perhaps, but a low, stealthy dread creeps over him like a cold shadow. He clambers back up into the saddle and tries to peer over the wall that he has had built ten foot high specifically so that no one might do this. Then he rides along to Thomas Digges's gate, where the night watchman lets him in.

"You have not seen Sarah?" Dee asks. "There seems to be no one at home? And no smoke from the chimney either."

William has no good answer, nor does Thomas Digges.

"Can I borrow your garden?"

Dee means to walk down to the river, and then back up to his own house, which is the only way in.

"Of course. I will come with you."

They descend to the river, and then through their adjoining orchard where the apples hang heavy and the grass is overlong. Digges holds up his lamp.

"What's that?"

Over by the water steps, lying in the grass is a long dark mound.

"Oh Jesu," Dee murmurs, for he knows what it is, but not who it is. Digges brings the lamp close and in its somber golden light Jiggins the boatman lies on his back, looking uncomfortable in his clothes, as if he has been dragged from the river by his collar. One eye is a dark whorl of blood, like a worm cast on the beach, and the stain of blood flares back across his cheek to matt the hair around his temple.

Dee bends and places the backs of his fingers on the bloodless cheek.

"Still warm," he says.

Dee and Digges exchange a quick look before each man's gaze flicks away, toward the house through the orchard.

"Do you have a knife?" Dee asks.

"No. Nothing."

They walk together following the familiar path past the vegetable and herb gardens, past the laboratories and the library and into the courtyard. Nothing stirs in the house save the low susurrus of wind and— Is there something else? Dee feels the hairs on his arms stand on end. The door to the buttery is open.

"Who's there?" he calls.

There is a fleeing stillness and then a streak of lithe movement that hurtles past them, terrifying both men so that Digges nearly drops the lamp.

"A fox!" Digges laughs. "Only a fox!"

They regather their wits.

"Hello?" Dee calls out, stepping into the cold darkness that smells strongly of its most recent visitor. Nothing else. A dish is broken; a tub of something is spilled on the stone floor and a net of cheese has been ripped from the beam above their heads. They turn back and take the lamp across the yard to the kitchen. The door is closed but unlocked. When Dee pushes it open he is greeted by a rush of cold air that smells homely enough, he thinks, of soup perhaps, but again, no woodsmoke.

"Sarah!" he shouts. His voice echoes as only in an empty house. "Sarah!"

There is only the slight scratch of mice.

"Here," Dee says, "let me light another lamp."

He finds the little stash of reeds and candles in the sideboard and lights one. The smell of soup is definite now. Leek. It makes Dee's mouth water. It is strongest by the fire, and that is where they find her, lying tangled in the shadow of an overturned bench on the flagstones by the side of the table.

"Oh Jesu, Sarah!"

Dee shoves aside the bench and bends over her. She lies on her back in a welter of still warm leek soup that spreads from the overturned cauldron and is smeared over just about everything within a three-pace circle around the body. There are signs of struggle—torn linens; kicked-up skirts; an overturned stool; a broken butter churn—and there are many footprints and scrapes in the puddles of soup on the flagstones. But Sarah's face is green with it, and it fills her mouth.

"It's like she drowned in it," Digges murmurs.

Or someone has drowned her in it. Pray God the soup was cold.

"We must raise the hue and cry," Digges says, and he makes for the gate that will lead him out onto the street.

Dee looks around the kitchen, the place where once his late mother used to bake strange flavored breads that only dogs would eat, where he and Frommond had brought up Arthur, and where they spent so many hours talking over the guttering flames of dying candles. Now it is transformed into some awful arena of incomprehensible struggle, and it gives off the same jangling atmosphere as—as a torture chamber, that is it.

And why? Why torture someone? To learn something. And what might Sarah have known?

"Murder!" he hears Digges shouting in the road outside his gate.

Only something to do with Dee and his family.

"Murder! Come one! Come all!"

The whereabouts of its members perhaps?

"There's been a murder at Doctor Dee's house!"

No, Dee thinks, he cannot be dragged into this just yet.

He must away, away and find Arthur.

Mortlake to Cheam under the moon is not ten miles, an hour's ride perhaps, but it is well after midnight before Doctor Dee arrives at Nicholas Frommond's gate to wake a dozing night watchman. The man jumps to his feet when he hears the horse and holds out his lamp and a stick.

"Whoa! Whoa! Who goes there!"

Dee is reassured. If an old man can sleep in the shadows by the gate, then surely nothing can be too far amiss? While a boy is sent to wake Master Frommond's butler, Dee asks if the old man has seen Arthur that day, but the night watchman's days and nights are scrambled.

"Most like," he says, and he leans back against the brick wall and closes his eyes. *Well, what does he know?* Dee thinks, and he clings to the bald fact that if anything had happened to Arthur, then surely the whole house would be astir.

"John?"

It is Nicholas Frommond himself, hastily dressed in breeches and shirt and a pair of cord slippers, and come to his gate holding up an old-fashioned rush lamp.

"Nicholas," Dee breathes. "Thank God. I'm sorry to have to rouse you like this."

They go into the yard. The house is newly built of brick in the Dutch style, and very handsome, with an ornate garden of low box hedging in a pattern enclosing different-colored stones. There is a face with another lamp at one of the glazed windows that might be Alice, Nicholas's wife. Dee's arrival can be the only thing that has disturbed the household, and he could weep as Nicholas shows him into the hall where the air smells of cooking, and baking, and under the cloche on the ashes of the fire, embers wink reassuringly.

"He's been happy all day," Nicholas is saying as he leads Dee up the stairs. "Though it is strange how much he loves the rabbits."

"You still haven't told him he's not eating chicken?"

Nicholas Frommond laughs.

"It'd break his heart."

Alice Frommond puts her head around her bedchamber door and asks if all is well. Dee can hardly see her in the globe of umber light, but he tells her there has been an incident at home, and that he is concerned for Arthur's safety.

"Here we are," Frommond says, and he starts up some wooden steps to the attic, where his children and Arthur sleep under the eaves. Dee must fumble his way, since Nicholas is blocking the light of the lantern, and the steps are almost as steep as a ladder up an apple tree. In the attic are arranged numerous palliasses, each heaped with a child under layers of blankets. When it gets cold, they will move downstairs, to be around the fire. It is the new way of doing things, about which Dee has no opinion one way or the other.

Frommond's oldest boy, John, wakes in the soft light of the lamp.

"What is it now?"

Now?

"Where's Arthur?" Nicholas Frommond asks.

"Arthur," Dee calls.

But there is no reply. Arthur's bed is empty. Dee feels the cold wind of dread.

"Did he come to bed?" Frommond asks.

The other children—three of them—are awake now. They look at one another, puzzled, not yet frightened.

"He was," one of them says.

"But there was a rabbit screaming and he thought a fox had got into the hutch."

"So he went down? On his own?"

The siblings look at one another with large eyes. One is older than Arthur, two are younger. Maybe one should have gone with him, or stopped him, but Jesu, they are just children, and Arthur is stubborn. If Arthur wants to go into the garden at night, then—well, what sort of example has Dee ever set? He's in the garden most nights, watching the stars and so on. So the children nod.

"I thought he'd come back," the oldest says.

"I was asleep," Claire says.

The smallest starts to cry.

Dee turns and clatters down the steps. He takes the lamp from Alice Frommond's unprotesting hand and continues back down into the hall, through the kitchen, past the buttery and the pantry to the back door. The drawer bar on the door is drawn back. He opens the door and steps out into the night.

"Arthur!"

No reply.

"Arthur!"

There's a steady breeze blowing through the night, bringing the unfamiliar smells of Nicholas Frommond's garden, and it takes a moment to realize the noise they can hear comes from the hutch where they find a rabbit dragging a leg that looks like it has been pulled from its socket. Such a thing would make any animal scream.

Nicholas Frommond doesn't know what to say. Alice joins them, hastily dressed; another rush lamp like a third glowworm in the dark.

"Perhaps—perhaps he is on the common?" she tries.

"Or perhaps he went home?" Nicholas wonders.

After a moment Nicholas can stand it no longer, and he sets aside his lamp and takes the rabbit and breaks its neck in a merciful act of delivery.

"Jesu, John," he says, "I am so sorry. If I'd known—"

"It is not your fault, Nicholas," Dee tells him. "Even if you had known, whoever has taken Arthur would have taken him somehow."

He saw Jiggins, saw Sarah. He knows it's true. And Nicholas

Frommond is a good and kind man, whom he has no wish to hurt, though by God he wishes to hurt someone. He sets off on another roaming tour of the garden, shouting Arthur's name and looking for the break in the fence, which he finds at the farthest point from the house, hidden behind some slender, silver-barked trees. Alice is with him and touches his arm.

"We'll find him, John, never you fear."

And how will you do that? Dee wonders.

There is a low woof from the house.

In fact it is Nicholas Frommond's oldest son, who has had the idea. He brings an old shirt of Arthur's, and a hound called Hector—a long-eared, low-slung thing, patched in black and brown—pulling at his arm on a leash. Better lanterns are brought, including a couple of bull's-eye ones, and the hound is taken down to the break in the fence. After a moment's sniffing it lunges toward the break and drags the boy through. Dee follows close on his heels, and then comes Nicholas Frommond. They follow the hound as it takes them snuffling up a lane bounded on both sides by high hedges, the lamplight throwing wild shadows everywhere and catching cats' and foxes' eyes in the undergrowth.

"They can't have got far," Nicholas Frommond says.

But of course they can. They could have had a couple of horses waiting. But if they do, they are not nearby, and the trail leads on. They stop a couple of times—at an intersection and then by some cleared common land where the lanterns catch a hundred rabbits' eyes and the hound becomes distracted—but John persuades it back on the scent and on they go into the night. Overhead the moon is dulling and sinking. Dee detects that they are tramping northward.

"Is Hector sure?" Nicholas Frommond asks, though how John is supposed to know is anyone's guess. On they go, across common ground, down lanes, and soon the air cools and the land slopes down toward the broad, impassable black ribbon of the river Thames.

"Oh Lord," Frommond murmurs. "They've taken to the river."

The hound sniffs and sniffs at the long parallel scratches that a boat being pulled up and then pushed out again has made in the patch of mud by the lapping water before it sits exhausted, defeated but knowing it has done as much as can be expected of it. John Frommond pats it and ruffles its ears. The sky behind them is lighter than ahead, and dawn can now not be far off. Over the river is Hampton Court Palace. The river is deserted for now, and whoever has taken Arthur can have gone almost anywhere.

Dee crouches and hangs his head.

He has never been so tired, never so sorry, never so fearful, or angry.

"Where have you gone, Arthur?" he asks the night. "Where can I find you?"

But the night has no answers, and at length he stands, and he looks about him, as if, he suddenly realizes, for Jiggins, the boatman who now lies dead in his orchard, and then he looks back at the group of ashen faces that stand waiting on his decision—Nicholas Frommond, racked with guilt; poor John Frommond, still in just his shirt; the exhausted hound—and for the first time in his life, John Dee does not know what to do.

CHAPTER FIFTEEN

Tutbury Castle, Northamptonshire,
day before All Hallows' Eve, October 1585

It is midmorning now, on another day that is sent to remind the world not to forget winter, and Jane Frommond stands at the frame of a poorly glazed window and stares over the thick glass down into the bailey below where Sir Amyas Paulet and his wife are walking, just as they do most days, both well-wrapped in dark woolenstuffs, their heads bent in earnest talk. They might walk in the parkland beyond the castle walls, or upon the castle walls themselves, where they would be afforded a view of the hills to the north, or the broad elms to the south, but they do not, choosing every day instead to take a turn of the bailey, limiting their view to the inner face of a stone-walled oval a hundred paces wide by a hundred and fifty long.

If they can endure this blinkered life they seem to be vaunting, then so surely can their charge, Mary, Queen of Scots.

After a moment Sir Amyas looks up, as if he knows he is being watched, and catches her gaze. Frommond steps back from the window: the wind down the valley is cold and almost constant, anyway, carrying the smell of the brimming middens into every nook and cranny of the rooms she has been given, on the first floor of a run of stone-built houses in which the rest of Queen Mary's household has been lodged, on the eastern side of the castle, abutting the old curtain walls. The plaster is damp, and the shutters do not fit, but there are chimneys, so fires can be nursed through the day and night, though this Frommond has to do herself, for Lucy Pargeter—her maid—cares nothing for her tasks, and if she had not been foisted on her by the Queen and proved herself such an ally against Queen Mary's Scottish ladies, Frommond would have sent her home and summoned Sarah.

It has been a month since the evening Queen Elizabeth appeared in the Dees' orchard to inform Frommond that she must for the moment forgo the curious privilege of being Mistress Dee—respected wife of an esteemed philosopher, yes, but also somewhat impoverished housewife and mother and rediscover what it is to be a lady-in-waiting. All those endless days spent in tight-pointed dresses and head-broiling confinement, trying to outdo every other lady in the room for the quality of her laugh at Her Majesty's jokes; for the beauty of her stitches; for the elegance of her dancing; for the melodiousness of her harp playing; and all the while waiting, waiting, waiting, and for what? For life to pass, for supper to come, for it to be time for bed, and the welcome oblivion of sleep, only for it to start again the next day.

And, of course, as she traveled up to Tutbury—in the very coach in which her friend Alice Rutherford had been killed all those years ago; the ball-holes now skillfully patched and repainted—she had had cause to dread Queen Mary's court even more than Queen Elizabeth's, for while there were certain distractions to be found in Whitehall and Greenwich and so on, she had been warned to expect no such thing in Tutbury.

"I am told she has a billiards table," Lucy Pargeter told her, which Frommond doubted, for she had been warned that Queen Mary's keeper, Sir Amyas Paulet, was the sternest man in all of Christendom, and unlikely to tolerate such things, but after five days' travel through the rain on roads that got steadily worse, they arrived in Tutbury to discover that there in Queen Mary's very small preference room was indeed a billiards table.

"Your Majesty." Frommond had bowed before her new queen.

Her Majesty had not looked very majestic, it had to be said. She looked as if she had been dropped into the chair that served as a throne from some height; she was slumped half asleep under a ratty piece of cloth, with a puffy, lopsided face, and one eye fluttering shut. She had glared at Frommond from that other eye, which was dark and glistened like a raisin in an underbaked cake. Frommond had stepped back and taken her place among those ranged about, merely staring at the queen, and nothing then happened for what must have been hours, and yet all stood waiting until Queen Mary lifted a finger, and one of the women brought a small struggling dog no larger than a cat and placed it on the queen's lap, from whence it promptly dived off.

"Cache-Cache!" the queen had bleated, heart-stricken, and everybody there set about corralling the yapping dog so that it could be returned to its doting mistress. This time it could be persuaded to settle, with a morsel of something, and at last the queen smiled a smile that gave the briefest, blurriest glimpse of what a lively beauty she must once have been before she became so enmired in tragedy and constraint.

The week that followed had been very bad. Frommond had been shunned, of course, just as she had expected, and glared at with naked hostility by Queen Mary's much-diminished household. On the fifth day, Mary Kennedy came to her and put into words the question that Frommond had been asking herself ever since Queen Elizabeth ambushed her in the orchard in Mortlake.

"What are you doing here, Mistress Dee?"

Mary Kennedy is one of those fierce, birdlike women, radiating a furious broiling energy. She wears a gingerish mustache and bright green silks, with the portrait of a man in miniature hanging on a long string of pearls around her waist.

"Her Majesty has sent me to cheer and console Queen Mary," Frommond had told her, which was the truth of course, though Mary Kennedy had not believed her and, again, nor could Frommond blame her: even if she had anything to say that might achieve either, Mary is usually sick, mostly in great pain, and her court naturally enough assumes Frommond to be some sort of espial sent by Elizabeth to gather intelligence on her. What that intelligence might be Frommond cannot begin to guess, for Sir Amyas has forbidden anyone in Queen Mary's household to leave the castle grounds—so Queen Mary can no longer hand out alms to the needy, which was once her wont, for fear the common people will come to love her—and nor are her people permitted to walk upon the castle walls in case they signal anything to anyone in the village below, and now, of course, no one may send or receive word from the outside world by letter.

One day close to All Hallows' Eve, Queen Mary manages a walk around the bailey, taking advantage of perhaps the last rays of autumnal sunshine, and when she comes in, her silk is damp with sweat and her face blotchy with the effort, and she takes to her bed the rest of the day until supper, when she rises with another great effort and when presented with the usual choices for first course, she takes soup, and veal and capon and goose and duck, and for second pheasant and tongue, and then an apple tart and two pears, all of which she washes down with wine.

After it, Mary Kennedy comes to find Frommond in her room.

"Her Majesty wishes to speak to you," she says, the first words she's addressed directly to Frommond since demanding why she was sent, and she turns on her heel. Frommond exchanges a look with Lucy Pargeter, who sits reading a book about plants, who raises her eyebrows, but says nothing, so Frommond follows Kennedy into the preference room where Queen Mary is slouched once again on her modest little throne under a newly embroidered cloth of state.

"Your Majesty," Frommond says, bowing in the penumbra of the late night.

The queen summons her closer.

"We are pleased to see you here, Mistress Dee," she says, as if Frommond arrived only this morning. "Despite appearances."

"I am very pleased to be here, Your Majesty," Frommond lies. The queen laughs gently.

"I'll warrant," she says, dropping the royal we, then adopting it again. "Tell us how fares our sister of England? Did she send any especial word for us?"

Frommond has to admit Queen Elizabeth did not say anything very special.

"Can I ask, Mistress Dee," the queen starts, "and I do not mean anything by this, or for you to take it in any way as a criticism of you, but why do you believe our cousin of England has sent you to us?"

"I was sent to cheer and console," Frommond repeats, "though I admit I am puzzled as to why I was chosen, for I have not been much use."

Queen Mary sighs.

"No, no," she says. "You are come as a boon, and we are glad to have you with us."

"How is that, Your Majesty?"

"Well," the queen says, warming to the subject. "You are polite and attentive, Mistress Dee, which makes us believe that for whatever reason you were sent, whoever sent you judges it to be in their best interests for you to be so, which makes us think that they must believe that one day we shall be Queen of England."

Frommond starts and wonders if that is true?

"Unlike Sir Amyas," Mary goes on, "who is so cruel to us that it is clear he cannot believe we will ever be his queen, for it seems he fears no retribution for his actions."

That is quite a point, Frommond thinks: if Mary ever does become queen, she will have a long list of scores to settle, first with men such as Francis Walsingham, perhaps, then with Lord Burghley, and then with Sir Amyas Paulet, and then—well, who knows? The list may well be endless. Every man who has ever slighted her. And when Frommond thinks about this further, she feels nothing but sorrow for this woman, for she sees that every slight Mary receives must land doubly: not just the injury of the slight itself, but the knowing that whoever slights her does so in the belief there will never be any repercussion, that Mary of Scotland will never become Mary of England. Then she thinks there is another layer: whoever has slighted Mary in the past will do whatever they can to ensure that she will never become their queen.

Conversely, though, Frommond supposes, any kindness is redoubled, for the same reasons.

But what a strain it must be, to have to judge the motivation of every act!

No wonder she is so ill.

Queen Mary asks more questions about the diverse intricacies of Queen Elizabeth's court, to which Frommond does her best to reply, though she has long since stopped caring who is in and who is out of Her Majesty's favor, which dance Her Majesty prefers, or where she went on her progress this year. Other questions are more difficult for different, but obvious reasons: the situation in the Low Countries, for example, where English troops are soon to fight Spanish troops, who would invade England to put Queen Mary on the throne.

"Strange times we live in, Mistress Dee; wild and scrambled."

She has a lovely accent, it strikes Frommond: French and Scottish, mixed, and English is her third language, though she can speak many more, and she sips a strong-smelling spirit from a silver cup and above its rim, the candlelight dances in her now awakened eyes.

"Do you have children, Mistress Dee?" she asks, moving on to safer ground, and Frommond confirms she does.

"Just the one, so far," she tells her.

"You are lucky," Her Majesty says. "I have one, but I had to leave him in Scotland, as perhaps you know. I miss him with the greater part of my body, do you know? I sometimes think the pain I feel in my arms and legs, in my side, has no other cause than my not being able to be with him or have him by my side. And the longer it continues, the worse it gets."

Frommond makes a noncommittal noise.

"If I might get some word to my son," Queen Mary says, those eyes catching the light, "then by God's grace, I do believe my pains might abate."

The unspoken question hangs in the air, unanswered.

That night Frommond dreams of her son, Arthur.

CHAPTER SIXTEEN

Crypt of Saint Dunstan-in-the-East, City of London, night before All Hallows' Eve, October 1585

They have gagged and tightly trussed the boy in ropes made from torn sackcloth, and he lies—still at last—bundled in the dead boatman's cloak, just out of the reach of the light from a lamp that Mademoiselle Báthory has set upon a tomb in one of the crypt's bays. Damp dust lies everywhere down here, like a soft beige cloth an inch thick, and it is obvious from the absence of footprints that no one has been down for many years.

"How did you know about this place?" Ballard asks. He does not mean Saint Dunstan-in-the-East, which is a large church just west of Tower Hill, well-favored by wealthy parishioners and with two large churchyards even above the one they have come through, but he means this extraordinary, inner crypt.

"When heretics ejected their priest, he came to the household of Duc de Guise, bringing with him the church's secret. And key."

She shows him the long silver spike she'd used to open the crypt's door.

"Why here? When we are so close to Walsingham's house?"

"This is family church of Dee. He was baptized upstairs, yes? Before his father stole gold plate from the altar and sold it in market like common thief."

She takes from her bag a few of those soul cakes that are made this time of year in readiness for All Hallows. She must have stolen them from Dee's kitchen, Ballard supposes, after she'd forced soup down the throat of that poor maid. She offers him one now, and after a long moment of hesitation, he takes it, for he is ravenous.

"What about the boy?" he asks, meaning to share the third cake.

She shakes her head.

"Is a waste of food," she tells him.

And for the first time he properly understands she means to kill the boy. She did not tell him that was her plan yesterday evening, when they had arrived in Mortlake to find Dee was not there, and Ballard had supposed they might have waited for him, or come back later perhaps, but by then Mademoiselle Báthory had already murdered the boatman and was stalking toward the house in search of Dee's wife or child or anyone she could find to kill. That was when they discovered the maid, and through her did they learn the existence and whereabouts of Dee's son.

She'd watched the boy in the garden in Cheam making sure all rabbits were back in their hutch for the night, and then, when night had fallen, and all the children had gone in, she struck again.

Ballard tells himself he would not have helped Báthory if he had understood she meant to kill the boy. He believed she meant to kidnap the boy, yes, which he knew was bad enough, though still, perhaps, just about within his undefined rules of engagement with the powers of Protestant England. He had believed she wanted the boy in order to extract something from the father, from Dr. Dee, or perhaps she wanted to lure Dee into a meeting when she would kill him? That too seemed within the bounds of acceptable behavior, because was this not, after all, a war? A crusade even? And Dee had, so Mademoiselle Báthory told Ballard, thwarted a plan that would have swung Emperor Rudolf's money behind de Guise's scheme to send an army to help replace Queen Elizabeth on England's throne with Queen Mary. So he could be counted as an enemy.

But when the sun went down last night, when the servants had covered both fires and the family had taken to their beds, he had seen Mademoiselle Báthory smile for the first time since she had pretended to be his lover in that alehouse in Margate. She'd stood and strode through the moonlit garden to the hutch from which she'd pulled a rabbit by the ears, and then with a twist, she had dislocated its leg. With no remorse, she'd cast the screaming creature aside, and its shrieks had been so pitiful that Ballard had had to clap his hands over his ears to block them out. When the boy came running in his nightshirt, just as she'd said he would, it was easy enough with the two of them to snatch him up, gag him with a cloth, and carry him, still squirming, back toward the river, where they had left the dead boatman's wherry pulled up in some undergrowth.

"Where will we take him?" Ballard had asked, once they were in the lighter, and he was with oars in hand, and she with the boy pressed beneath her feet, facedown in the gunnels.

"Downriver," she'd commanded.

And so he had rowed under the thin moon through the darkest part of the night with the falling tide past Richmond; past Mortlake—they could see the boy's house and, if he'd bothered to look, the dead body of the boatman she had stabbed in the eye for having served his purpose—past Westminster and Blackfriars, until just before dawn, when they'd slid under the bridge and were almost at the Tower, when Mademoiselle Báthory instructed him to take them between two boats moored to a still-deserted wharf where it stank of fish.

"Are you sure?" he'd asked.

He indicated the looming bulk of the Tower ahead, where the Queen's Yeomen carried torches in the battlements, and then the not-yet-waking city, where there would be night watchmen abroad. More to the point, he told her, Walsingham's house on Seething Lane was but a weak bowshot that way.

"Bring him," was all she'd said, taking the boat's lamp, and so he'd hefted the boy onto his shoulder, and in the graying night she led them hurrying through the streets to the churchyard of Saint Dunstan-in-the-East. Here, in a wall under a spreading yew tree that must have been planted in William the Conqueror's time, she had found a postern gate covered in ivy, for which she had pulled from her skirts a key as big as a child's hand. She'd unlocked it with a protesting squeal, and ducked through the gateway, and he could only follow for fear of attracting any night watchmen's attention. He had found himself in what must have been a long-deserted and overgrown churchyard whence there came the hair-raising squeak of alarmed rats. She had ignored them and led Ballard apparently unerringly along a path hidden by ivy, ducking under boughs and stepping over fallen trunks, to stand before the towering bluff of the church's buttressed southern wall.

More ivy. She'd put the lamp down and ripped that away to reveal a stone plaque, into which were chiseled letters too faint to read in the gloom, save for one brass-rimmed letter *O*, which had stared at them like a dark eye. Into this she had inserted another key, a spike as long and as slim as a reed, which she turned, and then removed, and she pulled on the plaque's edge, and lo: a hatch into some inner sanctum, a secret, hidden inner crypt, from which slunk a dense sepulchral air that smelled of cold earth and something long dead. After a moment's panic, Ballard had followed her in, stepping over the foot-high threshold and down a short flight of steps, and then she'd pulled the door to, sealing them in with the same key.

"No one will find us here," she'd said, "not until is time."

Ballard did not want to think about what that time might be. Instead he'd looked around him in the umber light of the lamp. The walls were close and the low ceiling barrel-vaulted, from which stalactites of unidentifiable matter hung along with blankets of spiders' webs. Deep alcoves were cut into what must have been church's foundations, and in each squatted a tomb of what might have been a past priest, topped with grisly memento mori: carved skulls and crossed shinbones in one; a full-size stone skeleton turning its empty orbs to the observer in another. *As I am now, so you shall be.*

The soul cakes are not the only things Báthory stole from Dee's house. She took a book of some sort, and a long black cloak with a hood from the back of the door to his library, and also something from the adjoining laboratory that she wrapped in the cloak, not to hide, but to save from damage.

"What now?" Ballard asks when he has brushed the cake crumbs away.

"We need freshly dead goat head," she says.

He starts. Her English is not perfect, but.

"What?"

"Head of a goat just dead. Must still have blood. And horns."

"Where the— Where are we going to find that? Why are we going to find that?"

"You find it," she tells him. "You go to butcher stall."

"We don't eat goats in England," he tells her, though he is not sure that is true. She does not care.

"We need," is all she'll say.

"And I have things I must do today," he tells her. "I have to give a man a pistol so he can use it to kill the Queen of England."

He loves how that sounds, but it is also true: he has to meet John Savage at Saint Giles-in-the-Fields to deliver him the one remaining pistol.

She nods, unimpressed.

"So go," she says, and Ballard almost caves in with relief, because for some reason he half supposed she might not let him, and he had no idea what he would have done then.

"But bring the goat's head on way back."

First, though, he goes over to touch what he imagines will be the boy's shoulder. The boy flinches and starts whining again, straining against his bonds. Poor little fucker's pissed himself, he sees. But so would he, he thinks, stepping away. Christ, it's heartbreaking. He has a child of his own who must be about that age, he supposes. In Paris, sired on a common prostitute before he was ordained, conceived and born under an onion seller's market stall, but he sometimes sends the woman money enough to keep the child in sausages and shoe leather.

He should take the boy and run, he thinks, that is what he should do. Take him and leave him somewhere he'll be found. Damn the Duc de Guise. Damn Thomas Morgan. It is all very well for them to send their fiendishly encrypted letters from the safety of Paris; they are not stuck here with a madwoman who has asked him to get the head of a freshly slaughtered goat, complete with horns.

Mademoiselle Báthory stands waiting at the hatch with that strange key, which she inserts into the lock and then swings the door open an inch, listening for any movement in the churchyard, and when she is satisfied, she steps aside to let him pass, though as she does so, she cups his cods; it's a brief clever squeeze that sends a thrilling jolt of alarm and pleasure up his spine and nearly knocks him off his feet.

"Be back by noon," she reminds him, "and with the goat head."

And the plaque closes noiselessly behind, and when he steps back to look at it, there is nothing to show it is there, save that strangely emphatic letter *O*. He steps out into the thick green early morning light of the churchyard and breathes it in like nectar, lingering a moment to relish his freedom. He wishes he had never met her; wishes that he had never been tasked with escorting her on this mission of hers, whatever it is, for it seems to involve killing anyone and everyone they encounter—the two Frenchmen in Margate, for example, purely to create a distraction; then the boatman, whom she stabbed in the eye with that rapier of hers the moment he had served his purpose, and then the maid, dear God, what a way to die, choking on soup just so that she would tell them where Dee's son was—and now this: the snatching of this perfectly harmless boy, in order, he is sure, to kill him in some strange and fearful way.

And by Christ, he is so tired! He can barely move his feet and he has not slept for—what? Three nights? Four? Not properly, anyway, and not properly since he witnessed her murder a man for the second time with her thumb in his back; not since she stabbed him in the throat that night afterward. Ballard touches his wound with a finger: it is the size of a ha'penny perhaps; a scratch and nothing more, but he did not expect her to have gone to bed with a bloody dagger, did he?

So he sets off, out of the postern gate, and onto the lane leading down to the river, his mind turning to his next problem, which is how he is going to explain to John Savage that he only has one pistol to give him? He had been so shocked when the first had gone off when he was robbing those men on the Portsmouth Road that he was almost blown off his horse, and then, when the bullet actually hit the man, and killed him, dear God! It was not as he intended. He had only been playing the part of Captain Fortescue, and he suddenly found himself floundering out of his depth.

But when he saw what the donkey was carrying—all that silver! More money than he'd ever seen in his lifetime. More than he'd ever hoped to see, too! Well, then, Ballard must admit it: he lost his head. It was pure naked greed, he knows that. A deadly sin. He would have shot the other man, too, had he come at him, but he did not—he cared more for the life of his friend than he did for the silver—and that is what swayed it for Ballard in the end: he was being given it! God had sent it his way to help His cause.

He'd taken the bags from the back of the cart and loaded them onto the donkey and ridden off while he could, all the while expecting to be caught, stopped, thwarted somehow, but nothing happened and a moment later he found himself under the shade of the trees, alone with a thousand silver crowns, and it was only that night, as he was pinned to a hay-filled mattress by the plump buttocks of an innkeeper's wife—whom he paid a silver crown for the pleasure—that he remembered the pistol.

But is he not now being punished? Is he not now shackled to a she-devil? She is his penance for the murder of that man on the road and for his subsequent greed, and if he runs now, if he fails this test and abandons the child, then he will have yet more innocent blood on his hands, and he will be damned for all time.

Ballard turns right along Thames Street, heading west, and he stops at a stall to buy a half-dozen fresh-shucked oysters with a thick slab of ashy bread and a mug of thin ale, and while he eats and drinks, he wonders how he can stop her killing the child. Realistically, he can do nothing, or nothing that does not risk his own mission, or future missions. And after all, she is sent by the Duc de Guise, whose encrypted messages were explicit: that for the sake of Holy Rome's enterprise of England, he—Ballard—must obey her every word in all things. That being the case, what then should he do?

There is only one thing for it: let her kill the boy, if she needs to, but pray God make sure he is nowhere near when she does it.

It is the coward's way out, he knows, but it is all he can do.

As he comes to this conclusion it turns nine of the clock. The city bells ring out, and the pigeons take flight, and so he pays the oyster woman a silver crown and since she has nothing like the change needed, he tells her to give half of it to charity.

"For I shall not need it where I am going," he says, though why he says this he will never know, nor she, and he sets off west along Thames Street, the briny oysters repeating on him, past the bridge where he buys another soul cake from a pretty hawker with her basket whose day—month! year!—he makes with another silver crown. Nearby he sees a herd of sheep; some law students in black, still drunk from the night before; crowds of beggars and urchins milling about in search of the slightest chance, and so it is that he spares not a thought for the man who detached himself from the crowd at the oyster stall and has trailed his footsteps since.

CHAPTER SEVENTEEN

Walsingham's house, Seething Lane, City of London,
morning of All Hallows' Eve, October 1585

Robert Beale arrives looking tired. From his unsuccessful excursion to find John Ballard in Surrey? Sir Francis wonders. Or from being woken so early by the awful news about Dee's boy and the murders in his house? Or from something else?

"What news?" Walsingham asks.

"I've set every man we've got searching the riverbanks, north and south," Beale tells him, "and questioning the lightermen and any fishermen and so on, and something might turn up but—pffft. There's no sign of him."

"And where's Dee now?"

"On the river, dowsing for a trace of Arthur."

"Dowsing?"

"Divining. He has some technique, he says, that will help find the boy. A golden ball, a pendulum he called it, on a piece of string. You hold it so."

Beale demonstrates, holding out his hands like a child playing a game of conkers with an invisible conker.

"He says it is more certain than prayer."

"But prayer will not get a man burned as a witch," Walsingham points out. "And if Sir Christopher Hatton hears? He'll have him roasting on a pyre before All Souls' is out."

Beale looks pained.

"It did occur to me, but surely not even Hatton would try that?"

Walsingham isn't so sure. Sir Christopher Hatton—despite their best efforts, still one of Her Majesty's favorites—has maintained a vendetta against Dee, who once sold him—reluctantly, apparently, which makes it worse—several tons of worthless black ore brought back from the New World, from which Hatton was certain his own alchemist could extract gold where Dee himself had failed. That Hatton's alchemist turned out to be a swindler who later absconded with thousands of pounds of Hatton's money only made Hatton angrier to have paid Dee's price, and he tried to have him burned, after accusing him of conjuring up evil spirits and scrying after treasure. But on that occasion at least, Dee was more useful to Walsingham alive than dead.

"Did you search Dee's house?" he asks.

"Both his and Nicholas Frommond's," Beale tells him. "We found nothing that you do not already know. At Dee's: a boatman by the name of Jiggins, stabbed through the eye, and a dead maid by the name of Sarah Johnson, who was drowned in leek soup she'd made herself. At Frommond's: a dead rabbit, but that has been explained as a mercy killing after they found its leg dislocated."

Beale is in very dark blue wool today—elegant, without being too much—and polished riding boots, but he does not look his usual self: something is distracting him, Walsingham detects.

"Can any of that have anything to do with our man Ballard?"

Beale tells him he cannot say anything for certain.

"Or anything to do with the two murders in Margate?"

Walsingham has Beale's report of that event on his desk: two men murdered; a man answering Ballard's description and a woman somehow involved, though how or why none can say, and both now vanished. What does it all mean? Walsingham does not bother to wonder aloud. Are they all connected? And if so, how? That's all he ever wonders, he thinks, about anything and everything, but the longer he has gone on in this game, the less he believes in coincidence.

"It is the sound of the woman that worries me most," he says with a sigh after a while. "Imagine if Ballard were planning to have her use the pistols."

"Jesu!" Beale mutters. "A woman assassin? We will have to—what?—double?—triple?—the guard on Her Majesty."

"Which she will refuse."

"Of course."

"We have to find the woman. That must be our priority."

Beale agrees and writes something in his ledger.

"And is there any sign of Phelippes yet?" Sir Francis asks.

"None so far."

Strange, Walsingham thinks. *Phelippes is usually so punctual.* Didn't he once threaten an employee who was late for something with a spell in the Tower? Sir Francis leans forward in his settle to hold his hands up to the first fire of the year. After a moment he glances over at Beale. There is another matter that has been preying on his mind, which he mentions now as if it were a mere afterthought.

"When you came to Barn Elms last month, Robert, when I was ill, you said you'd had word of our old friend Gilbert Gifford? He'd been causing trouble with that nasty little toad Allen at that college of his in Rheims, you said, and you were going to send word that he should move to Paris and offer his services to Morgan?"

He recaps the situation for Beale as if he were reading from the notes on their last meeting because there was something that Beale had said—or hadn't said—that day that had rung alarm bells, though Sir Francis has not been able to think how or why. Some reluctance to make an obvious move, perhaps. It might have been perfectly innocent, even sensible, but after the business with Ness Overbury, Walsingham knows it pays to keep an eye on his assistant.

And once again, Beale shifts on his stool, and he makes a play of looking for something, some note or other, when Walsingham knows that Beale's filing is meticulous, that he knows the whereabouts of every little piece of paper.

"It matters not, I should say," Walsingham goes on, "because in some strange state of heightened activity I actually managed to send him word myself. You'd had some objection to the plan that I could not then remember?"

Beale looks very briefly aghast, but then recovers his composure, and pretends to try to recall what that objection might have been, but before he can stretch his powers of deception beyond breaking point, a messenger comes thundering on the door.

Beale is swift to his feet to answer the door.

"Well?"

A message, parlayed from servant to servant, but originally from Master Phelippes.

"He's found Ballard."

"Where?"

"On Thames Street, heading west toward Holborn."

"Alone?"

"Didn't say. Just asked you to send men."

Walsingham watches Beale belt on his sword with grim enthusiasm, and he knows for certain that something is up with him.

"I'll send a company of Yeomen along Fleet Street," he tells him, "and another along Holborn. Take him, Robert, alive if you can; dead if you can't. But remember he has that pistol!"

It is impossible not to feel thrillingly alive on such a bright autumn morning as this—probably the last of the year—especially if you are raised up above the common throng in the saddle of a good strong gelding, and have a sword strapped to your waist, and are leading a troop of five Yeomen warders westward from the Tower toward Saint Paul's, with Her Majesty's principal private secretary's writ to scatter all before you.

They cannot canter, or even trot, of course, for people and things have a habit of not scattering as fast as you'd hope, and indeed the surface under hoof is not as reliably free of potholes as he'd like; but still, they ride until they reach Saint Paul's where the road forks either side of the cathedral, and where a clerkish-looking man in faded worsted shouts from his stall to attract their attention.

"Master Beale! Master Beale, sir! Over here!"

Beale reins in.

"Where's Phelippes?"

"Gone that way, sir," he says, pointing. "Toward Ludgate."

Beale heels his horse along the left-hand fork: Bower Row and Fleet Street, toward Westminster. He's relieved not to have to ride up Cheapside where the market is always heaving between cock-crow and curfew.

But it is not all unalloyed joy, is it? On its own, Walsingham's ordering of Gilbert Gifford to Paris could mean nothing—there was some confusion as to whether it was a wise move, and who was to send the order—but his careful recapping of the situation suggests he believes something is awry, that he knows Beale is up to something. Walsingham has a sense for this sort of thing, and he can spot deceit in the way most men can detect a hairline crack in a vessel by sound alone.

Jesu!

And what now will he tell Her Majesty? Because Beale knows all too well that Walsingham's aim in getting Gifford into Thomas Morgan's circle in Paris is to prove that Queen Mary is still somehow plotting against Queen Elizabeth. The exact thing Queen Elizabeth instructed Beale to stop.

Ducking under the Ludgate, the captain of the watch points him onward, and after a hundred paces they are past over the Fleet where the crowds thin and there are no more carts blocking the way. Half a league along Fleet Street and a boy stood at a corner points him the way.

"Gone up to Saint Giles's," he says.

Saint Giles's is an old church, once a leper colony, its grounds abandoned now and given over to low shrubs and rough pasture, notorious now for lewd acts and wayside robbery. Beale feels no anxiety. He has his sword and five Yeomen. On he goes, across Fickett's Field, where a six-foot crow's nest of branch and bone is already piled ready for tonight's fire. Strictly speaking these are banned as being popish, but in some places, the tradition of a fire at this time of year to mark the end of the harvest, and the beginning of winter, lives on, stripped of its connections with purgatory, perhaps—though who knows? Certainly not the Queen, who has made it clear she has no desire to make windows into men's souls—and instead treated the tradition as an excuse to drink ale until midnight.

Phelippes sees Beale before Beale sees Phelippes, loitering by a broken-down hovel. Phelippes points for him to stay back, and then points to the churchyard beyond the hovel. Beale swings down from the saddle, tells the Yeomen to stay back and on no account to come closer, and then creeps up on Phelippes's shoulder.

"Where is he?"

"Up by the church," Phelippes says, "talking to a new arrival. Someone who'd been waiting for him."

"Anyone we know?"

"Not sure," Phelippes admits. He has spent so long poring over minutely written codes and ciphers that his eyes are now ruined, and he should wear eyeglasses. "But Ballard has given him a saddlebag."

"What's in it?"

It can only be that pistol, Beale feels sure. So should this new arrival be taken first? Or should they follow Ballard to see if he leads them to the woman? Beale peers around the slumping corner of the hovel: the two men are a hundred paces away, both in dark cloaks, both tall, broad-shouldered, and rangy, and though not as young as they were, they inhabit the class Beale might categorize as "useful-looking," and talking so earnestly the brims of their hats touch.

Ballard must be the darker of the two.

"How did you know it was him?" he asks Phelippes.

"I saw him when I was in Paris this last year, and then today as I was down by Billingsgate getting an oyster for breakfast, there he was. I wasn't sure at first, only then he went and paid with a silver crown."

"For oysters? He could've bought half a hundredweight."

"Or more. So I sent word to Walsingham with a lad, who obviously found you, and I followed him here."

"Shall we take him?"

It is the sergeant of the Yeomen—Stevens—who's younger than the others and obviously been given the job as a favor to his father, and his voice is hoarse and plangent in Beale's ear. Beale turns. The fool is in his red doublet.

"No, of course you can't! Look at you! You're like the beacon on Shooters' Hill. He'll see you coming a mile off."

And it is already too late, perhaps, for when Beale turns back, the other man has vanished into the bushes behind, and so now it is just Ballard alone, half in, half out of a shaft of sunshine through the trees, and he stands there for a long moment, scratching his head thoughtfully.

"Shall we take him now?" Stevens repeats.

Beale holds his hand up.

"No," he says. "We'll watch him."

"It was the luck of the angels that I managed to follow him here," Phelippes tells him. "If we lose him now, Sir Francis'll have you racked."

"If we find that woman before she kills the Queen, then he'll have me knighted."

Phelippes wrinkles his nose. He hasn't read Beale's report from Margate.

"You'd risk the one for the other?"

Beale isn't sure. He turns to the Yeoman.

"Have your men take off their doublets, and take two that way around the church," he says, pointing left. "And send the other two that way. Meet at the far side and find that other man."

The Yeoman is doubtful.

"If you find him," Beale goes on, "then put him on this horse, and bring him to Sir Francis at his house on Seething Lane. If you don't, then keep looking until you do. Now go, for the love of God, go!"

Under his red doublet the man's shirt is horribly stained and no credit to Her Majesty. When he's gone, Phelippes has his weak eyes retrained on Ballard.

"He doesn't look too happy," he says.

Beale looks again. Phelippes is right. Ballard looks wilted.

"Tired maybe?"

"It can't be more than a mile's walk from the oyster stall," Phelippes supposes.

"Maybe he's come farther? From Rotherhithe or somewhere?"

Even without saying a word, Phelippes implies it is useless to speculate.

"How shall we do this then?" Beale asks. He means follow Ballard without losing him. "Was he careful on the way here?"

Phelippes thinks for a moment.

"Not nearly enough," he says, "no. Made me think he wasn't Ballard, for a bit, but it's him all right. He just seemed to plow on, not caring about anyone in his way, nor behind, following him, which I was. And he kept pausing, you know, clapping his hand on his head, too, as if he's got something on his mind?"

"Wouldn't you if you'd come here to kill the Queen?"

Phelippes supposes so.

"But it's as if he's come to kill her against his own will, isn't it? Look out, here he comes."

Ballard has turned toward them, and they have but a moment to slip into the hovel together. It stinks and its patchy framework of timbers and thatch is rotten and punctured with so many holes it's about to come down.

"If he comes in, pretend we're kissing," Phelippes whispers.

A pigeon coos from the rafters above, as if this is what he has come to see.

"I wish to God Arthur Gregory were here," Beale mutters.

"Come on," Phelippes goes on. "You know you want to."

He has his eye pressed to a hole and now he holds out a hand for silence as Ballard passes them, heading south, back toward Fickett's Field, and when he is past, Beale and Phelippes leave the hovel and follow, grateful that Ballard is so striking a figure. But Phelippes is right: there is something odd in Ballard's behavior, as if he is of two minds as to where he wants to go.

Eventually he seems to make up his mind, and he turns for the city. Beale and Phelippes swap hats and part: Beale going ahead, so that he is broadly parallel to Ballard, Phelippes lingering twenty yards behind, pretending to limp. Ballard takes them back down Fleet Street, toward the city, as if to enter through Ludgate, but just over the Fleet, he turns left, up along the Old Bailey, and now Beale and Phelippes swap coats, and hats back again, and they follow him north, and then through Newgate, down past Greyfriars into the shambles, where Ballard slows to a dawdle, examining the butchers' stalls.

"Can it be that he wants—what? A chop?" Beale asks. "Something for his supper?"

"Even assassins must eat," Phelippes supposes.

Beale presses his sleeve over his mouth, for even on a cool autumnal day such as this, the smell hereabouts is very bad, as cows and pigs are brought from Smithfield to be slaughtered and have their bodies hung on chains to drain over shallow coopered tubs before they are eviscerated, flayed, and butchered, and the stones below are glazed with hundreds of years of blood—fresh and dried—and one must walk sticky-soled between gutters that seem to erupt with coils of gray-green entrails, where dog battles rat and butcher's boy in a series of never-ending skirmishes, and where flies swarm in biblical numbers and provide a constant drone.

"Yeuch," Phelippes mutters.

Ballard does not seem to find what he is looking for in the first few stalls and he presses on. The market is busy, with hundreds of people milling about after their suppers, and everyone is shouting and gesticulating, and even though Ballard shows no sign that he knows he is being followed, there are so many shadows, side streets, cutbacks that he might easily take one and so lose them by accident. Beale's early elation dissipates, and Phelippes's warning about being racked rings in his ears.

Ballard stops ahead to inspect the wares of another stall and talks to the butcher. The butcher shakes his head and gestures farther along, and Ballard thanks him and moves in the direction indicated. Another stall, another conversation, this time satisfactory, for he's found what he was after and hands over a coin—presumably another of those crowns—but then seems surprised to be given what it is he has bought.

"What is it?" Phelippes breathes in Beale's ear.

It's a goat's head, complete with curling horns, still dripping blood from its neck.

"What in Jesu's name does he want with that?"

"Goat's headcheese soup?"

Ballard takes the head in outstretched hands, and then doesn't seem to know what to do with it, or how to carry it, but he's pleased, or relieved, to have it at least, and he settles on carrying it by one horn, down by his side, as if it were nothing out of the ordinary, as if he did this sort of thing every other day, and he sets off down toward Cheapside, the goat's head, swinging by his side, still dripping drops of blood that land like rose petals on the cobbles, which Beale, twenty yards behind, is able to follow with ease.

They follow him back east, toward the Tower, carrying the goat's head as if he is on his way to play bowls on Tower Green perhaps, and they hardly bother with subterfuge, for Ballard is walking purposefully, dead-straight, as if he has decided on his destination, so they walk together shoulder to shoulder, watching him follow the road around to the right, and head down toward the Thames. He's perhaps thirty yards ahead now, approaching Saint Dunstan's.

"How tall d'you reckon he is?" Phelippes wonders.

"Got to be at least six foot. Practically a giant."

"Not a profession you'd think of, is it, not when you're that tall."

"Being a priest?"

"Being an assassin."

Beale supposes so. They watch him pass the church, keeping on down toward where he bought the oysters, but then, suddenly, unexpectedly, he turns a sharp corner. Some sixth sense warns them both, and they set off, sprinting to catch up to him.

By the time they turn the corner, he's gone.

"What the—?"

The lane below the church, between the ivy-clad churchyard wall and the back of some warehouses, is about a hundred paces long, totally deserted.

"Where's he—?"

There's nowhere for him to go. They run the length of the lane, stumbling over the dried wheel ruts. At its end, the road runs left and right along Tower Street. Although there are some men and women and a couple of boys to be seen, there's no sign of Ballard.

"Jesu!"

They retrace their steps, quickly.

"Check the blood," Beale says, and the first drop they find is a ruby spot about the size of a raindrop on the ground at the churchyard side of the lane, but after it, no more.

"Fucker's just vanished!" Phelippes says.

But in among the ivy that hangs from the churchyard wall is a small, solid-looking postern gate, in planks of faded oak. He gives the door a shove, expecting no joy, but it swings open. Beale steps back and draws his sword.

Phelippes gives him an *after you* look and Beale ducks into the gateway, his breast clenched against a pistol ball, but there's nothing. It's dark in here, very overgrown, almost like stepping into a cave where everything—the walls; the tree trunks; the tombs and each of the tilted gravestones—is covered in moss, where thick creepers of ivy choke everything else. Even the air is thick and green, and cold as the grave, too, with a chill that seeps into the bones and makes Beale shiver and clutch his sword tight.

The ivy has long since covered the path underfoot, but it must once have wound between the graves, toward the towering gray stone buttresses at the flank of the church where stand two double doors, locked and covered in thick moss. Beale steps past, hacking at the ivy with his sword to clear his way, and after thirty paces or so he has reached the blank wall on the other side. There's no gate here, and no sign of Ballard.

Phelippes joins him.

They turn to look at the double doors.

"He can't have, can he?"

The doors don't even have a handle this side and their feet are thick with moss and ivy that has not been disturbed since the priests last carried one of their coffined brothers out here for burial.

"Where the fuck has he gone?" Phelippes asks.

They can only just follow the drops of blood in the gloom, but they peter out by the church's side, and they can find no more.

"He must've climbed the fucking wall!" Phelippes says. "Slyboots must've known we were following him all along!"

Then Phelippes turns to him and screws up his face.

"Chooooo," he says. "Can't wait to see what happens when you tell Sir Francis you've lost the man who's going to kill the Queen!"

Beale says nothing. He feels sick.

"But you saw him! You saw him come in; he—"

At that precise moment there is a crash, and the little postern gate behind them is flung open.

CHAPTER EIGHTEEN

Dee's house, Mortlake,
morning of All Hallows' Eve, October 1585

His son has been missing for six hours now, and Doctor Dee finds himself in a wherry being rowed eastward toward the city by Christopher Marlowe, who has come dressed for the day in a green leather jerkin, blue sailor's slops, and a russet cord cap, from which hangs a fat silver pearl.

"Just say the word, Doctor," he reminds him.

Dee says nothing. He is trying to focus, without focusing, on the small golden orb that he holds hanging on the end of a length of silver chain. But he cannot focus, even without focusing, for his mind is all ascramble not only with thoughts of Arthur, but for unfathomable reasons, thoughts, too, of his own father. Why? Why now, after so many years, has the shade of his father chosen to reappear? The last time he slept—when was that? on the roadside south of Blackheath?—he dreamed of the man, of Roland Dee, and woke up feeling pummeled not just by the hard ground below, but by anger, sorrow, and regret.

After a moment he gives up on the orb with a great frustrated sigh and sets it aside. He had bought it from a dealer off Cheapside—eight pounds—with the unearthing of King Arthur's treasure in mind, and the dealer had sworn to the orb's efficacy at disclosing anything, animal or mineral, quick or dead, even if whatever it was that was being sought did not wish to be found. He had taught Dee the right prayers to say, where and when to say them, and the preparations he must make, all of which took Dee the best part of an hour to perform in the darkness of his laboratory this morning, since when he has spent his time strenuously trying to clear his mind of every thought, good or bad, so that he can become the orb, and the orb become him, but to what end?

None.

Thomas Digges—also aboard, training the latest iteration of his spyglass on the river's southern bank for any sign of Jiggins's abandoned lighter, or of Arthur, though what this might be, no one wishes to think—offers Dee his costrel of ale.

"Got to keep your strength up," he says.

Dee takes a swig and tells Digges and Marlowe that he cannot concentrate, without concentrating, on the orb.

"My father seems to intrude," he explains, and Digges nods and leans in. He shares many of Dee's theories on the cosmology, and on optics, particularly, and it is he who has fashioned the eyeglasses that Dee claims give him extra insight into the unseen, and which do not just perch on a man's nose but are attached by sprung levers to the back of his head. The beautifully polished glass is heavy, and the frames press behind Dee's ears, and when he has had the leisure to think of such things in the past, he has told himself that he looks more than usually alchemical, and that if Hatton could see him now he would have him burned on sight, but today he has no time for idle thought.

Digges had allowed for the possibility, but right now he turns to speculating on the many ways in which the undisclosed mind reveals itself, and he wonders aloud, almost as a thought exercise, whether this reminder of the pain of losing the father is sent to distract Dee from the pain of losing the son, or to add to it?

Marlowe just shakes his head very slightly, setting that pearl dancing, and he rows on through the thinning whirls of river mist.

"Or perhaps it is because it is All Hallows' Eve?" Digges goes on, reminding them—as if they needed it—that at this time of the year the veil between the living and the dead is said to be at its most permeable, when ghosts are believed to walk the land, and Catholics say they can hear the bells ringing in purgatory, "as if they have churches in purgatory."

"The ancient Britons were the first to light bone fires around this time of year, did you know?" he goes on. "In gratitude for successful harvests, and in honor of a deity they called Samhain, their 'lord of death,' and the Romans of Julius Caesar likewise celebrated in honor of Pomona, their goddess of fruits and gardens."

From the bow of the boat Marlowe changes the subject.

"So what was he like then, eh, this old father of yours?" he asks, and John Dee must turn his mind fully to his father, to Roland Dee, to the man who left him with nothing save a bad name, debt and shame, and a single heirloom in the shape of an ornate silver rod. Roger Cooke later took the rod to riddle the embers under his crucible, and Dee could never think of a reason good enough to stop him and take it back.

"Sad, if I am honest," he now admits. "Life for him didn't go according to plan, and in the end, he had to leave London to live in Wales, where I never saw him again."

Digges reaches out to grip Dee's arm in a show of broader fellow feeling, while Marlowe touches the oars to send the lighter east again, around the river's curve toward Chiswick Eyot, where the rising sun shines straight in Dee's eyes. The river is deserted at this time of morning, and there is silence in the boat, though the birds are in full song. After a while, as the river winds south, and their shadows flicker away to their right, Dee picks up the orb again, and once more bends his mind to becoming it, and letting it become him, and he finds his mind is clearer now, cleansed of thoughts of his father for the moment, though the orb remains inert.

There are more boats on the river as they pass the Bishop of Fulham's palace on their left, and more still when they round the next bend past Chelsea, where the sun is now risen over Marlowe's head, and soon after they are abreast of Westminster, all astir with comings and goings of boats, and still the orb tells Dee nothing.

Dee fights his panic. Only by staying calm will the orb work.

But there has been nothing so far, not the slightest tremor to indicate life. What if this orb is a mere bauble, a skin of gold over a heart of lead? Or what if it will not work on water? Or what if *he* is the problem? What if he cannot read the signals it is sending? Or what if there is nothing to be read? What if he is going the wrong way? What if Arthur has been taken upriver? Or what if because he is a credulous fool, who believes in the power of divination when he should have been riding around Cheam shouting for his son, his son dies?

What then?

What then will he tell Jane?

He clenches his eyes and forces himself not to think such things, forces himself to be positive.

Stay alive, Arthur, that is all I ask of you. Stay alive, and remember that whatever else happens can be fixed with time and love. Only stay alive.

"Any thoughts, Doctor?" Marlowe calls. "Only the tides going out and I'm not convinced that ball of yours'll enjoy shooting the bridge."

Dee blinks.

"Yes," he says. "Over there. Why not?"

A moment later Marlowe steers them skillfully through the shadows between two towering river hulks, and into a small inlet known as Powell's Wharf. Dee breaks his nonexistent connection with the orb and steps ashore, and up the slimy steps he goes, at the top of which he stands for a moment of stillness amid the business of the dockside, adjusts his eyeglasses, and tries to clear his mind of all care and concern, before from his outstretched left palm he lifts the golden orb on its silver chain and holds it out before him until it is still, whereupon he awaits such guidance as it has to offer.

Which is none.

So he sets off eastward, with Marlowe clearing a path through the gawpers ahead and Digges keeping watch behind. Dee tries to glide along in long smooth strides so as not to joggle or interfere with the free movement of the orb, all the while remaining indifferent to his surroundings, trying to concentrate without concentrating; to listen without listening; to watch without watching; to create time and space where none exist, so that he is the orb and the orb is him, and it will communicate what it will communicate.

"Sort of like rubbing your tummy and patting your head," is how Marlowe confirmed that he understood Dee's description of what is required.

He walks as close to the water's edge as he is able, never once breaking the continuum, ignoring all the gibes. Together the three men make their way past the warehouses and across the quays and wharves that line the riverbank, each one dedicated to a different cargo, each populated by different craftsmen, and even by men speaking in different tongues when they come to the Steelyard—though here Dee's divination is treated with greater respect, for the Germans have always used such methods to discover subterranean deposits of lead and other ores—and soon they come to the bridge, where Marlowe stops the traffic and pushes people aside to let Dee pass unmolested.

Then they are down again, onto the wharves where the larger seagoing ships moor to unload and where the smell of fish is almost overwhelming and where a man must have his wits about him if he is not to be laid low by bellowing porters heaving their groaning trays of salmon and cod or what-have-you to market. Here it seems that among all the noise and riotous movement, the only thing that remains stubbornly still is the orb in Dee's hand, for it gives off not the slightest twinge, no tiny imbalance, no subtle little irregularity of motion to send that yearned-for vibration up Dee's outstretched forearm.

And so on they go, across the back of the market, where vendors and customers jostle and haggle and it is there, exactly where a man cannot pause for a moment just to breathe, and where Dee is finally beginning to believe that he has been rooked by the orb seller, and that because of his own credulity, his son will die, that there comes something from the orb: a tremor, as of life, as of a signal from a distant star or dying planet; a definite, definable, distinct something that creeps up Dee's fingers so that he almost drops the orb in startled surprise. Digges nearly bumps into him.

"John?"

Dee's heart rushes.

It is Arthur. He must have come this way, Dee is certain of it. It is his first link to his missing son. *Do not die, Arthur! I am coming!*

A moment later, he loses it again.

He retreats and crosses the line again.

This time it is less strong, but still there.

Does it wear out with use?

Marlowe makes some space among the crowd.

"Which way, Doctor?"

Dee turns away from the river and sets off slowly, following the faintest of thrums, the mildest of tickles, but his spirit and heart soar as he is led away from the market and onto Thames Street. Fifty paces.

And then, despite everything he had been taught about the orb, about ignoring the world around him, there is something about the shapes of the buildings; the width of the road; the degree of its slope up toward Tower Hill, and the way the shadow falls that makes him stop and look up, and there ahead is the bodkin-sharp spire of the church of Saint Dunstan-in-the-East. His heart suddenly turns and his spirits quail, for to him this is the very worst place in the world, the place he has run from, and come to hate more than any other; the sight of it reminds him of everything that he is most ashamed of in his life.

It was not always this way, of course. The church had once been the scene of so much pride, when Dee was a boy, and his family were parishioners, and his father had been made churchwarden. Everyone had known that Roland Dee was a coming man, favored by the king himself, with a household position and a sinecure as His Majesty's Packer, taking his rightful skim of every cargo both loaded and unloaded on every wharf from Queenhithe in the west to Clare's Quay in the east. But when the king died, his father had fallen foul of court and mercantile intrigues and was spat out by the machinations of much wealthier and wilier men.

Had that been the end of it, perhaps no one would have thought the worse of him, for such is life, and there but for the grace of God go we all, but in his desperation to keep his station and name, Roland Dee had used his position at Saint Dunstan to purloin pieces of gold plate from the sacristy to sell to a crooked goldsmith off Cheapside. His crime was discovered, of course, but even then he might have redeemed himself had he come clean and been willing to pay the money back, but he could not, or would not, and definitely did not, and so was the Dee family's name traduced, and their shame complete. Roland Dee took flight, leaving his wife and children to be put out on the street, and it was only thanks to Dee's progress at school and the charity of a schoolmaster that the family was saved.

Dee has never since been able to pass through this parish or look at that church without thinking that everyone knew who he was, even the stones, as if the mortification of those years were a brand on his forehead, and the shame of it dyed into his wool, breathed into his lungs.

And so—so why has the orb brought him here of all places?

Is it trying to tell him something about Arthur, or something about his father?

Or will it, dear God, merely lead him to those long-sought, but for now irrelevant pieces of gold plate that his father stole all those years ago and could or would never account for?

Dee stumbles, his tangled feet reflecting his tangled feelings, and he loses his connection with the orb, and it suddenly feels as if he holds in his hand a dead thing, a conker on a string, just as the wits had been telling him. He must close his eyes and step out of the slew of passing traffic of Thames Street, and he must absent himself from his past, and be here in the now, letting the orb swing freely, unimpeded by the debris of what is long gone. But, Jesu, it is hard.

"You look a touch peaky, Doctor," Marlowe butts in. "You all right?"

And Dee almost smiles at his well-meaning, well-timed clumsiness, and the distraction is like having a strangler's fingers prised from your throat, and a moment later, he achieves a more peaceful frame of mind, and then a little after that he feels that yearned-for-without-being-yearned-for supernatural thrill rising up the chain between his fingers, and he shuts off his earlier qualms about Saint Dunstan, and his father, and his past, and he steps out, allowing the orb to take him wherever it will.

Up Thames Street, from which he follows the orb left, up Saint Dunstan's Lane, up toward that awful church, closer and closer, and then just as it seems it is going to take him up the broad granite steps and through those daunting painted doors into the nave itself, Dee once more loses the connection. He has gone too far and must retrace his steps to find it again, and this time he knows only not to fear losing it, and sure enough, he does not lose it, for there it is, on the corner by the churchyard wall; he sets off along the lane that runs alongside it, only to lose communication again, ten paces along.

He turns back and stops before a sturdy little postern gate, up a step off the street, made of sun-faded oak planks, more than half-hidden behind a dense curtain of ivy that has been left to run riot since Roland Dee's day, though it is obvious someone has torn at it recently.

"Here," he says, nodding at the gate.

Dee has been here before, as a child, for the burial of the man who had baptized him, the man who gave him First Communion, the man who terrified the life out of him: Father Anthony. He shakes his head and shivers as if this will shake off the ghosts of the past, and he looks up at the iron spikes on the wall, the overgrown ivy, the overhanging yew trees, and he knows for certain that if Arthur is in here, then nothing good can come of it.

"In here is it, Doctor?"

Whatever happens, Arthur, Dee repeats to his absent son, *just please stay alive! We can fix anything and everything else, only please, please, please whatever else you do, do not die, my son. Only do not die.*

Dee nods, and Marlowe takes a step back and boots the postern gate hard enough to break any bolt, but the door is unlocked and flies open with a crack.

CHAPTER NINETEEN

Crypt of Saint Dunstan-in-the-East,
All Hallows' Eve, October 1585

Mademoiselle Báthory opens the plaque immediately, as if she had been waiting for his knock, and before Ballard can thrust the goat's head into her hands and turn and run, she takes his hand to pull him in as if for an embrace, and despite everything he knows, and despite everything he has decided, he still yields, and by the time he realizes she is just hurrying him along so that she might close the plaque behind him, it is too late. He is trapped with her.

He watches her lock it with that curious key and sees how she smiles to herself as she secretes the key somewhere in her skirts. *Probably in the same place she keeps that blade*, he thinks.

Then he looks to the boy.

Dead or alive?

Alive.

Part of him is relieved, part of him isn't: it means there is still that to come.

But she's been at work and has found and arranged a host of altar candles upon the tombs all around the empty space in the middle of the crypt—a few lit, but many more yet to be so—and in their light Ballard can see she has also swept the flagstones and arranged the lines of dust to make up the shape of—what? *Of a pentacle?*

"What are you doing?" he asks.

"What is needed," she tells him again. "Give me head."

He passes the goat to her, glad to be shot of the bloody thing, which smells hot and rustic, and he sees she has written around the pentacle—in letters made of that same thick beige dust—the words *Adam* and *Lilith*, and that in the center of the whole thing lies a small turd of gray wax to which is attached a hank of red hair.

"And where did you get all these?" he asks, gesturing to the candles, of which there must be a hundred.

"Sacristy," she tells him. "Steps up, behind tomb."

She points, but only because she needs his help in bringing something down.

"Don't step!" she barks as he starts after her. She means the pentacle. Ballard cannot take his eyes from the boy, who lies stripped of the boatman's cloak now but is still tied fast in sacking, still in his soiled linens. Even in the gloom of the crypt Ballard can feel the boy's eyes on him, hot and bright with terror.

"What are you going to do with him?" he asks for the hundredth time, and for the hundredth time she does not give a proper answer.

"What is needed," she repeats.

"But what *is* needed?" he presses. "What is needed with all this?"

He means the pentacle and the candles—and what is this? A rope? A bell-ringing rope? "What in the name of God are we even doing here?" he demands.

"What is needed to destroy Dee," she says. "So that is what we do."

"Why not just kill the man?"

She scoffs.

"That is not destroying him. He still have his name. He still have his reputation. If he is dead he will not know the loss. He will not know the loss of child, of his woman. He will not know loss of his name. When he knows the loss of those, then we kill him."

Ballard can think of nothing to say.

"Until then," she says, "come. Help. We need more things."

She collects a candle and disappears into one of the alcoves, shuffling alongside a tomb on which rests a skeleton.

Which leaves him standing there.

He should just walk out, shouldn't he? Take the boy and flee. Or find Walsingham's house; tell the porter on the gate how to find this terrible place, then run. That way the boy might be saved, though—dear God—she seems to hate the boy with a particular kind of spite, and if anyone should come stumbling about the church, he is certain she will see the boy dead, even if it is the last thing she does.

And also: she has the key.

After a moment's more indecision, the candle flames in the crypt flutter and Ballard becomes aware of the faintest draft wafting from the alcove into which Mademoiselle Báthory has disappeared. He peers down its length and sees in the back wall a square of pale light. He copies her shuffle down the side of the tomb where the angle of the roof makes him bend over the skeleton—he hopes it is stone—as if to kiss it. He holds his breath. The square of light is a half door, through which is a set of very narrow steps that wind steeply up toward another square of pale gray daylight above, and in the dust of each tread is imprinted the marks of Mademoiselle Báthory's shoes where she has gone up and come down with the candles.

He climbs them and finds himself rising through a hatch set in the beautifully tiled floor of a small, deserted room crowded with heavily reinforced wardrobes and chunky metal-studded coffers. The sacristy, he supposes, where the priests lock their precious robes and all the gold and silverware needed for their services. One of the coffers is open, its lock cracked apart, and on the floor below stands a chalice and its matching ciborium along with what looks like a thurible for dispensing incense smoke and a silver basin, which the priests would once have used to bathe their acolytes' feet on Maundy Thursday. Within that sits a hyssop aspergillum, which is used to broadcast Holy Water on the altar cloth and wherever else the rite demands.

Mademoiselle Báthory stands listening at a door ajar, which must lead to the nave. When she's satisfied there is nothing to be heard, she gestures—*come*—and slips through, and he can do nothing but follow. The nave is handsome enough: high vaulted and pillared and cool and gray, though without the presence of God it feels empty, which is just as well, for Mademoiselle Báthory is now dragging a stool across to the altar.

"You climb up," she instructs.

"Why?"

"To get cross," she says, indicating a large rosewood crucifix onto which is nailed an ivory Christ in his agonized death throes, set high up above the tabernacle on a long pole.

Ballard clambers up onto the altar, leaving his boot prints on snow white linen cloths, and stretches up to slide the pole out. It is probably the one they used to carry in procession when the parish bounds were beaten, he thinks, and he passes it down and then steps down himself. Instinctively he tries to brush the filthy dust off the altar.

"Leave that," she says, "and break this."

She means the crucifix from the pole, which is easy enough.

"Which bit do you want?"

She rolls her eyes at him.

"Both."

"What in the name of God do you want it for, and don't tell me you need it for what is needed!"

She turns back and looks at him under a cocked eyebrow, not even especially interested in his show of defiance.

"For what is needed," she says, very slowly.

He would hit her with the pole, except she is a woman, and also there is that blade in her skirts. He blinks. Behind him there comes a distant voice, in the street outside perhaps, or on the church steps; an everyday exchange of greetings between one man and another, coming this way.

"Quick," she says, and she turns and moves swiftly back to the sacristy. After a moment, he follows with the pole and crucifix, cursing her under his breath. Through the door she has gathered the altarware into her skirts, and she steps down through the hatch. Just before she disappears, she tells him to remember to put the hatch back after him.

"Is not time to be found yet."

Then she is gone.

Ballard turns a full circle. Not since his first schoolmaster has anyone ever spoken to him with such disdain, not even the Duc de Guise. He wishes now that he had kicked her head while he had the chance, just as she descended the steps.

Christ.

The hatch is very skillfully hidden in the tiled floor, but it is small and awkward to fit the pole and crucifix through, though he manages it. When he climbs back up to return the cover in place he pauses for a moment, half in and half out, caught between two lives, and he breathes in the old familiar smells of the church—not so very different from a Catholic church—and he cannot help but admire the beauty of the Cosmati pavement, and as he is doing so, he hears out in the nave an abrupt shunt and then the bang of a door, followed by brusque voices and hurrying footsteps. He should wait to be caught, he thinks, but instead he quickly ducks and slides the hatch over his head with a noise that must once have been satisfying, but to Ballard feels horribly final.

It leaves him in the absolute darkness, through which he must fumble, disturbing all that dust, and discovering that the skeleton he hoped was stone is not, and when he emerges with the crucifix from the alcove, his clothes and skin are smeared all over with that foul dust, with all sorts of matter in his hair. He breathes in the dust and starts to cough, and he can hardly get the words out to tell her that there are men astir upstairs.

"Someone's up there," he wheezes.

All she can do is to tell him to stop coughing so that she can listen.

They can hear nothing. The ceiling is solid stone. She decides to ignore the news.

She puts the crucifix to one side and starts arranging the silverware—the chalice and the ciborium—up on one of the tombs. After a moment, she barks words he has never heard before.

"Kurva anyád!"

It is obviously a curse, and she backhands the thurible, which clanks across the floor in anger.

"We need incense," she says.

"There must be plenty in the sacristy," he supposes.

"Which now full of heretic priests crying because they have lost silver cups!"

She rights the thurible.

"We get some when they gone," she decides, standing to take the pole. He passes it to her and watches her looking for a suitable way to secure it upright. There's nothing. Ballard cannot help because he is not practical like that, nor does he know what in the name of God she is up to. Eventually she sees a fix that requires him to push the stone cross off one of the tombs, onto the floor, where it breaks in two pieces.

"Is good," she says, and she makes him bring both bits to her, where she puts them on a step and arranges them into a base that keeps the cross upright. When she's satisfied, she stoops to lift the goat's head, and she carries it as if to crown a monarch, only then to impale it on the broken spike of the pole, like a traitor's head, before stepping back to admire her handiwork. The goat, its eyes open now, shocked at what has just happened to him, stands overlooking the pentacle as might a disappointed master of ceremonies.

Then she takes the crucifix and places it against a tomb, upside down, and he actually gasps, because that is sacrilege, and now he finally understands what she is about: creating the props of the Black Mass.

There is the image of Baphomet, the pentacle with the names of Adam and Lilith—who some say was Adam's first wife—and there at the center of the pentacle is a disgusting little homunculus that he now sees is intended to represent the Queen, Elizabeth, with her red hair.

"But why?" he asks, for surely Báthory is not going to conduct such a ceremony herself? And as an ordained priest, God forbid he will ever do such a thing.

At last she stops and turns to him, and at last she tells him her plan.

"It shows Dee is in league with devil, yes? That he will sell his soul to Satan. That he so greedy for power, he will sacrifice own son."

CHAPTER TWENTY

Churchyard of Saint Dunstan-in-the-East,
All Hallows' Eve, October 1585

"Quick!"

Beale takes Phelippes by the sleeve and spins him into the deeper shadow of one of the yew trees. They hear the voices of two men, and when Beale peers out through the low-hanging fronds of the tree, he sees three figures coming down the path in a knot, one of them in dark wool, another in green with a russet cap.

"Who are they?" Phelippes whispers.

"I don't— By Jesu! It's Dee!"

"What in the name of God is he doing here? And what is he wearing on his face?"

Beale sheathes his sword and steps out onto the path. Dee, who leads the party, starts, but his eyes do not focus; behind his glasses they seem to swim in his head. He holds the divining orb extended before him and Beale steps back to let him pass.

"Looking for his boy," the man in the russet cap tells them, and Beale recognizes Christopher Marlowe. He does not know the third.

"Here?" Phelippes interjects.

"He hasn't walked through the city wearing those eyeglasses and swinging that ball, has he?" Beale asks.

"Only from Powell's Wharf," the third man says.

Powell's Wharf is what? A mile?

"Did anyone see you?"

"What do you think?" Marlowe asks. "Whole bloody world saw him."

Beale intercepts a look from Phelippes. Both men hope Sir Christopher Hatton was not one of them: there's almost nothing he'd enjoy more than catching Dee in the act of conjuring. Each has half an eye on Dee, who continues to ignore them and has walked through the ivy toward the flank of the church, to almost the exact same spot they found that last drop of goat's blood. Now he's standing against the wall, looking from the conker to the plaque and back again, as if stuck. He leans his forehead against the wall and shuts his eyes. The conker is by his side now, hanging loose from limp fingers.

"Arthur," he says. "Arthur."

Beale and Phelippes look at each other, and then back at Dee.

"He's in there?" Marlowe asks.

Dee lifts his head from the plaque and nods. Then he steps back and extends a finger to touch the brass *O*.

"What's that, Doctor?" Beale asks.

"A keyhole," he tells them.

And when he takes his finger away, sure enough, there is a hole, but can it really be for a key? Dee steps another pace back to look up at the flank of the church that towers over them, smooth and implacable, and Beale steps into the space to put his eye to the hole. There's nothing there, of course, but is there a faint—the faintest—draft? He puts his cheek to it, then his wetted lips.

"But what does it open?" Beale asks.

Marlowe is trying to get his fingers around the edge of the plaque. He climbs up on the lower footing to see if he can pull it down from above.

"It's solid as you like," he says, dropping down and brushing his hands. "No joins or anything. Can't be a door, I swear."

Dee bends to peer closely at the keyhole.

"A quincunx," he says at last, tracing its edges with a spindly, inky finger.

"A what?" one of them asks.

"A quincunx," Phelippes explains. "Four circles joined by a single central circle."

Dee has stepped back again and is once more up at the thin sliver of sky between the church and the encroaching yew trees.

"We do not have long," he says.

"Till what?"

"Sunset. That's when they'll do it."

"Do what?"

"Kill Arthur."

All present flinch at these words.

Dee removes the eyeglasses and turns on Beale, and all trace of that soupy trancelike state is replaced by adamantine brilliance.

"Robert," he says. "I need a horse."

It is ten miles as the crow flies from Saint Dunstan-in-the-East to Roger Cooke's laboratory in Dee's garden in Mortlake, but many more if you're not a crow. First, Dee must lead his unfamiliar horse across the bridge, sticking to the left, head down against the crowd flooding into the city to see the bone fire on Tower Hill, and then he is in Southwark, where he must thread his way through the crowds of drunken idlers that choke the narrow lanes between the taverns and the brothels behind the Bishop of Winchester's palace.

Only then can he mount up and set his borrowed horse at a fast trot westward across the commons.

He believes he has taken twenty minutes out of his hour, easily.

On he goes, never a very accomplished horseman, clinging to the horse, his thighs burning, his head rattled; a burden rather than a master, through sour grazing, interrupted here and there by furloughs of turned earth; easily a dozen windmills, as well as an old friary or monastery that's been bought by a wealthy man with pretensions. He crosses a river that stinks of tannery waste, and then a mile later, another where the air smells fecund with malting barley, and where a man who wants to charge him pontage has to leap out of the way. The horse won't stop. Galloping now, it pounds away, eating up the distance, sweat flecking his neck, and still Dee kicks on, arguing for more speed, because the light has changed, and he knows sunset cannot be delayed.

More commons; goats and chickens; then a coppiced beechwood full of pigs; then a glimpse of the river on his right and he knows he is in Putney and that Mortlake lies four miles ahead and on he goes, the horse's pace less thundering now, the head beginning to toss, and its sweat is like a thick cream. Dee urges it on, for Arthur's sake, clumsily buffeting its neck because he is too scared to let go of the reins and pat him properly, making extravagant promises of wonderful rewards to come.

At length he sees the steeple of Saint Mary's, his own parish church, with its own bone fire in its yard, and the parishioners are beginning to mill about—children mainly so far, with their hollowed-out turnip lamps ready for the lighting—in anticipation of the vigil to come. Dee clatters up the lane, and he finally draws the exhausted gelding to a halt outside Thomas Digges's house where William the night watchman is there early, ready to catch him as he falls.

"You all right, Doctor?"

"Thank you, William, yes. I need to get to my house."

William opens Thomas Digges's gate and lets him through.

"Any news of Arthur?"

"Some," Dee calls, rightened up now and regaining the feeling in his legs. "I'll tell you later. Can you saddle Sparrow? And rub this fellow down? Feed and water him and whatever else it is you do?"

William takes the reins, still not sure, but Dee sets off down the length of Digges's garden, staggering on his burning legs, then he turns up into his own, through the orchard where the apples hang unpicked and where the deer have taken advantage of his absence to get into the vegetable garden. At first glance Roger Cooke's laboratory looks little better than a hovel in the garden, save the roof is sound; it has a very sturdy door and three glazed windows facing south to let in the light. It is locked, of course, but one of the windows—designed by Dee to help vent noxious fumes—needs only an unexpected twist and it is open, and through it a long arm may reach the door's turning bolt.

Once inside, Dee stands for a moment, the briefest flicker of time to acknowledge that the place is now cold to the touch, as it never was when Roger himself was alive, for there was always something on the go, even if it was just a charcoal fire to warm his clumsy old hands. He has not yet had the time to sit and mourn Roger and has none now. Instead, he must rifle through all the various alchemical tools that litter the much scarred and charred workbench, knocking aside cucurbits, alembics, lutes, and a stack of scorched crucibles in search of what he's after—the silver rod Dee's father gave him, and which Roger then took to use as a poker for his fire. He pulls out and upends the drawer of spoons and scoops and spatulas and tweezers and tongs, sending them to scatter over his boot caps.

Nothing.

"Christ Jesu, where is it?"

He rummages through everything else—the cold gray charcoal;

the shards of pottery and pieces of broken glass that Roger Cooke had hidden in a bin so that Dee would never know when he had broken something.

Nothing.

In one of the other laboratories perhaps?

Dee has his own, nearer the house and attached to his library, but Roger stayed clear of that, knowing it contained the last pieces of glass that Dee had brought back from Leuven. Still, though. He runs the twenty yards and must go in through the kitchen—still open after the coroner removed poor dead Sarah, and the smell of leek soup still strong in the air—through his library and then into his own alchemical house. There is no sign of anything out of place among all his equipment, no sign that Roger Cooke had been in here to break anything, or move anything out of place.

He must think.

What was Roger last working— Then he remembers. The cannon! Or, rather, the canisters. Jesu, it seems a lifetime ago now, lived in a different world, that saw them experimenting with the various charges in Digges's garden—blasting the dean of Saint Paul's water steps to pieces on that golden afternoon in June—before loading the cannon up into the bed of Nurdle's cart and taking the long road south to Portsmouth.

They had hope in their hearts, then, and were all three of them still alive.

Now, though, Dee is in a very different temper as he runs up his stairs and climbs out of his window, up onto the tiled roof of the library and along its spine, to leap the three paces needed to land him in the branch of Thomas Digges's oak tree that sticks out over the dividing wall between their gardens and that bows under his weight to drop him, less elegantly than in past times, on Thomas Digges's onion patch. From there he runs leaping over the fence to Thomas Digges's laboratory, only to find it locked.

He is breathless now, and weak for lack of food, and another setback will bring him to tears. But he doesn't need to think twice before he removes his boot, and he smashes a windowpane with its heel. He reaches in and lifts the latch. Inside, he knows exactly where to look first: by the bed of charcoal ash over which rests Digges's tripod on which sits a soot-smudged crucible, last used by Roger Cooke, but then, when he looks on the bench, it is not there!

Jesu! Jesu! Jesu!

Time is running out!

He tears through the neat orderliness of Digges's laboratory, unseating the ordered racks of various lens that Thomas uses for his specific line of inquiry and sending them scattering across the bench and floor, knocking over pots of polishing powders and upsetting a cupful of glass cutters and other tools of Digges's trade, but there is still no sign of what he is looking for.

At some point he will have to cut his losses and admit he has failed his son.

But he is sure he just needs to think, to think clearly.

And then he has it!

The spike!

The spike!

Christ!

He hurls himself out of Digges's laboratory just as the night watchman comes calling with the news that Sparrow is saddled, though he lacks a shoe, and William is not certain if— Dee bundles past him, and runs back down the garden, around the wall, and back up his own orchard again, and he crashes through his kitchen door, and runs screaming into his hall, and back into the library where there, tossed aside by the fireside and never looked at since Dee laid poor old Roger's body out after he'd brought him back from Portsmouth, is the man's bag.

He snatches it up, plunges his hand in, and there it is, the only tangible thing his father ever left him: a foot-long rod of silver, ridged down its length so that from either end it is the shape of a quincunx.

A key!

Who would have known it was that?

Not Dee when he left it lying around as if it were of no value whatsoever; not Roger Cooke when he used it to stir his charcoal; not Roger Cooke when he hit it with the hammer to set off the chemical reaction in his canister missiles.

Dee tosses the bag aside, stuffs the key in his doublet, and sets off running for Digges's stables and Sparrow, but then he asks himself, *Will it not now be quicker by boat?* Now that the tide is running out?

Boat.

He sprints down through his garden once more and takes the steps up to the jetty two at a time and then races to its farthermost point to stare westward, toward the sun that is not far from setting now, and to a river that is for once empty of any type of craft whatsoever. He falls on his knees and clenches his hands and offers up a prayer to God in which he promises to swap his own life for the appearance of even the humblest of rowing boats.

"A lighter, a skiff, a punt! A raft even!"

Jesu! Does he go back to the stables and find poor limping Sparrow?

Yes!

He is just setting off, and jumps the five steps to the ground, where he lands awkwardly, twists his ankle and throws himself forward, his hands outstretched, and the key spills from his doublet, and it is while he is crawling in the grass, fumbling for it that he sees from the tail of his eye coming sweeping around the bend from Richmond the barge he knows to belong to his old friend and patron, Robert Dudley, the first Earl of Leicester. His prayers have been answered beyond all expectation, so long as Dudley is aboard.

He is.

"My God, John, what a state you are in!"

Dee gulps the proffered ale and thinks that Dudley is one to talk: the man's arm is in a sling, and his shoeless foot is raised on a stool, but Dee has no time for niceties and blurts out his need for speed. When Dudley understands, he shouts at his bargemaster to up the tempo of the sweeping oars.

"As if we're to ram the Duke of Parma himself!"

And the barge lurches ahead, following the retreating tide downriver as if in some way mechanized.

After he's answered a fusillade of questions, Dee asks Dudley why his foot is up.

"Jousting accident," is all he'll say. He's on his way to Whitehall, though, where Her Majesty is to enjoy her own bone fire, and he is dressed in what looks like silver silk, with a short cape and a large-hilted sword to remind everyone that despite his injuries he will soon be leading an English army against Spanish tercios in the Netherlands. In any other mood, Dee might take pleasure in the experience of being rowed at such exhilarating speed, but he stands by Dudley in the stern, watching the sun become gauzy over the treetops to the west, and he knows he will miss the moment when the bells will ring out, when he believes that whatever is to be done to Arthur will be done.

The oarsmen are already sweating in their livery coats, but the bargemaster is warming to his task as they follow the sinuous meanders of the Thames north and south as it flows east toward the sea, and Dee curses every light that he sees being lit on the river's banks as a rebuke to his want of speed. He checks he still has the key in his doublet. Yes. They keep up the tempo past Whitehall, where Dudley is due, and there ahead skulks London, pinpricked with lamplight as it sinks into shadow.

"Happy to shoot the rapids, my lord? Tide's only just turned."

Dudley nods. Dee grips the gunwale. The bargemaster is hoarse with keeping his oarsmen in time, and despite himself, Dee becomes mesmerized by the motions of the blades. To and fro, up and down, in and out—the elegant red blades power the elegant red barge across the Thames's choppy broth. As they approach the bridge the oars become like insects' wings lying sleek to their sides as the barge gathers momentum and then punches through the flitting shadow of the arch to swoop down into the chaos of the outflow where the barge slews and seems to skid across the water until the bargemaster barks fresh orders and he heaves on the rudder to straighten her. The oars flick out in perfect time again, and dip, and dip, and the barge is brought under his control. Dudley nods his approval, and the bargemaster is satisfied.

And still the bell has not yet rung for six.

"Billingsgate," Dee says, pointing unnecessarily to the masts that mark the entrance to the wharf. The bargemaster adjusts and slows the pace as they approach, and with one last look around at the setting sun and the gathering gloom, Dee hurries to the bow, thanking the oarsmen as he brushes through their ranks and readies himself to spring onto the first fishing boat they come alongside.

"Godspeed, John," Dudley calls out from his chair. "Send word!"

Dee checks his doublet for the key one last time before he throws himself over the gunwale, his feet almost spinning on the fishing boat's slippery deck.

"Oy!"

But it is too late to apologize to anyone and he is across and off the boat's deck and onto the wharf before anything further can be said, and he sets off sprinting across the now quieted marketplace toward Thames Street, where the crowds are drifting toward the

Tower Hill bone fire, and his body is tensed for the first ring of the six of clock bell, but still it does not come. Up Saint Dunstan's Lane as once he used to as a child, when he was late for Mass, and likely to catch a thick ear from Father Anthony.

"Out the way!" he shouts at a group of already drunken guildsmen, and then he swerves right, along the tall churchyard wall, to the postern gate, and still the bell has not rung, and he thrusts the door open and keeps running up the ivy-choked path and there ahead of him stand Marlowe and Digges and both turn to him round-eyed with surprise, and they are holding out their hands as if to repel him, to warn him off, but he shrugs them aside and pulls out the key, slides it into the lock, and it fits just as perfectly as he knew it would the moment he saw it, and he manages to give it a half turn . . .

Before he feels two powerful blows falling upon his shoulders. His hand is torn from the key. He is driven to his knees. Before he can even cry out, his face is thrust against the wall and he's suddenly aware of five or six large men in red, all shouting at the same time, telling him not to fucking move an inch or they'll put a blade right through him so help them God, and he feels what might be a knee thrust into his spine and his arms are grabbed and pulled apart so that he's pinned to the wall, his face smeared against the plaque, and he hears a voice he recognizes as Sir Christopher Hatton shouting in his ear.

"I've got you now, Dee! You're mine, d'you hear? Conjuring for treasure all over the city! A hundred witnesses! You'll never wriggle out of this one, Dee! This time I'll see you burn!"

And all Dee can think is that the bells have started ringing for six, and that his boy will soon be dead.

CHAPTER TWENTY-ONE

Crypt of Saint Dunstan-in-the-East, London,
All Hallows' Eve, October 1585

The city bells are felt as the merest vibration through the stones down in the inner crypt of Saint Dunstan-in-the-East and Mademoiselle Báthory stands.

"Come," she says to Ballard. "First light candles, then we hook him."

"Hook him?"

"Mmm," she grunts and points with her chin to something Ballard has not bothered to notice before: a small stubby hook set in the ceiling where the apex of the arches meet, just as he saw in the shambles up on Cheapside. He watches her start lighting one candle from the flame of another, working her way around the crypt. He stands frozen, just watching.

"Come," she repeats over her shoulder. "Help."

"Just tell me what you are going to do," he asks again, knowing the answer already.

"What is needed."

She continues to light the candles. He remains where he is. She can't make him light candles, can she? She can't make him hang the boy from a hook. And now he finds he cannot take his eyes off the boy, who has stopped struggling, and lies there looking at Ballard with those terrified, imploring eyes, and in the silence, both hear something, he is sure of it, a little stir in the fabric of the church. The boy's eyes flick to it, too, over by the hatch to the churchyard, so he knows he did not imagine it: something like the first brush of a sword on its sharpening steel, but close at hand, almost intimate.

Ballard walks toward the hatch. He extends his fingers to touch the cool stone. It is a very clever piece of masonry work, he thinks, and except for their tracks in the dust below, there is no way to know that five or six of the stone blocks are not cemented in place. He traces his finger around the little brass escutcheon. So clever.

He is blocking out what is going on behind his back because he cannot stand it. Every sound from her makes his skin crawl, and now that he knows the rough outline of her plan, his every fiber is in riotous turmoil. He has been to executions, of course—who has not?—but never to see a woman burned, or a child hanged. There are some things the sight of which cannot be endured, still less participated in. He bends to peer through the keyhole, supposing he might glimpse the light from the yard beyond, but though he stares for some little while, there is nothing to be seen save absolute darkness, and soon he knows he must stand and turn back, to face what needs be faced.

She has the candles mostly lit now, and the scene is bathed in a golden glow that makes it appear even more horrific. Mademoiselle Báthory has looped the stolen bell rope around the boy's ankles, and for a fraction of a moment he believes that she has made a mistake, and for that he is glad, but then he sees she put the silver basin on the step with the chalice, and next to it the thing that she must have stolen from Dee's laboratory: a slim little knife such as barber surgeons use for bloodletting.

He knows now what she has planned: She will hang the boy by his feet, cut his throat to let him bleed him out into the basin, and then use his blood to fill between the pentacle. And she'll fill the chalices with it, too, and most likely paint more pentacles and symbols with the hyssop aspergillum that she brought down from above, and so create such a diabolic and degenerate scene that any man would be terrified and disgusted, but how is she going to tie it to Dee?

Then he sees she has that book she stole from his library—something in Greek—and Dee's cloak, too, put to one side to suggest Dee wore it to kidnap his own son, but put aside during this—this whatever it is supposed to be. Black Mass? Seance? It hardly matters. All anyone who finds it will see is the bloodless boy, the goat, the homunculus in the bloody pentacle; and when they find Dee's cloak and book—they won't care what exactly Dee was doing, whether he was conjuring Her Majesty's death or making a deal with the devil, and they'll not care if he was or was not following the exactly correct rites of the Black Mass.

"How will you make sure he is discovered?"

"We run into street, screaming hue and cry, yes? When people come running, we run other way."

Simple, he thinks.

She brushes her hands on the cloth of her blood-red kirtle.

"Help now," she says. "And careful of lines."

And he knows the time has finally come.

She stoops over the boy to check the knot on the bell rope is tight enough around his ankles. It is. Then she feeds the rope through her hands and passes it to Ballard, nodding at the hook: *you know what to do*. He feels as if his own blood were frothing and his fingers tremble as he takes the rope. He need only stand on the tips of his toes to feed it through the hook, and he pulls it, thinking of all those other innocent hands that have pulled on this exact same rope, only they have done so to set a bell to peal for the greater glory of God. He envies them now, for here he is, pulling the rope taut, and if he pulls another inch he cannot deny his active involvement in the death of this boy. But if he lets go the rope, and turns away, he will have to face her wrath, and the wrath of the leaders of Catholic Christendom, and he is already so enmired in this scheme that—and oh Christ Jesus he pulls, gently, and the boy slides across the floor toward him and lets out a muffled scream.

Mademoiselle Báthory stands watching the process, hands on her hips, in the way she might were she watching her horse being shoed.

And now the boy lies below the hook.

Another pull and he will rise.

Báthory looks at him expectantly.

He lets out a deep breath.

"I cannot—"

She seems to twist and harden, become almost metallic, and she steps up to snatch the rope from his hands. She leans into it, and the boy screams into his gag as his legs are lifted off the ground, and he follows until he is hanging with his head two feet from the flagstones, wriggling like a worm on a hook and swinging wildly.

Mademoiselle Báthory turns to look at Ballard.

"Tie it off," she says, indicating the loose end of the rope.

Ballard shakes his head.

"I can't," he says.

So she lets the rope go.

The boy drops, and the noise is a horrific clonk of skull on stone.

Ballard is almost sick with outrage.

The boy lies stunned, but Mademoiselle Báthory remains staring at Ballard, daring him to let her do it again, and she starts hauling on the rope. The boy hangs like a dead weight now, and there's already a blue bruise on that milky white forehead.

"Tie it," she says again.

This time he does. Two hard knots in the rope.

She lets go of the rope and stands back and it creaks as the boy turns a circle, limp and unconscious.

A blessing perhaps.

Ballard also takes a step back, horrified by what he has done. Something touches him on the shoulder. He leaps in fright. That fucking goat! Fucking Baphomet! Its eyes are open—terrifyingly judgmental pupils—and its tongue protrudes, very pale pink, while below its ragged ending, the pole is jammy with the last dribbles of its blood. Meanwhile Mademoiselle Báthory has used her foot to sweep the basin under the boy's tousled locks, and she is bending for that little dagger.

Oh Christ Jesus.

He cannot do this. He cannot watch. Ballard covers his eyes, his ears, but still he feels as if the air in the crypt has suddenly thickened, and is pressing him on all sides, and he cannot breathe and he knows the pressure will make his ears and eyeballs burst because what is being done is so foul and wicked that he—he finds he is gripping the horns of that infernal satanic goat, and with not a moment's further thought, he wrenches it off its pole and whirls around and he hurls it with every ounce of fury and frustration at Mademoiselle Báthory just as she is bending to slash the neck of Dee's boy.

He does not see which part of the goat hits her. Skull or horns, it does not matter. But as it hits her at the temple, she flinches and drops the knife to the floor and staggers away. Her fingers are pressed to her bowed forehead, and he watches her reel across the floor, kicking the basin, traipsing over the neat lines of the pentacle, until she loses control of her legs and goes over in a noisy tangle of limbs.

Ballard stands frozen.

He is suddenly master of his fate once more.

He pauses a moment, unsure of what to do first: the boy or the woman?

The woman first.

She lies facedown in the dust, alive, he detects from the vein beating in her neck, but limp, and when he has rolled her onto her back, unable, even in this most terrible of moments, to resist placing his hand on her buttocks, breasts, and cunny, because he knows she would hate that above all else, and he searches her closely to try to find that blade but he cannot see it or feel it anywhere. She must have hidden it elsewhere. But he does find that strange tubular key hanging from her belt on a thin leather loop in the folds of her skirt.

He stands and kicks the bloodletting knife somewhere she will surely never find it in the darkness, and he hopes never to see anything like it ever again. Then he goes to the boy, who is likewise unconscious, the bruise on his forehead swelling like a bubo.

"It's all right, boy," he whispers. "I've got you."

He ducks to lift Arthur onto his shoulder and then, with the weight off the rope, he unhooks it, and lays the boy down. He unties the rope and then takes him up again and he walks, carrying the boy toward the hatch. He inserts the key.

It does not go in.

He tries it every which way, turning it around and around but there is no way it will yield. Something is blocking it. Christ! He hurls the key away and hears it clatter against a tomb. He will have to carry the boy up the winding steps and out through the nave above. He can leave him where he'll be found—but what if she wakes up and finds him?

He realizes only now that he must kill Báthory. He knows that she would kill him in this position. He should find that blade of hers, or at least that bloodletting knife. Find it and slit her throat just as she would have slit his. But he also knows he cannot do it. He cannot kill a sleeping woman. She is too vulnerable, though perhaps if he had not given John Savage the pistol . . .

He has no time for this, he thinks. He must get the boy out of harm's way.

But where? Walsingham's house in Seething Lane? Leave him with the porter, and then run for it? It is as good an idea as any.

Up the winding steps then.

The boy has come to now, roused from his torpor, and Ballard has to drag him into the alcove, squeezing between the roof and that filthy old skeleton on the tomb's top, through all that foul dust.

"All's well, my lad," Ballard rumbles as reassuringly as he can. "Let's get you out of here, shall we?"

And the boy is pliant or does not scream, anyway. Ballard wishes he could carry the boy and a candle, for his body blocks any light at the back of the alcove, and he has to leave him on the tomb top while he fumbles for the door, patting the rear panel until he finally finds the slightest indentation and must hook his fingernails in and prise it open. Cool fragrant air drenches him and he breathes it in as if it is the sweetest thing, as if he is emerged from Hell.

He reaches back to collect the boy again.

The boy screams.

And oh Christ!

The woman! She is roused and conscious again, and she has risen to seize the boy by the heels!

"Get off him, you witch!"

She says nothing. He can just see her ferocity; feel it, even, as she wrenches on the boy's ankles. Praise Jesus her grip is upon the sackcloth bindings around the boy's ankles, and under pressure, they finally give, and Ballard and the boy tumble one way, while she tumbles backward into the crypt. Ballard grabs the boy, rights him.

"It's all right," he hisses. "It's all right," though, Jesu, is it?

The space is so tight he cannot bend his knee and hold the boy at the same time, so he must push the boy's body ahead, force him upward toward the hatch, and he knows the woman will come for him at any moment, and he curses himself for not searching her body more carefully for that blade. He can almost feel it slicing his ankles, his hamstrings. Now that the boy can go no further, Ballard must squeeze himself past him to unseat the hatch above their heads and for a long moment he cannot remember how it is done. His fingers scrabble at the mechanism.

"Come on come on come on!"

The boy is squirming, and it is suddenly as hot as hell in here, and Ballard finds the catch and pushes and pushes but it does not seem to be moving and he fears for a moment that for whatever reason someone has moved a coffer to cover the hatch from above, and then the hatch at the bottom of the steps is shoved open to let in a faint glow of candlelight through which her shadow comes crawling upward like a vast and malignant spider.

But in the glow, he sees what he has been missing: one more catch, which he flicks, and under his pressure the hatch flies up. Cold air and evening light descend, and he boosts the boy upward, using him to push the hatch off, and he almost hurls him out onto the tiles and scrambles up after him.

Ballard springs up the last few steps into the sacristy, and he grabs the cover and slides it over the hatch and presses it down with that now lifesaving clack as it falls into place, and he rolls onto it and lies there a moment to regather his thoughts and breath.

Then he feels her below, beating at the underside of the cover. It is a strange almost thrilling sensation to feel her scrabbling just an inch below him, but Ballard knows he cannot sit here all night. He stretches to reach one of the coffers—half the size of a coffin; probably as heavy as a man, studded and locked with a sturdy bar—and he hauls it over in increments until it half covers the hatch, then he steps off the cover, and slides another coffer across the tiles to butt up against it above the hatch.

She'll never lift them.

The boy is on his feet now, trembling with a mixture of fear and shock, his legs like a fawn's, and his eyes impossibly large.

"We're all right," Ballard tells him. "We're all right."

And he feels the gruff blood of Captain Fortescue beginning to flow again.

CHAPTER TWENTY-TWO

Churchyard of Saint Dunstan-in-the-East,
All Hallows' Eve, October 1585

"Leave him please, Sir Christopher! For the love of God, he is only looking for his son!"

Sir Christopher Hatton—in a low-pulled hat and a dark cloak lined with emerald green silk—stands in the evening gloom of the churchyard in no mood to hear anything from anyone in defense of Doctor Dee, and most especially not from Robert Beale.

"The last time he was discovered breaking Her Majesty's law, Master Beale," he says, "your master had him squirreled overseas, beyond my reach, and I swore then that I'd never let such a thing happen again, and nor shall I, so if it is all the same with you, I'll thank you, and your companions, to get out of my way and let the law take its course."

"But his boy!" Marlowe tries.

Hatton is briefly discomfited by Marlowe's sudden appeal, and he licks his narrow little lips and pulls on the tip of his beard, and for half a moment it feels as if the matter might hang in the balance, but Hatton's hatred of Dee overrides all other impulses, and he nods permission to the sergeant of his men, who still have Dee pressed hard and fast against the church wall, and at the sergeant's order, his men drag Dee back from the stones, as if it was he who clung there, and they carry him, a man on each limb, through the churchyard toward the postern gate.

"Robert!" Dee calls out from the center of this nest of well-muscled shoulders. "The key! Use it! He's in there! My Arthur!"

But Beale is too angry to listen.

"No," he shouts. "Hatton! By the powers vested in me by Her Majesty's principal private secretary, I command you to let him go. He's not conjuring treasure! You can see that! His son has been taken and we are trying to find out where he is before it is too late."

Even in his own ears this sounds pathetic, and Hatton thinks so, too, for he turns and stands in the middle of the path.

"Baaaaaaaa," he bleats. "Baaaaaaaa."

And then he makes an obscene gesture with his fingers.

"You whoreson, Hatton!" Beale shouts, and he is about to draw his sword again, but Marlowe is suddenly at his side, with an unexpectedly firm grip on his wrist.

"Not sure I like the odds, to be honest," he mutters.

Hatton laughs.

"Baaaaaaaa," he says one more time, and then he turns to hurry after his men.

Beale and Marlowe stand shoulder to shoulder and stare after him.

"Thomas," Beale calls to Phelippes over his shoulder. "Follow him. Find out where he is taking Dee. Go with them. Make sure nothing happens."

He doesn't trust Hatton not to ensure Dee suffers some painful accident while trying to escape.

"Hang on, Bob," Marlowe interrupts, "you'd best leave that

to me. I think me and the Dancing Chancellor have a bit of an understanding."

Beale hardly cares, just so long as it is one of them.

"Fine. Then Master Digges, can I ask you to run to find Sir Francis? Pray to God he'll be in his house in Seething Lane. Do you know it?"

Digges does.

"Tell him what's happened. Tell him to send us men here."

The two men bustle from the churchyard. Beale and Phelippes turn back to the church.

"Will we not need a lamp?" Beale wonders, for now in the gloom there is little to be seen.

"Let's just have a look, shall we?" Phelippes suggests.

They approach the plaque from which sticks the barely discernible stub of Dee's silver key. Phelippes takes it between his fingers and before he turns it they look at each other. Then Phelippes turns the key and then whistles under his breath as the plaque moves infinitesimally and cracks of very faint light appear around its edge.

"A door!"

They stare at it, then at each other.

"You ready?" Phelippes asks, nodding at Beale's yet-to-be-drawn sword.

Beale draws it.

"Won't be much good if he's got that pistol," he says.

Then Phelippes edges the plaque open.

"Christ alive," Beale breathes when they see the candlelit crypt.

Over the high threshold they step, Beale first, sword extended.

"Is he here?"

"Arthur!"

They walk up and down the alcoves, holding up the candles, sending crazy terrifying shadows, calling for Arthur, and it takes them as long as the Lord's Prayer to see that the crypt is empty.

"Look at all that dust," Phelippes says, pointing to the way it is scraped to one side in front of one of the alcoves in which the tomb is topped with a stone skeleton. Footsteps—two sets; one large and obviously a man's, one small and possibly a woman's—have come and gone, scraping away a path. No sign of a boy. Beale picks up a candle and holds it out to try to get it to shine on the far end, in case—what? Someone is hiding there?

"Arthur?"

Nothing.

At that moment there is a noise at the hatch through to the churchyard. A Yeoman puts his head through.

"All right, Master Beale?" he calls. "Sir Francis sent me to tell you he's on his way."

It's Stevens again, the one with the filthy undershirt, who looks as if he has already been demoted for losing sight of the man to whom Ballard gave the pistol.

"Stay there!" Beale tells him. "Do not let another soul even look through this door unless it is Sir Francis."

Stevens withdraws his head. Beale and Phelippes look around some more, baffled and lost for words. They are both beginning to hate being in this crypt. Perhaps it is the tombs and the paraphernalia of the Black Mass, but the atmosphere is close and sickly.

"Is it a worse crime to be a Catholic or worship Satan?" Phelippes wonders.

"Both as bad as each other" is Beale's opinion.

They step out of the crypt with gratitude and Phelippes swings the plaque back into place for Beale to lock. He slides the key into his doublet. Out here they can hear the bells ringing out in the churches that favor that tradition.

"If Sir Francis comes," he tells Stevens, "let him know we have gone to find the priest."

"Right you are, Master Beale, sir."

Out on Saint Dunstan's Lane there is nothing left to be seen of Dee's arrest and the crowds are thinner than they were, and Beale and Phelippes make their way to the church doors. The churchwardens and priests of Saint Dunstan have chosen to stick rigidly to the rule and not have a fire to mark All Hallows' Eve. Beale and Phelippes climb the granite steps and open the door to the church, which is not locked.

"Hello?"

No answer. It is dark within the nave, discomfiting, and deserted. It is as if it is holding its breath.

"Strange."

"Light a candle, will you?"

Neither man has anything with which to do so. Nor can they find any.

Outside the lane is almost empty now, just a couple of arm-in-arm drunks and a young woman hurrying home before the night watch make her life a misery.

"Wait here," Beale tells Phelippes. "I'll just see if Sir Francis is come yet."

Phelippes waits on the corner while Beale dips up the lane and pokes his head around the gate.

"Stevens?" he calls into the dark.

No answer.

"Stevens!"

Beale steps into the cold darkness of the churchyard. He can see the glow of Stevens's lamp, but the man still won't answer. The source of the light is not the lamp, but the open plaque, and in its golden glow he sees Stevens lying below, apparently asleep with his arm flung out. Beale draws his sword.

"Phelippes!" he shouts over his shoulder. "Phelippes!"

Phelippes comes thumping through the gate.

"What the—?"

They inch toward the hatch, each with one eye on the aperture, the other on Stevens. Beale takes the far side, Phelippes the near side, and they stop with their backs to the wall and listen for any movement within the crypt. Nothing. They peer around each jamb. There's no one to be seen, and nothing seems to have changed. The room is empty.

Phelippes crouches to roll Stevens over.

"Oooosh!" he cries, and steps back.

Stevens has been stabbed in the eye and is still bleeding.

"Like the lighterman in Dee's garden."

Beale pulls Stevens's sword from his belt and passes it to Phelippes.

"You wait here for Sir Francis," he tells him. "Tell him to search the crypt and the yard."

"Where are you going?"

"It must be Ballard."

Beale goes to the gate and steps out onto the now deserted lane. A moon is above the rooftops, mottled behind a veil of ill-smelling bone-fire smoke, but fullish, and enough to cast a wash of pale light and deep dark shadows.

"Oy!"

A night watchman with his lantern.

Beale tells him who he is. The night watchman looks utterly criminal, only saved from the gallows by being in Her Majesty's gang. He's seen nothing and no one.

"Give me your lamp, though," Beale orders, and the man reluctantly hands it over.

"But bring it back!" he shouts after Beale. "Corner of Eastcheap and Saint Margaret's. There's a hook. Ask for Skinner the Watchman. Everyone knows me."

Beale raises a hand and presses on up Tower Street eastward.

Here and there, in the deepest shadows, the probing finger of his newfound lamp settles on men and women with no homes and nowhere to go to, trying to lie low and evade the watch. They sit up, terrified, as his beam sweeps over them. He does not pause but hurries eastward past Cokedon Hall, where the upper stories of the houses are so built out over the road they almost touch one another, and he is glad of his lantern and his sword.

And whatever is he going to tell Sir Francis?

That he has lost Ballard, and his accomplice with the pistol, and the woman from Margate, and Dee's boy? And that Dee himself has been arrested for conjuring treasure? And that there is now a third body—Stevens—to add to the list of the dead?

But he might yet find them, Ballard and perhaps this woman; and if he can take them alive, then he stands a chance of redemption, but if not—and it is just as he is thinking this as he is crossing the bottom of Marke Lane, where it leads off from Tower Street, that he catches in the sweep of the beam of his newfound lantern a startlingly tall, humped figure that slips out of sight just a moment too slowly. He flicks the lantern back. But the figure is gone. He stumbles in the cart tracks, and nearly drops the lantern, and it takes him a moment to interpret what he saw—a man carrying a boy without a shirt.

"Arthur!"

He sets off after him.

CHAPTER TWENTY-THREE

Tower Street, Ward of All Hollows,
London, All Hallows' Eve, October 1585

In the light of the three-quarter moon, the boy clings to John Ballard as if he were his own father, and John Ballard carries the boy as if he were his own son, his skinny little body kept warm in the boatman's cloak, but the cloak is long, and its hem trails in the dirt, and when Ballard treads on it, he pulls it from the boy's naked back.

He curses inwardly.

"It's all right, lad," he soothes, hefting the boy higher on his hip, "I've got it."

He stoops to collect the cloak just as the beam of a night watchman's lantern rakes through the night and so nearly catches him, but by the time the beam flicks back, Ballard has the cloak pulled around the boy's bony little shoulders again and has ducked away down an alleyway into which neither the moonlight nor the watchman's lantern beam can stretch.

He's no real idea where he's going. He thinks again of dropping the boy at Francis Walsingham's house, which cannot be far, and the boy would be sure of care there, wouldn't he? For though Ballard has heard some terrible things about Francis Walsingham, the man can at least be relied upon to look after a child, whereas if Ballard just leaves the boy to wander the streets hereabouts he has a terrible fear that Mademoiselle Báthory will somehow escape the crypt and come and find him.

Jesu, that woman, he thinks. She is the devil incarnate and he wishes he had never met her. She has polluted the purity of his crusade against the Protestants who have taken over his country and made him feel dirty, debased, and wrong. He'd almost rather Queen Elizabeth ruled Christendom than fight on the side of someone like Báthory.

He follows the alley along, feeling his way as best he can, but he's lost now, no longer sure of his bearings. He can hear the bells of a distant church still ringing the vigil, and in the sky ahead is the glow of a bone fire that he hopes must be on Tower Hill.

"You all right, son?"

No answer, but the boy's alive, that's the main thing.

He emerges from the alley into a broad, moonlit thoroughfare that bends down the hill toward the river, and he sees he's come the wrong way. It was that night watchman who put him off, so he turns and just as he is starting back up the alley the beam of another lamp comes jagging toward him through the darkness. He turns back again and slips into the mouth of another alley, noisome and deep in shadow.

"We'll just let him pass," he hushes the boy from the safety of absolute darkness, and together they creep into the alley's depths past some broken barrels and pile of verminous old rushes. He watches the night watchman man hurry by, following his beam into the darkness, and still he waits a moment in case he should return, which he does. In the uncertain light, he doesn't seem the usual sort, Ballard thinks, who are always stolid and lazy. This man is in a cloak and tall hat, and he's determined. He's also carrying a sword—drawn—rather than a cosh.

Then he's gone.

After a few long moments, Ballard brings the boy out.

"We'll soon have you home, boy, never you fear," he tells him.

Ahead is a small crowd, mostly women boisterous with ale.

"Had too much has he? Ahh, the little one."

And that sort of thing.

He asks after Seething Lane.

"Follow along here keeping the Tower in sight," one of the men says. "Turn left when you see Custom House, only careful, as there's a night watchman up there."

He will have to risk it. He is so close. He walks on, and the boy is practically asleep and beginning to weigh in Ballard's arms by the time he turns into Seething Lane. Up ahead, raised over a serious pair of gates in a dauntingly tall wall, is a big glazed lantern in which a pitch torch flames, and under it is a fellow in a long coat moving beggars on. This surely must be Walsingham's house.

"Here we are, son," he tells the boy. "I'll be leaving you here with this gentleman, who will see you safe and sound home again. Sir Francis Walsingham's house, this is, heh? You know him, don't you? You'll be safe here."

Ballard stops before the porter.

"What you got there?" the porter asks. He's a hatchet-faced old soldier with a scar in his eyebrow and just a couple of teeth, like some old woodworking tool.

"Doctor Dee's boy," Ballard tells him.

"Doctor Dee's boy?" he says. "Fuck me! They've been looking for him all day!"

He holds the lantern to the boy's face. The boy cringes.

"How do I know he's who you say he is?" the porter asks. "You after a reward or something?"

Ballard has no time for this.

"If there is, you claim it for yourself," he says, and he tries to peel the boy's clinging fingers from his cloth.

"Who are you?" the porter asks Ballard.

"Captain Fortescue," Ballard tells him. "At your service."

The boy is tenacious and stuck fast.

"Now come on, lad," he murmurs. "You'll be safe here now."

"I'll get the butler," the porter says, and he's about to open the gate and maybe shout for someone in command.

"No," Ballard tells him. "I've not got time, but listen: tell your master there's a woman out here, from the Lord knows where, named Mademoiselle Báthory, who's been sent here by the Duc de Guise to kill Doctor Dee. She's locked in a crypt under Saint Dunstan-in-the-East. Tell your master to get himself down there with a troop of Yeomen and look in the sacristy where there's a hatch down into it, which I've blocked with a couple of coffers."

The porter is looking less credulous by the moment.

"You ask the lad," Ballard says. "He'll tell you. Saint Dunstan-in-the-East."

The he turns back to the boy.

"Now I'm sorry, lad," he says. "I wish we'd met in better circumstances, for you seem like a fine, brave young man and I'd've liked you to meet my boy, and him to meet you, but things being as they are, I must bid you adieu, as we say in France, and leave you with this gent here, who will take care of you handsome as you like."

He drags the boy from him and holds him in outstretched arms and thrusts him at the porter, who can hardly take him, with a lantern in one hand and a stick in the other, so Ballard must put the boy down and then the boy will not put his feet down and Ballard must deposit him on the floor and now the boy is mewling and grasping at him, and Ballard must bat his fingers away and step back and hold him off, for he still wishes to grip him, and it is as if this is the very last place the boy wishes to be left, and despite himself Ballard is almost weeping.

"Now, you be a good lad for this here gentleman, and you tell your old man all that's happened, but tell him to be careful of you know who!"

And he turns and he starts to run away, and he is startled to find tears blotting his eyes as he blunders on into the night.

CHAPTER TWENTY-FOUR

Herte Street, Ward of All Hollows,
London, All Hallows' Eve, October 1585

Robert Beale stands at the crossroads and hangs his head. He has to admit to himself that he lost them. Both. All three. Again. Twice in one day.

Christ. What will he tell Sir Francis? And what will he tell Dee? That he saw his boy, still alive, he was sure of it, being carried by John Ballard, the man he—Beale—has spent all day following, only to have since lost them both?

And Christ, what if Hatton's men have launched John Dee down some flight of steps and broken his neck?

What then will he tell Jane Frommond?

He checks where he is. Another night watchman is coming his way, but he's seen neither a man carrying a boy, nor a woman alone.

"Not this time o'night, even if it is All Hallows."

Beale decides he must return to Saint Dunstan to find Marlowe and possibly Sir Francis. It is best to get this sort of thing over and done with, yet even so he drags his feet. He turns a corner and there, suddenly, looms a man in whose face Beale instinctively points the beam of his lantern.

Ballard!

They are face-to-face, but there is no boy. No boy.

Ballard is as startled as Beale, only not so quick to realize his predicament. His sword is not yet drawn.

"One move," Beale tells him, "and I will run you through."

He raises his sword tip so it is just within the beam of the lantern so that Ballard can see it. Ballard raises his hands.

"Turn around," Beale tells him.

Ballard turns and Beale places the point of the sword in the back of his neck.

"Now," he says, "keep the hands up, and walk slowly back the way you've come."

Beale can feel the blood thrumming now, the heady excitement of a sudden, God-sent reversal of fortune.

"Where's Arthur?" he asks.

"Arthur?"

"The boy. And keep your hands up. I want to see them."

Beale can almost see Ballard calculating how to get out of this.

"I don't know who you're talking about," Ballard mutters.

Beale prods the sword into the soft roll of Ballard's flesh. Ballard flinches and lets out a hiss.

"Don't lie to me, Master Ballard. Where is he?"

There is a hitch in Ballard's step as he wonders how Beale knows his name.

"Who are you?" Ballard asks over his shoulder.

"Never mind that; where's the boy?"

"You're mistaking me for someone else, Master. I am John Fortescue, and I've never known a Ballard, and nor do I have any boy called Arthur or anything else come to that. I'm just—hssssss. Jesu, Master, you've drawn blood."

"Don't move your hands! Keep walking or it'll not just be blood I'll be drawing."

"There's no need to take on so," Ballard tells him. "I had one too many ales at the tavern and I am only trying to get home to Herne's Rents where if only I could lay my head I should have the chance to repent my foolishness—"

Beale prods him again.

"Save it, Master Ballard. I know you even in the dark."

"You mistake me for another, Master."

"I will kill you now, Ballard, unless you tell me."

"Jessusssss. All right. I left him around the corner, at Walsingham's house. With the porter."

Now it is Beale's turn to falter.

"What? When? Why?"

"I've just come from there now. The boy is safe. It wasn't me who took him. It was her."

"Her?"

"Whom you need worry about most. Mademoiselle Báthory. She is a fiend in human form."

They turn onto Seething Lane, and up ahead there is Walsingham's house, under its lantern, but there is no sign of the— But lying under the light of the torch is another low mound, blocking the same gate he's kept these last ten years. Ballard comes to a stop.

"Christ," he gasps. "How did she get out of the crypt?"

It sounds so genuine, Beale believes him.

"Who?"

"Her!"

Ballard ducks and starts looking around, as if Beale's sword in the back of his neck is now the least of his problems. He seems genuinely terrified.

"And where's the boy gone?" he goes on. "Where's the bloody boy gone? Oh Christ! She must have got him!"

Ballard doesn't seem to care when Beale presses the blade into his neck.

"For the love of Jesus," Ballard snarls, "whoever you are, this isn't about me! This is about him! About the boy!"

But Beale still has to look; he still has to see to the porter. He forces Ballard across the road and they stand over the facedown body.

"There, you see?" Ballard says, as if that proves anything. "Ten to one he's been stabbed in the eye."

"Turn him over," Beale tells Ballard.

Ballard bends and does so, brusquely, as if it is pointless because they already know he is dead, most likely stabbed in the eye, and time is fleeting.

And he's right.

"See?" Ballard asks. "She's got some blade. I never found it. She did this to me."

He points at his chin. Beale hardly cares. He rings the alarm bell that hangs on a hook by the gate. A sharp peal that will have the rest of Walsingham's household come running. Then he turns on Ballard, but before he can move, Ballard has whirled away and set off and is running for his life down Seething Lane toward the river.

Beale takes a breath.

"I've lost you twice already today, Ballard," he mutters, "and there will not be a third."

He sets the lantern down and sprints off after him.

Ballard is fast. At the bottom of Seething Lane he jinks hard right, back up Tower Street toward Saint Paul's. Groups of men and women are still drifting back from the bone fire on Tower Hill, and they shout at him but Ballard is running among them, knees and elbows pumping, scattering them.

"Stop him!" Beale bellows "Stop him! In the name of Her Majesty stop that man!"

No one does of course.

Ballard cuts left, just before accursed Saint Dunstan, making for the river perhaps but then he turns right again, running along Thames Street toward Billingsgate. Beale knows these streets intimately now. Could find his way through them even without the moonlight. Ahead is a man with a hand cart and two dogs that bark at Ballard and then at Beale and then there's another night watchman who might manage to— No. He's no match for Ballard and is still crawling in the mud as Beale hurtles past. Then Ballard hesitates ahead, on the corner of the market. He turns and sees that Beale is still only fifty or so paces behind, and then he sets off slowly, and there is almost a sense that he is waiting for him, or even looking for something or someone, and the thought fleetingly crosses Beale's mind that Ballard isn't trying to run but is leading Beale somewhere, and that it might even be to Dee's boy.

And so, astonishingly, it is: when he reaches the bulwark of Saint Magnus-the-Martyr Ballard stops and turns back to Beale, who is pounding to catch him, and he waits, poised to set off, but still . . .

Beale arrives.

It seems foolish to be waving his sword about, yet he cannot trust Ballard, who is the sworn enemy of everything Beale stands for.

Except in this.

"There!" Ballard points.

A woman, half wrestling, half dragging a bundle of cloth, just disappearing into the long tunnel of the bridge.

Beale looks at Ballard, Ballard at Beale.

Has Beale the time to kill him and then run after Arthur? Or wound him at least?

That is the calculation Ballard is forcing him to make.

And Beale decides without any thought. He lunges, a clumsy,

half-hearted thrash from an exhausted man. Ballard slips to the left. The sword skims his hip, its point tangling in the cloth of his coat. Beale is off-balance and staggers a step forward, and if Ballard had even so much as an eating knife, he'd be dead. Instead Ballard grabs his arm, gives it a twist that makes Beale gasp with pain and let go the hilt. Then Ballard gives him a firm shove and Beale is on his heels. Another, and he is on his arse, the air driven from his lungs, and his brain shaken loose.

Ballard extracts the bound sword from his cloak and passes to him, hilt first.

"Go," he says. "Go and save the boy, but for the love of God be careful of her!"

And with that, he is gone, disappearing into the darkness of Stockfishmongerow.

Christ!

Beale scrambles to his feet.

There is no way he will catch him now.

But Arthur? Perhaps.

He turns heel and starts off down the bridge, feeling that distinct thrum under his soles that tells him the tide is thundering out now and the starlings are quivering with the pressure. It's strange to be on the bridge at night, when all the shops are shuttered but there are so few people it is possible to move among the tight-pressing jumble of buildings. It is pitch-black under the arches and eaves, with occasional flashes of moonlight and glimpses of the river. Beale wishes he had the lantern still. He collides with someone who swears at him, and then with a couple, who are so engrossed they do not bother to swear at him and he does not bother to apologize. It begins to dawn on him that Ballard might be tricking him, until he sees what he had glimpsed earlier: a woman, in the clearing between Saint Thomas's chapel and Nonsuch House, just before the drawbridge castle, struggling with a load that might be the boy.

He speeds up, just as the woman drops the load on the ground and kicks it. The load thrashes and Beale glimpses a pale leg waving free from under the cloth. Arthur! The woman bends over the boy and uses her knee on him as if she's trying to pin a sheep for shearing.

"Stop!" he shouts.

She glances up and sees Beale.

She freezes and grimaces. In the moonlight, she is an unearthly being in a dark dress and pale linen partlet and were she not having to wrestle so hard to get what she wants, he might believe her a ghost or a demon, some devilish spirt come back through that veil that separates the quick and the dead. The boy makes one more desperate thrash, but now the woman springs into action and she hauls him up and begins bundling him in fierce and efficient buffets and shoves toward the bridge's stone parapet below which thunders the Thames.

Beale sees what she is about.

"No!" he cries.

But before he can run five paces, she has the boy on the balustrade, and she turns and bares her teeth at him, and with a shriek of exultant laughter, she rolls Arthur over the balustrade and into the torrent below.

CHAPTER TWENTY-FIVE

River Thames, night, All Hallows' Eve, October 1585

Robert Beale hits the surface feetfirst and is crushed by the colossal weight of the water. It clenches him like a fist and thrusts him down, deafening him absolutely, blinding him absolutely, seizing him absolutely; its power is so overwhelming that his every sense—including that of his identity, that he is a mortal man, a Christian soul—is submerged below the power of the water. He is nothing alongside it. He is nothing within it. He is caught in its maw and is of no significance. He might as well not exist.

How long after he emerges—barely alive, his lungs aflame and a hundred paces downriver—he will never know or be able to say, because it feels like a time out of mind, and anyway, he has no time to celebrate his deliverance from the grip of the roaring, sucking machine, for his release is temporary, and down it drags him once more into its pitching depths. He flails and kicks to defy the inevitable, but he can hear himself scream as his lungs erupt and he cannot tell up from down, light from dark until—

"Gah!"

He is suddenly rolled over and thrust up onto the river's choppy surface, where he is afforded the chance to gulp a mouthful of precious air before he is once more sucked back down into the all-encompassing darkness, where his mouth and ears and eyes and nose are stoppered, and he is tumbled this way and that. And as he fights, he feels his strength wane. He knows he cannot stand this much longer, and he is seeing stars and his lungs roar, but then he is churned to the surface again and given a brief blast of air before he is dragged back under.

On it goes, as if the river is toying with him, cat-and-mouse-like, until Beale finds the strength for one last thrash and he seems to slip from the current's grasp. He finds himself sidelined, washed aside into calmer waters, where the suck on his limbs lightens, and where for a few moments he is able to keep his head above the turbid water, spinning downstream past blurry lights on the riverbank, gasping for air to fill his aching lungs, still as helpless as a nut in a millrace, but able to give brief, thoughtless thanks to whichever saint the Catholics worship for the spirit of self-preservation that made him pull off his boots on the bridge before he jumped.

The depths of the river still pull at him, still weigh his pockets as with sand, and just as he is about to cry out for Arthur—"Arthur!"—he is dragged under again and must swallow a choking pint of the rich, bilgy, vegetable river water and find the strength once more to fight to the surface, and keep afloat, but it is a fight he can feel himself losing.

He rises up again, kicking as if to stamp on the shackles of the frigid deep.

"Arthur!"

There's nothing.

"Arthur!"

There's nothing.

Beale keeps beating the river's surface, knowing he can hardly swim, and Jesu! It is a struggle, and the few torches that mark Billingsgate slide by on his right, and he wishes he were back up there now, dry shod and facing a host of decisions he'd make differently, until he is spun around in the current so the lights are on his left and ahead is the Tower, where the curtain walls are pricked here and there by the Yeomen's torches in the battlements.

"Arthur!"

He sinks low, almost too tired to struggle now, his blood suddenly heavy and icy, his flesh pulverized by the rapids; as he sinks, Beale sees the lights of the Tower blur, and then with one last thrash he rises again to see them reflected in a thousand broken shards on the surface of the water, and in it, just over there, among all the other rubbish that floats on the surface of the water he sees something that looks like a seal.

"Arthur!"

He lashes his arms, kicks his legs, sinks; surfaces; and manages to propel himself toward the boy.

"Arthur!"

It is Arthur, clinging to some floating thing, and Beale takes a grip of a slick and spongy bit of it, and whatever it is dips below the surface and Arthur gives out a barely audible mew of despair and Beale sees they cannot both cling to whatever it is, and that one of them must—

He lets go.

Whatever it is rises, and Arthur clings on.

Beale sinks.

He cannot stop himself grabbing for the floating thing again.

It sinks.

He lets go.

And sinks.

Beale has swallowed so much water he is bilious with it now, weak, and so tired he wants to let go and let the delicious darkness take him, because he feels warm now, and there can be no time for regret for all the mistakes he's made just this day alone, and he emerges one last time to tell Arthur he is a brave lad, and that he loves him, and that he must cling on.

"That's all that matters," he says.

He can't see the boy's face.

It might not even be Arthur.

He's sinking now.

He supposes he might do one last thing, which is to push the floating object up, to support Arthur for as long as he is able, and he raises his arm as he lets his feet seek the riverbed, but it is not there. There is only depth and darkness.

And so it is that he doesn't hear the voice in the night or see the lantern on the boat's prow. He doesn't feel the strong hand that descends to grip his wrist or the weight of the pull that brings him from those depths and over the weed-slick gunwale of a lighter. He doesn't wince as his body is brought tumbling into the bilges to set the little boat rocking. He doesn't hear the three men already onboard telling one another to be careful for the love of God, "or we'll all go in." Nor does he hear one of them weeping as he embraces the boy or feel the rough hands that turn him on his back, and a man starting to squeeze his chest until the river water comes up through his throat and mouth in a jarring torrent. But he does feel the breath come back into him, and as he lies there, he sees Arthur wrapped in a cloak and held tight in Dr. Dee's arms, he sees bloody old Christopher Marlowe stepping over a thwart to take up the oars, and he hears a man he hardly knows—Thomas Digges, is it?—congratulating the doctor on his very intuitive use of the dowsing orb.

PART | THREE

CHAPTER TWENTY-SIX

Tutbury Castle, Staffordshire, November 1985

When the weather has been clement enough, and her legs have not been too painful, Queen Mary has on more than one occasion ignored her own ladies and favored instead Jane Frommond's arm for her very slow turn of the castle bailey. They walk with Cache-Cache at her side, and as often as not the queen seeks Frommond's advice as to how she should address her son on a matter in which no woman can possibly have any experience.

Today is one of those days.

"He is badly advised," the queen tells Frommond again, dropping the royal we when she is out of the Presence Room, and out of earshot. "I feel certain of it, and if I could but get word to him, then I am sure he would see sense."

Queen Mary is wonderfully unsubtle in her hints, and it is very obvious how much she would like Frommond to use her privileged position as one of Queen Elizabeth's women rather than Queen Mary's to send this message, but before she can spell this out in plain terms, Sir Amyas Paulet emerges from his house on the other side of the bailey and comes stamping in his proprietorial way toward them.

"A hard man," Queen Mary observes as he approaches, "and ignorant of the pain we mothers must endure."

Yes, yes, Frommond thinks. *Mothers*.

"Which is why," the queen continues, "I am training Cache-Cache to bite off his bollocks."

Frommond cannot stop herself laughing aloud, which Sir Amyas Paulet takes as being at his expense, and she cannot help retain her smile when Cache-Cache, smaller than most cats, growls at him. Sir Amyas doesn't like the dog—no one does, really, except Queen Mary—and stands on his dignity, but his barber has nicked his neck this morning, and there is a spot of blood on his collar.

He greets Queen Mary formally, comments on the weather—"passing fair for this time of year, though the days wear short"—and then tells Frommond she is sent two letters, which he ostentatiously produces folded flat from his doublet. It is unkind of him, of course, and Mary watches hawklike, a spot of color on each cheek, as Frommond takes them.

"I will save them for later," Frommond says, meaning to spare her.

Queen Mary is about to say something—*Open them now!*—but she feigns disinterest and asks Paulet if she might be permitted to take her caroche and visit the village, for she says her coachman has seen a poor beggar woman with no smock, and since she has smocks aplenty, she might take her one or two, for why should she need so many, when she is locked up so, with none to admire them?

Which Frommond thinks is a good question, but Paulet is having none of it, and tells her that the laws of the realm already provide for the adequate relief of the poor.

"No man need want for anything save by cause of his own lewdness."

Mary is unconvinced.

"You fear lest by giving alms I should win the favor of the people," she tells him, "but you ought rather to fear lest the restraining of my alms animates the people against you."

When Paulet takes his leave, Mary sighs, and directs their steps back toward her enforced lodgings.

"I do not wish to know every last detail, Mistress Dee," she says in her soft fluting Scots accent, "but you will let me know something of what is going on in the outside world, won't you? One or two details per letter perhaps? Only when you've had the time to read them, of course. You might bring them along to our Presence Room? Only please do not bring that maid of yours; she has altogether too speculative a look, as if she is already measuring me for my weeds."

Frommond knows what she means about Lucy Pargeter, who has a very strange manner, and she seems to look right through you, when she can be found to look at you at all, for she seems to be able to absent herself from any situation with the skill of a cat. She is like no lady's maid Frommond has ever met, not merely for being tall and bony, and strikingly handsome, but for greeting every day-to-day task that Frommond gives her with a wryly cocked eyebrow—*Really? We're doing this, are we?*—as if she has an eye on some greater objective than merely folding clothes, brushing hair, fetching embroidery frames, and so on. She regards Queen Mary's Scottish courtiers with a delighted, skeptical mien, as if marveling at their antics, and she remains so uncrushably aloof that every black look they dart her way seems to bounce harmlessly to the floor.

When Frommond is back in her rooms, she sits at the lectern and breaks her husband's seal first to find a long letter, but its first sentence makes her start:

Arthur is safe!

She reads on, increasingly horrified, conjuring up airborne devils from between the detail-sparing lines that by the foot of that first page become all too ground-bound when she reads that the whereabouts of the man and the woman who kidnapped her boy—for purposes about which Dee is maddeningly opaque—and then threw him off London Bridge are still unaccounted for; they could be anywhere.

At this she stands.

She rips open her brother's letter, hoping for more details, or sense at least, only to find a long, heartfelt but boring mea culpa for the loss of Arthur under his aegis, followed by an expression of his profound relief that John managed to track the boy down, and to pluck him from the river before he was drowned, and this at night, too, which must be reckoned a feat of rare genius. He alludes to certain unconventionalities, and to certain charges being dropped, and a death sentence being mercifully suppressed, and he signs off with a fraternal plea for forgiveness, and so she returns to the rest of John's letter, but finds him infuriatingly oblique until the last sentence where he writes that Bess—what he always calls the Queen—has charged him to bring Arthur north to join Frommond, wherever she may be, so that the boy may be afforded the sweet cherishment of his mother. He signs off by saying that this letter comes with love, from Δ.

And that is it.

Frommond is now more turbulent of spirit than she has ever been and then is startled to find Lucy Pargeter staring at her, one eyebrow raised, from where she has been lying on her bed, watching her over the toes of her pink knitted stockings, this whole time.

"Jesu!" Frommond cries.

"Sorry," Pargeter says.

"I did not hear you come in?"

"I was here first," Pargeter explains, "and did not wish to startle you."

What kind of maid lies on a bed, with— What is that? A book about plants? Before Frommond can inquire about that, Lucy asks when Doctor Dee is coming to join them.

"But how do you know he's coming?" Jane asks, fearing her letters are already tampered with.

"You read aloud."

Frommond sits back at her stool and stares out of the thick glass of the window, stunned, seeing nothing, and the letters lie loose in her fingers until her brother's slips to the floor.

Dear God, she thinks.

"So which of those details of the outside world will you parlay to Queen Mary then, do you think?" Pargeter wonders. "Which will Mary Kennedy deem suitable for Her Majesty's tender ears?"

As promised, Dee arrives two days later, with Arthur. She's seen John in some parlous states, of course, but when he steps out of the carriage, he seems to have aged years, or been bleached perhaps, for he carries neither weight nor color.

"I have seen hell," he admits, "but he has visited it."

He reaches back into the carriage to help the boy out, and she rushes past him to fold her son into her bosom, and when Arthur does not respond, but stands with his arms stiff by his sides, Frommond weeps the first of the many tears that will be wrung from her in the days to come, for the boy has become frozen and mute and only stares and starts.

"As if his mind has been ravaged," Dee whispers, with dewdrops on his eyelashes. The boy's eyes are fixed on Dee and they never once leave him, not for a moment, all the rest of that day. It is only when at long last he is asleep in her bed, and she and Dee are able to murmur by the fire, that Frommond learns the full horrors.

"How did you get out of Hatton's clutches?" she asks when he is done.

Dee is not quite sure.

"Something to do with Christopher Marlowe," he says, and she registers this as something to smile about later, if she ever smiles again.

"And so what do you think that woman was doing in the crypt?"

Dee cannot be sure, because he never set eyes on it.

"I couldn't leave Arthur alone, and I could never have taken him back there, could I? But from Robert Beale's description, she was trying to make it look as if I had sacrificed my own son to Baphomet—"

"Baphomet?"

"A goat-headed deity the Templars were accused of worshipping. Quite an interesting character, in fact—but . . . Anyway."

"Why?"

"Why? I think she wants to destroy me."

"But who is she?"

"I do not know for sure. Someone sent by the pope, perhaps? Or King Felipe?"

Frommond thinks of the Duc de Guise, and how he tried to manipulate the Holy Roman Emperor, Rudolf, into attacking England by making him fall in love with a prostitute. She remembers that woman in the castle gardens, pinching Kitty de Fleurier, as if she hated her, with venomous intent.

But Dee is going on, telling her that the crypt was set to look as if he had been performing a Black Mass.

"And to make it look as if I were putting a curse on Her Majesty with a wax likeness. She wanted to make it obvious to whoever discovered the scene that I was implicated; she even stole my gown and a book from the library."

"She was in our house?"

Dee has a cup of wine very near his lips. He stops and turns to her, absolutely stricken.

"Oh Jesu," he says. "I did not tell you. In the letter."

He puts the wine down.

"No," she says.

"No. Not that she was in our house. That she— She killed Sarah. That Sarah is dead."

"No!"

Dee can only nod. Frommond sinks back on the bed and cannot stop herself crying aloud, is for some time inconsolable, and cannot even abide her husband trying to comfort her. There are many more tears.

"How?" she eventually snivels.

"I-I don't know," Dee lies, and she knows he's lying, but she does not want to hear how Sarah died, for she has had enough horrors for one day. She claps her hands to her face as if she means to burrow into them and she cries out to God.

"But why?" she finds she's crying. "Why Sarah? Why Arthur? And why you?"

"The man—Ballard is his name, who I believe killed Roger on the road from Portsmouth—"

And she starts keening again when she remembers poor Roger Cooke, lain out on the laboratory bench with a blood-stiff doublet and a great gout taken out of his chest. Dee doesn't finish his sentence, and she doesn't ask him to because she has finally heard enough for one day. Later, in bed, Frommond lies next to Arthur, and she does not sleep until she hears the birdsong, and she dreams he will wake up and be his old self, and that the healing can begin, but when she wakes her dream is proved to be just that: a dream.

⌖

"So what shall we do with you?" she asks Arthur when they are all three walking on the castle walls in what might be the last of this year's very thin sunshine.

He says nothing. Only looks at his father.

"You can come with me?" Dee suggests.

Frommond is surprised.

"Where are you going?" she asks.

Dee looks awkward.

"I have to find a new ironmaster," he admits. "There are supposed to be some in Shropshire, that way."

He indicates east.

"None in the Weald had the necessary skill," he goes on, "or were prepared to extend credit, and Master Hawkins—of course—still expects his cannons."

Of course.

She had almost forgotten about Hawkins and the cannons.

"You cannot take Arthur," she tells him. "Not with that woman still alive out there."

"No," Dee agrees.

Then he stops and turns to face the boy.

"How would you like to stay here and look after your mother, Arthur?"

Arthur's gaze does not waver from Dee's face and so that is a no. Frommond wipes the tears from her cheeks and stares out over the parapet toward the hills in the north. Despite the sun, the wind is sharp and wintry. She places her hand on her son's shoulder, and he flinches, and she feels physically sick. Dee puts his arms around her shoulders and hugs her close.

"It will take time," he says. "That is all."

She prays he is right.

"So we'll stay, shall we?" he asks Arthur. "Look after your mother for a week or two?"

Arthur's gaze remains fixed.

Dee shoots his eyebrows.

"Right," he says, "so that's agreed."

They walk on a bit and see Sir Amyas Paulet walking with a man whom neither recognizes, hands behind their backs, out in the open parkland beyond the moat.

"He only goes there when he doesn't want Mary's people to overhear."

Paulet sees he's being watched, and he glares at them, and so they turn away and are rewarded by seeing Lucy Pargeter emerge from her quarters across the bailey, in a sage-green dress, carrying what looks like another book, this one very large and serious. She has of course not been on hand as she should be for a day or two, and when Dee sees her, he does a double take, and clicks his fingers.

"That's who she is!" he says.

"That's who who is?" Frommond wonders.

"I knew I knew her, but I could not remember where from. She's Lucy Wingfield."

"Her name is Lucy Pargeter. She's supposed to be a maid, the one Her Majesty foisted on me along with a lot of equally useless dresses."

"Humph," Dee says. "Perhaps Pargeter is her maiden name?"

"She's married?"

"Well," he says. "She was. I knew her husband: Humphrey Wingfield. In Leuven. He studied pharmacology and was much feted for having translated Dioscorides's *De Materia Medica* from the Greek into Latin, and this before his twentieth winter, only afterward, when it was looked into, it was discovered that he could no more speak Greek than he could converse with a dolphin, and that it was his maid who had done all the work."

"And his maid was—Lucy?"

"Exactly. They married before it all emerged, and then . . . well. It is sad. After his disgrace he was drowned trying to swim across the Scheldt."

"The Scheldt?"

"Huge river. Runs through Antwerp."

"Hmm."

"Hmm indeed. It was very out of character. Anyway. I wonder why Bess should have sent her with you?"

They are silent a moment, watching Lucy hurrying along.

"Perhaps," Frommond thinks aloud, "Bess didn't so much as send her with me, as me with her?"

Dee is struck by this possibility.

"Let's go and find out, shall we?" he suggests, only by the time they are down in the bailey, Lucy has disappeared into one of the houses, and instead Mary Kennedy is there standing at a door, fists on hips, fierce as a wren.

"Her Majesty has summoned you," she tells them, without preamble.

"Very well," Frommond says. "We'll come now."

"Not the boy," she says. "Her Majesty will not wish to have a boy presented."

Arthur understands he is about to be separated from his father, and he begins to shake as with the ague.

"You go," Dee tells Frommond.

"She wishes to see you both."

"Well, she cannot see me, and not my son," Dee tells her.

"She will not like that."

She'll be fine, Frommond thinks: it's Mary Kennedy who has the problem. It's like this in any court, though: everyone so jealous of their access to the monarch, they must invent absurd rituals and beliefs to justify their position. Dee hardly seems to care whether he meets Queen Mary or not—he is looking about the bailey, presumably for signs of Lucy Pargeter—which Frommond knows will be taken by Mary's courtiers as a sign of lèse-majesté, just as oftentimes his indifference is interpreted that way at Queen Elizabeth's court, to the detriment of his prospects.

"I will come and explain," Frommond volunteers, which Mary Kennedy grudgingly permits.

"But we wish to meet this boy of yours!" Queen Mary says when she does. "And he will wish to see our billiards table, and play a game with Master Nau, we are certain of it. Though you must warn him not to make any wager on the result, for Master Nau is determined to make back the money he lost to your maid."

"He's been playing billiards with Lucy?"

"She's been playing billiards with him," Queen Mary replies with a laugh. "Isn't that so, Master Nau?"

Claude Nau, standing over the billiards table, colors.

Queen Mary is in very good spirits today. Her legs seem not to bother her, and more than that, Sir Amyas Paulet has announced this morning that the queen's household is at last to move from Tutbury.

"We have been petitioning for months now," the queen explains, "for this is a noisome little seat."

No one knows where they're to go, but all agree that it cannot be worse than where they are. Frommond is not so sure.

"Have you been to Yorkshire?" she asks.

"Mistress," one of them starts, "we're from Scotland."

A good point.

"So, please, Mistress Dee," Queen Mary asks, "please summon your husband before us, and bring your boy, whom we are determined to make smile, for we are given to understand he has of late been in the wars."

The thought of Mary trying to make Arthur smile is disturbing, but Frommond cannot refuse, and so Dee is sent for, and he comes to the shabby little Presence Room, with its opaque windows and smoking fire, where Arthur will still not leave his side, but clings there, frozen and watchful. Dee performs a bow, which Queen Mary acknowledges with an expansive gesture. She is in blood-red silk today, and as lively as Frommond has seen her for days if not weeks, as if the thought of leaving Tutbury gives her hope, and a moment later, behind Arthur's shoulder, there comes the softest click of billiard ball against billiard ball, and Frommond sees Arthur's focus slip from Dee for the first time since he came here and slide to—and quickly back from—the billiards table on which, at Mary's nod, Claude Nau has rolled one ball to click against the other.

Which is something, perhaps.

CHAPTER TWENTY-SEVEN

Robert Beale's house, Barnes, December 1585

"You are not so much fun as you used to be, Robert, I have to say."

It is somewhere around four in the afternoon, maybe already dark outside, and Devereux is lying in Beale's bed at his house in Barnes, where the curtains are drawn against the winter winds that come off the marshlands to the south.

"I'm not exactly well," he reminds her.

"Well, you should be," she tells him. "Plenty of people nearly drown, and they don't make a monthlong song and dance of it, do they?"

"Don't they? And anyway, it's not the near drowning, I think, so much as all the bad water I swallowed."

Which is true: God knows what was in the Thames, but since that night Beale has been racked with spasms, and delirious, as if with the bloody flux, and now, weeks later, he has wasted to next to nothing, a gaunt specter.

"Well, I am getting up," Devereux says, and she rolls out of bed, and he makes no effort to stop her, but lies there, watching her dress, and thinking of her husband's imminent release from the Tower. He clenches his eyes and prays once more that when Her Majesty releases Sir Thomas Perrot, it will be to send him to Holland, where, sad to say, he will killed by a stray bullet or horribly maimed by a Spanish pike.

It is properly dark by the time Beale rouses himself, and by the time he comes down to his hall, she is gone, and sitting in her place at the kitchen table is one of the Queen's pursuivants in Her Majesty's colors, eating soup.

He is there, he says, to escort Master Beale to Whitehall.

"To Whitehall?"

"To see the Queen. If you believe yourself well enough?"

It is obvious what the man thinks: that he is well enough. He has not been here while Beale has lain with the ague, sweating and shaking and—according to his servants and physician—shouting some very unsuitable things. It is true that that stage seems to have passed, but strange symptoms linger still, including the stench of the river always in his nostrils, and the taste of it, too, lacquering his tongue.

"But at this time of night?" he wonders. "It will be dark on the river."

The man shrugs.

Well, Beale supposes, he was always going to have to brave the river again at some point. And probably, one day, he would have to cross it—either by boat, or by bridge—at night, so why not now? Although it seems to him that Her Majesty has brought forward this reckoning to a purpose.

Why not leave it until tomorrow morning, say?

Because she wants him ill at ease, which means she wants to talk to him about his efforts to stop Walsingham ensnaring Queen Mary.

Christ, he had hoped she would have forgotten that.

Or found someone else to do her bidding.

Why not Thomas Phelippes?

Why not any of the other men Walsingham employs?

Because they are not sleeping with the wife of a notoriously violent maniac like Sir Thomas Perrot, of course, so the Queen has no easy thing with which to blackmail them.

The pursuivant dunks a thick wedge of bread into the soup and then squashes it into his mouth, and then he gets up to go. And so for the first time since All Hallows' Eve, Beale gets himself properly dressed, and though his shirt and doublet now hang like a farmer's smock and his breeches flap like sails around his skinny shanks, he is soon stepping out into the night with a half-dozen Yeomen, all carrying lamps, making their way through the dark toward the river.

In the end it is not too bad. He muffles his face to mask the river's smell, and he sits in the boat with his eyes closed, gripping the gunwales as if every tiny movement means the boat will turn over and he will be plunged under that glossy black surface that is, mercifully, at least still tonight. At Whitehall, he is taken straight from the water steps up a set of back steps to Her Majesty's library.

"Master Beale."

"Your Majesty."

She is in very dark silks this evening, with a veil to match, and her skin is alabaster white, even in the umber glow of the lanterns, and Beale wonders if the effect of seeing this apparently floating skull would ordinarily be so unsettling or if it so only because he has spent so long cooped up alone.

"Well?" she asks. "What progress have you made?"

"I have been in bed at home these last weeks, Your Majesty," he reminds her.

"I suppose at least you cannot have abetted him," she says, "being abed."

Beale manages a weak chuckle.

"Oh, very good, Your Majesty," he says.

She waits.

"And given that is the case, Your Majesty," he continues, "might it not be better to instruct someone else to take over my role as—as—as your agent in this matter? Thomas Phelippes, perhaps? He is altogether closer to Sir Francis in this affair than I ever was."

"But we need someone we can absolutely trust, Master Beale," she tells him. "Someone who is almost as invested in our cause as are we."

By which she means: someone with as much to lose as herself, and sure enough, she then asks after Devereux.

"How she must look forward to Sir Thomas's release!"

"Indeed, Your Majesty, I am sure she does."

And so Beale must once again bow and scrape and promise that he will see to it, and that Her Majesty shall not be disappointed and so on, and after some few minutes of this, the floating skull seems to relax somewhat, and from the shadows by her side extends a lily white, much beringed set of knuckles over which he is invited to bend his head and very nearly place his lips.

And just as he is about to take his leave, she actually smiles.

"And Master Beale," she says, as if this is a matter of the gravest regret, "if you should perchance encounter Lady Perrot, please forewarn her on our behalf that should we be moved to pardon her husband, it will be on the understanding that he will take his place alongside our lord of Leicester's army sailing this month for Holland?"

And she looks at him as if to say: *You see? We are not a monster.*

⌖

The next day Sir Francis Walsingham comes to find Beale back in bed, not having managed to convey the good tidings to Devereux, but apparently poleaxed by the mental rigors of facing the river at night.

"Robert, my boy," the old man breathes as he settles himself into a seat by Beale's bedside. "How are you?"

His quick brown eyes traverse the pillow arrangements, and look, there on a table is Devereux's very fine silver-backed hairbrush, from which Beale knows the old man will manage to pluck a sample, and deduce, as if he has not already, that Beale is still in some sort of relationship with a woman with long blond hair that grows dark at her temples when she sweats, and whose husband will soon kill him.

Then Beale wonders if Walsingham has been before to the house, while Beale was ill, and if so what he learned then, poking around, unobserved, or from whatever he was shouting while he was delirious.

And if Walsingham has not been then, why now?

Ahhh, that is it: he has learned of Beale's visit to Whitehall. How? A spy on the back steps? One of the oarsmen? Mistress Parry or even Her Majesty herself perhaps. Beale decides to play it straight, and he admits he is worn out from having been summoned by the Queen, who wanted to hear his version of what had happened that night.

"What did you tell her?"

"I think the truth."

Walsingham nods. His eyes seem to glister in the low light and Beale can tell that Walsingham doesn't believe him.

"But you did a very good thing that night, Robert," Walsingham tells him. "You saved a boy, which was one thing, but more than that you diverted us from devouring our own, which we would have done had we believed what that woman wanted us to believe. Dee would be nothing but a greasy black puddle in Smithfield, for one thing, and there would be no telling where else we would have gone in pursuit of Her Majesty's enemies."

Walsingham pats him on the shoulder, and Beale does not know what to say. Should he ask for a knighthood?

"And no sign of Ballard? Or the woman?"

Walsingham shakes his head.

"Not a trace. Which is both good and bad, of course. No more corpses turning up stabbed in the eye, at least, but unless she's gone back to France—unlikely—then she must still be out there somewhere. And nothing of Ballard either. No Captain Fortescue entertaining the drunks in the Dog and Duck with his exploits at Brielle."

Beale nods soberly.

"So," he says.

"So we must revert to our earlier plan."

Which Beale has forgotten, of course, or otherwise put from his mind.

"Which is?"

"Gifford," Walsingham reminds him.

Ahh. Gilbert Gifford. Yes.

"Did I— Did I forget to ask Phelippes to send word that he should move to Paris?"

Walsingham smiles at him as if he understands such things happen when in fact, of course, that is why Walsingham employs him: to ensure they don't.

"Perhaps it was I who forgot to tell you," Walsingham says, letting him off the hook, "but it matters not. One of us sent word, and Gifford is Paris-bound. More than that, I've sent Phelippes up to Tutbury to see if we can somehow inveigle the man into Queen Mary's household, and he's suggested moving Mary's household to better quarters, to encourage her to believe her fortunes are on the up."

"But they aren't?"

"Well, they are. You'd not keep your worst dog in Tutbury. It's damp, and the middens have long since overflowed. I'm putting her in Chartley Castle. It is slightly more comfortable."

"So what has that got to do with Gifford?"

"Gifford grew up around Chartley. When he gets to Paris he is going to volunteer to act as the link we've broken in the chain of Mary's correspondence with her agents there. He can insinuate himself into Mary's happily expanded household, and then— Are you all right, Robert? You look suddenly very feverish?"

Beale feels suddenly very feverish too.

"It's nothing," he says. "Hot flushes that come and go. Cold flushes too. Nothing to be alarmed about."

Walsingham claims to suffer similarly.

"But I think I had best leave you be then, my boy: you are not yet strong enough, and so I shall see if I cannot twist Arthur Gregory's arm to go in your stead."

"Go where?" Beale asks. Walsingham takes some persuading, but he lets on in the end, because of course he wants to.

"Rye," he says. "Down in Sussex. I knew you know it, you see? Having been there before."

Beale does know Rye. He liked the little village perhaps above all others that he visited on his travels along the south coast, for there was a very good inn there, with a clean and comfortable bed in a private room with a view of the sea, and he had always promised himself that one day he'd take Devereux there to revisit their own odyssey, only this time at greater leisure, and in greater comfort.

"What needs to be done down there?" he asks.

"Gifford's to land there as soon as the weather permits, so I need someone I can trust to meet him off his boat. Make sure he makes it unmolested by the searchers. Escort him to London. From there he can make his own way up to Chartley."

Walsingham looks very concerned, and Beale lies sweating with guilt for a moment, thinking of the sorts of things that might be reasonably expected to go wrong in that scenario. Enough, surely?

But now Walsingham reaches into that old leather bag of his and pulls out—of all things—that wheel lock pistol that Ballard dropped on the road, the one carved with *Deus Vult*. For a moment Beale believes Walsingham has read his mind, seen his disloyal thoughts, and is going to turn the pistol on him. He nearly barks that it was Her Majesty who made him do it, but in fact Walsingham is just showing it to him.

"I was going to give you this to take with you," he says, holding it up to admire it. "So you could have passed yourself off as a good Catholic should anything go awry. I imagine someone else will be sent to meet him. It might even be Ballard."

Beale sees the opportunities to scotch this scheme mounting up.

"I believe I can manage the journey," he says, his fingers stretching for the pistol.

CHAPTER TWENTY-EIGHT

Herne's Rents, Lincoln's Inn Fields, west of London, December 1585

Since his escape from Mademoiselle Báthory John Ballard has stayed within doors, too terrified to venture out lest he see her awful visage grinning at him in the street. As a consequence he has put on so much weight that his clothes can no longer be stretched to fit, so he has followed Anthony Babington's advice and visited his tailor, a Dutchman who works in Clerkenwell, to be measured up for some silver-shot breeches with red silk panes; a velvet jerkin that the tailor promises him will see him out; and a beautiful copy of his old green coat, in felted wool, faced with similar silver brocade. A hat, too, tall and black with silver buttons. Quite striking.

He is told the work will take a week, and once it is ready, Ballard decides to pay a long-overdue visit to the French Embassy, at Salisbury Court, which he enters via the servants' entrance, as per their arrangement, from which, when he states his name, he is conducted via a back passage up to the ambassador's office. Here the ambassador inspects him very closely and then asks a series of questions, the answers to which only Monsieur John Ballard is believed likely to know.

This new ambassador—Monsieur de l'Aubépine—is an old fellow with a broad forehead of the sort you often see scarred by an old wound, wise eyes, and a stubby white beard that ends in a neat point above an old-fashioned collar and gown.

"You are here to take all her letters?" he asks hopefully.

He means Queen Mary's.

"Only those for me," Ballard disappoints.

"Pity," de l'Aubépine says. "Now that Walsingham has cut off Queen Mary's correspondence, we are experiencing something of a glut."

He gestures toward a pile of sacks in one of the room's corners.

"All for her?"

De l'Aubépine nods.

"We lack for a courier to make the final link," he says. "So it all stops here."

"You'll need a carter not a courier," Ballard tells him.

"Or we'll burn it all, when the weather closes in."

Probably wise, Ballard thinks.

But there is among all the piles of letters addressed to Queen Mary one addressed to him, to John Ballard, Esq, from Thomas Morgan in Paris, which he takes back to his lodgings to decrypt in the light of a candle, with a jug of fresh urine and a bottle of good strong brandewijn from one of the Flems across the fields. Ballard fears the worst, and dreads hearing what the Duc de Guise will say about his rupture with Mademoiselle Báthory, but after an hour spent poring over the page, he finds not one mention of her, and he drinks the spirit with relieved pleasure. He is given another altogether easier-sounding task, however, which is to travel to the village of Rye in Sussex, to pay off the searcher and escort two men who are dedicated to the enterprise of England back to London. One brings news from the new pope of the confirmation of Queen Elizabeth's excommunication, and the other—named Gilbert Gifford—will reveal his uses, by and by, and he particularly is to be cherished.

"God's stones," John Ballard tells Anthony Babington, "imagine if this one is worse than the last. As if Báthory was Saint John to his Jesus."

Babington is chewing the end of a feather and does not answer. Ballard is not sure Queen Mary's supporters believe him when he tells them about Mademoiselle Báthory and the crypt. Part of him wants to take them all back there to show them where it all happened, even though by now it will have been discovered and presumably tidied away, the chalice and ciborium packed away and the goat's head thrown to the pigs. He can't, though, of course. He's had to shut himself away in these ratty little rooms until the clamor has passed, which he now thinks it must have, though by the mass he remains terrified of encountering that woman again.

Where can she have got to? And what did she do with that boy? Nothing good, of that he can be certain, but though he has asked Babington and the others to keep an ear out for news of such, there has been nothing. Nothing in the inns they frequent, nothing in the pamphlets.

Ballard sighs, but not unhappily, for he is relieved to learn that he is still trusted enough in Paris to be sent to Rye on this hopefully quite simple task, and though the roads will be bad at this time of year, he is warming to the thought of quitting these rooms, and this company, for a week or so during which he will once more be able to break out his Captain Fortescue persona. There is also the small matter of digging up some of those silver crowns, the supply of which he has blasted through these last weeks on a new cloth, brandewijn, and pies.

CHAPTER TWENTY-NINE

Sir Francis Walsingham's house,
Seething Lane, December 1585.

Arthur Gregory is one of Francis Walsingham's most reliable agents, with an astonishing skill in passing undetected in places he should not be, but tonight he is where he should be: bringing his master an urgent message just landed at Custom House.

"From Nicholas Berden," he says. Walsingham sits up and reads the slip of decrypted paper from his chief handler in France.

Humph, he thinks when he has read it. So Morgan has sent *two* men across the Narrow Sea. Gilbert Gifford *and* Alan Everard. How will that complicate matters for Robert Beale? Gravely, probably, especially since this Everard is not unknown to Walsingham: unlike John Ballard, he is genuinely an old soldier, with years of experience serving with the Duke of Parma, and famous for fighting, and winning, duels.

Damn.

He knew he should never have let Beale go alone to meet

Gifford off the boat in Rye. He knew he was up to something, but supposed it might be to do with Mistress Devereux—a last hurrah before her husband got out of the Tower, perhaps—and he felt he had interrupted the course of true love once too often already, so he had let him go, but now Sir Francis regrets it. He should have sent a battalion of Yeomen.

Yes. That is what he should have done.

But it is not too late.

"Gregory," he calls. "Send for Captain Druthers. I need a troop of Yeomen down in Rye as fast as is humanly possible."

CHAPTER THIRTY

English Channel, December 1585

December is not the worst time to cross the Narrow Sea, but it is not the best either. The day is short, and the wind a steady roar before which the boat runs in impatient zigzags across heaving mountains of spume-flecked sea. At the tiller the master is encased against the rain in sailcloth, but huddled in the bow, Gilbert Gifford and Alan Everard are in wool and cord, both soaked to the skin.

"Can you see England?" Everard asks.

Gifford clamps his hand on his hat and sticks his head up over the gunwale to find no sign of the chalk cliffs, only heaving sea under darkening skies.

"I think so," he lies, though he is not sure why. He needs time. Time to work out what the hell he can do about this man Everard, whom Thomas Morgan has foisted on him, to bring English Catholics the news that Pope Sixtus has confirmed his predecessor's bull excommunicating Queen Elizabeth, and to remind the English that they are duty-bound to kill the heretic and will even get time off in purgatory if they do so. Everard has hardly said a word since they left Boulogne; not really since they left Paris, when he told Gifford that he recognized him.

"From where?" Gifford had wondered. "I was in Rome some time, and in Rheims, too, of course."

Everard had shaken his handsome head and said no he could not think where for the moment, but it was neither of those places, since he himself had never been to either.

"It will come to me though."

"Home then?" Gifford pressed. "Back in England? My family are from Staffordshire?"

Everard had not been there, either, but just as they were climbing onto the boat, and perhaps there was something about the way Gifford wrapped his cloak about him that sparked the memory, Everard had remembered.

"That was it," he'd said. "I saw you with Nicholas Berden, in the undercroft of Saint-Nicolas-des-Champs."

By then the rain was already coming in hard, so Gifford had not needed to hide his telltale blush.

"I don't know who you are talking about," he'd said. "And I've never been to Saint-Nicolas-des-Champs."

Which Everard—rightly—did not believe, and still does not believe, because Gifford had indeed met Walsingham's chief agent, Nicholas Berden, in the undercroft of Saint-Nicolas-des-Champs, to receive Sir Francis's instructions to come to England. And though what Everard himself was doing there is a good question, the answer hardly matters, does it? Because the thing that matters now is that Everard will warn every recusant in England that Gifford is a spy, and so his mission to insert himself into the chain of communication between Queen Mary and the French ambassador in London is dead in the water before he even sets foot in the land!

God damn it!

Unless he can ensure that it is Everard who becomes dead in the water?

Which is the exact same conclusion that Everard has also made, which is why he is watching Gifford so carefully, and the problem is that Everard is very obviously capable of looking after himself: he moves with the ease of a trained swordsman, and he is able to balance well enough against the boat's movement through the rough seas so as to relieve himself overboard and keep an eye on Gifford, without once staggering or pissing on himself. Even the crewmen were impressed and clapped as he made his light-footed way back to the bow, where he sat watching Gifford as he might a snake, and in a way to make the basket of his sword hilt very obviously to hand.

And so the boat plows on, its sails straining overhead and its hull down below as it buffets through heavy seas toward landfall in England, and Gifford finds himself staring at Everard, becoming increasingly desperate.

CHAPTER THIRTY-ONE

The George and Dragon Inn, Rye, December 1585

It is seventy miles of bad road between London and Rye and against all sense and advice, Robert Beale rides them alone, head down into the teeth of a southwesterly gale, and when he finally arrives at the George and Dragon Inn, three days later, he falls in the stable yard and needs be helped to a bed where he lies shivering for the next two days, wishing that he had, after all, asked Devereux to come with him. He is fed mutton soup that tastes of the sea, and ale that tastes of kelp, and all the time he has one ear cocked for the temper of the wind that howls in the chimney.

On the third day the gale blows itself out, and so Beale must rouse himself.

"You're going out in that?" the maid asks. "You'll catch your death."

It is still raining very fine needles when Beale reaches the castle and identifies himself to the constable.

"You want a detachment of men? On horse?" the constable asks, as if Beale has asked for unicorns and angels. It's barely eleven and he's already been drinking, but the place is so damp and desolate Beale cannot blame him.

"I need a show of force that will stop a boat landing."

"When?"

"The boat's coming from France. Probably set off this morning, and with this wind, she'll be in sight by sunset."

While the constable grapples with this, Beale takes to the battlements above, where a single Yeoman stands considering the harbor a hundred feet below, and together they stand under his miserable thatch cover and watch woolly rain clouds sweep in from the sea almost at eye level.

"Be dry once all this rain's passed" is his opinion.

When Beale comes down the constable tells him he can raise five men, well-mounted, ("well; mounted,") and will bring them to meet Beale in the yard of the Sailmaker's Arms at sunset.

"With arquebuses?"

"Aye, though if you want to see Christmas, stand well back: they cannot hit a barn door."

Beale thanks the man, returns to the George and Dragon, where he changes his clothes and takes a fresh gelding from the suddenly busy ostler.

"I've oiled his legs," the man says, "but keep him out of the mud."

Beale leads the horse out of the yard and onto the lane that will take him down to the harbor. The rain is beginning to let up.

If Gifford sees a welcoming party, he'll never land, will he? He'll go back to France, and Beale will never have cause to use that wheel lock pistol.

Just in case, though, he loads it.

CHAPTER THIRTY-TWO

The George and Dragon Inn, Rye, December 1585

"You can't have that room because there's someone in it already," the maid tells him. "A gentleman."

John Ballard smiles his broadest Captain Fortescue smile and produces from behind her pretty little ear a silver sixpence, which he twiddles between his forefingers.

"Why," he says, "I am sure this fine gent might be persuaded to move to a lesser room, were the price right."

Her eyes are drawn to it, and a moment later it is gone into her jerkin.

"Or you can ask to share it with him," she supposes.

"But why should I wish to share it with him when there is another with whom I would far rather be?"

The girl does not even blush.

"I'll ask him when he comes back, or you can ask the master."

God damn it.

Ballard is in no mood for being messed about with.

His money—nine hundred silver crowns—has been stolen.

Dug up, and taken away, every last one of them, and now, once he has paid off the searchers, he will be down to his last few crowns and have once more to live like a mere mortal.

And he knows who has done it.

Mademoiselle Báthory.

Why did he tell her where the crowns were? It is true that he did not know how truly devilish she would reveal herself to be, but she had by then already shown her teeth, hadn't she? Stabbed him in the throat, just for trying to squeeze her titty. He should have known then not to trust her, but he had blundered on, hadn't he? Playing the role of boasting, devil-may-care Fortescue, always so casual. Along the old pilgrims' route, he'd told her, under a rock between the coppiced beech and the badger's sett behind the burnt-out windmill half a league out of the village of Friday Street on Leith Hill, in the direction of the Tillingbourne waterfall. "If anything happens to me, dig it up, m'dear! It is all yours!" That is what he'd told her. And she'd done it.

He knows he has no one else to blame but himself.

Dear Christ.

And now this: an unwilling wench, and some gent in the inn's best bed.

Still, he is not entirely destitute, is he? And there is always the hope that Gifford will bring funds for him from Morgan in Paris, why not?

He smooths his beard and makes for the buttery, after which the stables, where he hires the last gelding and takes her out into the lane and along to the castle to find the constable in his tower, already flushed with wine though it is scarcely midday.

"What do you want?" he asks.

"To make you a rich man," Ballard says, closing the door behind them.

"Go on?"

And the deal is done, for the usual price: forty silver crowns.

A heartbreaking moment for Ballard as he counts out the coins, but needs must, and he consoles himself with the thought that should this thing come off, his reward will not only be in heaven, but here on earth, too, where he supposes anything short of being made an earl would be an insult.

"When do you expect him?" the constable asks, raking the coins from the table. Ballard has no exact information as to when Gifford and Everard will arrive, but he once spent three weeks in Dieppe waiting for a favorable wind to come over, so he's broadly familiar with the winds and the tides here in the Narrow Sea.

"Might be this evening," he supposes. "Sometime after sundown perhaps."

"And where don't you want us looking?"

"The harbor," Ballard says. "They're coming in on a fishing boat."

"All right," the constable says. "I'll make sure we're on our way to Winchelsea."

"Good man," Ballard says and leaves him to it. It is not a bad way to make a living, he supposes—just looking the other way—but the constable doesn't seem especially happy, does he? So Ballard must suppose there is a different sort of price to be paid.

CHAPTER THIRTY-THREE

Off Rye Harbor, same day, December 1585

The boat master interrupts Gifford's thoughts again, to ask for perhaps the hundredth time if he is certain the searcher has been paid off?

"I am," Gifford lies.

"Because we are putting our heads into a bear's mouth, you know? Look: harbor lights."

He points to the two burning braziers that mark the channel ahead.

"Once we are between them, only one way out, and not until morning, by which time—pffffwp, dufff."

Which is his impression of a headsman's ax hitting a block.

"Keep going," Gifford tells him.

The boat master grunts and issues a muffled order, and in the gloaming, the crewmen are quick about their business, taking in the sail and putting out chunky knots of rope as the boat slows between the two flaming torches and begins its sluggish drift toward the lights in the middle distance that mark the quay.

"You are sure, Englishman?"

"Yes, yes, I'm sure."

It's stopped raining, and the clouds have parted to reveal a cheerful plump moon, and in its light, Gifford dares another glance at the stern face of Alan Everard, who has still not said a word to him, though he has been cheerful enough with the master and his crewmen. He decides that it is now or never, and he leans forward as if he has come to a long-mulled-over decision.

"You are right, Master Everard," he says, masking the quaver in his voice with a cough. "You did see me with Nicholas Berden. I wish you had not, because it does not reflect well on my skills in this trade, or perhaps it reflects well on yours. I have been meeting him every couple of months on Thomas Morgan's orders, to supply him with chickenfeed about the tensions between the English and Welsh priests and the Jesuits."

Everard says nothing.

"You need not believe me, of course."

Still nothing.

"When we land, we can go straight to the new ambassador in London. Have him send word to Morgan to confirm what I say."

Still nothing.

"Bravo," one of the crew murmurs to the boat master as they bump up against the second or third hull with a gentle creak of compressing rope buffer.

Everard says nothing, but gathers up his cap and canvas bag and with a quick round of muscular farewells to the crewmen and the master, he steps nimbly over the gunwale and is swallowed up in the dark. Gifford stands wondering what in the name of God that means, until the master tells him to follow.

"Allez-y, Englishman, and good luck."

"Everard!" he shouts. "Wait!"

The fucker must not get away.

CHAPTER THIRTY-FOUR

The Sailmakers' Arms, same evening,
Rye Harbor, December 1585

It is quiet in the hall of the Sailmakers', but even quieter outside in the intermittently moonlit yard, where Robert Beale has been standing, shivering slightly, behind an empty firkin watching the fishing boat come in, praying to God that Gifford is not aboard, but knowing in his heart of hearts that he probably is, and cursing the constable and his five imaginary troopers who have not turned up. If he's seen the boat, then surely the constable has. And so where are his horsemen with their lanterns and poorly aimed arquebuses? Why haven't they been charging about the place making themselves very obvious?

That was the whole point of Beale's plan! To put Gifford off the landing!

Christ! He hadn't liked the look of that constable and knows now he should never have trusted him: he's either a villain or incompetent. He will see to him in the morning, whatever else he does.

But until then, if that is Gifford aboard, then Beale's options have shrunk to more or less one.

He carefully takes the wheel lock from his bag and starts off through the piles of old fishing nets and broken crab traps toward the Custom House.

CHAPTER THIRTY-FIVE

Custom House, Rye Harbor, same evening, December 1585

John Ballard manages a satisfied smile in the dark, for there, across the river from where he has chosen to hide—in case the constable is playing him for a fool—two figures steal quickly through the shadows.

Gilbert Gifford and Alan Everard.

Well met, he thinks, *well met indeed*.

And the constable seems to have kept his word, too, so Ballard decides it is safe. He steps out and moves quickly to intercept them. This is what he is made for! None of that skulking about in crypts! This is his realm, where he is most comfortable, striking a blow in the struggle against the dour old Calvinists who would seek to take his country from him!

He is about to holler a hunting cry.

When, from the corner of his eye, he sees a further movement. And then there comes walking past him—he believes he has gone mad, or that someone is playing a trick—for there is the very man who—he is certain of it: the very man who pressed the sword into his neck in London the night with Mademoiselle Báthory! The man who had known the boy's name was Arthur.

What in the name of God is he doing here?

He's stopped ten paces ahead, waiting in the shadow.

And what is that in his hand?

A dag! A wheel lock dag! Ballard is certain of it!

God's stones!

The man raises the pistol and points it along the causeway toward where Gifford and Everard are coming, and a moment later there is a whir, a flash, then a boom, and the pistol leaps in the man's hand.

There is a cry up on the wharf.

He's hit one of them!

Dear Christ, the man must be an extraordinary shot, or very lucky.

Ballard feels his blood singing. He is about to draw his blade and run the man through, to save at least one of his fellows, when behind him he hears the clip of hooves and the jingle of harness, and he knows that that bloody constable has reneged on their deal.

Forty crowns in silver!

Gah! He hesitates. He could do it. He could stab the man with the dag, and then run. But no. It is too risky. He slips back into the shadows and turns and runs back along the harbor front into the darkness.

[illegible]

his neck [illegible]
man who had known the boy [illegible]

[illegible]

[illegible]

[illegible]

PART | FOUR

CHAPTER THIRTY-SIX

Chartley Castle, Staffordshire, Christmas Eve, 1585

"God's blood, this will not do!" Mary Kennedy shouts. "Look at it! A man has been murdered in this bed!"

Jane Frommond cannot help but look and is relieved to find only a horribly stained palliasse within the frame of a very broken-down bed, not a body in sight.

"Her Majesty cannot be expected to lie on that," Kennedy continues. "It is beneath her dignity."

And yet, needs must: for Queen Mary must lie somewhere, and fast, or she'll keel over where she stands, which is in the middle of the hall, for it has been a long journey made longer by Sir Amyas Paulet's refusal to let her take her carriage through Uttoxeter lest she should prove unable to resist exercising her natural, charitable largesse.

"Can we not just turn the mattress over?" Frommond wonders.

"Already done that," the maid tells them. "You don't want to see what's on the other side."

She's one of Mary's laundresses, with stranglers' forearms and lye-reddened hands as big as plates.

"Go and tell Paulet we need a new mattress," Kennedy demands of Frommond, though she has no right to talk to her this way. "Tell him we need a new mattress and a new bed frame."

"He couldn't help even if he wanted to," Frommond says with certainty. "It is Christmas Eve. Just put a blanket on it, or two, and then a sheet and she'll never know."

"She'll never know? She is a queen!"

Frommond almost laughs, and she leaves them to it and goes to find Arthur and Dee, who are standing outside in the dusk, waiting for the stars to appear and taking stock of their new surrounds. Chartley, like Tutbury, is raised up upon a man-made hill above the low-lying countryside, but here at Chartley the Earl of Essex has abandoned the old stone fortifications and has had built next to the curtain walls a handsome manor house, complete with four brick chimneys, glass in most of the windows, and a tiled roof. It is still encircled within the moat, though, which is why Sir Amyas chose it.

Arthur is looking anxious again, for the moat is supposed to be very deep and there are also numerous large stockfish ponds away to the west.

"It means we will have carp breakfast, noon, and night." Frommond sighs.

"And is there space for the billiards table?" Dee wonders.

"There had better be."

For it is the only thing that brings Arthur peace. He plays standing on a stool, and not only against Claude Nau and Lucy Pargeter, who is the best in the household, but occasionally, when her legs are up to it, even Queen Mary, whom Mary Kennedy has forbidden him to beat. While playing it, Arthur seems to forget the great freight of his recent terrors, and he manages to tear his gaze away from his father and place it on the balls as they are sent ricocheting across the table's dusty green surface.

He still has not spoken, but there is nothing wrong with his voice, for every night he cries out in his dreams and if Queen Mary ever took to her bed before two of the morning, he would wake the whole household.

They stand in silence for a while, getting used to the new view, and despite the moat, however deep it might be, Frommond feels very exposed up here; very out in the open now that she is no longer surrounded by curtain walls the height of two men, for she cannot help but imagine that *she* is out there somewhere—that woman, the one who stole Arthur—and that she is even now watching them, her schemes as yet incomplete.

"You do not seem scared, John?" she whispers.

He half laughs.

"I am absolutely terrified," he tells her. "She is all I think about. Everywhere. All the time. What is she planning next? Jesu."

They had better go in, they both agree, into the house that all Mary's people now must share for the foreseeable future, in which the Dees' room is under the eaves, up a flight of dizzyingly steep steps. Lucy Pargeter is to sleep on a truckle bed that rolls out from underneath their frame, which Dee believes will finally give him the chance to find that book he saw her carrying across the bailey of Tutbury Castle, which has intrigued him since.

When he finally encountered Lucy on his third day in Tutbury—after she had feigned two days of illness to avoid it—she had acknowledged she was the widow of Humphrey Wingfield, and she admitted that she did recall meeting Dee, but she'd been very vague about what had brought her to Her Majesty's service, reduced to the status of a maid. When Dee told her that he had been sorry to hear of her husband's death, she had flinched, but not—Frommond thought—because she did not like to be reminded of it, but because she did not wish her business known.

"I still miss him," she'd said.

Which had not rung false.

"His was a very fine mind," Dee had said, making a couching motion with his fingers by the side of his head to indicate a large brain. She had lowered her eyes demurely, as if to bring the conversation to an end.

"But what possessed him . . . ?" Dee had blundered on, but if Frommond might have supposed Lucy would be upset by Dee's uncharacteristically insensitive line of questioning, she was wrong.

"He had been reading of Hero and Leander," Lucy had told them with a rueful laugh, "and was prompted to re-create the swim across the Hellespont."

"Just like that?"

"Just like that."

"Extraordinary," he had breathed.

"Extraordinary," she had agreed.

And that had been that.

Or so it had seemed, but Dee had still not been convinced all was as it appeared. Not only was Lucy incapable of looking after Frommond as a lady's maid ought, she seemed incapable of looking after herself, and she was oftentimes to be found looking about as if for her own maid.

"But you said she was Humphrey Wingfield's maid?" Frommond had wondered.

"Well, perhaps she was never really his maid? That was just what he told us?"

When they take Arthur up to bed that night, Lucy is already in her own low truckle bed, pulled out from beneath theirs so that they all four lie side by side, but at different levels, and Lucy has fashioned an eye mask against the light of the rush lamp that Frommond holds up while Dee carries Arthur.

Does she tut?

Frommond believes she does.

And she rolls over, as if they have disturbed her, which they must do to get into their own bed, which is pushed up against the wall beyond hers.

And in the morning, she is gone.

"Forever?" Dee asks.

No. When she emerges at midday to greet the bringing in and the lighting of the yule log, as well as the installation of the billiards table, Lucy admits she has discovered the oratory, a private little room where one might find peace and quiet, and she has spent all morning there "quite content."

"Doing what?" Frommond asks.

"Reading."

"But I had to dress myself," she tells her.

"And you have done it beautifully, if I may say so."

Frommond does not know whether to punch her face or pat her back.

Later that day, Queen Mary sends for Frommond, and Frommond climbs the stairs to find her in bed, lying unknowingly—she hopes—on that awful bloody mattress, looking terrible.

"The exertions of moving houses," her attendant Barbara Mowbray explains.

The room is very warm and close, with the fire banked but scarcely a lamp lit, and Queen Mary ushers Frommond forward with a soft patting of her fingers on the sheet beside her.

"They say I do not have long," she manages to wheeze.

Which Frommond has heard once or twice before from those lips.

"How fares wee Arthur?" Mary asks with the softest, wettest cough.

Frommond tells her he is fine so long as he stays with his father, and that now the billiards table is leveled to Master Nau's satisfaction, then with God's blessings they should continue to see improvements.

"And who knows," Frommond finishes, "he may yet talk to us."

At which Mary's eyes water. Barbara Mowbray is on hand with a piece of absorbent silk and when the royal eyes are dried enough, not too much, Mary starts weeping again, only this time when Mowbray reaches in for a dab Mary moves surprisingly fast to slap her hand away.

"Och, don't fuss so," she implores. "In fact, leave us."

Which earns Frommond a foul glare from Mowbray, and after she has taken her mincing leave, the two women are left together, and Queen Mary very slowly regathers her breath.

"Can I get you anything, Your Majesty?" Frommond asks, in part to delay what she knows is coming, but Queen Mary shakes her head, setting tears leaking from the corners of her eyes into the fine hair at her temples. After a while she reaches for the gold clip that Frommond has oftentimes seen near her person, and she passes it to Frommond.

"Open it," she says.

Frommond does so, to find within two portraits that in this light might or might not be by John Dee's old friend Nicholas "Points" Hilliard. A very beautiful woman on the left, and a very finely dressed young man on the right. Her and her son, Frommond supposes. The son looks like the sort of man Frommond trusts least.

"Isn't he handsome?" Mary wheezes.

"He is, Your Majesty. Very fine."

"We have been meaning to show you for some time."

"I am glad that you have, Your Majesty."

Frommond passes it back.

"We know we have been boring you with all our talk of him," Mary says.

"Not at all, Your Majesty."

"But we have no one else to turn to."

She says this with such significance, it would have been perverse and unnatural not to ask what she means, although Frommond knows precisely what it will be.

And so it proves.

A letter to her son in Edinburgh, to be sent via the French ambassador in London, to tell him that she would renounce all claim to the thrones of Scotland and England, if only she might be let free.

"We have had in mind," she says, more content now that the matter is broached and not refused, "for some little time now, a very simple life. Before that day at Langside, we happened upon a manor house, stone-built, very comely and pleasing to the eye, with a small garden and a wood behind, and a view of a loch below, which we were told was Loch Doon. And at the time this pleasant seat struck us as being most serene, and we wished to linger, but alas, the hand of destiny was upon our shoulder, and we were impelled to march to war."

With all that that entailed, Frommond thinks, but does not say.

"With all that that entailed," Mary says, rolling her eyes.

"But that humble spot has stuck with us," she goes on, "and oftentimes have we dreamed of it."

"And that is what you wish for yourself, is it, Your Majesty? A simple manor house where you might be left in peace?"

Queen Mary clenches her eyes and squeezes out the last tears, and Frommond thinks she has offended her, but Queen Mary is laughing.

"You are laughing at us, Mistress Dee!" she says. "Laughing at us for having the modest tastes of a farmer's goodwife!"

Frommond joins in the laughter and promises her she is not.

"But what we wish above all other things," Queen Mary admits, more seriously now, "is that our son takes up our throne in our place, and that he is permitted to rule unencumbered by our past mistakes, or by our present state. If he achieves that and would grant us the chance to find ourselves such a place as that humble dwelling, then we believe and most earnestly hope that something might yet be saved of this wreckage of our life."

And there is a silence while both women weigh up what the other has said, and what comes next.

"Only we cannot hope for it, unless it is known that we have renounced all claim to our royal throne."

"Can you not just tell this to Sir Amyas?"

Mary's face clenches.

"Sir Amyas is no well-willer," she says. "He wishes us dead, or unhappy, or both. He will no more grant us this wish than he will bring us a gift this Christmas."

That is probably true. And it is hard to imagine Paulet handing out any presents come the new year.

Another lingering silence ensues, which only Frommond can break, and finally she does: "If I were to do that, Your Majesty, how would I go about it?"

CHAPTER THIRTY-SEVEN

Sir Francis Walsingham's house,
Seething Lane, London, January 1586

"Here he comes," Arthur Gregory cries, "the man of the hour!"

Robert Beale sighs inwardly and steps into Sir Francis's office where the fire smolders against the cold of the day, and the atmosphere is one of imperfectly restrained excitement.

"It was a lucky shot," he assures them.

"You're telling us!" Gregory laughs. "I've seen you play bowls, remember!"

"How did you know to shoot?" Walsingham wonders.

Beale shrugs.

"I saw he was drawing his sword," he lies, "and that he was going to kill me or Gifford. It was a warning shot, really, if I'm honest. I could never do it again."

Gregory whistles and shakes his head.

"Some balls you've got, Master Beale," he says. "I shall look at you in a new light from this moment on."

Walsingham manages a gentle laugh.

"But do you know, Robert, that as astonishing as your shot was, it was still only the second-most-extraordinary thing to happen that day in Rye?"

"Really?"

"You wait till you hear this, Master Beale," Gregory jeers while Walsingham picks up a piece of paper from his lectern.

"From Robin Poley," he says.

"Poley?" Beale needs reminding.

"The fella that's tracking Babington," Gregory obliges.

"Yes," Walsingham goes on, "and he writes to say that the most extraordinary thing is that there was a witness to your marksmanship. A witness apart from Gifford."

Apart from Gifford? Beale's mind races. Did he betray himself in any way? He cannot think so.

"Who?"

"Our old friend John Ballard. Your old friend John Ballard."

"Ballard?"

"Yes. He was in Rye, apparently, according to Poley, who has spoken to him since. He was on the quay, sent to bribe the searchers and to see that Gifford and your dead man made it safely ashore."

"He saw it all!" Gregory crows.

"My God! And so where is he now? Ballard, I mean."

"Living in Herne's Rents, apparently, out by Holborn, and still raving about the woman who tried to kill Dee's boy."

"Raving in a good way?"

"Bad. Says she's sent by the devil, if she isn't the devil herself."

"Does Poley know who she is? Where she's got to?"

"No. But wherever it is, it is with the money Ballard stole from Dee, which it seems she's stolen from him. We've got men looking for her, of course, but you know—women: headdresses, veils. Not easy. Also she is not running with the usual recusant crowd."

"She was tall, that I remember."

Walsingham and Gregory exchange a glance.

"Tall," Gregory repeats as if that is logged and recorded as being anything other than not very helpful.

"Why do we not bring him in?" Beale wonders. "Babington, I mean."

"We're waiting to see where he takes us," Gregory tells him. "And if it turns out that it's him to whom Queen Mary's writing, well, then we'll have got him, and her."

"Bloody hell," Beale breathes.

"Poley says Ballard has been sent over to help run a cell," Walsingham says. "One which we knew about, but had not until now taken too seriously. One of them's a poet, and the self-styled leader—a man named Anthony Babington—is more romantic than recusant."

"He's supposed to be absolutely obsessed with Queen Mary," Gregory adds. "He knew her when he was a boy, apparently, and now he wanks himself blind every night thinking of her as his queen."

"And what's their immediate aim?" Beale presses.

"Undefined so far, but Poley says Ballard was sent over from France to spur them into action. He's telling them a lot of lies about their names being mentioned in the pope's prayers and a fleet of Spanish galleons just waiting 'pon their word."

Beale's heart stalls.

"So Ballard was in Rye to take Gifford to this Babington? In order to put him in touch with Queen Mary? To put her in touch with him?"

Walsingham blinks a slow unspoken yes.

So there it is, Beale sees, laid out before him: the extent of the snare that Walsingham has set for Queen Mary; its maturity, and proximity. It is the very thing to which Her Majesty demanded he put a stop, which he has abetted with his poor aim. He swears silently.

"Are you all right, Robert?" Walsingham asks. "You've gone very pale again."

"Must be all that river water you drank," Gregory says. "Here, have some ale."

"Yes, please. Thank you."

He drinks.

"And so where," he asks when he has finished, "is Gifford now?"

He prays he is in the Tower, or dead; anything other than already on the road to Chartley.

"Already on the road to Chartley," Gregory chortles. "But he was still singing your praises, Master Beale, even as he set off up north: says without you shooting Everard, then this whole scheme to get him into Queen Mary's household would be dead in the water. Ha ha! His words."

"Ha ha" because that is how Everard actually died: in the water. He ran when Beale's pistol ball hit him, blinded by the pain or by the blood in his eyes, and he stumbled off the quay's edge, between two fishing boats, where there was nothing anyone could do for him, or would do for him. Beale and Gifford had stood there, trying to decide who was who to whom, and by the time Captain Druthers and his Yeomen arrived, the drowning man's cries could be heard no more. Druthers had arrested them both, despite Beale's protestations, and when the local constable turned up, drunk, it was his men who fished Everard's body from the harbor.

"Cheer up!" Gifford had cajoled Beale all the way back up to London with the Yeomen guard. "You did a brilliant thing. The fucker was on to me, I tell you. He was about to let Ballard know that he'd seen me with bloody old Nicholas Berden! I'll never know how you picked him out in the dark, but Sir Francis'll give you a pay raise when he hears, that's for sure."

Beale had been aiming for Gifford, of course, because with him dead, Sir Francis's plan to insert him into Chartley would be stillborn, but not only had Beale missed Gifford, he had managed to hit and somehow kill the only man who could have stopped Walsingham's plan moving on to its next stage. Basically, it would have been far better if he had done nothing.

Thank God Her Majesty will never learn of this.

"You wait until Sir Francis tells Her Majesty what you pulled off!" Gregory now says. "She'll knight you on the spot."

A pulse of pure panic enlivens Beale's bloodstream when he hears this, because of course if she hears what he's done, then the Queen will release Thomas Perrot from the Tower early, to give him plenty of time with Devereux in London before he takes a ship for Holland. And she'll probably also tell him what's been going on while his back has been turned and where he might find Beale, and then—oh God. But then he calms himself, and he remembers there is no earthly way Walsingham will ever tell Her Majesty of his part in this scheme to snare Queen Mary, because Walsingham doesn't want her to know anything of it in the first place.

"And is there any news from Holland?" Beale asks, his voice a little bleaty, as if his mind is set on higher things than a title.

CHAPTER THIRTY-EIGHT

Stepney, east of London, January 1586

John Ballard has summoned them all to a frowsty old studio in Stepney, to have their likeness painted by a man named Marcus Teerlinc, an old acquaintance who owes him a favor.

"Well met!" Ballard cries whenever another new one arrives. "Well met, indeed, sir!"

"Quite a throng," Teerlinc mutters, looking steadily glummer as each new arrival adds to the number of men already shuffling awkwardly around the studio's limited space. The padded couch—the scene of so many of Teerlinc's triumphs—is turned on its side and pushed to the back, and when Ballard believes they are all here, there are fourteen faces to be painted, which Teerlinc thinks outweighs the favor owed by at least five times.

"Just get a likeness of me then," Ballard murmurs, "and Master Babington, perhaps, and maybe also the poet, Tichbourne, or he'll write some awful poem about how he was left off. The others you can just rough out or whatever it is you do."

Teerlinc is still reluctant. Ballard's third last silver crown is passed over.

"I promise you will not regret this, Marcus," he assures him, putting an arm across his shoulders and turning him so that it seems they are studying the men gathered before the easel. "Do you not recognize greatness when you see it? Have these men not got it stamped all over their features? Mark my words, Marcus, these men—these heroes—will change the course of history."

Marcus remains limp under his hand, but Ballard doesn't care. The old pornographer is no judge of character, and what he—Ballard—says is true: these men will change the course of history. Soon they will be raised up to exalted positions in government, and this likeness—made before the defining act—will soon be worth far, far more than its weight in gold. Marcus will soon be begging, begging, to have another chance of painting each of them.

Ballard goes to stand among them, inhaling wet wool and sour breath, and turns to face Teerlinc. *Actually, what a pathetic squirt the man is*, Ballard thinks. *He should not be allowed to paint such men.*

"Stand like this please, gentlemen," Teerlinc instructs, his breath a white smudge in the freezing studio. "Yes. You there. Tallest at the back, please, Master Ballard. You will wear your hat, sir? Even within doors? Very well, I am not one to judge, only it blocks your fellow's face. Stand to the left a bit, yes, you, sir. And turn this way, as if you are looking at something over my left shoulder. Perfect."

Ballard can feel the low-level roiling tension rising among the men.

"I still say we undertake a grave and needless risk," Babington says from the corner of his mouth. Others agree.

"Keep still, gentlemen, please," Teerlinc says, as if it matters what he paints.

"It is a calculated risk, sirs," Ballard tells them. "Copies of this painting will be sent to the pope! To King Felipe in Madrid! To the Duc de Guise! Imagine that! You will be heroes! Blessed by the

Holy Father himself. He will be able to look at this and pick you out and say 'Look you, sirs, there be the hero Sir Chidiock Tichbourne! There be gallant Sir Edward Harington'—"

"Habington," the man in question corrects.

Whatever, Ballard thinks.

When the first (and last) sitting is done, and after he has inspected the drab smear that captures no discernible likeness, Ballard feels the blood of Captain Fortescue pumping through his veins, and despite his dwindling resources he decides that now is not the time for penny-pinching, and he leads all the sitters to the nearest inn, where he pays for a private room and orders the cooks sent out to find the finest—freshest, anyway—meats, wines, and ale.

"Nothing is too good for my heroes."

When dinner is served, he jams a stool against the door and invites an intimate hush while he tells them why he has gathered them together today, why they are having their likeness done—because the plot is quickened and thickened.

"For Master Gilbert Gifford is come!"

The reception to this snippet is disappointing because none know who Gifford is.

"He landed in Rye the week before last, and so much does Walsingham fear him that they sent a reception committee, and I saw with my own eyes one of those devils try to shoot him with a wheel lock pistol! But with God's grace, Gifford evaded the heretic bullet!"

It would have been all the more remarkable if the ball had hit its target, of course, from that range and in the gloaming, but he does not tell them that, and nor does he tell them about the ball actually hitting Alan Everard.

"After which he was seized by a party of Yeomen," Ballard continues, "who wanted to bring him back to the Tower, save, again thanks to God's grace, he managed to escape!"

"He escaped?" a doubter asks.

"They are still searching every hedge in Sussex for him!" Ballard laughs. "High and low!"

"How?"

"I do not know the exact details, but within the week he was taking wine with the French ambassador at Salisbury Court!"

"And what was he doing there?" Babington asks.

At which Ballard beams.

"That is it, sir!" he says. "That is it! Gather close, gentlemen, for what I am about to tell you is not for lewd ears: Gilbert Gifford is come to England to take letters to Chartley! To Her Majesty the Queen that will be!"

There follows a silence while they consider the implications: that there is now, at long last, a conduit to Queen Mary; they can let her know that they stand ready to ride to find her and set her free just as soon as she sends word. But before they can start to celebrate as Ballard hoped they might, Babington reminds them of the other matter:

"And what of the Queen that now is?" he asks. "Last time we met, you said there was a marksman sent from France?"

Ballard might laugh, for at that exact moment there comes a circumspect knock on the door, and he holds up a finger to get them to keep that thought in mind while he leaps to his feet to open the door with a flourish to reveal none other than John Savage, looking a touch unkempt now, having been living wild in the woods beyond Saint John's, practicing with the pistol, which Ballard sees he has brought with him in the bag he gave him what feels like months ago now.

"Well met, Master Savage!" Ballard cries, just as he always does. "Oh, well met, indeed!"

And he folds him into the fondest hug despite the fungal reek.

The room is silent, all faces turned.

"Who is this?" Babington demands, as if this newcomer might jeopardize the safety of the entire scheme. But when it is explained, he and the other men become self-conscious, shy even, and they queue to touch the hand that will pull the trigger of the pistol that will kill the Queen of England. After which Savage sits, very self-contained, perhaps conscious that he is a man apart, in a realm apart, and he takes a modest piece of bread and a cup of ale, and Ballard wonders if such a man might really be relied upon to seize the moment? He will need bolstering, that much is certain. But how?

Well, he will come to that, perhaps.

Today, though, is a day for fellowship; for good cheer; for stirring speeches and a toast to the queen that is to come.

CHAPTER THIRTY-NINE

Doctor Dee's house, Mortlake, January 1586

Mademoiselle Katherine Báthory has spent the last five days and nights sitting alone in Doctor Dee's laboratory, waiting, with no joy, for his return. She has not permitted herself a fire. She has hardly permitted herself to sleep, or eat, or drink, and she knows she is weakening fast and that she must soon change her tactic and go out to find him, or she will pass out and perish.

Only she does not know how to find him.

After she had witnessed the saving of his son, she had known that she was right and that John Ballard was wrong about the man being a wizard. She had stood there on the bridge, trying to work out how John Dee had done it, and why it had all gone so suddenly wrong, and whose fault it was. When she'd shaken her head in wonder, the pain reminded her that it was Ballard's fault, of course, for throwing the goat's skull at her and then taking the boy. When he'd blocked the hatch into the nave, she'd returned to the hatch to the churchyard, only to find that locked, too, and she must admit that she screamed when she saw she was entombed, but then she saw, lying in the dust, the key, tossed aside.

She'd slotted it in and opened the door to find an astonished Yeoman standing dumbstruck in the churchyard. He was so slow to move that the key was already through his eyeball and into the back of his skull before he'd blinked twice. After that, with so many men around, she had just run, never expecting to find Ballard or the boy ever again, or at least not that night, but she had turned a corner, and there, astonishingly, he was, standing mute before some kind of porter who did not know what to do with him. She had killed the porter with the blade in her sleeve, and taken the boy, picturing him crucified in Dee's orchard, but he began to struggle and then the Englishman appeared, and tossing the boy's body from the bridge had served two purposes: a tiny thrill, and a means to divert him from following her.

After watching both rescued, Báthory had walked south, into a small town dedicated to vice, where she had had to draw that blade twice, once to kill a man who looked at her with intent, and once to kill a dog. Then she had carried on into the night, heading southward, in the direction of the village of Friday Street, formulating a new plan.

Traveling alone had been difficult, and with daylight, very swiftly dangerous, but the second man who tried to rape her had a very fine horse, and a voluminous cloak, and once she'd dragged his corpse into a ditch, she mounted up and made very good progress and came, by and by, to the stone behind the burned windmill, from which she took all Ballard's ill-gotten silver. Then she reburied eight hundred and fifty crowns of it behind the coppiced beech before retracing her steps back to London in search of Dee, with whom—whatever else she decided—she had a score still to settle.

When she reached Mortlake, the house was deserted. Someone

had carried away the bodies of those she'd killed last time she was here, though the kitchen still smelled strongly of soup, and Mademoiselle Báthory had allowed herself a pang of regret for having had to kill that maid, however necessary it was.

And then she had settled down to wait.

Days have passed now, and her patience is whittled to nothing, when suddenly there is a thunderous hammering on the gate to the street beyond the small yard in front of Dee's house. She is on her feet and ready instantly, though for what she does not know. No one will answer the gate, and if no one answers, whoever is knocking will go away.

She opens the gate.

A fat bruiser of the type she is familiar with from her home country stands there with an equally ugly boy and dog.

"Oh," the man says, snatching his hat from his bald head, and he's instantly uncomfortable before her beauty.

Báthory says nothing.

"Is the doctor within?" he asks, turning his hat between his fingers.

"No," she tells him.

"Oh," he says.

"What you want with him?"

"I just came to give him a bit of good news," the man explains. "Hoped he'd be back because I wanted him to know soon as, didn't I?"

"Go on," she says.

"Well, I wanted to tell him we've found his cannon."

"His cannon?"

"We heard he'd taken his young'un up north to find his missus, but I thought he'd want to kn—"

"Up north?" she interrupts. "What is north?"

"What? Up north. We heard—"

The man wilts under her gaze.

"We heard he'd—taken Arthur. Up north. After the lad's dip in the drink. A troop of Yeomen came by for them both, and— Well. We've found his cannon."

He trails off. A bead of sweat pops onto the taut skin of his crown and rolls down his temple.

"Gone to look after the Scottish queen, she has," the boy chips in. "Mistress Dee, that is."

She closes the gate in their faces and stalks through the house to collect her cloak.

CHAPTER FORTY

Chartley Castle, February 1586

A hard white winter, with the moat frozen over and bursts of icicles erupting from the gargoyles' mouths, and one day at the beginning of February a crow falls from the pale clouds to land with a thump in the snow before Dr. Dee and Arthur as they take their walk in the castle's bailey. Some might believe this sudden splash of jet black is a bad omen in a world turned otherwise only white and gray, but neither Dee nor Arthur is superstitious.

"Well, Arthur," Dee says, "thank God cows don't fly."

Arthur manages a small smile at the repurposed joke, and Dee thinks his heart might burst, for it has been a few weeks since he's seen one of them.

"Shall we take it in to see if the cooks can make anything of it?" he asks. "A soup? A pie?"

Arthur shakes his head. Dee stoops to pick it up, and they examine the bird together. Its irises are a strikingly pale blue, and it is steaming, as if letting its soul out through its feathers. Arthur takes it from him.

"Let's bury it," he says.

It will be a shared endeavor even if a little unusual, and it will give Arthur a purpose now that Masters Nau and Curle are suddenly too busy to play billiards with him. In the bailey they meet Sir Amyas Paulet coming from one of the few sound buildings left remaining within the castle walls, a steward's lodgings perhaps. He doesn't notice them because he is being very careful to close the door behind him, and Dee wonders what's going on in there? Woodsmoke sifts from the chimney and there are plenty of footprints coming and going.

When Paulet sees them, he starts, as if caught out.

"God give you good morrow, Doctor Dee," he recovers and stalks over to join them. "What have you got there, my boy?"

"A crow," Arthur tells him, his voice still heartrendingly quiet.

"Fell from the sky," Dee explains. "Must have frozen in mid-flight."

Paulet tells them he is not surprised.

"A hard frost last night. What'll you do with it?"

"Bury it," Arthur whispers.

"Ha. Ground's frozen. You'd be better off throwing it in the moat. Though that's frozen, too, of course. But anyway. Come on. Chuck it from one of the towers."

He is trying to lead them away from the house where the fire is lit, Dee can see, but Arthur likes the idea of giving the bird one last flight, and so they follow Paulet wheezing up the ice-rimmed steps to the battlements, where Dee hesitates a moment before sticking his head up above the parapet.

"What's got into you, man?" Paulet barks.

What has got into him is the fear that she'll be out there. That she'll see Arthur, and Arthur will see her, and that will be enough. Of course it doesn't make sense. It is just the fear she has engendered in them all. And of course, she's not out there. All there is are miles of mist-haunted snowfields and forests of naked trees, and in the lane running along the bottom of the slope beyond the moat comes a cart laden with barrels, pulled by three horses in the old-fashioned way, nose to tail.

"Ah," Paulet says. "The brewer. I had better—"

They watch Paulet for a moment as he doesn't quite know what to do. He doesn't want to leave them here, but for some reason he feels the need to meet this brewer, and Dee knows with a curious little thrill that he has stumbled upon something covert.

"You go, Sir Amyas," he tells him. "Arthur and I will give our friend here its final flight, and then we shall repair to the fireside in Queen Mary's Presence Room, if she'll have us, and play a game of billiards. How does that sound, Arthur?"

Arthur nods approval.

They watch Paulet stamp back down the steps and bustle across to the castle's gatehouse where he bangs on the door and rouses the porters and guards. Dee and Arthur turn back to watch the brewer whip his horses up the slope, and then they turn their attention to the dead bird again.

"Shall we?" Dee encourages, and after a murmured prayer, Arthur launches it with two hands, as a pigeon trainer might release a prize specimen, only this one tumbles straight down through the skeletal shrubs to bounce once and then skid across the ice. It is strangely disappointing, and Arthur pulls a face. The cold has turned his cheeks rosy, and the wind his eyes watery.

"Ah well," Dee says. "No harm done, and perhaps a fox will find it now, and so you will have given him his dinner."

He takes the boy's frozen hand, and they retrace their steps, past the stables where Queen Mary's coachman is helping the brewer and his lad unload his barrels in a cloud of steam from his stamping horses, and out through the gatehouse where there's no sign of Paulet, but when they reach the Presence

Room, Queen Mary is risen from her sickbed, and is even up to playing billiards with Lucy Pargeter while her ladies cluster near the fire, drinking hot spiced ale and complimenting her on her shoes.

After the perilous dip in her condition brought on by the effort of the move from Tutbury to Chartley, in the last few weeks Queen Mary's health has improved beyond measure. Her physician, Monsieur Bourgoing, is delighted and puts it down to the beer she has started drinking, in which the whole household has joined her.

"It is an elixir," Bourgoing says, which usually provokes a titter from Queen Mary, and again, Dee is conscious that he is on the outside of something, something that might come from being a stranger in a tight-knit court, or—?

The feeling grows over the following weeks, until he knows it is not a species of hypersensitive paranoia, and when he speaks to Frommond about it she knows what he means.

"It is more than that," she is sure. "They've become smug, haven't they? As if they know something we don't."

Then she tells him about the letter that Queen Mary asked her to send.

"Did you?" he asks.

She shakes her head.

"I've not had a single chance," she tells him. "You've seen what Paulet is like: he'd have me stripped if I tried to leave the castle."

"So you still have it?"

Again, she shakes her head.

"That's the thing; she asked for it back. Said she no longer needed it sent."

"Needed?"

"Exactly."

"Who was it addressed to?" Dee wonders.

"To the care of Guillaume de l'Aubépine, but it was intended, she said, to be sent onto her son, relinquishing all claim to the thrones of England and Scotland if she might be left in peace to go and live in a farmhouse overlooking a loch somewhere."

"Jesu," Dee says. "Did you read it?"

"The seal came apart in my hands," Frommond tells him. "It honestly did. As if she wanted me to read it."

"And what did it say?"

"Exactly that. And that she wanted to live there in peace, she said, just her and a few ladies. She was very smitten with the idea."

Dee strokes his beard until she stays his hand.

"You look like you think you are a wizard," she reminds him.

"But there was something strange about it," Frommond goes on. "About the paper, I mean. It was stiff, and slightly shiny, as if—you remember you told me about that Italian, and his method for writing on the inside of cooked eggs?"

That was a long time ago now, but it still makes Dee smile to think of Giambattista della Porta, and the ways in which he—Dee—once wooed Frommond.

"It made me think there might be a secret hidden within, a code or some such. Invisible writing or something, and I was very wary about sending it, even if I'd been able."

"So why has she decided she does not now need it sent?" he wonders aloud.

"Because she no longer wants to be set free to live by a loch? Or because she has found another way to send the letter?"

"Or both of those things?"

"That doesn't make sense," she tells him.

"I mean, she's found another way to send messages; different messages."

"Ahh," she says. "Yes."

"And that would explain the change in mood around here and

why Nau and Curle are suddenly burning the midnight oil: they are back to enciphering her letters."

At first the satisfaction of finding an explanation is pleasing.

"But then to what end?" Dee wonders.

"Pray God she is not attempting some plot!" Frommond says, clapping her hands to her cheeks. "Some scheme to get herself freed!"

But of course she is, Dee thinks, and he tells Frommond about Paulet in the bailey of the castle, trying to keep them away from a particular house.

"They are all up to something," he says.

"And we are caught between them," Frommond supposes. "Ooof. It makes me feel sick."

He knows what she means because the truth is he has come to admire Queen Mary. She is sharp and perceptive and courageous in the face of the frankly unnatural limits that are placed upon her person. Before Dee joined her strange court in exile, he thought of Mary just as other men such as Walsingham and Burghley thought: that she was a serpent in England's bosom, and that she must be got rid of one way or another, but now he has come to see her plight: forced out of her own country by the usual sorts of power-hungry lords, she came to England in desperation, and where for no other reason other than for who she is, she was clapped in gaol by right of—what? Nothing. Dee has seen worse gaols, of course, and spent time in them, too, but Mary's gaol is a gaol nonetheless, and though she has done nothing yet to conclusively prove they cannot trust her, they do not trust her, and they have steadily squeezed the life out of her, as if to ensure their prophecy becomes self-fulfilling. It is a horrible lesson in power, and fear, and inevitability.

"I shall write to the Queen," Frommond says, "and ask her if she will let us leave."

Dee nods. *Pray God she agrees*, he thinks, for the threat of John Hawkins's deadline is beginning to weigh very heavy, and he is yet to find a single ironmaster able to forge the cannons to his design. Frommond has told him he must go. But he can read between the lines. He will not leave her by herself with Arthur, for which she is pitifully grateful.

CHAPTER FORTY-ONE

Walsingham's house, Seething Lane,
City of London, April 1586

Gilbert Gifford is sleeping like a dog on the floor before the fire when Robert Beale comes back from Whitehall Palace, and Beale kicks his foot.

"Wake up."

"Didn't realize it'd be such fucking hard work," Gifford tells him, yawning and stretching. "Six weeks I've been taking messages up and down that fucking road, with nothing to show for it save saddle sores like you wouldn't believe and flea bites you can put your finger in."

"Why don't you ask someone else to do the Chartley end?" Beale suggests. "I'd do it, even."

And he would, too: it would surely give him greater opportunity to scotch this scheme of Walsingham's, as well as get him out of London, so that he wouldn't be here if and when Sir Thomas Perrot gets back from Holland, whence Her Majesty sent him as a reward for Beale's apparent heroics in Rye, and this morning threatened to summon back, claiming that she was still hearing reports that Walsingham was plotting to ensnare Queen Mary in some treachery. Beale had denied it, of course, but this wasn't a court of law, Her Majesty told him.

"I will summon Sir Thomas back today, Master Beale, if I hear word of any more of your espials riding up and down the York Road."

He had promised her this morning that he was doing all he could to stop it, and she had given him one of her gimlet stares that reminded him that although she said she had no wish to make a window into men's souls, she could if she wanted to.

And now here is Gifford, lying on his office floor, complaining about being tired.

"It's that fucking Paulet," Gifford goes on. "'I'd rather trust one person than two.' Making a martyr of me, he is. And Snibbet, the brewer. He actually makes me do the work he's not paying me to do. Deliveries and that. Not sure how long I can keep doing it, to be honest. Don't tell Sir Francis I said anything though."

Beale shuffles some paper.

"It's only been a couple of months," he says.

Gifford groans.

"Feels like forever," he says, and "Has there been anything yet?"

He means anything of interest implicating Queen Mary.

"Only that Claude Nau is negotiating to marry Bess Pierrepont, but as I say, early days. This could go on for years. Not that I mean to dishearten you."

He does.

Gifford blows out a long sigh and climbs wearily to his feet. He is covered in dried mud, and his cheeks are aflame with chilblains. He slumps in a chair that squeaks in protest.

"Sometimes I wish you had hit me in Rye," he says. "Nothing too drastic. Not like you done to Everard. Just a nice little tickle, something that'd put me out of action. I could spend a couple of weeks in bed, being looked after by some sweet little nurse or other. I bet Walsingham's got a fleet of them."

Gifford twaddles on for a bit; the drifting nonsensical words of a man done in from being in the saddle for five days out of six, and Beale's thoughts leave him, and return to his own problems: specifically, how to scupper this plot of Walsingham's.

He has to admit that Gifford has shown rare ingenuity in pulling the various strands of this plot together; first getting Morgan in Paris to vouch for him to the French ambassador here in London, and then getting the French ambassador to vouch for him to Queen Mary, too. Once he had their guarantees, and a packet of the letters that had been waiting at Salisbury Court, he took them first to Phelippes to decipher—to discover not very much they did not already know—and then to Arthur Gregory to reseal. Then Gifford took them north, to the little town of Burton, three leagues from Chartley, where Sir Amyas Paulet had contracted a brewer to supply some of the town's famously good beer to Queen Mary's household. Paulet had chosen this brewer not because his beer was especially good or cheap, but because he was known to have recusant tendencies, and, crucially, to be as dishonest and greedy as the day was long.

"A man after my own heart," Gifford had laughed.

Gifford had played the part of a wealthy Catholic and bribed the brewer to take him on as his apprentice, horse boy, servant, whatever, and take him on the wagon to deliver beer to Chartley. While Gifford was unloading the barrels of ale, Queen Mary's coachman, John Sharp, came out to admire the horses and to lend a hand if necessary for he was bored, and it took but a moment for Gifford to show him that one of the plugs was marked, and to tell him that he must check it, later. Sharp had understood. The barrels were unloaded and stacked in the buttery, and Gifford jumped back up onto the cart and off they went back to Burton.

Sharp then must have returned to the buttery and found that into the plug of the marked barrel was pinned a greased leather envelope, and in this were the letters from Morgan in Paris, and the ambassador in London, sending their blessings to Her Majesty, and informing her that she could trust Gifford, and that she would now be able to communicate with them in this same manner, but in reverse.

After all the cruelties and privations that Mary had endured, the thought that she would now be able to resume contact with the world beyond Chartley must have come as a pleasure beyond compare, so overwhelming that all caution and sense was blown to the wind, for Mary set to straightaway drafting her reply, which included a new cipher that they were to use from then on, in case the letters should fall into Walsingham's hands.

Beale had been with Phelippes when Gifford brought them the first packet that he had plucked out of the Burton brewer's barrel, and Phelippes had sighed.

"Ah well," he'd said. "I always thought it was too good to be true."

"She is mocking us," Walsingham had said, poring over all the little details of which Greek letter replaced which Roman letter, which number which word, and so on. "No one can be this indiscreet, surely?"

But they'd still copied the crib sheet and resealed it and delivered it to the French ambassador, and a week later Gifford had gone to collect another batch of letters from the ambassador, which he brought to Gregory to open and for Phelippes to decode using Mary's new cipher, and lo, it all made sense. She was not trying to fool them; she really was that indiscreet.

"Or desperate," Beale had suggested.

Which was why, of course, Walsingham had cut her off from the outside world in the first place.

"Anyway, what does it say?" Beale had wanted to know.

In all honesty: nothing much. The messages were carefully phrased expressions of love, and reassurance that Mary was not forgotten by her well-willers, but the French ambassador did sign off with the promise that something was brewing—"a joke?"—that would bring Mary great succor. Gregory sealed it all up again and Gifford took it back up to Chartley, where he received another batch from Mary, which when deciphered, was full of questions as to who was doing what where, and complaints about Paulet, whom they called Corvus—the crow.

This went on for two months, all through the tail end of that filthy, lingering winter, and slowly the truth began to percolate through to Her Majesty's principal private secretary: that nothing will come of this venture; not because it is not a meticulously executed plan, with all angles covered, but because there is nothing there to find, that they are wrong about Queen Mary, and that she is as she says she is: an innocent victim who wishes only love and friendship between herself and her cousin of England.

Toward the end of March Walsingham's health faltered and he had retaken to his bed in Barn Elms, though every morning a tirade of furious messages from him kept arriving at his offices in Seething Road demanding that something—anything—be discovered, done, provoked, anything.

"Our whole service has been bent as if with one mind toward this one single thing, and I cannot believe that with all the resources employed and brainpower deployed that we cannot see behind the facade to the truth of the thing. We are missing something, gentlemen, of that I am certain, and what is required is greater diligence."

"He's about to tell us failure is not an option, isn't he?" Arthur

Gregory had laughed, and the subject matter of the next day's missive from Barn Elms had been "Failure is not an option."

Meanwhile Phelippes has started to believe that the cipher that Mary had sent in that first packet can only have been an elaborate trick, or perhaps but one stage in an encrypting process, and that he lacks insight into the other. His eyes have become startlingly red-rimmed and he stinks of tobacco, and he, too, is intent on driving himself toward an early grave.

But as each inconsequential banality had crossed their desks, Robert Beale had felt better. The weight lifted from his shoulders, and all the more so since the news from Holland was that the English and Spanish armies would soon engage. Sir Thomas Perrot, the fighting machine, would surely be wherever the fray was hottest, and the Spanish tercios were not likely to offer quarter. Also Devereux was back in London, and it would soon be May.

But then in late April, something happens.

"Wait!" Phelippes shouts. "Look at this!"

Beale feels the blood drain from his face, and all pleasure flees.

"What is it?"

"Someone here from the French Embassy is saying that there is a packet of letters from Scotland and from France, addressed to Mary, being kept at the house of Anthony Babington."

"Babington?"

"That's the fella Robin Poley says is obsessed with her," Gregory reminds them as if Beale needs reminding. "Him who's putting up John Ballard."

They have to wait a good long moment for Phelippes to decrypt the next sentence. When he has, he laughs.

"The French are suggesting she contact him directly!"

The three men stare at one another, each aware that something significant has just happened; the first inkling of the hidden, interlocking design they've been desperately searching for has revealed itself, like stones emerging from under wind-washed sand. Connections have been made at last: Babington-Ballard-Gifford-Queen Mary.

"This is it!" Phelippes breathes, rapping the page with his knuckles. "This is it!"

"Shit the bed," Arthur Gregory murmurs.

That afternoon the Queen summons Beale again.

He refuses to go.

"Tell Her Majesty I have the plague."

"You do look a touch peaky," the pursuivant says, backing off.

Beale sits in his house and wonders what to do.

Gifford will collect the packet from Phelippes, then ride north to Chartley. He'll get the letters to Mary. She'll send word through Gifford, who will take the letters to Phelippes, who will decrypt them before returning them to Gifford to take to the French ambassador, who will then pass them on to Babington. Babington will reply the same way, but in the reverse! And if Babington is as Poley describes, he will make some extravagant offer to save Queen Mary, to spring her from captivity, and put her on England's throne.

And that will be that. Walsingham will have his proof, and Beale will have failed in his mission on behalf of Queen Elizabeth.

So where in among that chain of events can he insert himself?

CHAPTER FORTY-TWO

Saint Giles-in-the-Fields, west of London, May 1586

John Ballard has come hotfoot from Salisbury Court and is laughing when he passes the message to Anthony Babington late that morning.

"Wait until you read this, Master Babington!"

He watches Babington's face, waiting for his reaction, and when it comes it is very gratifying and Ballard takes the credit as if it has all been his own doing, which, in a way, it has been.

"And this comes from her hand? She wrote this herself?"

Babington is looking at the letter as if it were some precious relic.

"Yes indeed," Ballard says, before qualifying that answer with a more accurate description, which is that Queen Mary will have expressed her meaning in French to Master Nau, who will have taken it down and tidied it up before passing it on to Master Curle, who will have translated it in English, and then encrypted it, and then folded it into Master Gifford's ingeniously crafted leather wallet, which he will have given to John Sharp to bung in the empty barrel, which would then have been loaded aboard the wagon and taken to the brewery in Burton where Gifford would have retrieved it and brought it south to Salisbury Court where the Baron of Chateauneuf's private secretary—Claude Nau's brother-in-law, as a matter of fact—would have decrypted it onto the piece of paper that Ballard is now gazing at as if it were touched by the hand of an angel or some such.

"But basically yes."

"Have you read what it says?"

"Of course not," Ballard lies, astonished once again how naive Babington really is.

"She says merely that I am to give you the packets that I brought back from France?"

It isn't much, is it? Ballard thinks. Certainly not what he was hoping for. But it is a start!

"She is being discreet," he tells him. "She cannot put down on paper that she has heard of you and your gallantry and so on, can she?"

Babington supposes not—though why not?—but he is a bit winded.

"The point is that she is in touch, isn't she? See?" Ballard continues. "She doesn't write to just anyone. She wants you to write back. So you do. Tell her that you have given me the packet of letters and that I have sent them with Master Gifford, and that they shall soon be with her. Something like that."

"But that doesn't begin to cover what needs to be said!"

Oh Jesu, Ballard thinks, but cannot say.

"I see that, Master Babington, but this is not like sending a marriage proposal to a fair maiden in another county whose father doesn't approve, is it? This is deadly serious. If you write anything that can be misconstrued, then you bring mortal danger upon us all, and most especially upon Her Majesty."

Now Babington looks almost ecstatic to be mentioned in the same bracket as Her Majesty. Ballard sighs. He is a fool, this boy, and will squander his gifts, and his life and the lives of those of them around him if he—Ballard—is not careful.

"So let us compose this letter together, shall we? I have an appointment with Master Gifford here tomorrow, before nine of the clock, so we can work on something appropriate this evening at the Plough, if you've a mind? Only I may be—?"

He means short of funds.

Babington doesn't care about that. He hands over some coins with a faraway look in his eye.

"How is the likeness coming on?" he asks, apropos of nothing, it seems.

"Likeness? Oh, the portrait. Very well, I do believe. Master Teerlinc has been in touch to say how pleased he is with it so far. Maybe we will need one more sitting? And now, Master Babington, you must excuse me for I have another man whom I must meet."

The man with whom Ballard has the appointment is John Savage, the man to whom he was sent to give the gun so that he—Savage—can get close enough to kill Queen Elizabeth, but who has sent word that he is losing his nerve, not to say his mind. He needs money and reassurance, and so Ballard bids Babington farewell until the evening and walks down through Fickett's Field to the Cock and Bottle, the inn on Fleet Street where he was last with Mademoiselle Báthory, the night he truly learned her nature, and where he now finds John Savage sitting with neither food nor drink, tapping his hands on the table, jittery and infirm of purpose.

"Be of good cheer, Master Savage!" Ballard announces, a hand upon his shoulder, and he tells him about the letter from Queen Mary.

"I do not have it with me or I would show you how in her own hand she sends her blessings on your enterprise, and how she says your name in her prayers. She bade me wish you courage, for you are chosen of God, and she also bade me remind you of our Holy Father's injunction against the heretic queen that is, and that with your single blow you will be breaking the shackles of this false religion, and setting free this realm of England, thus assuring your place among the saints and martyrs in Heaven."

And Ballard says a great deal of other things besides, not all of them logical or consistent, for Savage is only alive to certain words and sentences. He looks very wild now, with his hair and beard grown unkempt and his linen in dire need of attention, and he has lost a lot of weight, too, so that he appears ferociously messianic; he's the perfect person to deliver the wrath of God to this false Jezebel Elizabeth of England.

"She also bade me give you this."

His very last silver crown.

Savage snatches it up and then he stands and grips Ballard by his shoulders and gives him a blazing look.

"Go with God, Father John Ballard!" he says and turns and flees the inn, and Ballard is left not knowing what to think or do. He sits. Sitting opposite the man is like going to the Tower, he thinks, and looking down into the lions' cage, and catching one of the great beast's eyes. Is that a good thing in an assassin, or a bad thing? He thanks God the inn is empty this afternoon save for whorls of woodsmoke that rise and fall in the light of the early summer sun through the windows.

A moment later the innkeeper brings him ale and a pie.

"I did not order these," he tells the man, though they are welcome.

"It's my lady over there what bought 'em," the innkeeper says, and he nods at someone behind Ballard's shoulder, and there is something about the innkeeper's look—fixed but puzzled—that makes Ballard's fingers stop before they touch the mug or the bowl. He feels a sluice of hot ice down his back, and his thoughts seem to fizz as he slowly sits back, turns and looks over his shoulder, and there she is.

CHAPTER FORTY-THREE

Chartley Castle, May 1586

Her Majesty's reply to their request to leave Chartley comes very slowly.

"She says no," Frommond tells Dee.

Behind his eyeglasses Dee's eyes widen and he swings his feet off the bed where he has been reading a book about fish to Arthur. It is a book he himself has written and Arthur is somewhat somnolent.

"No?"

She shakes her head. She feels a great weight of guilt, for she knows he is becoming ever more concerned about meeting John Hawkins's order for those cannons he promised. He has once or twice suggested he take Arthur with him to the Shropshire forge masters who might give him credit, and then cast some guns to his specification, but she cannot bear the thought of parting from the boy, not while that woman is out there, and so Dee has had to content himself with writing long letters to Thomas Digges, down in Mortlake, about the possibility of re-creating Roger Cooke's canisters for the gun, and with much solitary pacing, with much on his mind.

"See for yourself."

She passes him the letter. He reads silently, then passes it back.

"She asks after Lucy" is all he says.

"It is what I was saying: Lucy's business here is more important than mine, and we shall not be allowed to leave until it is done, but what is it? I never see her from one day to the next."

"She is oftentimes in the kitchen," Arthur tells them.

He is so silent sometimes they forget he is there, and now they both turn to smile at him, so delighted to hear his voice regaining its strength they hardly care what he says.

But then: "The kitchen?"

"Why?"

"She has told the cook that she likes to cook."

Frommond and Dee look at each other.

"Lucy?"

She does not look the type to interest herself in such things.

"We could ask?" Dee supposes.

They cannot find her, of course. Or not until they remember the oratory, the narrow door to which is always locked, and so the room has more or less been forgotten. It has not really occurred to anyone why it is always locked, or who always locks it. It turns out that it is Lucy who does so, for she is the only one with a key, but to discover what's inside, they need to ambush her just as she is either coming or going.

"Lucy!"

She flinches to find them all three there outside "her" door and she tries to lock it behind her and move away down the passage as if suddenly very busy, but when she looks down Dee's foot is in the door. She pulls it sharply to, but Dee's boots are solidly built.

"Mind if we take a look?" Dee asks, pushing the door wide.

Lucy backs into the room, and they follow. Inside, it smells medicinal—more laboratory than oratory—and in the sill under the tall thin window stands a stack of glazed crucibles and various pestles and mortars, and there's a little brass brazier and tripod, and numerous bunches of herbs hang drying from the rafters above. Dee's attention is caught by the book that stands upright on the lectern, thick and handsomely bound in yellow leather, with an unusual hasp and lock. He had mentioned seeing Pargeter carrying it the week he arrived, but she—Frommond—hadn't taken much notice at the time.

Now Dee springs on it and snatches it up and studies it closely, not as one might a book, by opening its pages, but as one might a box of something. Lucy looks calculating, but then she sees Arthur has followed them into the oratory, though they can all four hardly fit, and he is about to touch a jar of something on the prie-dieu.

"Don't touch that!" Lucy shouts, and she pushes Dee aside and pulls Arthur's hand back. She is as sinuous as a snake.

"What's going on, Lucy?" Frommond asks. "What is all this?"

Lucy looks around for some reasonable explanation but if she finds one, it emerges stillborn, and meanwhile Dee has sprung the lock on the book and within it are not pages as you might expect, but a series of small drawers, each labeled in neat letters, and a chubby glass bottle set in an alcove. Painted on the inside cover is a skeleton with a battle flag extending from its mouth on which are written some words in Latin.

Dee reads them out.

"*Statatum est hominibus semel mori*?"

It is given that all men must die.

Lucy purses her lips and says nothing.

Dee then reads out the labels on the drawers: "*Hyoscyamus Niger*; *Papaver Somnif.*; *Aconitum*; *Bryonia Alba*; *Datura Stram.* These are all poisons."

"Yes," Lucy says, and she holds up her hands. "Yes, they are, and so?"

Dee pulls open one or two of the drawers, each hardly bigger than a man's thumb. They are mostly full and there's a clear liquid sloshing in the bottle. Frommond wonders what the drying herbs are, but she is beginning to feel lightheaded from the fumes.

"Outside," Dee says. He leaves the book and holds his hand out for the key to the oratory door. Lucy tells him she is not going to give it to him.

"Why should I?"

"Because we have— Because you are practicing to poison someone."

"And what has that got to do with you?"

Frommond is startled. If that were true, then she would suppose Lucy would be repentant, but she's not. She leads them out into the bailey, and Frommond asks Arthur to stand back a little, so they may speak of sad matters. The boy does, but he seems to slip back into that defensive, closed posture of frozen watchfulness.

"Just what in the name of God are you doing here, Lucy?" Frommond asks, which makes Lucy stop to consider her shrewdly before she decides on a story, which may or may not be the truth.

"Her Majesty sent me," she decides. "Queen Elizabeth."

"To poison Queen Mary?"

"Yes."

"To make her ill, or to kill her?" Dee asks. He has experience in this of course.

"Both," Lucy tells them. "To poison her slowly, so as not to give any cause for suspicion, so that she is ill, and then dies."

"Why would Her Majesty do that?" Frommond asks. "Want her dead, I mean. She has refused every effort to have her executed— I've seen her with my own eyes reject all of Walsingham's pleas to allow him to have her executed—"

"She does not want her executed," Pargeter interrupts. "She just wants her dead, and she wants her dead before Sir Francis Walsingham can put her on trial."

Dee is more interested in the method of the poisoning.

"In tiny doses," Lucy admits. "In the Queen's wine to begin with, but now she only drinks beer, and I cannot get at that for it is doled out by Mary Kennedy, not Barbara Mowbray, who is with Curle's child and cannot stand the smell, so was happy for me to bring the queen's cup to table."

She shows them a ring and pops it open to reveal a tiny reservoir.

"What were you giving her?" Dee asks.

"A mix of my own device," Lucy says. She is proud.

"Does Sir Amyas know?"

Lucy shakes her head.

"Queen Elizabeth asked him if he would not rid her of what she called her troublesome queen and blamed him for not throwing her out of a window or down some stairs, as would happen in any other country in Christendom, but Paulet refused. Said he would not make a wreck of his conscience. A nice way with words, and meanwhile he withdraws everything from her and kills her by neglect. Hypocrite."

At least you cannot say that about Lucy.

"So what now?" Frommond asks. "You cannot expect us to just stand by while you poison a woman."

Lucy shrugs.

"Can't I?"

"Of course not!"

"Even though Her Majesty has ordered it done?"

"But—"

But what? There is no but.

"It is still murder," Frommond tells her.

"She's dead anyway," Lucy argues. "And this way she'll know

nothing of it. I would make it painless. In her sleep. And then she—and we—are spared all this."

"All this what?"

"All this stalking; this trapping of a woman. It is filthy. Far worse that what I have in mind."

"Jesu!" Dee mutters. "How many people have you killed, Lucy?"

"I don't think of it as killing, Doctor."

"What do you think of it as then?"

"I merely shorten lives," she says.

Dee snorts.

"Well, yes," he says. "But that is just another way of saying the same thing."

Lucy shakes her head.

"My father was a hangman," she says. "I am a hangman's daughter. I only execute the guilty."

"Your father was a hangman?"

Hangmen are usually men who have been found unsuitable by the butchers' guild.

"My mother's family brought me up," Lucy answers the unasked question.

"And what happened to your mother?"

"My father burned her."

Jesu. Frommond finds she has stepped back.

"And was she guilty?" Dee asks.

"Of being a Protestant, yes."

"And what then happened to your father?"

"I killed him. With poison. He was the first person whose life I shortened, and I only shortened it by a day, for he was in the Tower, condemned to death for the murder of nearly forty men and women whom he was ordered to execute by Queen Mary."

She means a different Queen Mary, of course, this one of

England, whose reign had seen hundreds of Protestants burned. But it all makes a terrible kind of sense.

"If Scottish Mary lives and comes to power," Lucy continues, "then it is likely we must return to the Catholic faith once more, and once more men like my father will be ordered to burn more women like my mother. If the death of one woman prevents that, then so be it."

Dee and Frommond stare at her, and she gives them a weak smile, turns her heel, and is gone.

"Well, at least now we know," Dee supposes.

"Why she is such a terrible maid?"

Neither laughs.

Now Frommond understands that Lucy is not fully human. She is a device, aimed at Queen Mary.

"So we are drawn even deeper into the mire," she says. "On the one hand, in here, we must sit and watch Lucy circle Queen Mary with her book of death, and on the other, out there, we know that Walsingham is tightening the threads of his scheme, and we will know that every little skip of joy that Mary makes is in fact a step toward the headsman's block."

In the silence that follows they hear what they can only suppose to be music coming from Mary's Presence Room, and a little whoop of joy, which neither has ever heard since joining the Scottish queen's household.

CHAPTER FORTY-FOUR

The Cock and Key, Fleet Street, west of London, May 1586

They sit at one end of the long table, and she forces herself to look at him, just as she can see he is forcing himself to look at her.

"Well, well," he says. "This is ill-met, Mistress Báthory."

"I need help," she tells him.

"And you come to me?"

"I have letter, from Duc de Guise."

"I don't care," he tells her with his mouth, but when she holds it up, his eyes betray the truth.

"Read," she says, and she passes it to him.

"How did you come by it?" he asks. "Through the French ambassador? He should have told me."

"Not matter," she tells him.

She wrote it herself, of course, in her most careful French, but in fact she has had to visit the French ambassador, because after a long and extremely trying trip north to find this place Chartley, where Dee was hiding, she discovered it to be a castle, surrounded by a moat, and guarded all hours of the day and night. So she returned to Salisbury Court to send word of her progress to the Duc de Guise.

Here she learned of Gifford, and his access to Queen Mary in Chartley.

"So he wants me to introduce you to Gifford?" Ballard asks.

She nods.

Who will introduce her to the brewer, who will get her into the castle, even if she has to hide in a barrel, where she will find Dee.

CHAPTER FORTY-FIVE

Walsingham's house, Seething Lane, London, June 1586

"Gifford's late," Walsingham says.

Beale hopes he has had an accident. Fallen off his horse. Been murdered by thieves.

But he hasn't. He comes running up the steps to Walsingham's office, a look of wild jubilation.

"Babington's replied," he says before he has managed to regain his breath, and he pulls a letter from his doublet. Walsingham makes an indescribable sound of relief overlaid by triumph.

"He brought it to Salisbury Court late last night, they said, and you know what these fucking Frenchies are like. No chance of working by candle, is there? Not when there's all that wine to be drunk, so they kept me waiting this morning while they put it into code."

"What does it say?" Beale demands.

"I don't know, do I?" Gifford barks. "It's fucking sealed."

Beale should remind Gifford that he only recently saved his life.

"Pass it here," Arthur Gregory tells him, and he gets to work with some boiling water and a whisper thin blade. A moment later, the letter is open.

"God damn it!"

It's in code, of course.

"Phelippes! Phelippes!" Walsingham shouts. "Where the hell is Phelippes?"

Thomas Phelippes has gone up to Chartley.

"Maybe we should try ourselves? I mean, how hard can it be? We have the encryption right here."

But it is a long letter, and just looking at the cypher makes Beale's eyes dance.

"Robert—" Walsingham starts.

"I'm on my way. Come, Master Gifford."

They ride hard all that day, and the next, and the one after that. At the end of the third day Beale is a broken man and once again must be helped down from the saddle by Thomas Phelippes and Sir Amyas Paulet himself.

"Told you it was hard," Gifford says.

They pass the letter to Phelippes, who leads them to a room in what must have been the castle steward's house where he has set a lectern under the west-facing window. He has about two hours of daylight left, so he lights his pipe and perches his heavy eyeglasses on his nose and sets to. Beale hobbles back through the gatehouse.

A moment later he sees Dr. Dee and his wife and son emerge and cross the bailey toward him, and Beale would admit to slipping a tear to see Arthur looking not just alive but well. But Beale soon becomes aware that something is going on, that they may have something to tell him. Dee suggests to Arthur they take a walk along the wall to watch the crows roosting in the elms and so it is Mistress Dee who will do the telling.

"Do you know Lucy Pargeter?" she asks when they have walked

a few paces to a carved mounting stone on which she allows him to sit. Beale does so with some relief and tells her he does not.

"Her Majesty has sent her here in order to . . . in order to make sure that if Sir Francis does find evidence of Queen Mary plotting against Her Majesty, then Queen Mary will not live to face any kind of trial."

Beale takes this in for a moment.

"How will she do that?"

Mistress Dee tells him about a book that isn't a book, but made up of drawers filled with different sorts of poison. *Aconitum* and so forth. Beale says nothing. He sits, Frommond stands, in the slanting sunlight, and he has that same sensation of finally glimpsing some considered design carefully hidden in the pell-mell of daily life.

"And you're certain?" he checks, though obviously she is.

"We found the book"—Frommond is matter-of-fact—"and she admitted as much. And I know Her Majesty sent her up here, because she sent me, and there was no reason to do that unless she wanted an excuse for Lucy to be here too."

What does it all mean? A year ago and Beale would have had no idea, but this past year has confirmed in him the growing conviction that men and women such as he and Mistress Dee and this woman poisoner are no more than pawns to be pushed around and used up in the service of someone else's purpose.

"I can tell Sir Francis, of course," he supposes.

"And he will put a stop to it?"

"I should think so," he says. "Don't you?"

"Because he wants to see Mary tried?"

Beale nods. Sir Francis does want that, and though Beale has never quite put it into words before, even within the confines of his own private thoughts, over these past few months he has also come to see why: Walsingham's immediate priority is of course to keep England safe from the Catholic powers, but he is also looking beyond that, and his long-term aim is to break the spell of the widespread belief in the divine right of rulers to rule. Just as the reformed faith has done away with saints and martyrs and such hocus-pocus that only confirms privilege and concentrates power in priestly hands, so Walsingham and his kind wish to break the monarchy's stranglehold on power over the people. If Queen Mary can be brought before a court of mere subjects, and found guilty of some breach in their laws, and be held accountable for that breach in the most extreme and public manner, then so might *all* queens and *all* kings be held likewise accountable. And so is it really any wonder that Queen Elizabeth strives to thwart Walsingham's aim and avert any trial and execution of a fellow monarch in any and every which way she can?

But it means their next steps must be guided by whomsoever they wish to win this struggle: the people, in the shape of Walsingham? Or monarchy, in the shape of the Queen?

Mistress Dee is looking off after her husband and son, who stand two small shapes on the distant battlement, watching the crows, when she lets out a small gasp of realization.

"She is already dead, isn't she?" she asks. "Queen Mary?"

Beale opens his mouth to answer that maybe she is not, but at that point, Phelippes emerges from the steward's house and waves to Beale: *Come quick!* It can only mean one thing.

Beale hesitates a moment and looks her in the eye.

"Yes," he says. "I think she is."

CHAPTER FORTY-SIX

Saint Giles-in-the-Fields, Holborn,
west of London, July 1586

John Ballard has been looking for Anthony Babington all week, but now here he is, beautifully dressed in linen the color of a fresh duck egg, with a resolute smile and rosy cheeks under the broad brim of his silver-buckled hat.

"God give you good morrow, Master Ballard!"

Yes, yes, Ballard thinks.

"I've been looking for you everywhere!" he says instead. "I've left word with everyone I know. We need to draft your reply."

He dares not say her name aloud, even out here in the dappled shade of these woods. But Babington takes his arm and makes him walk alongside him just as he would if he was about to explain his plans to build a new house with a view of a lake, and Ballard has a horrible sinking sensation.

"Fret you not, Master Ballard," Babington tells him, "for I have already written it."

God's stones! That is what Ballard most feared. Still, it is not the end of the world.

"May I see it? I know you young gentlemen are fond of flights of fancy, and it would not do to overtax the ambassador's secretary."

"You need have no fear on that account. The letter was short and punchy and stuck to detail."

"Was?" Ballard snaps.

"Yes. Was. It has been sent. After you failed to appear at the Cock and Bottle that evening I took it to Salisbury Court myself."

Ballard wrenches his arm free.

"Tell me you're joking!"

"Not a bit of it. I left it with the ambassador's secretary, M'sieur Fontenay."

"What did you say?" Ballard demands. "What did you write?"

Babington is almost delirious with the pleasure of having been in touch with the Scottish queen himself, but he is still a gentleman and does not like to be shouted at by a man such as Ballard.

"What someone needed to say when Her Majesty was first imprisoned eighteen long years ago, Master Ballard: that she must have her freedom! That the country cries out for a release from this Protestant bondage! That now is at long last the time for all good Catholic men to rise up and put an end to the heretic Queen that is! Something you should have done years ago!"

"You put that on paper?"

"Yes! And more besides! What you call discretion, I call cowardice! I am done living so insipid a double life as this! I told her about the armies across the sea, poised to invade! I told her how an army of Catholic Englishmen will rise up; how I will come to release her personally; and how six good men will be sent to dispatch the heretic usurper."

For a long, turbulent moment Ballard thinks this is some joke aimed at his controlling self, and that perhaps he has been treating Babington too much like a child, not trusting him enough, perhaps; but then the full horror dawns: he means it! He has genuinely written all that down on paper! Paper that might so easily fall into Walsingham's hands!

Ballard grabs Babington by his beautifully tailored lapels and snarls into his handsome face.

"Tell me you are fucking lying!"

But he can't because he's not. Ballard thrusts Babington away. He looks flushed and sulky suddenly, like a sulky scolded boy.

"Oh good God, Master Babington, you had best pray to God the ambassador has not sent that letter, because if he has, then never mind putting your head or my head on the block, it'll be Her Majesty you've sent to her death!"

Ballard says no more, but sets off running for Salisbury Court.

"But I did!" M'sieur Fontenay says when Ballard is taken to his chamber. "Last week. M'sieur Gifford waited for it and then took it straight up there."

Ballard curses silently.

Christ, he thinks, *why was I not there to make sure Babington wrote something sensible? Something deniable? Something vague that would not risk all our necks?* Then he remembers: Mademoiselle Báthory. He was with her that night, for despite everything he knew about her, and despite his hatred for her, he had been unable to resist. Christ. The things she did to him, and the things she made him do to her. She had rented a house on the Strand—though God knows how and from whom—and she put a pheasant's tail feather up his backside that she had pulled out just as he was making his vinegar strokes, and he would swear he actually fainted. That had only been the first time he had emptied himself that long night, and in the morning, he had been scourged with guilt, and in no fit state even to think about Anthony Babington.

Once more he curses her. She is a Jezebel who has brought nothing but ruin upon him, he tells himself, and he should have killed her while he had the chance, while she was splayed facedown on that bed perhaps, and as he is thinking that, he remembers that in fact it was *him* who was splayed facedown on the bed, and that he never, for one moment, was in control of her: it was always, always the other way around.

He wonders where she will be now?

Halfway to Chartley, he supposes, and he cannot help but wonder what inducements she will offer Gifford if Ballard's vouchsafing of her bona fides does not entirely sway the man, or what she will do if he refuses entirely.

But then he stops, and thinks, and realizes that she might, just might, in fact, end up doing him a favor, even if it means the temporary cessation of communications with Her Majesty in Chartley, because there is every chance that Báthory will kill one or the other of the brewer or Gifford. That might, just might, pray God, mean that Babington's absurd letter either does not get delivered, or even better, if it gets delivered, it stays with Her Majesty, whose answer must also necessarily stay with her.

CHAPTER FORTY-SEVEN

Walsingham's house,
Seething Lane, July 1586

The packet from Phelippes in Chartley sits on Francis Walsingham's desk, unopened, and he stares at it for a long moment, focusing on the small gibbet that someone—Phelippes himself presumably—has drawn on its cover. He wishes Robert Beale were with him now, or Arthur Gregory, or his wife even, how nice that would be, for this is a moment that he would prefer to share with another, to defang it of any great significance with some workaday inconsequentiality; some ordinary little observation about the weather, say, which has been good, hasn't it? Though that is not always welcome, of course; after a week under the sun, London needs a proper deluge to get the drains moving again.

Sir Francis places a finger on the packet and spins it.

If he opens it, his covert struggle with the Queen will be out in the open. It will be an act of defiance that she will interpret as a declaration of war.

He will remember this moment for the rest of his life, he knows that. It is its defining moment. From now on there will be life before he opens this packet, and life after.

Oh, just get on with it, he tells himself.

He opens it.

CHAPTER FORTY-EIGHT

London, August 1586

Babington has lent him a silver crown, so John Ballard buys a good lawn shirt with a spreading collar and, it being a non-meat day, he takes a dish of sand eels and lampreys at an alehouse near Clerkenwell where he also buys a pipe and some tobacco, which he feels is the sort of thing old Captain Fortescue would do, and, it being a warm day, he sits at the long table farthest from the smoking fire, and he drinks his ale and he eats his lampreys and he allows that his mood, for the first time in a month or so, has tipped from being full of nameless dread into one that might almost be called optimism.

For in among the shipwreck of these last few weeks, he has glimpsed what might be the slightest chance of a distant possibility of the opportunity to turn disaster into something that cannot quite be called a triumph, but might at least lead to him finding a way out of all this with life, limb, and dignity intact. And every day that passes during which he hears nothing from the French ambassador, or—most of all—nothing from Mademoiselle Báthory, makes that possibility ever more likely.

It does require Mademoiselle Báthory to murder Gifford and the brewer, of course, so burning the channel of communication between Her Majesty in Chartley and the outside world, but Ballard believes that they were more or less dead men the moment he gave Báthory their names, and what else could he do? He still has not discovered where she keeps that blade, and he had known very well that had he demurred during that night together, she would have killed him in an instant.

Perhaps he overreacted to that business with Babington writing his letter to Queen Mary anyway? Perhaps it had not been that bad? Babington is a deluded young fool, of course, with wildly romantic notions about all this, but isn't that more or less exactly why Morgan chose him? No man with all his wits would ever willingly embark on such a venture. Perhaps it just sounded as if he had committed far more to paper, and to the Enterprise of England, than really he had? Perhaps he was merely boasting?

Ballard feels like something sweet and orders a cup of sugared wine.

When it comes, a new man brings it, not the innkeeper, and he plonks the cup down with such little ceremony that it slops. Ballard is about to give him the rough edge of his tongue, but when he looks up, their gazes lock, and Ballard sees the man has eyes like certain hunting dogs, and that he leans forward to rest both hands spread upon the table and he continues his staring, like no innkeeper ever stares, and he smiles like no innkeeper smiles. Ballard can look nowhere else except into those eyes. He knows who he is. He knows why he has come, and his blood turns to ice, and his bowels loosen, and he loses all grip of himself.

CHAPTER FORTY-NINE

Presence Room, Manor House, Chartley Castle,
Staffordshire, August 1586

Sir Amyas Paulet's disgust is biblical.

"Such an unholy and undignified racket," he says, "and such a waste of money."

Frommond and Dee are sitting with Arthur on the stone mounting block outside the house, just far away enough not to be driven mad by the raucous creak and squeal of the strange musical instruments that Queen Mary and her household seem to enjoy.

Lucy Pargeter is with them, a strange, disquieting presence.

"Bet you wish I'd done her in now, don't you?" she mutters in Frommond's ear.

This joke is too close to the knuckle, of course, but before Frommond can say anything, Sharp the coachman emerges, ruddy faced and very much in his cups, and he weaves his way across the grass to ask Pargeter to come in and dance with him. She refuses and the humiliation makes him angry with them all.

"What's wrong with all you English, eh?" he demands. "Sitting here like you'se shit in your porridge!"

He's about to do something unwise perhaps when Sir Amyas barks at him and he retreats within, muttering words they cannot catch over the bagpipes in the Presence Room. Then they are left, just the five of them, all knowing what they know, and all save Arthur are glutted with the irony that Queen Mary's party—supposedly held in honor of Barbara Curle née Mowbray being delivered safe from childbed, but really to celebrate some secret development they believe to be a step toward freedom—marks instead a great unknowing stride that Queen Mary is taking toward the scaffold.

After a while Paulet shakes his head.

"I cannot stand it," he says, though it is not clear what he cannot stand.

And he departs.

The tension among the English in Queen Mary's household has risen steadily, day by day, since Thomas Phelippes had deciphered the letters in the steward's house. Frommond had stood in the yard, waiting for a word with either Beale or Phelippes when they emerged, but when they did, neither had broken stride on their way to the stables.

"Did they say anything?" Dee had asked afterward.

"Nothing," she'd told him. "Not even a farewell."

"Oh Jesu," Dee had murmured, for now they know the noose is tightening fast. It will be some letter they have found, she supposes, something definitive to prove Queen Mary is conspiring against Queen Elizabeth. Something that will leave Queen Elizabeth with no choice but to act against her cousin or lose the services of Walsingham.

"I could still do it, you know?" Lucy says. "It would be a blessing. One big dose of poppy juice and then a little concoction of my own device and she'd be with her archangels before she could say Loch Lomond."

"No!" they both cry, and Arthur starts.

"Fair enough," she says. "Though I shall have to explain to Her Majesty why I failed her."

⊕

That night, in a lull between Arthur's night terrors, the Dees turn to each other.

"Perhaps we should let Lucy do it?" Frommond whispers. "We would be saving Queen Mary whatever Walsingham has in mind for her?"

Dee shakes his head in the dark.

"Bess will never let Walsingham have her tried, let alone executed. She's a fellow monarch. A prince, Bess would call her, remember? And also, what for? Treason? You can only commit treason against your own country. And Bess will never sign the warrant because of that bloody Bond of Association law."

"It is all so grim," she murmurs. "Mary deserves none of this."

"No one deserves it."

There is a long silence.

"Do you ever think of her?"

"Of who?"

"The woman who—"

"All the time."

"She'd deserve what waits for Mary."

"And more."

Frommond wishes she had not mentioned her aloud. She knows there will be no more sleep for either of them that night.

⊕

The next morning, Frommond climbs out of bed as if her limbs are bags of sand, and she goes down to the hall where Mary Kennedy is slicing bread and singing a jarringly cheerful song. She stops when she sees Frommond, and there is a note of triumph in her voice when she tells her she looks tired.

"I did not sleep," Frommond admits.

"Well, you had best sleep well tonight," Kennedy tells her, "for you will wish to be up bright and early tomorrow to see Her Majesty off!"

"Really?" Frommond asks. She cannot stand Kennedy, and she now actively wishes to lie abed tomorrow. "Where is she going?"

"Hunting!" Kennedy beams. "We are all going ahunting!"

"Hunting? What do you mean hunting?"

Queen Mary has not been permitted to walk beyond the bailey for months, and now she is permitted to go hunting? *Something is very wrong*, Frommond thinks. Can Mary Kennedy not see it?

"Sir Amyas has permitted Her Majesty to go hunting with her bow. What is wrong with you? Do you doubt Her Majesty is still able to shoot a bow?"

Frommond turns and runs to find Dee.

"It will be tomorrow," she says. "They will take her then."

He is chewing something, and he closes his eyes, and nods very slowly.

"They are all so caught up with the thrill of it. The whole household is. And none have stopped to think what it might mean."

"None know what we know," he reminds her.

She sighs, helpless.

"It was always going to happen," she supposes.

And it does.

Queen Mary is up startlingly early, but she takes an age to be got ready, and when she comes down, she is beautifully turned out in midnight silk, with her hair just so, for it seems she believes she is to be hunting with some local gentry. She is so touchingly nervous that Frommond cannot bear even to look at her as she stands among those in her household who are not coming with her but wait in line by the door to wave her off on her day out.

"Why, Mistress Dee," Queen Mary starts when she sees her there, "what can be the matter?"

Frommond finds tears are streaming down her cheeks.

She shakes her head.

"Nothing, Your Majesty," she says. "Nothing."

"Oh, but there is!" Her Majesty is correctly certain. "I cannot bear to go out and enjoy myself thinking of you like this, Mistress Dee. You shall come with us. We shall demand another horse! Or, no! You shall take my spare pony and we shall proceed sedately so as to tire neither out entirely."

"No! I couldn't!" Frommond is too loud.

"You refuse the command of an anointed queen, Mistress Dee," Mary jokes, "albeit of a remote and occasionally inhospitable realm?"

"I would slow you down too much, Your Majesty."

"Nonsense," the queen tells her, and she even takes her arm. "Sir Amyas is coming with us, and between you and me, I do not entirely trust Cache-Cache to behave himself should I have to entrust him to Sir Amyas's care while I take my shot, so I insist!"

Frommond is helpless.

"There!" Queen Mary announces. "It is settled."

And all proceed out into the yard where the horses are waiting, and there is Sharp the coachman, brought to draw and load Her Majesty's crossbow when the time comes, and he is so excited to be venturing beyond the confines of Chartley at last that when he sees that Pargeter has turned out to watch them go, he forgets her snub over the dancing, and heels his horse over to talk to her.

"I shall bring you back something special, Mistress Lucy," he tells her. "And maybe a tail feather for your pretty wee cap."

Pargeter just shakes her head and catches Frommond's eye and makes a face that asks her what she's doing. Frommond can only shrug, and she wants to shout that the queen mustn't go, for can't they see it is a trick? Can't they see that Paulet just wants to separate Mary from her courtiers so they do not cause him any trouble, but meanwhile the queen is in impossibly high spirits and wondering if Arthur would like to come, too, and surely there is a spot for him with the footmen on the coach that will follow along? And Frommond is praying that Dee keeps the boy clear until they are gone. Meanwhile all the queen's ladies are bustling about, ensuring the coach is packed with everything they will need against every conceivable eventuality of the day, except the one that Frommond is sure is to come.

She can say nothing, but hangs her head and refuses an offer of help up into the saddle as they set off with a gentle cheer and a fusillade of claps from those staying behind. They clatter down the track toward the lane that will take them west, toward the moors. Claude Nau drops back to ride next to her, wearing brocade on his waistcoat, and a broad straw hat against the sun, and he wonders why her husband is not joining them today. Frommond tells him that Dee is not much of a one for blood sports, and even as she says the word *blood* she feels her voice waver, but Nau doesn't notice, and instead tells her he doubts they will catch anything.

"For Her Majesty is too long rusty in the saddle."

But her physician, Bourgoing, is more optimistic.

"She has the royal luck," he suggests. "So long as she puts aside that infernal mutt."

Cache-Cache is contentedly tucked into a sling against Queen Mary's breast and might even be asleep.

And then alongside them comes Master Curle, cradling a fearsomely powerful-looking crossbow and wondering why Sir Amyas has not given them any bolts?

"He fears you will put one through his brainpan, Gilbert."

"I would, too," Curle says, laughing, "had he not yielded and let Her Majesty out this day."

But he would not, of course, for they are surrounded—albeit at a polite distance—by two dozen mounted Yeomen who would quickly chop him down. Spirits are very high, however, and they gallop off the road and ride through the bracken with the sun in their eyes, laughing, and halloing and giving outlandish Scottish hunting cries so that surely there is no chance of ever catching any kind of beast unawares, and every now and then the queen must summon one or the other of them back to wait for Sir Amyas, who has not been well, she tells them, and can they not all see he is not a natural rider? When they have ridden five miles or so, and Her Majesty is feeling it in her unused legs, they come together and in a loose bunch they ride through a broad swath of sheep-cropped grass that rises toward some wind-tutored trees on the hilltop. Frommond notes that Paulet has deliberately dropped back now, and that is when they see the men, five of them.

Frommond is close enough to hear Mary's gasp, and she grasps Bourgoing's forearm.

"Who are they?" Bourgoing asks.

Curle turns to Nau, wide-eyed.

"Can it have started already?"

He means the queen's rescue.

Nau cannot be sure. They turn to Mary, who lifts her chin as befits a queen, and heels her horse forward to meet the men, who are now riding slowly toward them. One leads the other, a man in dark green, with flashes of gold brocade, of whom Her Majesty is approving.

"God give you good day, sir!" she calls from a little way off. "Are you perchance sent to greet us by Sir Anthony Babington?"

The man snorts.

"I am not, madam," he says. "I am Sir Thomas Gorges, sent by my mistress, the Queen of England, to tell you that she finds it strange that contrary to all pacts and engagements, that you have been conspiring against her—"

Mary lets out a strangled cry. Cache-Cache starts yipping.

But Gorges carries on.

"A thing she would not have believed had she not seen the evidence of her own eyes and known it for certain."

Cache-Cache keeps up the barking and Mary sends confusing and contradictory signals to her horse, who paces and frets, and she appeals to her secretaries, who are caught with faces aghast.

"Tell him, gentlemen, please!"

Her accent is suddenly much stronger now, and she plucks at her bosom, where she usually keeps her crucifix, and all her gentlemen sit thunderstruck in their saddles, openmouthed with nothing to say other than "no," and "no," and it takes the arrival of Sir Amyas to come and take Queen Mary's reins for anything different to happen, and Frommond hangs her head as Kennedy turns to her and snarls, "You knew!"

CHAPTER FIFTY

Burton-on-Trent, August 1586

The brewer is a disgusting heap of flesh, with the eyes of a tortured pig, and he smells of yeast, but Mademoiselle Báthory will consider anything to get up onto that hill and into the castle, and so she briskly services him among the empty barrels in the store while his wife is raking the barley in the oast house. It is only afterward, as she is wiping her hand, that he tells her that Gilbert Gifford is gone.

"Fucked off back to France, hasn't he, and that fucker Sir 'Am I an arse? Yes' Paulet has canceled my fucking contract so there's no—"

He is dead before his body hits the floor.

The wife she spares, and then Báthory thinks again and returns to stab her in the eye too. She falls into the heap of barley, staring upward into the chimney. Báthory hears children playing over the wall, down by the river, and supposes they might belong to the brewers and she thinks of ushering them into the water, like ducklings, to drown, but decides that will cause too much fuss.

She locks the gate, though, so that they cannot come back

into the yard, and then steals one of the horses, a sad unkempt thing that will do for now, and a shabby traveling cloak to hide her form and her dress, and she mounts up and plods slowly westward toward Chartley. She must pull over at one point as a troop of Yeomen ride past escorting some sorry-looking gentlemen eastward, which makes her think.

She has been to Chartley before, to find Dee. That journey had ended in her riding slowly around the castle and that manor house raised on its hill behind its moat, unable to see a way of getting past the guards, who were unusually alert thanks to a pucker-faced man in black who scuttled about the place shouting at them as if his life depended on it. Even before she had seen how impenetrable Chartley was, she had scaled back her grander plans for Dee's death, and knows now that she will have to be satisfied with merely killing him, and his wife, too, of course, and that boy.

Standing under some elm trees in the fields she had actually seen him and his boy walking on the castle wall, and for a moment she thought they had seen her, but it had been getting on for dusk, and she was in the trees, and they hadn't reacted, so she stayed stock-still and considered if it would have been possible to shoot them with a crossbow, before discarding the idea. You can't shoot three people with a crossbow unless there are three of you, and you all have bows. She has seen it done, against the castle wall at home in Ecséd. It started with a clerk who had ideas above his station, and they chained him and his family together, and her father used only one crossbow bolt to kill the man, who was the heaviest, and when he was pushed into the lake, his weight had dragged the rest of his family in one after the other, like dominoes, all the way down to a babe in arms. Everyone had laughed to see it done, and her father had boasted that he had killed ten people with a click of his fingers, and they had looked about to find another family to do it to, an even larger one, but when they had found one, the smith had to admit that he had not forged enough manacles, or length of chain, so it was him and his family they shot against the walls, in the old-fashioned way—after lunch, with each of them taking up a bow.

Today she ties her horse behind the elms again and waits and watches and notes that while last time she was here there was almost nothing happening—no comings, no goings—today there is a constant stream of men on horses, and carriages rattling up and down the track that winds up to the manor house. If her instincts do not fool her, she would say the household was being disbanded, and she thinks back to those men on the road she saw, and she feels that an opportunity will soon present itself.

So she leaves the horse contentedly cropping the long grass under the trees, and she strikes out around the moat, heading for the road that will lead her up to the gatehouse, and sure enough, she is right. No one thinks to stop her at the guardhouse now, and in the yard before the manor house there is a great commotion as some gentlewomen are being led in tears from the house and induced to climb protesting into caroches or put up on horseback, and they are all demanding to know what has happened to Her Majesty, and none of the men or the Yeomen can help them, for it seems no one knows what has happened to her, only that she is not coming back from wherever it is she's been.

Mademoiselle Báthory cannot understand their accents, and she supposes the women to be the Scottish queen's ladies, and the boxes of papers and clothes that the Englishmen are carrying out to stack on the wagons that wait must be her clothes and her papers. The operation is being carried out as they might a grim chore, overseen by a thin clerkish-looking man with scarred cheeks and red-rimmed eyes.

"Not the beds in that room," he shouts up at someone who is leaning out from a window above. "Leave all that. It is Doctor Dee's chamber."

The head vanishes.

The man turns to her and looks at her closely, and she readies the blade in her sleeve, but at that moment two men ask her to mind her back, and then they ask the first man where he wants this.

"It's fucking heavy, Master Phelippes," one of them says, "so if you've a mind?"

And as he turns to tell them to put it on that wagon over there, Báthory slides quickly through the grand double doors and into the hall where two more Yeomen—who are perhaps supposed to be guarding the stairs—are playing billiards. She is quickly up the stairs, and she opens a closed door to find a large room from the boards of which the carpets have been recently lifted and in its center a bed from which all sheets and blankets have also been taken to expose a horribly stained mattress. The room already smells faintly of a perfume that Báthory recognizes from somewhere in her childhood.

It is not the room she is looking for.

She tries other doors and it is only on the fifth that she discovers the room in which there are still sheets and blankets on the bed, some clothes on a stand, and a hat she recognizes as belonging to Dee's woman. There's a truckle bed pulled from under the bed, which she supposes must belong to a servant.

She hears footsteps in the passage outside.

She slips to the floor and slides across the truckle bed and under the main bed, where she lies in the dusty dark, her nose nearly touching the web of string ties and the feather mattress above. The door opens, and she hears footsteps coming and going, light and ladylike. The woman's? She moves very slowly to slip the blade from her sleeve, but by the time she is ready, the footsteps are gone and the door is shut, and she is alone.

She does not bother to resheathe the blade, but lies there, to wait for nightfall.

CHAPTER FIFTY-ONE

Chartley Castle, Staffordshire, August 1586

Forewarned of what the day will bring, Dee has taken Arthur down to the river to study the eels, and when they come back, weary after their long day, it is to an almost different house. All the guards are gone, and the house is stripped bare, as if robbed by very thorough thieves.

"Even the billiards table!" Arthur says.

Dee puts his hand on the boy's skinny shoulder.

"Well, Queen Mary will want a game now and then, won't she?"

"But where has she gone?"

Dee has no idea. He is more concerned with Frommond. Where is she? He saw how she was suborned into joining Queen Mary's hunting party this morning, and he waved her off unseen from the riverbank, but it will be dark soon, and she is still not back.

"Let's go and see if there is anything left to eat, shall we?"

There is. Leek soup. Dee feels his stomach turn. But the cook is still in residence, and a maid and a footman, and Dee asks if they may join them in the kitchen.

"Bit sad, eating alone in the Presence Room."

They nod and clear a space at their table. The evening light feels almost watery, and they are all of them subdued, and none so much as the maid, who weeps continuously until the cook tells her she will make her soup too salty if she carries on so, and she may go to bed if that is all she can offer, and the footman sighs and rubs his face and then begs Dr. Dee's pardon.

"Not much company, are we, Doctor?"

"Not a bit of it," Dee says. "We shall all miss her very much."

There is some ill-informed guessing as to where she is gone, and Dee asks if they've seen Lucy Pargeter.

"Cleared out, she did," the footman says. "Took all her books and herbs and that, and Sir Amyas's second-best horse, and set off for Burton."

It sounds as if he will miss her almost as much as he will miss Queen Mary, and the cook ruminates that it was quite a thing, wasn't it, serving a queen?

"Don't suppose it'll happen again soon."

Then at last there are hooves in the yard and they are all on their feet and pressing out through the back door to find it is Sir Amyas and Frommond and a single guard dismounting after a long, long day. Sir Amyas retires to his lodgings, and the guard to the stables with the horses, but Frommond sits at the table and wine is brought from the buttery and as soon as Arthur sits in her lap and falls asleep, she tells them how it happened.

"They took everyone away," she says. "Nau and Curle and Kennedy and all the others. They left her with just Bourgoing. And Cache-Cache. And she got off her horse and sat under a tree and refused to move. She told them she had always been a good sister to Her Majesty Elizabeth. Then she started praying and asking God to deliver her as he had once delivered David from his enemies, and then—dear God! Bourgoing started trying to tell her that Queen Elizabeth was dead, and that all this was to ensure her safety, and thank God that none of the soldiers spoke French or they'd have struck his head off there and then."

"Did Mary believe him?"

Frommond drinks deeply.

"Not for a moment," she replies when she's put the cup down. "She threw herself on the ground and wailed that she was of no use to anyone on this earth and that she no longer sought anything save the honor of God's holy name, and the liberty of his church and of his Christian people."

Jesu, Dee thinks, *that is just the sort of thing that gets anyone killed.*

"So where did they take her then?"

"To a house a few miles away. I have forgotten its name. Very handsome, and new-built, but without her maids, or her clothes, and she'd even forgotten that crucifix she wears. She left it here. Asked me to find it for her."

"They've taken everything," the cook says. "Like locusts in the Bible."

"Also her cloth of state. The new one: *En ma fin gît mon commencement*."

It is dark now, and lanterns are lit.

"And she told me about that little house again," Frommond tells them. "The one she'd seen with the view of the loch. I believed her this time."

Dee sighs.

More stories of Mary follow. The cook will never forget her generosity. The footman, her laugh when things went well. Neither liked Mary Kennedy. Mary never went to bed before midnight, and often as late as two o'clock in the morning, but it has been a long day, and at last it is time to turn in.

"Can you manage?" Dee asks Frommond.

She can't, so Dee takes the boy from her lap, and hefts him onto his hip with his head resting on his shoulder. He's still mostly asleep. The cook gets the kitchen door and they cross the yard to the house, which waits in unaccustomed darkness. Frommond carries a rush-dip lamp and she shunts open the scraping door with her shoulder and within the air is still and heavy, still haunted by what is missing, and Dee can almost hear those awful bag and pipes and their terrible screeching sounds.

"Here we are, Arthur," Dee murmurs as he starts up the back steps that leads to their bedchamber, but Arthur suddenly wakes. His head snaps up, his nature changes from soft dough to braced steel in a trice.

"Whoa! Arthur!"

Dee nearly drops him.

Arthur lets out an eerie scream, as he used to during the worst of his nightmares in the weeks after his ordeal, and he thrashes at Dee and tries to spring free, to launch himself away and out of Dee's arms, but Dee clutches hold of him and Frommond is there to try to soothe but the boy is beyond that. He is hysterical and will not stop thrashing and screaming.

"No no no no no no no no no no!"

It gets worse with each step, with the boy's fists and heels flying, so Dee retreats, all the while making soothing noises but having to wrestle to keep ahold of his son, and then back out into the yard where the boy seems to calm a notch, though he still whimpers and weeps; and in the light of the lamp they can see Arthur's eyes are open but he is not awake, and he gives off a choleric heat that almost hurts to touch. It is all so unsettling that Dee feels his hair rippling on end and he, too, starts conjuring up the terrors in the night. When he looks up into the darkness of the landing above, he cannot supress a shudder.

"We can stay out here all night," Dee tells her.

"He'll soon calm down. He has to."

They stand with him for a long while, and let the heat and spring seep out of the boy's weary limbs, then they try again, in through the door and toward the steps, but again the boy stiffens and starts to fight as he babbles and screams, and this time Dee turns about instantly.

"What's got into him?" Frommond asks. "He's as bad as he ever was."

The cook has locked the kitchen, and it is just them standing there now; no night watchman, no porter. It is a lonely position. A broad yellow moon and the distant screech of an owl. They try again, and again, and each time Arthur erupts into agonies, until eventually he exhausts himself, and at the fifth or sixth time of trying they get him up the stairs and into the bedroom, where Lucy Pargeter's truckle bed is still pulled out. Dee shoves it halfway in with his foot, and he uses it as a step to help him lay Arthur's inert body gently on the mattress, fully dressed. Frommond puts the lamp on the sill and lifts the window shutter to block out the night miasmas, and then they themselves quickly undress down to their shirts, and Dee helps Frommond to carefully clamber over Arthur to lie on his one side while he takes the nearside, and they lie there like that, staring at their poor boy in the low aura of the rush-dip lamp.

It is impossible to sleep.

Arthur's breathing is ragged, and he whines and struggles as if against bonds, or as if he is back being tortured in his state of delirious semiconsciousness. He will not settle, but writhes and lunges, and all Dee can do is stroke the boy's sweaty forehead while Frommond sings a gentle lullaby and the lamp dies and the moon sends its light around the shutter to creep across the rushes of the floor to mark the passage of time until at last the boy closes his eyes and he seems to settle into something like a natural sleep, and Dee lies back and rests his head and shuts his eyes.

A moment later he opens them again.

When the bed was pushed in, Báthory was sure they would find her, but she had been lucky, she thought, until the three of them lay on the mattress and it sagged down to press her to the floor. While the boy struggled and they strived to soothe him, she had inched over, so that she could at least breathe, and she wondered what to do. She rejected all other ideas save to slowly try to edge the truckle bed out from under the bed above and slowly set to, expanding herself, and nudging it with her shoulder, elbow, and knee. Every time the boy above thrashed or moved, she would shuffle it half an inch.

But then they seem to have calmed him.

If only she had enough space to unsheathe the blade and stab up, once, into where she is certain the boy is lying, he'd soon be dancing again.

On she goes, inch by painful inch.

It is frustrating, of course, but she does not mind. She imagines they will all be sleeping on their backs, and she can see herself killing them quickly now, with three short stabs, plonk, plonk, plonk, before she can go and find a horse, and set off back home under the light of this well-sent moon.

What was it? What has he heard? Something not right. Some movement in the guts of the house—a sound, a vibration, a shift, an approach.

Dee's heart thunders and his blood crackles in his ears and he very slowly lifts his head. In the sliver of moonlight from around the shutter, he sees that Frommond and the boy are asleep, their faces like alabaster angels, relieved of a greater part of their cares, but when he looks the other way he— His heart races, for there it is again. A noise. A shift. It came again. What was it? A footstep? A whisper? The sound of a sword being eased from an oiled sheath?

He looks down the length of his body, past where his toes tent the linen sheet, and then down to the bed's side. He starts. Dear God! Can it be? The truckle bed is moving? He clenches his eyes, for he knows they are playing tricks on him and what he sees is a projection of some inner fear; of Lucy Pargeter perhaps, he vainly hopes, and when he looks again, the bed is not moving of course.

But then there is the noise again, or no: a different noise, from elsewhere in the house. But it does not feel innocent.

He lifts his head off the pillow.

His eyes continue with their tricks.

The pale sheet of the truckle bed is moving again, he is sure of it, but how can that be? And the noise is coming from somewhere else in the house, and it is coming closer, and the bed is moving again though when he stares at it he is certain it is not, and then when he extends his arm to touch the sheet, it is not moving, and now next to him on his other side Arthur is waking again, and suddenly the bed moves again, he feels it this time, and he feels every hair on his body stand on end and a bellow of terror is about to erupt when with equal force the door of the bedchamber blows open and there is lamplight and suddenly three or four large men in the room, towering over him, up on that truckle shouting.

"Here he is!"

"Got him!"

"Get his legs!"

"Fucking hold him down and if he moves, hit him."

And Dee feels rough, strong hands on him, and bodies weighing him down, pressing him into the mattress. He tries to shout but nothing will come, and now Arthur is awake and he is screaming, and Frommond, too, is sitting up and bellowing at the men to unhand him and get out, and Dee can do nothing else while he tries in vain to fight the gloved hands off him.

"Stop fucking fidgeting," one of the men barks at him, and he is delivered a firm buffet across the face from a gloved hand, and then the lamp is brought closer so he might be inspected and its glow fills the room and gives shape to the men who have him pinned to the sheets. They are of the broad-bodied brigade, bullish blunt instruments.

"Have you got him?" a voice comes from behind their backs. "Where is he?"

And another, thinner, older face inserts itself between the brawny shoulders.

"Where's my cannon, John Dee?" he shouts. "Where's my money?"

It is John Hawkins, early, here to shove his arm up Dee's fundament to pluck out his liver.

CHAPTER FIFTY-TWO

London, August 1586

Anthony Babington is caught five days later, after the city and its attendant villages have been turned upside down and after every house, hovel, and dungheap of every suspected recusant has been thoroughly ransacked. He and Chidiock Tichbourne and a couple of the others appear starving hungry and begging for food from a family in Harrow, and the household servants spread the news. They have spent the days hiding in the woods at Saint John's, living on herbs and whatnot, covering their elegant tailoring with sackcloth and using green walnut shells to darken their otherwise rosy cheeks so that they might pass as commoners. When they are brought back to the Tower, fires are lit, psalms are sung, and the bells of London ring out in celebration.

And one by one the other gentlemen are rounded up, just as Arthur Gregory had predicted they would be, though the last is caught in Worcester, two hundred miles away, and not until two weeks after John Ballard's arrest, but by then Sir Francis Walsingham and Thomas Phelippes are more or less done grinding their way through the other conspirators' testimonies, and there is not much more to be learned, if there was anything there in the first place.

There is no doubt of their guilt, of course, but that is not what Her Majesty's principal private secretary is looking for. Walsingham needs incontrovertible proof that Queen Mary knew of their plot to kill Queen Elizabeth. The hurdle to that, though, is exactly that which Queen Elizabeth identified: there is no proof that the messages "from Queen Mary" were actually from her, for despite the trick of depriving her of her means of communication, and then returning it in the hope she would not be able to resist putting her own pen to her own paper, she has not been half as foolish as has Babington, say, and has insulated herself against any implication in the plot by dictating what she wanted said first to her French and Scots secretary Master Nau, who then passed his notes to her other secretary, Master Curle, to translate into English before enciphering them.

"It's all very well," Walsingham tells his wife as he is getting into bed one night, "but none of these men can prove it one way or the other. For definitive proof we need Nau and Curle to tell us all they know."

"And what will happen to Babington and his gang?"

"Pfffft. Let's not talk about it now, not just as we're going to sleep."

CHAPTER FIFTY-THREE

Residence of the French ambassador,
Salisbury Court, London, September 1586

Mademoiselle Báthory has been in this country almost a year now and has come to hate every square inch of it, but if there was a particular part of it she hates most, it is this road down which she finds herself traveling for the second time, once more on her way to Salisbury Court to see the secretary to the French ambassador, and once more filled with contempt for herself for her latest failure.

To be trapped hiding under a bed while Dee and his family were arrested and taken off like that! Dear God, if the Duc de Guise ever heard of it! She will never tell a soul how when the soldiers finally trooped off, she had to push the bed out and roll out after it and she had been so furious she had cut the ropes of the bed, and slashed the mattress open, and had carried on at it until there were feathers floating everywhere. Then she had left the house in the dark, stolen another horse from the stables, and set off after Dee, save that she did not know which way they had gone, and after an hour in the faint moonlight on unknown roads, she had given up and found a hovel by the side of the road where she'd slept wrapped in her cloak. In the morning she'd woken up being stared at by a black-and-white dog with honey-brown eyes and a boy who kept asking her something in an accent she could not understand. She mounted up, pointed her horse south, and all that day kept finding feathers in her clothes and hair.

At Salisbury Court there was nothing for her from the Duc de Guise, who usually sent her messages care of the ambassador's secretary, and the absence had felt like a whiplash. And she had also had to endure the humiliation of admitting to the ambassador's secretary that she had lost the man he knew she was supposed to be putting an end to, once and for all: John Dee.

"Arrested you say?" he had asked.

She had thought so.

"By who?"

She had not known.

"Then how do you know?"

She had seen.

"Were they Walsingham's men? Or Yeomen? I know the chancellor Sir Christopher Hatton has been trying to have him burned as a conjurer for many years now."

She doesn't know.

"What were they wearing?" he asks.

She had heard, she had corrected herself.

"And what did you hear?"

The secretary—M'sieur Fontenay—had guessed she was hiding something, but he would never have been able to guess what.

"I have my spies," he had said. "I will ask around, and see if he has turned up in any of the usual places. I understand he is no stranger to the Tower, except the cells there are full to bursting."

It had been an invitation to discuss what else was happening in the wider world, but Mademoiselle Báthory was not interested in that.

She wants only Dee and his family.

She still had plenty of money, and that which she needed but could not afford, she stole, and she had found a house on the Strand that belonged to a man—Sir Nicholas Something—whose wife had taken all the house servants and gone to her family's home in somewhere and would not be back until whenever, with a gate onto the road and also one onto the river, so that the porter on the front gate thinks his master leaves by the river, and the porter on the river gate thinks his master has left by the road, when in fact their master lies dead in a culvert in Willesden. It has meant that she has been isolated, though, and knows only that London is in the grip of some tumult, for troops of men in red thunder along the road beyond one gate, and beyond the other, well-appointed barges pass up and down the river at all times of night.

Every day Báthory has the watergate porter hail a lighter to take her to Mortlake, where she finds Dee's house exactly as she left it the night before, with the grass grown long in the orchard, and every other day she goes to see M'sieur Fontenay to discover if he has learned anything about Dee.

"He is in none of the London gaols," Fontenay tells her. He is looking very bleak, and believes she should know why, but she does not care.

"Where can he be?"

"Perhaps he was not so much arrested as kidnapped?" Fontenay wonders.

She thinks about that night, trapped under that bed. Men stamping about the chamber, kicking the truckle bed back under the main bed, and half crushing her against the back wall. There had been something strange about it, hadn't there? The noise, that was it. Apart from the shouting, the men were very quiet. That was it! They were none of them wearing boots. Why ever not? Who doesn't wear boots?

"Sailors," Fontenay tells her. "Sailors never wear boots."

CHAPTER FIFTY-FOUR

Tower of London, September 20, 1586

"How's that poem coming along then?" John Ballard asks.

Chidiock Tichbourne looks up from his scrap of paper with an expression of such infinite pain that Ballard cannot help but roll his eyes.

"Cheer up," he says. "We'll soon be with the heavenly choirs."

"I still believe Queen Elizabeth will pardon us," Anthony Babington tells them. He is leaning against the bars of their cell, seeking the sliver of daylight that comes from a well above, and since the trial ended this last week with a guilty verdict, he has been clean out of his wits.

"That's the problem with people like you," Ballard tells him. "Maybe it is a good thing, actually? You just assume everything will turn out all right, because nothing ever goes wrong for you, does it? You've never had to go hungry day after day, or sleep by the roadside, or watch a child die, and you think it'll go on like this forever, and I suppose it does, until it doesn't, and then you find yourselves in a place like this."

The two men ignore him, or they don't have an answer.

"I met a girl once who put a feather up my bum, did you know that?"

Tichbourne sighs theatrically.

"Oh, get over yourself," Ballard tells him.

Later, when Tichbourne is asleep, Ballard steals the poem and holds it up to the lamp.

" 'My prime of youth is but a frost of cares; my feast of joy is but a dish of pain'?"

Babington is still awake but says nothing. Ballard cannot be bothered to read any more and he leaves the poem where it was, but he might just as easily have burned it, for the atmosphere in the cell is febrile, as if the air is heavier than normal, pressing on them, making their ears buzz, and each man deals with the tensions differently at different times. There are moments when Ballard wishes to beat Babington's smooth handsome face to a bloody pulp, and there are moments when he wishes to embrace him as a brother in arms and tell him that none of this was his fault, that it was Robin Poley who betrayed them, and that they should kneel together, side by side, shoulder to shoulder, and pray for the life of the queen that will be.

Not Tichbourne though. For some reason Ballard cannot feel for Tichbourne as he does for Babington. Perhaps it is because he is ginger? No. It is because he's so long-bloody-faced. Yes, he oftentimes feels like crying, yes! We are all going to die! But that is no excuse to mope about the place blaming others and penning poetry, is it? No reason not to pay the guards to bring brandy, even if it is watered down, and sing songs and try to capture some joy in this world before our candle's snuffed out, is it?

The real problem is that they blame Ballard for it all, for urging them on, for telling them they must kill Queen Elizabeth. As if there was any other way!

Fools.

⌖

The next morning, they come for them. Fifteen Yeomen, five for each, crowding through the narrow confines of the lower dungeons.

"Where are the others?" Babington asks.

He means Savage, Barwell, Tilney, and Abingdon.

"Don't you worry about them," the sergeant of the party advises.

They are taken up the steps, where Tichbourne is tripped, and then out into the Tower's bailey where a small crowd is gathered in silence around a handful of packhorses. Ballard feels very empty and cold, and the world seems thin and wintry, as if in hibernation, or mourning, and he is glad the sky is a scrim of flawless gray the color of a dove, because he does not think he could stand to die under blue skies.

"What about breakfast?" he asks. "Do we not get that?"

The sergeant pulls a face.

"Headsman don't like it," he says. "Gets all over the place. Can I have your coat, sir?"

Ballard hesitates. He'd rather wear it. It is still in good nick and— Hang on, what did he say? About the headsman? He looks down at his belly, at where his breakfast might reasonably be expected to fit, but still can't imagine that what is within will soon be without. The sergeant is behind him, already easing his coat off his shoulders.

"Shame for it to be ruined on the way, though, eh?" he supposes. "And it'll fit me a treat."

Ballard shrugs himself free of it and is now in shirt and breeches.

"I suppose you want my boots?"

"Well, you won't need 'em, will you?"

Ballard crosses to sit on one of the woven hazel hurdles that lie on the ground, and he removes his boots and passes them over, and then he remains there, barefoot, waiting, until he realizes he must shuffle farther up the hurdle, and then he lies down and extends his arms upward, as if stretching in the morning, and the guards use leather thongs to tie his wrists to each of the hurdle's top corners.

He has to stop himself asking them if this is really happening.

They lift the hurdle and hang it by a loop of rope to the horse's saddle, so that he is propped up and can watch the same thing being done to Babington and Tichbourne, who being slighter and smaller must share their hurdle, and he asks Tichbourne if he ever finished that poem about the frost and Tichbourne ignores him.

"Writing a poem, he is," Ballard tells the guards. "About how his life is cruelly cut short."

"Shouldn't've plotted to cut the Queen's short then, should he?" a younger guard asks.

When the others are tied to their hurdles and raised on the back of their horse, there's an order and a drum beats, and the procession sets off with a jerk.

"Christ!" Ballard calls out. "Slow down! We need some wheels on this thing."

Still no one laughs.

The journey really begins when they are through the lion gate, where he can smell the beasts, and he remembers John Savage's eyes in the inn that night, until he sees the crowds waiting for him, armed with every kind of filth that they then throw over him, and the roar of their hatred is horribly sobering.

Save some for the other fellows is what he'd planned to say, but he is so shocked at their loathing of him that he raises his eyes and looks to the heavens just in time to pass under a window and receive a bucket of piss and turds across his legs. The hurdle skids through the mud of Thames Street and the crowd's roar becomes almost impossible to bear but there's nothing to be done. He must just take the blows, and on it goes, and every yard is a freshly enthused stretch of crowd where everyone has saved up their worst missiles, and he flinches and bucks as he is hit by stones, and bones, and bits of old wood, and a dead rat and everyone shouts at him to tell him he's a fucking traitor and they hope what is about to happen to him hurts like where he will be spending eternity for what he planned to do to Her Majesty. And on it goes, on and on, until he is battered, bruised, and covered in every filth imaginable and he cannot even make his bellows of rage and pain heard.

Ballard is too shocked to wonder where he is being taken, but eventually he sees the underside of one of the city gates and realizes it must be Ludgate, and then they are out of the city but here the crowds are even worse and the Yeomen must fight to stop men and women beating him with sticks, until he is dragged into a clearing where the crowd are held at bay by two lines of soldiers and more wicker hurdles, in what must be Fickett's Field, he supposes. He knows he has crossed this exact spot many a time, on his way to and from meetings with Savage and Babington and even Mademoiselle Báthory, and he realizes perhaps this is why they've chosen here to kill him, in sight of Saint Giles-in-the-Fields. When he looks up he sees a tall scaffold—twice the height of a man—above which tower some even taller gallows, over which a few ropes are looped and against which are propped three or four fruit-pickers' ladders.

The din of the baying crowd is tremendous, but at least they have stopped throwing things, and when he is untied and helped to his feet, he turns to face the people and has never in all his life seen so many gathered anywhere at once. It is as if the world has emptied and sent everyone here to shout at him and wave their fists. Babington and Tichbourne need help standing, but then Babington collects himself and raises his chin, and Ballard thinks, *Well, here's to you for that, at least.*

"Come on, you," a florid-faced butcher calls in his ear and he is pulled along by a couple of equally big, bald men with leather bracers on arms as thick as legs, and heads like gunstones, and they turn him and tie his hands very firmly behind his back and then steer him almost gently toward where a priest waits, trying not to look terrified by the noise and crowd and thoughts of the spectacle to come. The butchers take him to some steps and lead him trudging up the sanded treads and Ballard wants to tell them that this has all been a mistake and that something should and could be worked out. But before he gets the chance he is out onto the scaffold, suddenly towering over the sea of upturned faces, and he cannot resist turning around to look at the places he knows all too well, but never seen from this exalted position. He fancies he sees the exact bush behind which he gave Savage the pistol, but then he notices the dark tub of an iron brazier half full of glowing coals above which the air dances and part of him is surprised to see it, and another part of him seizes up, and it is impossible really to believe, and then there to one side is a chunky-legged, much scarred and stained butchers' table on which are spread the grim black implements of the shambles' trades, and he thinks back to the buying of that goat's head almost fondly.

The priest arrives up the steps, quailing as if he is also afraid of heights, and then after an awkward moment when he, too, takes in the brazier and the knives and the axes, he holds up his hands for silence from the crowd. He is granted some, though those at the back will never hear anything said, so they keep up a riotous hubbub, and he turns to address Ballard and to tell him to kneel, and Ballard kneels and the priest asks him to acknowledge his faults and confess his sins.

"For the matter of which I am condemned," Ballard announces in his strongest Fortescue voice, "I willingly do."

"And will you ask Her Majesty's forgiveness?"

"If I have offended her, then I do humbly beseech it."

"And will you renounce your Catholic faith?"

"I will not," Ballard says, rising from his knees now and turning to the crowd, who seem to enjoy a show of something from their dead men, even if it is heretic defiance, and he asks as many of them here who are of the Catholic faith to pray for him, for he hopes to be with the angels of heaven before the half hour is out. There is some booing from the crowd, but that is to be expected, and then one of the sheriffs takes his elbow and pulls him back from the edge toward the foot of one of the ladders and a heavy necklace of rope is dropped over his head and tightened before he can even think of ducking out of it, and he is grateful, for he would have tried otherwise, and spoiled his show of bravery, and ruined the reputation of gallant old Fortescue.

"Come on then, sir," a man standing three or four rungs up one of the other ladders says, "take a few steps. You'll not fall."

He can feel hands hovering behind him, and then a third man on a third ladder is by his side to hold his shirt just above the elbow, and that is enough to balance him as he takes a step up the ladders, wishing that he had not given his boots away. Someone is pushing him from behind now. He can feel their hands on his buttocks, and the cool fat rope starts to pull him up, too, and he can hear it creak against his ear.

"That's it," someone encourages, "you're doing fine."

He has to take more steps and he finds himself scuttling up the rungs all in a rush and all the prayers that he had meant to pronounce aloud now seem to stick in his throat. The words fly from his mind as the rope tightens and then one of the men next to him, whose hand had been a reassurance that he would not fall backward, turns traitor, and gives him a hefty shove. His feet slip. His toes lose contact with the ladder rung as it is pulled from under him and the rope hits him across the throat like an iron bar. His brain erupts in stars and flames and he lunges to get a footing somewhere, but there's nothing, and his heart thunders in his ears and the world thickens and blackens, as if being burned, and something monstrous seems to be growing within him, crowding out his innards. He sees fantastical shapes as his eyes roll into the back of his head. His chest roars with pain for something that does not come and cannot be gotten and—and then it is as if he has crested a hill, and he achieves a moment of accord with the pain, and his blood feels aglow and the darkness is no longer to be afeared and he has no more fight in him, and the acceptance of the pain under his tongue is an inkling of perfect peace—and then he is falling suddenly and he lands in an abrupt and agonizing jolt that shakes him and he can suddenly breathe but he is also winded and his ankles must be broken. The noise comes roaring back to him like a wave breaching on a shingle shore and light breaks in, too, as he is recalled to life and dreadful pain.

Someone frees him of the weight of the rope, and he feels almost delirious, as strong hands cup his arms and legs, and he is lifted and carried and he believes he might be with angels, and there will be no more sorrow, no more tears, no more pain. He will be lain in a feather bed and his mother will be there to stroke his forehead, and he will be warm under down-filled quilts while the room is cool and he remembers his boy, and he will be there, too, and someone will be holding his hand in her cool palms, but then he is thumped down on a hard surface, and his shirt is wrenched up and his breeches are tugged down and dear God! Someone is handling his nethers and he is able to let his eyes open a flicker to see a bald man coming at him with a huge, chipped, filthy knife, and thus does he learn the meaning of real pain.

CHAPTER FIFTY-FIVE

Portsmouth Harbor, England, September 1586

They have been given a small house, and a servant, and nine armed guards to make sure neither Frommond nor Arthur leave without John Hawkins's permission. The house smells of fish guts and rotting seaweed. It possesses not one stick of furniture save a stained palliasse on which lies a woolen blanket impregnated with what might be whale oil.

"I will not be long," Dee promises Frommond. "I will get the money somehow, even if I have to sell everything we own."

Which will not raise the thousand crowns he owes Hawkins, perhaps, but despite feeling sick with guilt at the pain and misery he has once more inflicted on Frommond and Arthur, Dee is strangely confident of his success. He cannot tell them that it is because of the golden orb, though; that it has been giving him strong signals that what he seeks—King Arthur's treasure—lies not in Glastonbury as was commonly supposed, nor indeed in Wales, but to the north, somewhere toward London. He cannot talk to Frommond of it, of course, and how he misses Roger Cooke at moments like this. Roger would have sat and listened to his theory with just the right level of skepticism, one that did not nix it completely but prompted a higher striving.

Hawkins very reluctantly lends him a horse.

"It's on the bill, Dee," he tells him.

Yes, yes, whatever.

And Dee sets off plodding up the London road, just as he did with Roger the year before, save this time alone but for his golden orb that swings in its curious, unnatural way, as if the chain were a rod, toward the northeast. He rides on all day, and even stops in the White Hart, where they recognize him as the fellow who slept in the stables, and then he sets off again and rides briskly past the spot where Roger was killed, for what point is there in lingering?

When they had ridden this road south to Portsmouth, after three days and nights spent crammed into a caroche rattling down from Chartley, he had pointed out where Cooke had been killed. Hawkins had still not believed him, for the most part because he had not wanted to.

"Get me those bloody missiles, Dee, or I will have your wife's liver too!"

"But I keep telling you, Hawkins, that I can't. Cooke invented them and he is dead."

"But we had a deal, Doctor! You shook my hand in the Pelican Inn. Walsingham bore witness."

"I don't know what else I can tell you, Master Hawkins. God knows I would love to satisfy the terms of our agreement, but as I keep trying to explain to you, the man who invented the canisters is dead, and he has taken their secret to his grave."

It had been unstoppable force moving immovable object.

"Then I want my bloody money back," had been the best Hawkins could do. "With interest!"

Which had seemed astonishingly reasonable, given Hawkins's

reputation, and his threats, and for a brief moment Dee had hoped his would then become just another to be added to the long list of names to whom Dee owed money—near the top perhaps, for his threats were colorful and persuasive—but Hawkins had other plans, and so rather than drop Dee and his family by the side of the road and leave them to make their own way back to Mortlake, he had effectively kidnapped them and taken them all to his property outside Portsmouth where they were to remain until every last penny of the thousand crowns was repaid.

"Is that legal?" Frommond had wondered.

Hawkins had looked disgusted just to hear the word.

But the sailors had been kind, especially to Arthur, and though he had not left Dee's side since it had happened, he had not needed to, and there must have been enough succor in being with both his parents that he did not succumb to the paralysis that had once again risen up to grip him the night Hawkins came for them.

And so now here Dee is, riding with the sun on his back once again, only this time alone, and at the behest of his orb. Every now and then he dismounts, to see if it is the rhythm of the horse that influences the minute signals that travel up the chain to his ungloved fingers. Dee is curious about where the orb is taking him, but some say that Camelot was in Winchester, so there is every chance that King Arthur came this way, on his way up to Westminster, of course, or, wait, Canterbury? The orb is now taking him eastward in that direction, along the old pilgrims' path that winds through the Weald of Sussex and Kent.

Well, why not?

He rides for a day until he reaches a small stream and he stops to let the horse drink and rest and he takes the orb from his purse and sets it swinging again. The movement almost startles him it is so strong. He takes the horse's reins and leads it along the stream until they come to a small village below a hill. The orb takes him up the hill toward a burned-out mill, and it is easy to imagine King Arthur standing there, doing—something, but perhaps not burying treasure. Though why not?

The orb takes him to the mill, past a badgers' set to a rock that has been turned over to reveal some diggings, where if something had once been buried, it has been recently unburied, and Dee stands there and stares down at the mud for a few long moments. So the orb has brought him to the exact point where King Arthur's treasure *was* buried? The exact spot where it no longer is? He looks at the orb as if it might have some sort of expression on its entirely smooth spherical face. It doesn't, but nor is it entirely still.

Dee has an idea and finds in his doublet the eyeglasses that Digges made him, and he puts them on, and looks again at the orb, and then back at the hole in the mud, and then, after a moment, there comes the faintest tremor. It feels as if the orb has been thinking, deciding what to do, or waiting for him to put the eyeglasses on, and now it has decided what to do, and it guides him toward a coppiced beech tree, where the leaves have been well scattered, but there is a distinct mound, the earth of which yields under Dee's toe cap.

A moment later and he is reunited with most of John Hawkins's silver crowns, and he sits for a moment, feet in the hole, staring at the muddy bags, and thinking what a strange world it is.

"Now if you could only find me that cannon," he tells the orb, but then he supposes that is asking too much of it, and really, that he should be grateful for what he is given, which is after all, nearly all the money he needs to repay Hawkins. He acknowledges that the orb has more than earned its keep, but then—human nature being what it is, he supposes—while he is loading up the saddlebags, he cannot stop himself thinking about that cannon, and the irritating mix-up with the bailiffs and the scrap metal dealer and the ironmaster, and he is still thinking about this while he leads the horse back past the burned-out windmill and down the hill toward the village and it is only when he is back on the pilgrims' path, heading west, back toward Portsmouth in the hope Hawkins will accept the lion's share of what he is owed, when by newfound force of habit he takes out the orb and lets it hang for a moment, expecting nothing, only to feel that telltale thrill through his fingers and up his wrist, telling him to go not west, not back toward Portsmouth, but east.

"Well, well," he says, turning the horse around.

CHAPTER FIFTY-SIX

Tower of London, London, September 1586

It is the week after John Ballard, Anthony Babington, and the other dozen conspirators were executed, and the atmosphere in London, especially among Walsingham's men, remains flat and peculiar. They try to justify what happened—to tell themselves that Babington and his men were merely served their just deserts—but none can really believe that, and when they are alone, or at night, or in their cups, then guilt will gnaw their innards, and the grisly spectacle of that first day will return to play itself out again, and again, and again.

It took two days in total: seven men on the first; seven on the second. But by the evening of the first it seemed the whole world was sickened by the sight of the castrations and the eviscerations, by the sounds of men screaming as they were cut and gutted, and by the smell of blood and roasting offal, and so by the second day the Queen was persuaded to incline toward mercy, and the butchery was ordered to be stopped. The last seven men were still dragged to the scaffold but the crowds kept away, and then they were hanged until they were dead and carted off to be thrown in the river, because by then anyway, they already had more than enough heads to fill the pikes on the drawbridge castle, and the lad they paid to carry the sack of tar-dipped skulls up to the leads had to chuck the old ones away into the river first.

"Like planting a whole new crop," Robert Beale now observes from the battlements of the White Tower where they are waiting for the bringing up from below of Queen Mary's secretaries, Masters Claude Nau and Gilbert Curle.

"Hope he washes his hands afterward," Walsingham murmurs.

Beale tries to follow the heads, tracing the exact path he took through the water that night last year, but they sink, or he loses them, and anyway, it is time to go below to resume their questioning of the two men on whose testimony Queen Mary's life can—with just a little more effort to clarify things—no longer depend.

It all hinges on the letter that Queen Mary had sent to Anthony Babington in reply to his very rash boast of troops coming from abroad, and his promise that he would personally rescue her while six noble gentlemen would undertake the tragical execution of Queen Elizabeth. Phelippes had taken barely an hour to decipher it, and it was this decryption on which he had penned a small drawing of a gallows to signify its importance, but it was not conclusive proof that Queen Mary had conspired against Queen Elizabeth because there was no incontrovertible proof that Queen Mary had written it herself, or dictated it herself, or even seen it or knew what was in it.

Under close questioning Queen Mary's secretary for English matters, Gilbert Curle, has told them that he translated the letter as it was written in French by Claude Nau, first into English and then into code, which sounds plausible, but when questioned about this, Queen Mary's secretary for French matters, Claude Nau, told them that Curle translated it from French written not in his hand, but by Queen Mary herself, and that this piece of paper is to be found somewhere among all the piles of paper they took from Chartley on the day of Queen Mary's arrest. So they have become fixated on this piece of paper and have been going through all her papers for the third time of asking, and still with no luck.

Without that piece of paper, it can still be argued Claude Nau had composed the letter. Or Gilbert Curle. That is vanishingly unlikely, it is true, but as Walsingham does not need to remind either Beale or Phelippes, they are dealing with some complicated standards of proof, and they know the only way Walsingham will ever be able to force Queen Elizabeth to sign Queen Mary's death warrant is with definitive, undeniable proof that it was Mary who composed the note to Babington, that it was Mary who conspired to have her killed.

Which they cannot find.

"So let's try another way," Phelippes says as they resume their seats around the table in the constable's office.

"Bring up Master Nau."

Later, in Walsingham's office, with warm wine and a good salmon pie, they raise their cups to Phelippes's skill at copying the letters so carefully that Curle thought they were the originals, which Babington had in fact burned.

"And another funny thing," Sir Francis tells them, finding again the report from one of his agents, "John Hawkins has kidnapped our old friend Doctor Dee, and he's holding his wife and child hostage in Portsmouth until Dee repays the money Ballard stole."

"Oh dear God," Phelippes says, laughing, "they'll be there until doomsday!"

CHAPTER FIFTY-SEVEN

Mortlake, west of London, October 1586

The first properly cold day of the autumn and Mademoiselle Katherine Báthory has the watergate porter hail her a lighter to take her upstream, but at this time of day, with the tide so far out, the river can be very quiet, and they must stand and wait for one. The porter takes the opportunity to chat.

"Mortlake again, is it, Mistress?" he asks.

"Yes."

"And Sir Nicholas not about again?"

He means the owner of the house, the man still lying dead in the culvert in Willesden.

"No."

"Only I ain't seen him for a week or two, and I was talking to Master Clayton, the porter on the other gate, and he ain't seen him neither?"

She does not ask him to elucidate his meaning, but he goes on anyway.

"So we're thinking that maybe Sir Nicholas ain't here? That he's gone somewhere, and maybe he don't even—"

It looks like he's slipped and fallen into the mud below the steps, and she watches his body sink into the ooze, and there is a moment when all that can be seen of him is the pink tip of his nose but that is soon gone and by the time a lighter finally appears, and by the time she steps down into it, there's no sign of the man save for a few bubbles and his hat, but since that is almost exactly the same color as the mud, the lighterman does not wonder at it.

As he pulls her westward, she has the feeling that something is coming to its end. Not just her living in Sir Nicholas's house on the Strand, but something more fundamental is about to conclude, and so she is not precisely surprised finally to see signs of life in Dee's house. There is smoke from the chimney, and a door is open in one of the huts nearer the river.

"Take me in," she tells the lighterman, but only once they are farther upstream, so that she can survey the situation, and she gets out onto a built-up gravel bank that might once have belonged to a monastery. She ushers the lighterman away and walks back along the river after him. When he is out of sight, she lets the blade in her sleeve drop.

By the time she has made her way back along the riverbank to Dee's garden, the shed door is shut and locked, and the house is deserted once more.

She rests her head against the gate and closes her eyes.

After Dee and his family were taken by the barefoot men whom M'sieur Fontenay supposed might be sailors, Báthory had almost given up hope: he had been taken to sea, and there was nothing further she could do. Fontenay suggested she send word to the Duc de Guise, but that felt like an admission of failure, which she was not yet prepared to entertain.

"I will ask such contacts as we have in this country," Fontenay had said. "Find out if there are gangs of sailors who kidnap families."

It had sounded hopeless, even then, and in the meantime, all she could do was wait.

But now someone was here. Someone is back.

Will they come back?

Yes.

So she will wait.

PART | FIVE

CHAPTER FIFTY-EIGHT

Fotheringhay Castle, Northamptonshire, October 1586

It is raining hard on a filthy evening when after four days and nights on the road, Queen Mary sees Fotheringhay Castle for the first time, and she cannot help but gasp.

"What is it, Your Majesty?" Mary Kennedy asks.

Then she, too, sees it, and her instinct is to cross herself.

"We've seen worse, surely?" Master Bourgoing claims. "Lochleven? Craigmillar? Dunbar even?"

"Och, they were grim," Mary Kennedy agrees.

But Fotheringhay is grimmer yet: ancient gray stone, like a widow's tooth, set high on a motte and with its feet encircled by sluggish river and sheets of flooded fenland that are so flat and so alien to Queen Mary of Scotland that were she more superstitious she might believe they were approaching the very edge of the world.

The caroche rattles over the castle drawbridge, in through the gatehouse, and is taken in a neat circle of the yard to be left facing the steps that lead up to the keep. The door is wrenched open. Since she has been accused of conspiring against Queen

Elizabeth's life, all her guards are permitted to express their hatred of her, and anything and everything that needs be done for her is done with brusque contempt, so that now this Yeoman standing holding open the door of the caroche looks as if he might slam it on her before she is halfway out, and kind Master Bourgoing steps forward to shelter her from the possible blow.

When they have climbed the steps to the keep they are drenched, and Queen Mary is exhausted, but they are met by Sir Amyas Paulet, who makes them keep climbing.

"Your rooms are to be at the back, ma'am," he tells them.

And when they find them, they are so small that Cache-Cache growls when he enters.

"Why are we not allotted the staterooms?" Mary Kennedy wonders aloud, and it strikes Queen Mary that she knows why: the staterooms are reserved for others.

"They are for my judge and jurors," she tells them.

And so it proves.

The silence in the makeshift Presence Room at the back of the castle where the windows are unglazed and closer in size and shape to arrow loops is profound and sorrowful as her much-diminished household members consider what this means: the next stage along the path to death.

"There is no point in weeping," she tells her women. "Let us at least see to our legacy."

They assume she means her will, and she does, but she is now reconciled to the fact that her son, James, is not going to change his course; he is not going to intervene, to ask her back to rule with him. He has abandoned her for the chance to become Elizabeth's successor, and so there is the matter of her inheritance to consider, specifically her claim to the English throne. Her son inherits his claim through her, but what is there to stop her passing it not on to him, but to someone else? To Felipe of Spain?

Nothing.

Except she still has no way of promulgating her wishes.

If she wrote it in her will, and left it to be discovered, then the English would suppress it, so her problem remains the same as it always has: How shall she get word out there?

And she thinks back to the time to just before they began to use the brewer to get her letters and messages out, and how she had written a will divesting her son of his claim to England and had actually put it in the hands of Mistress Dee. She had believed it was a letter to James, pleading a mother's love—and it was that—but included in the visible text was a clue that would have alerted the French ambassador to hold the letter over a candle, and had he done so he would have discovered the new will, leaving her claim to England to King Felipe of Spain.

As soon as the letters began to flow again, she had been relieved to learn that Mistress Dee had not managed to send the letter and so she had asked for its return, meaning to send similar through the brewer, and she had destroyed it—thanks be to God—for fear that should the English find it, they would privily show it to James, to further increase their estrangement.

Now, though, what has she to lose?

"Mary," she says, summoning Kennedy to her side, "let us ask Sir Amyas if he will permit us one more member of our little household, shall we?"

CHAPTER FIFTY-NINE

Whitehall Palace, October 1586

Robert Beale has never seen the Queen so enraged.

"So despite our most earnest beseeching, Master Beale," she shouts, "you have done precisely nothing to prevent happening that which we very specifically instructed you to prevent happening."

It is not a question he can answer by telling her that he tried to shoot Gifford and then became so sick of his duplicity that he threw himself into other tasks—the wrapping up of Babington's plot—little realizing that in doing so he was only abetting Sir Francis's scheme to entrap the Queen of Scots.

He can only hang his head.

"And so now it seems our royal cousin, the Queen of Scotland, is to be brought before a commission of commoners who, though no doubt the highest in the land, are still in no position to pass judgment on an anointed queen and have no right to do so!"

Now she gives in and hurls a silver ewer of wine to crunch against the wainscoting, splashing the tapestry above and the Turkey carpet below.

"And more than that! They will then condemn her to death!"

Beale stands staring down at the buttons on his doublet and cannot hang his head any lower. He has heard of men being dragged from this room to spend years in the Tower—Sir Thomas Perrot was one of them—for the slightest indication of lèse-majesté, and now here he is, accused, however unfairly, of defying a specific order. She will have him beheaded, or worse, set Perrot on him, who is on his way back from the battle of Zutphen with a pike wound to his right buttock that is a source not only of great pain but also profound humiliation, and there is only one way a man like Perrot assuages things: by inflicting the same on others.

"Which is the thing," the Queen continues in a rising shriek, "the very thing, the only thing, above all else that we wished to avoid!"

Another something smashes elsewhere in the room. He can hear her breathing very heavily just behind him, and he believes for a moment that she will brain him with what? A scepter? He stands clenched, ready to receive the blow. But she walks around in front of him and stares at him long and hard, but he dares not look up. He can almost feel the heat of her anger as she stands before him, and then, with a very sharp movement, she drives a knee deep into his testicles.

He reels back and falls to the polished floor and lies there jackknifed while pain and nausea compete to kill him. Before either succeed, or yield, he is aware that she has come to stand over him, and when he opens his tear-filled eyes, she bends to glare at him, her eyes like chips of fire and her mouth a crimped line.

"That is like nothing compared to what you can expect when Sir Thomas Perrot gets back, Master Beale, so we suggest you get up off our floor and get to work averting this catastrophe!"

CHAPTER SIXTY

Portsmouth, October 1586

If John Dee has ever been more tired, he cannot remember when, but here he is at last, at the lodge house of Hawkins's estate just outside Portsmouth. It has been raining hard, and he is in clothes that will not be dry properly until next summer, but it is Nurdle for whom he feels the most pity. The poor horse has come all this way from Mortlake again, once more with the cannon in the bed of the cart and the silver, though this time without the weight of Roger Cooke, and he needs a proper rubdown followed by a month under cover with a sack of oats. Will Hawkins give him that? Probably not. Also, Dee has promised to get him back to Thomas Digges's brewer within the week.

The gatekeeper waves him on, and Dee flicks the switch over Nurdle's flanks, and the horse sets off at a trudge toward the little house where Dee knows he will find Frommond and Arthur, but before he can reach it, here comes a party of horsemen straight from the stables of the main house, led by none other than Hawkins himself, who looks half as comfortable on a horse as he does on the bridge of a ship.

"Where's my money, Dee?" he shouts while still fifty paces away.

Dee gestures wearily to the bed of the cart.

"The most part of it," he says.

Hawkins has a face the color of goose fat, from which the rainwater runs in streams, and he rides around the back of the cart, where Dee turns to watch him dismount and flap the sailcloth off the piled bags.

"And the cannon," he notes with grudging approval.

Dee nods.

He taps the bags as he counts them.

"Three bags shy, Dee," he tells him as if Dee did not already know. Dee hangs his head. He had hoped that Hawkins would take the cannon as the difference, but he's too tired to try to strike a bargain with Hawkins right now. He just wants to go and lie down out of the rain, and he wants to lay eyes on Frommond and Arthur.

"Can we talk about it afterward?" Dee asks.

"After what?"

"After I've at least seen my wife."

"Well, if it is her you're looking for, you've come to the wrong place, Dee. She's not here. Yeomen took her off in one of the Queen's caroches. Wanted urgently apparently, up north, with the Scotch queen. Taken that boy of yours with her, too."

Dee cannot believe what he's hearing.

"Where?"

Hawkins consults one of the other horsemen.

"Fotheringhay."

"Where's that?" Dee asks.

"Pfffft," Hawkins says, gesturing northward. "I don't know. Don't care."

"Why did you let her go?" Dee wonders.

"Couldn't say no; she was sent for by Her Majesty."

Dee shakes his head. Raindrops fly from his nose. Nurdle hangs his head. So many questions, and Hawkins never likes to answer any of them, even if he knew the answers.

"But I'll keep the money, Dee," Hawkins tells him, "and the cannon."

CHAPTER SIXTY-ONE

Mortlake, west of London, October 1586

Mademoiselle Báthory had answered the gate to the pursuivant four days ago, and his question had taken her by surprise.

"Mistress Dee?" he'd asked, supposing her to be she.

"No," she'd said.

"Where is she?" he asked plaintively.

The man—he had been no more than a boy really—had been in red and blue wool, with a big embroidered badge that read ER above a crown on his doublet, and though he was already quite road-splattered, his horse had been fresh, contentedly cropping the weeds at the foot of Dee's wall.

She'd quickly sized him up and had smiled.

"Within," she'd said, opening the gate.

He'd misinterpreted her intentions and a moment later he'd lain dead in the courtyard with a hole in his eye and in his purse she'd found the message intended for Mistress Dee: at the request of the Scottish queen she was to repair to the castle of Fotheringhay.

Báthory had started with the buttons on the pursuivant's doublet, and a little later had swung herself up into his saddle, pleased to think of all the Queen's messengers now scouring the country looking for Dee's wife so that they might send her to Fotheringhay, wherever that is, where she—Mademoiselle Báthory—will be waiting for her, and her husband, and her son, who will surely be trailing along behind.

All she needs to do is to find this Fotheringhay place.

CHAPTER SIXTY-TWO

Fotheringhay Castle, Northamptonshire, October 1586

Jane Frommond and Arthur do not reach Fotheringhay until after the trial has finished and the commissioners and all their various servants have dispersed back to their various counties to consider their consciences.

"Just as well," Sir Amyas's chamberlain tells her. "We've had men sleeping in the corridors of the stables."

He is not displeased to see her, though, and gives them a room at the back of the castle, facing south, with a Turkey rug and moderately soiled mattress in a bed with curtains on, which someone has painted scenes from the expulsion of the Garden of Eden.

"No maid this time?" he asks, and when she shakes her head, he confides that he thought her last one was useless, and he is not surprised she got rid of her, "but I've never seen anyone so lucky at primero."

That is not the reason I got rid of her, Frommond nearly tells the man.

It has been a long, long journey, on very bad roads, through

Reading and Oxford and then east through lands so flat and low the caroche wheels seemed to be rolling through the sea, and every dwelling was raised up upon an island. It had rained all the time, and now everything that she and Arthur possess is sodden and growing mold.

"Why are you here?" Mary Kennedy had bristled when she first saw her, as if Queen Mary had not warned her she was coming, and Frommond had had to pretend she had no idea, though she does: she believes that now that Queen Mary's conduit to the outside world is once more blocked, she once again wishes to use her to send word to her son. Frommond has more or less decided she will not, since she is become certain, for reasons she cannot explain, that Dee was right, and that there was more to the letter than appeared.

The warmth of Queen Mary's welcome confirms something anyway.

"Mistress Dee!" she cries, standing rather than sitting in the middle of her stateroom and seemingly restored to health now that the trial is done with, and seemingly blithe about the verdict, which the world is still to learn. "Welcome back to our little world! Shrunk since last we saw you, owing to the unkind vicissitudes of time and tide and Lord Burghley and Sir Francis Walsingham, of course, but we still have our billiards table, Master Arthur, look, and though we lack the company of Masters Nau and Curle, we have been practicing daily, and fancy you will find us none too shabby in that department!"

She seems relieved of her past burdens, as if she believes the trial went well, and that it may lead to her freedom, but later, on a tour of the views from the stateroom windows while Arthur plays billiards with M'sieur Bourgoing, Mary confides that her cause is in the hands of God.

"I did not attend the second day," she admits. "There was no point. There were twenty-four of them, and they had all sorts of letters that I was supposed to have written in my own hand but would not show me, as well as the testimonies not only of M'sieur Nau and Master Curle, but of this man Babington, too, whom they have already put to death, did you know, along with all his friends whom they claimed I had encouraged to put an end to our sister of England?"

Frommond had heard.

"And so now we await their verdict," Queen Mary says with a shrug.

Her change of circumstances, which to the outside eye appears disastrous, seems to have changed some inner clock in Queen Mary. Gone is the heaviness, the anchored purposelessness and instead there is a light steeliness, as well as a genuine cheerfulness. She seems reconciled to something. Perhaps because she has learned her real enemy is Sir Francis Walsingham, and she has seen his moral squalor? Or perhaps it is as simple as the fact that after eighteen years she has something, anything, that genuinely matters to look forward to? Either way, she no longer stitches her tapestry with complicated little hints, but lays out her design with bold insistence.

"Mistress Dee," she asks, "we asked our sister of England to permit you to come to us to give us succor in our hour of need, and though she has never been one to dip too deep into her own purse, if something costs her nothing, she oftentimes provides, and so she has with you, for which we are grateful."

"It is my pleasure, ma'am."

"But we were not being entirely candid with our sister of England, because although you are a boon companion to us in this our hour of need, we hope there is a more tangible service you may be prepared to do us."

CHAPTER SIXTY-THREE

Fotheringhay Castle, Northamptonshire, October 1586

Nurdle gives up the ghost in heavy rain on the road just north of Aylesbury. The poor horse is exhausted, and when he cannot take another plod, he keels over in his traps and is dead before his head hits the ground. Dee had been walking alongside him, along a causeway between two water meadows, and there is no one in sight to help pull him off the road, or take the cart, so after a prayer and an apology, Dee must leave him to it and continue along the road northward.

He can move faster without Nurdle, and the next day he sees the castle from leagues away; and in a break in the weather, Dee appreciates the way it is designed to dispel hope in anyone thinking of trying to gain entry without permission, an impression that is only confirmed up close, for it is raised up above a moat, up on an island in a broad river, with towering curtain walls, and a double-towered gatehouse at each drawbridge. You would stand more chance of taking it with a navy than an army.

Dee walks through the little village with its new built bridge across the river where each bank is lined with reed-cutters' punts and he approaches the northern gatehouse and is rebuffed, of course, for he hardly looks the part, but he manages to persuade the sergeant of the Yeomen to send word to Sir Amyas Paulet, and Paulet sends a servant who recognizes him to be whom he says he is.

"Still got to search you, Doctor, up and down, in and out, if you know what I mean?"

Dee does.

"Very thorough, thank you," he tells them when it is done and he must put his sodden clothes back on.

Then he is permitted through the gates, which close behind him with a definitive boom, and he is escorted by five Yeomen past the various outhouses and the chapel where more guards wait under awnings, and up the steps of the motte where a bored Yeoman knocks on the huge doors for him, and he must send for the porter to find the chamberlain, and while he waits, Dee sits on the steps and studies the featureless countryside.

"Quite something, isn't it?" a young Yeoman tells him, meaning the castle, and Dee supposes that while it is not the Tower, or Windsor, its position and its size, and its rain-darkened stones make a powerfully imposing statement of intent.

"Old King Richard was born here, did you know? Crookback what murdered them princes in the Tower."

Dee did not.

"And there's crayfish in the river and all," the man tells him, and Dee wonders how he knows.

"Seen 'em with my own eyes," the man says. "Eaten 'em, too. You've got to cook 'em, mind."

The chamberlain arrives, with Frommond and Arthur in tow.

"You found us!"

CHAPTER SIXTY-FOUR

Sir Francis Walsingham's house, Seething Lane, London, November 1586

"So there it is," Beale says. "Guilty."

Walsingham nods.

"I expected to be exultant, didn't you? But I suppose it is often the way when you achieve the very thing you've conspired at for so long: you feel a bit flat."

Walsingham is looking very somber in his usual black and white, and his barber has cut his hair very short, and on this damp afternoon, with the shadows deep and long, all the lamps going, and the fire, too, the two men sit in gloomy introspective silence for a moment, each of them trying to comprehend what has just happened.

"Eighteen years it's taken me," Walsingham goes on eventually. "Ever since she landed in Cumbria."

"I often wonder what would have happened if when she left Scotland she'd taken ship across the North Sea instead of the Solway Firth," Beale admits. "That was the mistake she made, wasn't it? To come to England. And it's cost her eighteen years and now, finally, her life."

"Who can say?" Walsingham asks, throwing up his hands. "She might have drowned in a squall at sea, or she might have been crowned Queen of England. There's no way to tell.

"And it is not over yet," he goes on to remind Beale. "It will take one last heave to get Her Majesty over the line to actually sign the death warrant."

"Would you like me to take it to her?" Beale asks, nodding at the paper on Walsingham's desk.

Walsingham looks at him very levelly for a moment.

"No, thank you, Robert. There is no need. I'll do it myself and when she's signed it, I will send it to Sir Amyas with a pursuivant. You look tired and you should stay here in London and get some rest."

CHAPTER SIXTY-FIVE

Fotheringhay Castle, Northamptonshire, December 1586

Mademoiselle Báthory's first attempt to get into the castle is a failure.

"Leave it with me," the sergeant of the guard on the gate told her when she said she had an urgent message for Sir Paulet.

"It must be delivered by hand only," she had said.

The sergeant had shaken his head.

"Let's just have a look at it, shall we?"

"*Kurva anyád!*" she had been unable to stop herself spitting, so near and yet so far, and the Yeomen had known something was wrong. There had been ten of them on the gate: six too many to kill there and then, and of course she didn't have anything by way of a letter to hand over, so Báthory pretended she had muttered that curse because she had discovered that she must have dropped whatever it is she had brought for Dee on the way and would now have to retrace her steps in the slim hopes of finding it.

"Back to London? That's three days' ride, mate!"

She knew that, of course, having just ridden it. It was much easier traveling while passing as a man, and especially as one of Her Majesty's pursuivants, who she learned were given the best horses in the inns, and free ale, but were content to accept the worst beds, and on that first night with a tanner and the innkeeper's daughter, who obviously intended to rut next to her until they found themselves staring down the length of a two-foot blade of Toledo steel.

So she had retraced her steps, to give it some thought, and on a long stretch of the road she had come to learn was called the North Road, she had met another of Her Majesty's pursuivants, riding hard and looking grim. He slowed his horse and greeted her.

"Going to a place called Fotheringhay," he'd said. "You ever heard of it?"

"Is up there, yes," she'd said, her gloved thumb over her shoulder.

"Something big," the man had said. "Ever seen so many seals?"

And from his bag he'd taken and shown her a document that was festooned with ribbon and sealed with half a dozen fat disks of imprinted wax. She caught it as it fell from his lifeless hands and put it in her own bag, which had been empty until then. Then she dragged him off the road and rolled him into the ditch where he floated into a patch of teasels and bulrushes, which she thought would do for a while, and then she took his horse, turned tail, and repeated her steps back to Fotheringhay.

"Found it, have you?" the same sergeant asked the next day. "Fucking lucky, you are, son, and look at all them seals. Something important I'll warrant. Imagine if you'd lost it for good! They'd fucking skin you alive!"

"I give it to Sir Paulet," she tells him.

"No, no, son, you hand it over here. Not a fucker goes in and out of these gates without being searched top to toe, crack to crevice, and everything in between. We've got the queen of the Scots up in that Tower, and if she gets word in or out, we'll have the fucking Inquisition knocking our doors down and setting us alight. So no. No one in, no one out, without the express permission of Sir Amyas Paulet himself."

Báthory had swallowed her curse this time and handed it over. Who cared? And she had set her horse for the nearest town, pondering once more, and thinking that it will soon be Advent, and that she will have to pass a second Christmas in this horrible Godless country, facing precisely the same old problem: Dee is hiding in a castle she cannot get into to kill him and his family.

So she will have to draw them out.

But how?

CHAPTER SIXTY-SIX

Fotheringhay Castle, Northamptonshire, December 1586

Snow on the ground again, and it is hard for Frommond to believe it has been more than a year since she has been home to Mortlake. Time seems to have elongated and compressed at once, but Arthur is more or less back to his old self, and now restive at being kept within the confines of the castle where there are neither cousins to play with, nor even a rabbit hutch, but today is not the day for complaints of any sort.

Today a pursuivant has come and delivered grim tidings, and all Her Majesty's household women as well as M'sieur Bourgoing are gathered in the stateroom on the first floor to hear Sir Amyas Paulet announce the commission's verdict.

"Guilty, ma'am," he tells her.

Mary Kennedy gasps, as if she can possibly be surprised, but Queen Mary squeezes her eyes shut as if to seal in the tears, and she sits stiff-backed on her makeshift throne under her newly completed cloth of state, her knees and feet together, cocked slightly to one side, and her hands clasped in her lap, and there is total silence, even from Cache-Cache, as her strange court in exile stands and watches a single tear escape and slide into her partlet.

Then she claps her hands together

"Well," she says, "it comes not as a complete surprise."

And she stands, as if she must now be about her business, and an hour or so later, Frommond is unsurprised to be summoned to her privy room.

"Mistress Dee," Queen Mary greets her from the window, "come take a last look at your husband and child before they catch their deaths of cold."

Across the wall she can see Dee and Arthur in a small skiff with one of the Yeomen guards. They at least have been granted license to come and go as they please, and now they are lowering in and out of the water a long tube of what might be leather; Frommond suspects there will be a sheet of glass in the bottom and they will be studying some sort of fish.

"Crayfish, perhaps? John mentioned there were supposed to be some in the river. And he has a theory about keeping meat fresh by freezing it."

"Has he now," Queen Mary supposes. "It is good for a child to have an interest."

"I meant Dee," Frommond interrupts, and Queen Mary laughs.

"Still though," she says, "my own son, now, I do not know where he started to go wrong."

And so they are back to James again, and Frommond cannot help but smile as she absently listens to Mary's interpretation of her son's shortcomings, and she watches Dee and Arthur's explorations of the very limited flora and fauna of the winterbound river Nene as it flows out toward the North Sea.

She's right: they will catch their deaths of cold.

CHAPTER SIXTY-SEVEN

Fotheringhay Castle, Northamptonshire,
January 1587

If it were not such a strange thing to say, John Dee might say that being found guilty of encompassing the Queen of England's death suited Queen Mary, for she seems to have regained her purchase on life, and while all those around her weep down long faces, she plays billiards with Arthur and lets him win.

"Aaargh!" she cries. "A three-cushion cannon! How could you? And we a crowned head!"

And she gives him his winnings: a silver crown that has been sent to her, she says, by her mother-in-law, Catherine of Medici.

"She would not wish you to have it, because she is a horrible old woman, so you may take double the pleasure in it."

The queen has spent much of the last few weeks looking to her legacy with various bequests and wills drawn up, tidying up her life, tailoring her legacy, reinventing herself as a devout Catholic when she was, in past times, practicable about such matters, but she is yet to bring Frommond the letter she wishes her to take to the French ambassador, and Dee suspects that she is still trying to source some alum to make the writing invisible.

Sometime after Christmastide Mary Kennedy confides in him her theory that the delays between the trial and the proclamation of her guilt suggest there are forces at play that he—Dee—does not fully comprehend.

"Divine forces?"

"Aye. Could be."

He does not need to be told that she has never met Sir Francis Walsingham or Lord Burghley, who are unlikely to be swayed by such things, though Kennedy may have a point about Bess, who he knows will be fighting against any official execution with every fiber of her being to prevent any for the damage it will do her image as a perfect Christian prince, and for the precedent it will set. That is a more likely cause of delay than any divine force, he thinks, but it does raise the question of what else Bess will be doing to prevent it.

They had managed to prevent any poisoning of Queen Mary while they'd been in Chartley, and when the household was disbanded Pargeter seemed to have disappeared, though Dee still half wonders if it was her pushing the truckle bed from under theirs that night Hawkins kidnapped them, but who else may Bess have sent to fulfill her task?

Another poisoner? A strangler? A smotherer?

But the members of Queen Mary's household are fixed, and no one new has joined them since he himself arrived. He has once or twice wondered if perhaps Frommond has been sent to kill Queen Mary, but he is certain she could never do it. She has come to admire the Scottish queen and even love her, as has Dee, if only for the kindness she has shown Arthur and indeed everybody around her, when she has been enduring great agonies of body and soul. Also: it was not Bess who sent Frommond here, but Queen Mary who summoned her.

And so with every passing day, Kennedy's belief in the power of divine forces grows stronger and stronger, until three days after the feast of Candlemas, in those first few days of February, when in the gloom of another freezing afternoon, Robert Beale arrives.

CHAPTER SIXTY-EIGHT

Fotheringhay Castle, Northamptonshire, February 1587

Robert Beale has spent a week on the roads of middle England looking for the Earls of Shrewsbury and Kent, who are necessary to the proceedings but have suddenly made themselves very scarce undertaking out-of-season surveys of their various far-flung estates, but now, at last, here they are, riding toward the castle gates where Sir Amyas Paulet waits for them in the snow, hands on hips, like a stone doorstop.

"So it is to be done, is it?" he barks.

"It is," Beale tells him, gratefully swinging down from the saddle. "The headsman is on his way by caroche. He will be here before nightfall, and it is to be achieved tomorrow morning. Is she expecting it?"

Sir Amyas blows out a long plume of steam.

"I think not," he says. "She's been wearying cheerful these last few weeks, as if she believes the delays between trial and pronouncement indicated an infirmity of purpose, and the longer this dither and delay has lasted the more cocksure she has become."

Sir Amyas really hates her. Beale wonders why.

"Come on then, let us go and break the news," he says, leading the two earls past the chapel and up the steps to the keep.

In the Presence Room on the first floor, the remaining men and women of Queen Mary's household cluster at the windows and watch the three men come. Some—Mary Kennedy especially—cling to hope:

"They are here to set you free, Your Majesty!"

But Jane Frommond knows Robert Beale. She knows he does not stamp along like that unless he has a great weight on his mind, and so she is not surprised when the door is thrust open without a knock, and while Sir Amyas marches through the room as if he would set everybody ascatter and rips down Queen Mary's cloth of state, Beale and the other two enter more slowly to stand before the little throne with faces grim as gravestones.

"Sirs!" Queen Mary beams at the other three from her throne. "I detect by the gravity of your demeanor that you bring tidings?"

Beale coughs into his fist and then fishes from his doublet a square of paper from which hang two seals. He begins reading and with every word the clamor in the room from such as Mary Kennedy and Barbara Mowbray, and even, God save her, Frommond's own throat, increases; but Queen Mary remains calm, and poised, with no trace of fear, nor of false jocularity. She is ever honest, even in this most extreme of circumstances.

When Beale has finished, he seems not to know what to say.

No one does. Perhaps there is nothing to say? Everybody in the room is weeping, and Frommond is relieved that Arthur is elsewhere, with Dee, in their room studying geometry, rather than here to witness this.

Queen Mary merely stares at the window, and then she has a thought.

"Sirs," she says, "we have of late had much time on our hands and have made a study of the history of this noble realm, and in particular its kings and queens, among whom we once hoped to number, and we are reminded that your King Richard the Second was quietly done to death in Pontefract Castle, which is not so far from here, and we are concerned that you may have in mind such a fate for ourselves?"

Queen Mary seems resigned to her death now, Frommond sees, and her remaining fear is that it will be brought about by some shabby murder in an oubliette such as King Richard II endured, not in a blaze of pious glory, an act of martyrdom for the one true Catholic faith.

One of the earls tells her that she need have no such fears, for she must know she was in the charge of a Christian queen, and again, Frommond thinks it is just as well Queen Mary never questioned the presence and then the absence of Lucy Pargeter.

Queen Mary seems to take great heart from this strange reassurance, and it becomes clear that she has used the time since her guilty conviction to prepare for this moment, for she stands now, fearlessly facing down the Englishmen sent to kill her, and she is ready, it seems, to claim her place among the saints and martyrs for the Catholic faith.

"I am quite happy and ready to die, and to shed my blood for Almighty God, my Savior and my Creator, and for the Catholic Church, and to maintain its rights in this country."

After which there is more said but from the tail of her eye, Frommond sees a movement through the window, as a caroche rolls to a halt in the bailey, and from it step five or six men and women who mill about while servants remove their luggage, and then they begin making their ways slowly up the steps below to the doorway ten feet below where Frommond stands. One of the men carries something that in other circumstances she might mistake for a harp, but today, here, now, she knows can only be an ax. She is about to gasp, and clap her hand to her mouth perhaps, but then her gaze meets the gaze of another woman walking a few paces behind, staring straight back up at her.

Lucy Pargeter.

Who puts her finger vertically to her lips.

Shhhh.

CHAPTER SIXTY-NINE

Approaching Fotheringhay Castle,
Northamptonshire, February 1587

After all that, it is not difficult. The party of riders with the caroche are loose knit, dropping back, riding forward, answering calls of nature and even stopping for food in an alehouse, and so they do not seem to know one another, and there is a very grim atmosphere, as if they are riding to a funeral she thinks, and they do not question her or wonder why they are joined by one of Her Majesty's pursuivants, who merely tags along, looking young and weary, and one of the men even offers to buy Báthory a pie.

"Feed you up a bit, sonny."

She takes him up on it, and eats quickly, turned away from the others. There is one woman there, sharper than the rest, who she is sure has detected something not quite straight about the young pursuivant who joined them—when? But she is undecided whether she should say anything about it, which is as well for her, of course, because Mademoiselle Báthory has already decided what to do about her if she does.

In the end, the woman decides there is nothing to say about it, and so nothing happens and they are all of them still alive when they reach the gatehouse where that fat sergeant who had twice turned her back and who she will kill if she has to is not there, and his replacement stands watching, a grim expression on his face as she troops in behind the caroche and the other riders and follows their lead to the bailey, where the woman and the two men get out, while those on horseback dismount and lead their horses around to the stables.

Once she has passed the horse to the ostler's lad, Báthory tags along with the other servants, up the steps and into the great hall of the castle where carpenters are at work erecting a large square dais, and everything else including the floors and walls and a large lump in the middle of the dais are covered in billowing sheets of linen dyed black as night, and where there are benches laid out as if for spectators of a tournament.

She studies it for a while and has an idea.

But first she must find Dee. And his boy.

CHAPTER SEVENTY

Fotheringhay Castle, Northamptonshire, February 1587

"John! John!" Frommond whispers so as not to wake Arthur.

Dee looks up from his book, alert and interested, his eyes much magnified by his eyeglasses.

"They are going to execute her tomorrow," she tells him.

Dee closes his book.

"I heard something," he says. "Some people on the steps, but I didn't want to leave Arthur. How has she taken it?"

"Very well. She is pretending she is being martyred for reasons of her faith, but listen: Robert Beale is here and he has brought Lucy Pargeter."

"Jesu! Surely it is too late for that?"

"We have to find her."

But at that moment Mary Kennedy knocks and summons Frommond to Queen Mary.

"You go," Dee says. "I'll go and find Mistress Pargeter."

"You can't leave Arthur."

"He's asleep," Dee tells her. "He will be all right."

⌖

He finds Lucy Pargeter alone in the light of a lamp in the otherwise deserted buttery, on the second-lowest floor of the castle, just above the dungeons. She is pounding something in a ceramic mortar.

"Mistress Pargeter."

She heard him coming and keeps grinding away with the pestle.

"Please do not try to stop me tonight, for all our sakes, Doctor Dee," she says. "Her Majesty wishes this done, and if you try to dissuade me again, you are preventing me complying with her orders."

"I understand that," Dee tells her.

"So there is nothing more to say, is there?"

"I am merely interested what poison you intend to use?"

"I have the one of my own device," she says, proudly gesturing to the mortar. "A mixture of *Scopolia carniolica*, *Hyoscyamus niger*, and *Mandragora officinarum*."

Dee whistles.

"Jesu," he says. "That must pack a punch."

"My mixture induces intense well-being and a willingness to cooperate, only after perhaps a quarter of an hour do the physical symptoms become noticeable, by which time the patient merely wishes to sleep."

"Patient?"

"We've already had this conversation, Doctor."

"It sounds wonderful. Are there any side effects? Other than death, of course?"

Pargeter stops pounding and looks at him quite seriously.

"Apart from death, none," she says. "The only drawback is that there is a period of what I call radical loquaciousness after perhaps as long as it used to take to say the rosary, that I find very boring, but then comes the coma."

He wonders if she would be interested in hearing of his experiments with the Calabar beans that Sir Francis Drake brought him from his voyages to the Bight of Benin? But perhaps that is for another time.

"And did you give this to your father? When you shortened his life?" he asks.

Lucy Pargeter hoods her eyes and nods.

"What about your husband?" Dee wonders. "What about Humphrey, before he took to the waters of the Scheldt?"

She stares at him a long moment before shaking her head.

"The something else?" Dee presses.

"More *Scopolia carniolica*," she admits.

"And that is what made him so suggestible? When you suggested he swim the river?"

Again, the pause and then the slow nod.

"He wanted to hang himself," she says now. "And I wished to spare him the pain and the disgrace."

"So how will you do it tonight?" he asks.

"I will put it in her wine."

Dee nods. It is well known Queen Mary likes wine, and she likes to stay up drinking it until midnight, and tonight of all nights, why not?

"So she will not wake up tomorrow?"

Pargeter shakes her head.

"Do you think that a pity, Doctor Dee? Given what she must otherwise face?"

"I wish there were a way she might avoid both, of course."

Pargeter surprises him now.

"I too," she says. "I have come to admire her more than I ever thought I would."

There doesn't seem much more to say and yet Dee does not want to leave her, to let this thing come about, and yet why not? Pargeter waits patiently for him to go.

"I am not sure if I told you about the Calabar beans that I—"

He is interrupted by a rising screech from up the stairs.

Frommond.

He sets off at a sprint.

CHAPTER SEVENTY-ONE

Fotheringhay Castle, Northamptonshire, February 1587

Jane Dee, née Frommond, stands on the steps outside that back bedchamber and she shrieks to rouse the house.

"Arthur!"

There is no sign of the boy. Soon every lamp in the keep is lit, and the search of the castle begins from top to bottom. Queen Mary interrupts her prayers and her letter writing and comes to the Presence Room door in her socked feet.

"I will help look in the hall," she volunteers, but M'sieur Bourgoing, who has just seen what has been built down in the hall, forbids it.

"You will catch your death, Your Majesty."

She can only shake her head as if to dislodge the peculiarity of her position.

"Where is Sir Amyas?"

Sir Amyas is in the lower part of the castle, along with Robert Beale and the Earls of Shrewsbury and Kent. Someone is sent. Dee goes through every room, along every corridor from dungeon to attic. He rips through everything he finds. Overturns beds, coffers, tables, cupboards, and wardrobes. He shines a lamp down the privies and up the chimneys. His voice is hoarse with shouting.

Arthur cannot have left the keep, of that he is certain, because at the front door, even though it is bolted from within, stand five Yeomen, all awake, kept warm by a brazier, and at the postern door at the back of the castle, likewise bolted from within, stands Jonas Digby, the Yeoman whose brother owns the punt from which Dee and Arthur studied the crayfish.

"No one nor nothing's been out this way, Doctor."

Dee believes him.

An hour after Frommond found Arthur missing, Dee returns to the hall where he finds his wife weeping inconsolably, being supported by Mary Kennedy and M'sieur Bourgoing, who has a fresh lit lamp, but the thought that it might be his fault for abandoning Arthur for perhaps the first time in a year has not yet formed itself into words in Dee's mind. He tries to think and then his fingers once more seek out the golden orb in his purse. It has worked before, so why not again? They stare at him as he holds it out, so dainty in such a place, and he lets the chain swing and is unsurprised to feel nothing unusual in response.

He turns his back on them and then takes out Digges's eyeglasses. He knows now they look absurd, but he was not lying; they really do help him think. They seem to permit him an insight into the subtle chains that underpin the universe. He takes up the orb again, and the lamp, and he commits himself to a compressed version of the rituals that the dealer on Cheapside taught him, and he attempts to clear his mind and recapture that state of nothingness that allowed him to find Arthur that first time. He concentrates without concentrating on the boy, and he takes those smooth elongated paces about the darkened hall, around that black-smocked dais, one hand holding the orb, the other the lamp.

And so— And so at length there is something, the faintest stirring.

The orb wishes him to attend to the back wall of the hall, by the fire. To the right of the fire. Dee walks around the dais. The orb stills. There is nothing to be seen save an expanse of black linen. Save what is that? A small bright dot of something in the linen, just above waist height. A golden button? A hole? He holds up the lamp and bends and puts his eye to it.

CHAPTER SEVENTY-TWO

Fotheringhay Castle, Northamptonshire, February 1587

With the boy now fainted and lying at her feet, Mademoiselle Báthory stands behind the black drapes that curtain the walls of the hall, the blade already extended from her sleeve, so sharp it has made a small nick in the linen, and she waits for the fools to give up and go and look for him somewhere else. She should have left some doors open, or broken a window, she sees that now; then they would be out in the courtyard and she would be left in peace to arrange what she has in mind on this dais.

Lucy Pargeter concentrates on what needs to be done. Ever since she shortened her father's life, and then Humphrey's, and since then a dozen others, she has prided herself on her clarity of thought, and her superiority to muddle-eyed affection. She had loved both men and wished to spare them pain that was inevitable. She likes Queen Mary and wishes to spare her. So let her die happy, and painlessly. She deserves it.

Dee bends to peer, and the blade comes at him a split second after he realizes what he is looking at.

Báthory is so used to the sensation of the blade slipping through a man's eyeball and into his brain that she is startled by the click of its tip against something hard and then the way it is dragged aside, diverted, and she finds her arm is seized fast.

"Kurva anyád!"

CHAPTER SEVENTY-THREE

Fotheringhay Castle, Northamptonshire, February 1587

The point cracks against the lens of John Dee's left eyeglass and snaps his head back, but the smooth surface of the glass directs it beyond his ear, and as Dee falls back, he grabs at whatever struck him and tries to keep upright.

An arm!

He hears a cry, and he pulls the arm past him, and twists so that both he and the owner of the arm must fall crashing onto the floor, tearing the linen sheets from the walls, but he is on top now, and he envelops the thrashing body in the linen, smothering the struggling figure.

Frommond is suddenly there, and Bourgoing, too, and everyone is shouting incomprehensibly, and Dee is using all his weight to keep the body down and the blade wrapped in more linen, and the body still bucks and pulls and tries to wrench the arm free until Bourgoing snatches up the lamp, and then times his step to perfection and stamps on the writhing arm, pinning it to the floor. Then he stamps with his other foot on the arm holding the blade and there is a terrible guttural cry from under the sheet and Dee knows where the head is now and uses all his weight and anger to hammer his elbow into the face and there is a terrible noise and at last stillness and silence.

"Mama?"

Dee looks up to see Arthur in his mother's arms, awake now, but still mute with terror. Frommond is shushing him and bouncing him as if he were still a baby on her shoulder, and she is caught between taking him away, and finding out who it is who stole him, and who it is who has just tried to stab Dee.

"Who is it?" Frommond asks, turning the boy away so that she can look back at Dee over his shoulder.

Dee doesn't know.

He removes the blade from its spring, but it's useless for cutting cloth. Bourgoing passes him his knife and holds the lamp over Dee while he cuts away the sheet around the man's face to reveal, not what he expected at all.

"A woman!"

At that moment there is a terrible shriek from Arthur, and Frommond must turn and run away with him. Dee takes the lantern and holds it close to the face. The woman's cheek is broken, perhaps, by the force of Dee's elbow, but the rest of her is preserved in all its hard beauty, and it takes him a long moment of mental strain to remember where he has seen her before.

Then it comes to him: Prague. In the palace of Emperor Rudolf. It was this woman who held Kitty de Fleurier captive. The one who snarled at him and called him a Jew wizard. He'd laughed at the time. Now though. Jesu.

Dee has never had cause to hate anyone so much in all his life, aware that he is looking at his personal Satan; but he is aware, too, that even so, he will never be able to bring himself to kill her.

He rolls her over onto her front and ties her hands with cut-up pieces of the linen. He does this as roughly as possible, and it wakes her and she writhes and spits incomprehensible consonants and tells him she will still do awful things to him and his wife and his boy.

Dee gags her, but still she hammers her toes on the floor and keens against the cloth pulled tight between her teeth. Thankfully M'sieur Bourgoing is still there, a dark-eyed little Frenchman who understands what is needed, and he kicks her face until she stops her thrashing about.

And it is at that moment that Lucy Pargeter comes through the hall with an earthenware jug, on her way up the steps to Queen Mary's bedchamber.

"What have you got there?" she asks.

CHAPTER SEVENTY-FOUR

Fotheringhay Castle, Northamptonshire, February 1587

The plan, when it comes down to it, is made up on the spot and is fraught with uncertainty. After long consideration, Pargeter and Bourgoing agree it is worth a try.

"What have we to lose?" Bourgoing asks.

Pargeter is less easily convinced, but her objections are more practical.

Dee talks fast.

"We do it now, or not at all," he says.

Pargeter shrugs acquiescence.

"On your head be it," she says, and she returns to the kitchen for her book of poisons.

While they wait, they watch the woman in the pursuivant's uniform, who lies there, stunned perhaps, and giving off a terrible heat of hatred, and Dee thanks Bourgoing.

"No," Bourgoing says. "Thank you. I will talk to Queen Mary's ladies. They will see it as a last chance. And they will do it. They love her."

Dee nods in the darkness. He thought so.

When Pargeter returns, she takes charge.

"Turn her over," she instructs.

They do so.

"Sit on her, and take off the gag, but you hold her nose, Doctor Bourgoing, and her chin."

Dee sits across the woman and removes her gag. Bourgoing holds her nose and chin. Pargeter waits with the spout of her jug by the woman's lips, and when she tries to draw breath, she slops some of a new mix down her throat.

The woman chokes and froths.

"Think about how Sarah felt when you did this to her," Dee tells the woman.

Lucy pours more down her throat. And more still.

"Gag her and leave her for a moment. Then we'll take her to the Presence Room."

Dee asks what is in the jug.

Pargeter will not tell him.

After a few moments, she kicks the woman.

She's out cold.

"But she's not dead?"

Pargeter shakes her head.

"She'll be this way for a few hours. Is that long enough?"

Dee thinks so.

"Let's get her upstairs."

He takes her shoulders, Bourgoing her boots, and in the light of the lamp held by Pargeter, together they carry her up to the deserted Presence Room, where they drop her behind a settle. Bourgoing throws a cloth over her.

"You go," he tells Dee. "Go and see to your wife and Arthur. I will stay here and start with Mary Kennedy."

Dee finds Frommond in their chamber, sitting with Arthur

lying across her, his back turned to the door, possibly asleep. He puts a hand on her shoulder, and she puts hers on it.

"Is he dead?" she asks, quietly, but with her chin thrust forward, so that Dee knows that this is what she wants.

"Not yet," he tells her.

"How did he get in?"

"He is a she," he tells her.

"Who took Arthur that first time?" Frommond wonders. "And it is she who killed Sarah?"

Dee thinks so and tells her that he remembers her from Prague.

"She's the woman who controlled Kitty de Fleurier."

Frommond frowns and brings her to mind.

"She was the one I thought looked clever?" Frommond wonders. "Why? Why is she even here?"

"Come to kill us, in revenge for getting Kitty de Fleurier out of the emperor's clutches, is what Ballard told Beale."

Frommond shakes her head.

"So what now?"

He tells her his plan.

She shakes her head and then starts to half laugh—and half cry.

"Well," she wonders, "why not?"

CHAPTER SEVENTY-FIVE

Fotheringhay Castle, Northamptonshire, February 1587

The next morning, when it is light enough to need no candles, Robert Beale leads the sheriff of the county of Northamptonshire up the protesting stairs to the door of Queen Mary's privy apartment where the sheriff knocks and they wait. Beale's entire body is tingling and his skin feels aflame, but the sheriff looks worse, as if he will vomit any moment.

"Not used to this," he admits.

"Who is?" Beale wonders. Certainly not him.

Mary Kennedy opens the door dressed in plum-colored velvets with a white linen veil that is long enough to reach the floor. Behind her, Queen Mary kneels at her prie-dieu with her eyes closed.

"It is time, madam," the sheriff says.

Queen Mary looks up.

"I am ready."

CHAPTER SEVENTY-SIX

Fotheringhay Castle, Northamptonshire, February 1587

It takes a long time before the sheriff is finally able to lead Queen Mary through the anteroom and onto the black-clad dais in the black-clad hall, but when she has finally said farewell to her servants and the junior members of her household staff she steps up onto the dais, and she stares at all the men who have come to watch her die, and particularly Sir Amyas Paulet, who sits in the first row. She shakes her head in what might be interpreted as pity, and there is a great wave of murmuring among them, for she is in black, in such a beautiful velvet and silk and lace-edged dress it would bring tears to anyone's eye, but like all her women this morning, she wears a full-length linen veil in the Catholic style, and so the details of her expression are for her, and for her God, alone. She carries a crucifix and a prayer book, and after she has stared down the crowd of gentlemen for some little discomfiting time, she turns to the two masked men who stand to one side, hiding the ax, in long black gowns such as scholars wear, and white aprons.

One of them, the senior of the two, bows, and then gestures to a chair that Mary is to sit on.

She does so.

It is Robert Beale's task to read the death sentence, and when his voice has settled, the air stills, and time seems to stop, and all through it, Queen Mary appears calm, even cheerful, as if he might be reading a pardon. He turns to her and bows one last time, and there are tears in his eyes, and not merely for her, perhaps, but for himself, for he knows he has failed Queen Elizabeth. He steps off the dais and walks to the back of the hall, to stand by the fireplace, in which the logs are piled high, from which someone has ripped the masking sheets and put them back badly. He wonders where Dee is, and where Frommond is. Perhaps they are with Arthur? He heard from one of the guards that the boy had taken to sleepwalking in the night and had caused quite a stir.

Up onto the dais now steps the dean of Peterborough Cathedral, who has been sent to give an admonition to Queen Mary for her treasonous Catholicism, and who will then lead the entire assembly in prayer for her forgiveness, but he stammers when nervous or anxious, and cannot get going though he tries three times and at the fourth, Queen Mary calls him Master Dean and tells him she will not hear him.

"You have nothing to do with me," she says, "nor I with you."

And she turns her back on him just as if he were boring her.

He persists, telling her to repent of her wickedness, and she tells him to be silent, but he will not, and he begins praying, but nor will Mary be silent, either, for she holds up her crucifix, and starts praying in Latin. The two pray alongside each other for a moment, raising their voices, competing, until some men in the crowd join with the dean, at which point Mary slips off her chair to her knees and she continues to shout her prayers above the astonished hubbub, until eventually the dean yields.

When it is done, Queen Mary switches her prayers to English, so that all may hear, but she is growing very weary now, and though she prays for her son, and her sister of England, by the end it is clear she can contrive no more, and she concludes by petitioning God to spare this silly little island from plague.

That is enough.

At Shrewsbury's signal, the headsmen step forward to undress her, and at this Queen Mary's women move in one block onto the stage to defend their mistress, even though she can be heard joking that she had never had such grooms before to undress her, and Beale wonders if that can be true, from some of the things he heard about Queen Mary when she was in Scotland. But the headsmen are seen off by Queen Mary's women, who cluster about her, mobbing her like birds, until at last they are ready: her outer garments are removed and they step aside to reveal Queen Mary clad in a velvet petticoat and satin bodice, both stained the color of dried blood, which Beale knows to be the color of martyrdom in the Catholic Church, and despite himself, despite the situation and despite the linen veil, Beale cannot stop himself noting that she is far comelier than he had believed.

But now the queen is very tired it seems, as if exhausted by the performance of defiance she has put on, and she seems somewhat confused, and her gentlewomen must gather around her again, a cluster of women, all circling her, and there is some confusion, and to Robert Beale's untrained eye there seem to be more than is necessary, but whatever they tell her seems to work, and though she is confused, and somewhat unsteady on her feet now, she permits herself to be steered toward the cushion that has been laid out for her. One of the women steps in front of the queen as her veil is removed and she covers Queen Mary's eyes with a piece of silk that hides almost all her face, and when she tries to take it off, the same gentlewoman stays her hands and then places them upon the black-shrouded block. They must even place her chin where it should go, and only then do they step back.

She is in the hands of the headsmen now. And while one of them holds her down, the other swings his ax.

And at long last, Queen Mary's troubles are ended.

CHAPTER SEVENTY-SEVEN

Fotheringhay Castle, Northamptonshire, February 1587

Dominique Bourgoing and Lucy Pargeter pass the queen's unconscious body out through the kitchen window, where John Dee takes her and holds her to him as he slides on his back down through the snow that lingers on the north side of the motte to the bailey below. At its foot, he considers how to pick her up, and so, just as he did with Roger Cooke, he lays her out on her back in the snow, with one knee cocked, and then he steps back, and falls on her, rolling over her and pulling her with him so that he now lies facedown in the snow with her on his shoulders. Cache-Cache arrives, yipping and dancing about in defense of his mistress, and Dee has to calm the dog before he can lift Mary onto his shoulders, considering as he does so that nothing is ever wasted on a curious mind.

Just then, a muffled cry from the great hall above.

"God save the Queen!"

"Amen to that," he murmurs, and he turns and begins his crouching run through the mist-shrouded orchard with the Scottish queen over his shoulders, to the postern gate of the castle, where the drawbridge is down, and where Jonas Digby stands waiting with Jane Frommond and Arthur, saucer-eyed and frozen cold, and below them is Jonas Digby's brother's punt pulled up among the dead reeds.

"Is she sick?" Arthur asks.

"Just tired, I think," Dee tells his son.

Frommond is more concerned that she's not dead, and they help him lower the queen's body to the ground above the punt. Her eyes flutter open and she looks at them, her eyes swimming and vague, and Dee wonders if she is imagining herself in the afterlife, and if so, looking up at him, Frommond, and Arthur on a mist-shrouded riverbank in February, whether she imagines herself in heaven or hell?

"*En ma fin gît mon commencement*," Queen Mary murmurs, and then her eyes roll back and she is asleep, snoring heavily.

"A good sign, I think," Dee says.

Lucy Pargeter's poison is working just as she predicted: a period of intense well-being and a willingness to cooperate, followed by a period of radical loquaciousness, then coma. Poisoning the queen had been a risk, but she would never have been able to carry off a performance such as she had on the scaffold had she not genuinely believed she was about to be martyred.

And was in the grips of a low-level dose of *Scopolia carniolica*, too, of course.

After that, as the effect of the drug changed from radical loquaciousness to confusion, Queen Mary's women had gathered around her. They'd bundled her aside and coaxed Mademoiselle Báthory to take her place at the block. Dee wonders what Lucy Pargeter had forced down her throat to make her so pliant?

And then, that was that.

And so now they lower the queen into the punt, wrapped in her warmest traveling cloak, and then they slide the punt down into the slow-moving river Nene, and after Dee has given his wife and son both a hug, he steps down into the punt after her.

"We will meet in Peterborough," he tells them. "This day or the next."

Frommond smiles at him as bravely as she can, and Arthur gives him a somber little nod. Just before Dee pushes off and out into the mist, Cache-Cache slips into the punt and stands, one forepaw raised, guarding his mistress.

Jonas Digby gives the punt a shove.

"Godspeed, Doctor Dee!"

CHAPTER SEVENTY-EIGHT

Hampton Court Palace, February 1587

Ice on the Thames and a good six inches of snow on the ground have brought the world to a stop. The river, the earth, and the sky are indistinguishable, the same frozen shade in which only a swan's beak would give it away. Robert Beale, heavily shrouded in dark lambswool piled upon his shoulders to the height of his ears, hears a crow cawing above the noise of his thick-soled boots crunching as he walks across the gritted ice toward the gatehouse, and the inspection of the Yeoman warders.

"Master Beale," the extravagantly bearded, blue-nosed sergeant greets him with a puff of cloud for his breath. Beale wonders if the man knows anything, if he knows why Beale is summoned this morning? Probably not. Why should he? And yet, isn't there some look in his eye, some glimmer of black pity, if such a thing exists? Or is it a frozen tear?

Before he steps in through the archway, Beale takes one last look around at the world he believes he may never see again, or at least not as a free man: Hampton across the river under its smudge of woodsmoke; two boys throwing stones at a goose; and upriver a woman pulling at a branch stuck in the ice. Through the archway, in the inner courtyard, braziers are lit, and there is the usual bustle around the kitchen. No one looks up to see him standing there, which he takes to be a good sign. On his way up here he had become convinced everyone he saw, and who saw him, knew that he had failed the Queen, and that she had summoned him with the specific intention of having him arrested and executed. He began to wish Sir Thomas Perrot would jump out of a bush and kill him there and then, saving him much pain and disgrace, but no. Nothing. Only a slow, clopping ride on a steaming horse along the banks of the frozen Thames and now here he is, being called to across the doorway of the Great Hall by another sergeant of the Yeoman warders.

"This way, Master Beale!"

Robert takes a breath and steps out. *Crunch. Crunch. Crunch.* That is when he notices a platoon of Yeomen standing warming their hands on a brazier, their halberds resting on their shoulders, all turned to stare at him walking by. He feels as if he is walking to the gallows of his own volition. He should turn and run. *Crunch. Crunch. Crunch.*

"God give you good day, sir," the sergeant says. A page appears at his shoulder.

"Her Majesty awaits, sir, in her private chapel."

What does that mean? A private interview. Is that a good thing? Beale cannot decide. At least he is not to be disgraced publicly, before all the courtiers in the Great Hall. He gathers himself, thanks the Yeoman, and steps in after the page, up the steps toward his fate. Only here is a surprise: Sir Francis Walsingham.

"Robert."

He feels his heart turn. But has Walsingham come to help condemn him, or save him?

"Sir Francis. I did not expect—"

"No. I came when I heard you were on your way. Not far from Barn Elms."

"Of course."

But how did he know Her Majesty had summoned Beale to Hampton? This is a question he cannot ask, and even if he could, he knows Walsingham would not answer. Instead Walsingham falls into step with him, up the stairs.

"So, Robert," he begins quietly, so that the page does not hear, "I understand Her Majesty is displeased with us both?"

Beale wonders about denying it, about telling him that Her Majesty has nothing with which to reproach him, but he is at sea, and Sir Francis is a rock, or a piece of wreckage, to which he wishes to cling.

"I am sorry," he says, thereby admitting he had been trying to undermine Sir Francis's efforts to bring Queen Mary to trial and execution.

"There is nothing to be sorry for, Robert," Sir Francis reassures him. "Her Majesty gave you your orders."

Beale feels a wash of warm relief and cannot help but turn to his master.

"How long have you known?" he asks.

"Since your fever," Walsingham tells him. "You spoke aloud. But before then, really. I suspected she'd try to stop us."

"Us?"

"Us. We. All of us who are not kings or queens."

"So that is what this is about? You bore no animosity to Queen Mary?"

"Some," Sir Francis admits. "She was not the cause of our troubles, but you know how she inspired them."

He means the assassins. Men such as Babington.

"And now that she's gone?"

Walsingham looks at him soberly, his hand on the chapel door. "Well," he says. "That is the question, isn't it?"

The chapel is warmed by two fires and a hundred candles, but there is no sign of Her Majesty until they walk the length of the aisle to the altar and turn back to look up, where she stands raised twenty feet above them in her privy balcony, overlooking the chapel, so they are forced to bow upward, as it were. She is in wools dyed the color of summer aubergines—almost but not quite the color of mourning—with sable and ermine wraps and a muff for her elegant little hands, but there is high color in her cheeks, and her eyes are bright with some passionate opinion. She is surprised to see Beale is not alone.

"Sir Francis? We were not expecting you?"

Walsingham bows.

"Nevertheless, Your Majesty, here I am."

They stare at each other for a long moment, a struggle the nature of which Beale can only guess. It feels very significant, almost elemental, and it is finally the Queen who capitulates, and she exhales a long, resigned sigh.

"Yes," she says. "Here you are."

Ordinarily she might now summon a servant to bring them spiced wine, or something warm against the cold of their journey, but today is not to be that sort of day, not that sort of interview.

"So it is done?" she asks.

Walsingham turns to Beale: *Well, is it?* he asks without words.

"It is, Your Majesty," Beale replies.

The Queen nods tightly.

"And you saw it? You saw her—body?"

"I did, Your Majesty, yes," he lies. He saw her head chopped off, but thereafter there was some confusion: it transpired that Mary wore a wig, and so when the executioner held up her head by her hair, the head fell, and rolled, and one of Her Majesty's women—

Mistress Kennedy perhaps?—gathered it up and thrust it into the waiting coffin.

Her Majesty stands watching him now, hawklike in her aerie, waiting for him to apologize for failing to stop Queen Mary's death. But Beale feels he cannot, or now, thrillingly, need not, not with Sir Francis by his side.

"And?" the Queen presses.

Beale feigns being at a loss.

"And she is dead, Your Majesty."

"She was guilty, Your Majesty," Walsingham intervenes. "She broke your law."

He does not remind her it was a law that he forced her to put into statute, does not remind her how unfair the law is or how it cannot possibly have applied to a foreign national such as Queen Mary. Instead he reminds her of the trap he set.

"She signed a pledge that she would hunt down and put to death anyone who conspired to kill you. In this case it was herself."

This only makes the Queen lose control of her already barely suppressed temper.

"We told you, Sir Francis," she snaps, banging her fist on the rail. "We told you not to seek her death."

"You told me not to seek her *trial*, Your Majesty," he corrects. "You were unconcerned about her death."

The Queen's eyes now become slits of pure fury.

"Do not presume to tell us what we were and were not concerned about!"

Walsingham bows, but there is something, some line in his leg, or back, or neck that signifies some irony, and the Queen throws the cup she had been carrying. It smashes out of sight.

"You shall see what happens now, Sir Francis!" she shouts. "You shall see what happens when you cross a divinely appointed monarch! You, too, Master Beale; you shall reap what you have sown when the Spanish come crashing at our door. You have loosed the Spanish wolf, do you not see? Do you not see that it was Mary who was the only thing holding them back!"

Walsingham stands straight. None of this is new to either man, of course, nor the Queen. It has always been the calculation: Would the Spanish send their ships and soldiers to evict Elizabeth if it meant they must to put a Frenchwoman on the throne? But however she dresses it up, that is not what has so vexed Her Majesty, is it? It is Sir Francis's successful challenge to her authority; his suggestion that a monarch is just as much bound by the law as is a commoner, even when those laws are made by mere commoners.

"We will deal with the Spanish when they come, Your Majesty," Walsingham tells her. "You need have no fear on that account."

She stares down at them, furious, cornered, having lost control of the route the interview with Master Beale was supposed to take, and perhaps it is being here in Hampton Court, so beloved of her father, that makes Beale wonder if Sir Francis would have ever dared challenge King Henry like this.

"Get out!" she snaps. "Get out!"

Again the two men bow. Shoulder to shoulder they hurry from the chapel, passing under her, and Beale flinches in case she should drop something on their heads; they continue through the Yeomen gathered, awaiting an instruction that never comes.

"Not today, I think, gentlemen," Sir Francis tells them, and the Yeomen watch both men pass, indifferent. They walk together, free men, out into the courtyard.

"Thank you, Sir Francis, thank you," Beale breathes, knowing how close he came to being dragged off by those Yeomen.

"Not a bit of it," Walsingham soothes, as if it were nothing, but now Beale sees sweat is pouring down the man's forehead. The confrontation cost him dear. They walk in silence a moment.

The crunch underfoot seems to have a different register now. Less ominous. He feels as if they are walking back to life. And Walsingham is actually humming some tune or other.

"Of course," Beale says, "she is right, you know. About the Spanish."

"Oh, yes," Walsingham agrees. "We are absolutely skewered. The Spanish will send a fleet, and they'll crush our navy, Hawkins or no Hawkins, Drake or no Drake, but we will have set a precedent, won't we? And perhaps one day, someone somewhere will take that to heart. No man or woman, whoever they may be, is above the law. It trumps everything and everyone."

They walk on.

"That would be nice to think," Beale says.

"Mmm," Walsingham agrees.

"But in the meantime?"

"In the meantime, I think we had better find Doctor Dee, don't you?"

EPILOGUE

Loch Doon, Galloway, May 1588

Mary Stuart stands with her arms outstretched by the loch shore, the spring sun on her face, the iodine-tinged breeze ruffling her loose hair. Her eyes are closed, and she smiles while a small dog capers on the stones by the brown water's edge, and she gives not a thought to her cousin of England, for she is, at long last, free.

AUTHOR'S NOTE

English schoolchildren are routinely taught that in 1586 Anthony Babington plotted to replace Queen Elizabeth with Queen Mary; that he communicated as such with Queen Mary via a brewer from Burton but was caught in the act; that both Babington and Mary were tried, found guilty, and deservedly executed for treason. We are taught that Queen Mary's death triggered King Felipe of Spain to send an apparently invincible armada to punish England, the fate of which was greeted as a ruling handed down from the court of divine justice.

The truth of what is known as the Babington plot, which underpins the events of *The Queen's Lies*, is, of course, far stranger, more nuanced, and infinitely more baffling than the story we are told, and literally no one emerges from it with their reputations intact, save perhaps Doctor Dee, whose involvement goes largely unrecorded. Part of the problem is that what we now think of as the "intelligence community" was then so fluid and compromised that it is impossible to say if any one man was loyal to any one cause or not. Not even Sir Francis Walsingham, whose interests ran contrary to those of his Queen, nor the Queen herself, either, who in trying to stop a fellow divinely appointed monarch being put on trial by mere commoners was acting not in the interests of England or the Reformed Faith, but in those of Christendom's kings and queens.

And that is before one starts to look at what motivated men such as Gilbert Gifford, who switched sides two or three times at least and ended up working against the Catholic church, even as he was preparing to be ordained a Catholic priest. What was he thinking? John Ballard was a more straighforward character, in that he at least remained constant, if a liability, to his own self. But why did he commission that (now lost) portrait of all the conspirators? And why did he wear clothes guaranteed to attract attention?

Anthony Babington himself is a puzzle, too. His fateful letter to Queen Mary reads as if he might have dashed it off after a good lunch, and after sending it, he seems not to have understood what was in it, or entirely certain about his whole enterprise, because he made overtures to work for Walsingham against his fellow conspirators, little knowing that some of them were already working against him. I get the impression—though from nowhere specific—that he did not think anyone would take him seriously, and so didn't realize the depth of his danger until it was too late. I have also inferred from the ether that there must have been any number of nascent conspiracies to remove Queen Elizabeth and replace her with Queen Mary being dreamt up all over the country, of which Babington's was only one. It was his ill luck to become useful to Sir Francis Walsingham in the old spymaster's deeper, hidden struggle with monarchy in general and Queen Elizabeth in particular.

Walsingham's scheme was extremely cunning, and extremely ruthless—and perhaps quite farsighted—but it was also extremely risky, since in having Queen Mary tried and judicially executed, at one stroke he not only removed the principal reason for Spanish reservations about invading England—that they'd have to put the next Catholic in line of inheritance on the throne, which was Queen Mary, who, being part French, would naturally favor France rather than Spain—it was also such a provocation that King Felipe was more or less duty bound to send an invasion fleet. Although John Hawkins was hard at work building an English navy that might match the Spaniards, there was still a long way to go, and few would have betted on England winning that fight.

Queen Mary is often portrayed—not least by me in *The Eyes of the Queen*—as a conniving villain, but the facts of her life are heartbreaking, and though there is no evidence of the old switcheroo that Dee perpetrates on that fateful day in Fotheringhay Castle, it would be nice to imagine her living out the rest of her days with the sun and wind on her face, free to come and go as she pleased, undisturbed by the turbulence that had governed her earlier life or the frustration that must have characterized the eighteen years she spent under Elizabeth's lock and key in England, for no other reason than for being who she was to whom.

The law that Walsingham forced through Parliament in 1584—the Bond of Association—was an outrageous piece of legislation aimed squarely at catching Queen Mary out, and once she had put her signature to it, she had more or less signed her own death warrant. It is often argued that in any other country she would have met with an unfortunate accident or been poisoned before her first year in captivity was out, which may be true, but keeping her under lock and key for so long, and then killing her, is not really any better, is it? Especially as there is evidence that when it was clear Walsingham and Cecil were going to put her on trial, Queen Elizabeth did try to pressure Sir Amyas Paulet into pushing her down the stairs, only for him to refuse, saying he would not make a shipwreck of his conscience. There is no evidence for the existence of Lucy Pargeter, I hope that is obvious, although there is for the book of poisons she carries. A Viennese book dealer is selling the model for Mistress Pargeter's through Abebooks, for just over $10,000, if you are interested.

Mademoiselle Báthory is not quite made up but is intended as a sister of Elizabeth Báthory, a Hungarian noblewoman who may or may not have been a vampiric serial killer living in the last half of the sixteenth century, who was accused of bathing in virgins' blood to prolong her youth, and to whom the *Guinness Book of Records* has awarded the title of most prolific female murderer. As ever with these sorts of things, the truth is probably slightly more mundane, and she was more than likely slandered by her family's enemies and debtors, but that is not to say her sister, Katherine, did not come to London to kidnap poor Arthur Dee.

And as for John Dee at the time of the historical record, he was necessarily operating behind the scenes, under cover, because he was, for reasons discussed in *All the Queen's Spies*, pretending to be in Prague, but there is no doubt that with England in such peril he would have been there, sometimes out of his depth, but always on hand, eventually, with the right solution, at the right time, especially when his Queen and country were about to face their greatest challenge yet.

Oliver Clements
January 2024

ACKNOWLEDGMENTS

I thank ye:

To my warrior queen, Lisa Gallagher, who is at the front lines of my world.

To my incredible publisher, Libby McGuire.

The glorious editor Kaitlin Olson and her passionate editorial assistant Ife Anyoku.

I want to thank the wildly talented designers Kyoko Watanabe and Esther Paradelo.

Our frontline marketer Aleaha Reneé and towering publicist Camila Araujo.

To the book-architect production editor Jason Chappell and wondrous copyeditor Laurie McGee, who has copyedited every single book in the series—we hope she will continue with this adventure!

Thanks to ALL

þancie • Gracias • εὐχαριστώ • Takk • TLAZOHCĀMATI •
kamsa hamnida • grazie • Merci mille fois • Dankeschön •
Dankuwel • Çok teşekkürler • 多谢 • Cảm ơn bạn rất nhiều •
Wielkie dzięki • धन्यवाद • ありがとうございます • Mulţumesc •
ขอบใจนะ • תודה • Adúpẹ́ • Diolch • Xtyozën yuad • Ngiyabonga •
kha-em-per-ankh • yusulpayki • gratias tibi ago • 謝謝 • gràcies •
დიდი მადლობა • hvala • баярлалаа • Ahéhee • Dhanyabaad •
تشکر از شما • obrigado • спасибо • Waad ku mahadsan tahay •
rahmat • tapadh leibh • A- key-yeh

ABOUT THE AUTHOR

Oliver Clements is a novelist and screenwriter based in Mortlake, London.